ALMONDS & RAISINS

'The first in a trilogy of novels, a
family saga of Jewish refugees
from the pogroms and
persecution of Eastern Europe at
the turn of the century, settling
in the slums around
Strangeways gaol because that
was as far as you could carry
your baggage from the station,
working their way up through
the garment trade sweat shops'
THE GUARDIAN

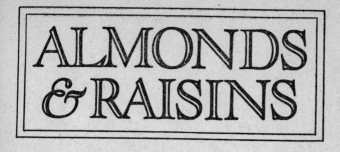

ALMONDS & RAISINS

MAISIE MOSCO

NEW ENGLISH LIBRARY

For my mother and in memory of my father,
Nathan Gottlieb

Acknowledgements
The National Union of Tailors and Garment Workers
(Manchester Office), for information kindly supplied.

Those members of the Manchester Jewish Community
whose recollections of times past have enriched this book

Samuel Woolfe, H. R. Gouldman and Ethel Bernstein,
for assistance with research.

My daughter Marilyn Selby for help and encouragement.

_____

First published in Great Britain 1979 by
New English Library
Copyright © 1979 by Maisie Mosco

First NEL Paperback edition August 1980
Reprinted October 1981
Reprinted February 1982
Reprinted June 1982

NEL Books are published by
New English Library,
Mill Road, Dunton Green,
Sevenoaks, Kent,
Editorial office, 47 Bedford Square, London WC1B 3DP
Printed and bound in Great Britain by
Collins, Glasgow

0 450 04609 6

Under Yidele's cradle stands a snow-white goat,
The goat has been to market,
That will be Yidele's calling, too,
Trading in raisins and almonds.
There will come a time when railroads
Will cover half the earth
And Yidele too will earn great wealth,
But even when you are rich, Yidele,
Remember your mother's lullaby
And the raisins and almonds.

From an old Yiddish lullaby,
'Rozhenkes mit Mandlen'

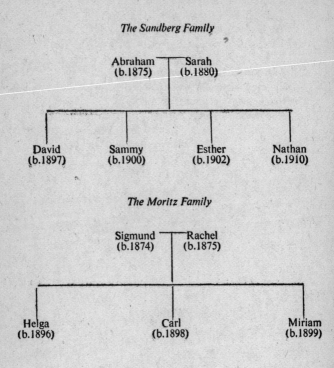

The Sandberg Family

Abraham (b.1875) — Sarah (b.1880)

- David (b.1897)
- Sammy (b.1900)
- Esther (b.1902)
- Nathan (b.1910)

The Moritz Family

Sigmund (b.1874) — Rachel (b.1875)

- Helga (b.1896)
- Carl (b.1898)
- Miriam (b.1899)

PART ONE:
HOPES & DREAMS

CHAPTER ONE

Each time a horse and cart turned into the approach Yossel Lensky hoisted his belongings onto his back expectantly and put them down again when the vehicle rumbled past him. After a while, he began doing this even when it was a carriage.

'You think your relation can afford to hire a *droshky* after only two years here?' Sarah Sandberg asked him, but Yossel just mopped the sweat from his florid face and continued the charade without replying.

'He's making me nervous,' Sarah said to Yossel's wife. 'And I'm nervous enough already.' She shifted little Esther to a more comfortable position in her arms and glanced maternally at David and Sammy, her aquiline features shadowed with concern. Her children had not slept in a bed for more than a week and there was no certainty that they would tonight.

'Who isn't nervous?' Hannah Lensky answered. 'On the train, I felt excited, I couldn't wait to get to Manchester. But now we're here, the thought of beginning again, with four kids, and hardly a penny in my pocket! Well it won't be easy, will it?'

Gittel Lipkin wrapped her shawl closer about her bony shoulders and grabbed her youngest child by his coat tail as he was about to run away. 'You want to get run over by a cart, Moishe! Remember on the boat how you nearly fell overboard?' She smiled at the other women. 'When was it ever easy?'

'Yankel and me, we're just glad to be here,' Zelda Cohen said thankfully. 'Easy we don't expect it to be.' She touched her full breasts and winced. 'I'd have fed my baby on the train if I'd known we'd be hanging around this long.'

They were huddled by the wall outside Exchange Station, waiting for Yossel Lensky's third cousin the rabbi, whom he had hoped would come to meet them.

'What will we do if he doesn't turn up?' young David Sandberg asked. The October twilight was fast thickening to dusk and a

11

yellowish mist, carrying with it a smell that reminded him of bad eggs, was making his face feel cold and clammy. There was, too, the stink of horse dung in the air, and the gas they used to light the trains was drifting from inside the station.

Sarah licked her dry lips. They still tasted salty from the spray blowing up into her face when she staggered on deck, nauseous, during the sea crossing. She felt David tug at her skirt.

'Mother, what will we do?'

'Me he's asking!' Her husband was watching a horse relieve itself, with a bemused expression on his face. 'You never saw such a spectacle in Russia, Abraham?' she inquired caustically. 'David wants to know what we'll do if Mr Lensky's cousin the rabbi doesn't come. It's a good question!'

Abraham Sandberg pushed his black fedora to the back of his red, bushy hair and thought about it. 'The same as we'd have done if we hadn't met Mr Lensky.' He gazed apprehensively at the stretch of cobblestones in front of him, which sloped down to a main highway. He could see the flickering streetlamps and the traffic moving along and dark clumps of buildings rising against the sky. 'But I hope we don't have to. A stranger could get swallowed up here!'

'The first Jews who came had nobody to meet them, did they?' David pointed out.

'In those days cities weren't as big and busy as they are in 1905,' his father said as a trainload of passengers began jostling through the station exit.

David watched two little boys get into a hansom with a lady. Their neat jackets and knickerbockers made the clothes he and his brother had on seem like baggy old sacks and the lady's coat was dark-green velvet, trimmed with shiny fur. He glanced at his mother's shabby shawl and skirt and wished she could have one like it.

'We wouldn't get lost if we took one of those, would we, Father?' he said as the hansom moved away. 'They're smaller than the Russian ones and they've only got two wheels, but we could manage to squash ourselves in.'

'A plaster for every sore, my son David's got! An answer for everything! What can you do with him?' Abraham exclaimed exasperatedly. 'Also he thinks I'm made of money.'

12

Shloime Lipkin let go of little Moishe whom he had caught by the scruff of the neck as he was about to make off again and wagged his forefinger solemnly at David. ' What you'll spend on a *droshky* today, my lad, you won't have in your pocket to buy bread with tomorrow. None of us can afford to say no to a free ride.'

'You still think we'll get one?' Sarah asked doubtfully.

'My cousin the rabbi will come,' Yossel Lensky insisted as if the honour of the clergy was at stake. He heaved his bundles aloft again as another vehicle turned into the approach. 'Didn't I send him a message with that other rabbi, the one who caught the boat before ours? Ministers don't let people down. Have patience everyone and you'll soon be taken to where you're going.'

'To tell you the truth, Yankel and me we don't know where we're going,' Zelda Cohen hee-hawed edgily. Her laughter always sounded like a donkey braying.

Gittel Lipkin stopped slapping little Moishe. 'You came without an address, Zelda? How could you do such a thing when you were pregnant?'

Zelda gazed tenderly at the infant cradled against her. 'I'm not pregnant now.'

Her burly young husband put his arm around her. 'And a live child with no place to go is better off than a dead one. They were setting fire to the houses when we left.'

'Ours also,' Gittel said quietly.

'So what do you mean, how could we do such a thing?' Yankel demanded. He tied another knot in the piece of old rope which belted his patched coat, as if he must do something to busy his hands.

A single tear coursed down Zelda's pale cheek and splashed onto her baby's face. 'I saw my mother squelching through the mud in the marketplace, everyone was running for their lives.' She looked at Yankel despairingly. 'God knows where she is now.'

Shloime Lipkin tugged at the peak of his heavy cap and tried to hide the anguish in his eyes. 'Our parents died at Kishinev. So we don't need to worry about them anymore,' he added in a hard voice.

'If Moishe hadn't had a fever we'd've been there ourselves,' Gittel whispered. 'They went to spend *Pesach* with my niece who married Shloime's nephew and we were going also. Sheba'd just had a baby and she wasn't well enough to come home to the family for the Passover.'

Sarah's heart skipped a beat, but whose would not at the mention of Kishinev? The pogrom there two years ago had been the worst yet, with Jews torn from their beds and tortured, nails driven into their flesh, their eyes gouged out, left in their agony to die. A special prayer had been said for them in the synagogue in her townlet and everyone had wept. She saw Zelda clasp her infant closer to her breast and remembered hearing that many babies were tossed out of upstairs windows during the three-day slaughter, that the pavements in the Jewish quarter had been spattered with their splintered skulls. Zelda must have heard about it, too.

'So what can you do?' Gittel shrugged breaking the pensive silence. It was a question to which there was no answer and one they were all accustomed to hearing.

Zelda sighed and went on with her story. 'I must've fainted after I saw my poor mother. The next thing I knew, I was wrapped in a blanket, shivering with cold and Yankel was pushing me across a field in a handcart, with all our things crammed around me, bumping me up and down till I thought the baby would burst through my stomach.'

Her husband tapped the enamel pail which was slung around his neck by the handle. 'Before she fainted, she reminded me to bring this. My Zelda thinks they don't make pails in England!'

'It was a wedding present, why should I leave it behind? And can you give me a guarantee they do?'

Sarah stroked the infant's fuzzy, dark head. 'Pr'haps being bumped about in the handcart brought on your labour early, Zelda.'

'Don't remind me about my labour, Mrs Sandberg. What a place to have your first child! When I think of the lovely clean sheets my mother prepared for my lying-in. A fine lying-in I'm having!' Zelda tried to smile, but shuddered instead. 'All my life I'll remember that filthy hold, with the boat tossing like a bobbin and you Mrs Lipkin kneeling in front of me so nobody would see, while Mrs Lensky delivered her.'

'I was trembling all over,' Hannah Lensky confessed. Her pasty complexion flushed with pride as she eyed the child. 'I never delivered a baby before.'

'Now she tells me!' Zelda brayed and everyone chuckled with her, as if it was the best joke they had ever heard.

It's a wonder we can still laugh, Sarah thought. How do we do it? Up to now, there hadn't been much to laugh about, but even at home people had kept their sense of humour.

Once, when the dreaded marauders had ransacked her parents' house and ripped the *perinehs* on the beds with a sharp knife, scattering the down filling everywhere, her mother had joked about it afterwards and said her father looked like a snowman, covered from head to foot in white feathers. She fingered the small gold brooch at the neckband of her blouse, lost in recollection.

'Don't look so miserable, Mrs Sandberg!' Zelda chided her. 'Listen, everyone's got their packet.'

Sarah looked at the seventeen-year-old girl who was counselling her like a great-aunt and smiled. Gittel Lipkin was telling her children a folk-story to keep them quiet and Hannah Lensky had just split an apple into quarters for hers, as if they weren't all waiting to be carried off heaven-knew-where by a rabbi who might not turn up, but were having a carefree outing. The four families had been cooped-up together travelling since they met by chance on the quayside in Hamburg, but nobody had mentioned their experiences in Russia until Yankel was goaded into it just now. Why am I thinking about this? Sarah asked herself. Maybe I thought the others hadn't had such a bad time as Abraham and me, because they didn't talk about it. But we didn't, either and we still haven't. You don't rush up to another Jew and say, 'Listen, I was lucky to escape with my life.' It wouldn't surprise him and the details don't differ too much from place to place.

'How much longer must we wait?' David asked. 'People're staring at us.' He glanced around furtively. 'Last time I got stared at they set about me, don't you remember, Mother?' He touched the silky, black ringlets which hung one on either side of his face, alongside his ears. 'And tried to pull these off. It's not my fault I have to wear them, is it? That our religion forbids me to cut that part of my hair?'

Sarah wiped a smut off his nose with her fingertip. 'In Russia that happened to you, David.' She smiled into the soft, dark eyes which were exactly like her own. 'You're in England now.'

'Do they like Jews in England?'

'How do I know when I've only just got here? All I know is they let us live and to live is enough.' Sarah eyed her frail younger son anxiously and pulled his muffler higher around his neck. It wasn't like him to be so quiet. 'Is your leg aching, Sammy?'

'Only a bit.'

'Lean against David, it'll take the weight off it.' She averted her eyes from the crippled limb which nothing could heal. The yellow mist had settled on her shawl like a layer of moist muslin and the children's garments were beginning to feel soggy, too. 'Do something, Abraham!' she instructed her husband. 'I'm very grateful to Mr Lensky for offering us a ride, but we can't stand here all night.'

'You won't have to!' Yossel exclaimed joyously. 'Look! My cousin the rabbi is here!'

David tried not to laugh. The scrawny little man was clinging to the front of the cart precariously with one hand and holding onto his big, flat, brimless *streimel* with the other.

'That's the same hat he used to wear in Rostov,' Hannah Lensky whispered to Sarah. 'It always was too large for him.'

'Oy vay!' he shouted when the horse halted abruptly and he was flung to the rear end. Then he righted his hat and his grey sidelocks, smoothed the collar of his black caftan and said what he had intended to say, '*Shalom Aleichem!*'

Peace be unto you, how lovely it was to hear that familiar greeting in this strange place. Everyone crowded around the dilapidated vehicle. '*Aleichem shalom*, Rabbi!' their reply resounded. Unto you be peace.

'Allow me to welcome you to Manchester,' he smiled.

Sarah wondered if he was going to deliver a sermon, some ministers never lost the opportunity.

But Rabbi Baruch Lensky was not that kind and it was not too long since he had stood where they were standing, he remem-

16

bered how it felt. 'What're you waiting for?' he said brusquely to hide the emotion these arrivals always evoked in him. He rapped on the cart with his rolled umbrella. 'Put in your things already and let's be off. My supper's waiting and the driver's also.'

'I can't see anything,' little Moishe Lipkin complained as the horse began to tug its heavy load.

'Peep between the slats like Sammy and me're doing,' David advised as they rumbled past a chestnut-vendor who was stirring the glowing coals in his rusty brazier and an old crone in a man's flat cap, shouting her wares from beside a barrow of oranges.

The rabbi was seated on a stool the driver had provided for him. Everyone else had to squat on their bundles and boxes. 'So many little boys we have here,' he said after Yossel had introduced the other families. 'So they'll say their Bar Mitzvah portions in England instead of Russia, God will still hear them.' He polished the handle of his umbrella on his cuff thoughtfully for a moment. 'But will He forgive my Cousin Yossel for expecting me to meet a train at sunset, when I should be saying prayers with my congregants?'

Yossel exchanged a shamefaced glance with the other men. The evening service had slipped their memory. He swallowed hard, it was a serious oversight. 'You know how it is when you're on the move like we've been, Baruch. You lose track of time.'

Rabbi Lensky smiled, he knew it was the truth. 'Even if God doesn't forgive you, on this occasion I'm sure He'll excuse you.'

'What's the difference between being excused and being forgiven?' David asked his parents, but they were too busy peering over the side of the cart to answer him.

The bad-egg odour grew stronger as they neared the bottom of the slope.

'We're on a bridge, David, look!' Sammy piped. 'There's a river flowing underneath.'

David gazed down at the rank, brown water and grimaced. 'It doesn't look like the Dvina, does it?'

Sammy held his nose. 'It doesn't smell like it, either!'

'The River Irwell has a perfume all its own,' the rabbi chuckled. He turned to Sarah and Abraham. 'I have in my congregation a couple who talk of the Dvina. A Mr and Mrs Berkowitz.'

17

'It's them we're going to.' Sarah felt in her reticule to make sure she had not lost the address.

'So you're also from Dvinsk. It's good you have *landsleit* here, people from your hometown.'

'My wife isn't happy about us going to them,' Abraham said hesitantly. 'We don't know them very well and she doesn't like to bother anyone.'

'We're going to *landsleit*, as well. A family called Mishnik,' Shloime Lipkin said. 'Do they belong to your congregation, Rabbi?'

The rabbi shook his head and chuckled. 'Wait till you find out how many there are here! Places to pray are the only thing we're not short of.'

'Everyone at home says over here a person from the same place as you'll do anything for you,' Shloime told him.

'We heard the same,' Abraham said.

'What you heard is true.'

'But my Gittel and Becky Mishnik never got on together at home,' Shloime sighed.

Gittel smacked Moishe's behind to stop him from using the slatted side of the cart as a ladder. 'Who could get on with Becky Mishnik?'

'See what I mean, Rabbi?'

'Set your minds at rest,' the minister reassured them. 'You won't stay with them forever and coming from the same place is a strong bond, believe me, when you're miles away from it.'

'But the Berkowitzes don't know we're coming, there wasn't time to let them know,' Sarah said in a troubled voice.

'Can they turn you away when once they were in the same position themselves? How would they have the heart?'

'It makes sense,' Yossel declared.

'For you it's all right,' Shloime said enviously. 'You've got the rabbi here, he's family.'

'When it comes to it, we're all family,' Rabbi Lensky said quietly. 'Aren't we all cursed with the same inhuman affliction, which causes our blood to spill whenever a scapegoat's needed? Who are those butchers taking it out of just now because this year they tried to throw out the Tsar with a revolution and didn't succeed? I don't have to tell you. Instead of counting sheep to

18

help me fall asleep at night, I lie counting all the pogroms there've been the last few months and it keeps me awake. And last time it was the Tsar himself who arranged the blood-letting, we get it from all sides!' He stared into the dusk, sorrowfully. 'These days a Jew who's lucky enough to be in England never knows who he'll find on his doorstep asking for shelter. So what can you do? It's making houseroom hard to find.'

David gazed at the imposing edifice which stood directly opposite the station approach. He could not see it too clearly in the gathering darkness, but there was something holy about it. 'Is that a *shul*, Rabbi?' he asked as they turned left into the main road.

'That? A synagogue?' The little minister's homely features crinkled with amusement. 'One that size we don't have yet! Mine is a room with the ceiling falling in, but God doesn't mind, a snob He isn't. That beautiful building is Manchester Cathedral.'

A flicker of apprehension crossed David's expression.

'Here, there's no need to fear the Church, my boy. It's not like in Russia.' Rabbi Lensky took a tin of snuff from his pocket as they jogged under a railway bridge. 'We've left the Irwell behind, it's safe to clear my breathing tubes!' he joked inserting a pinch into each of his flaring nostrils. 'And now we're entering Strangeways, where our people live.'

Everyone began peering into the dusk to get a glimpse of the locality. Gloomy expanses of brick and deserted streets met their eyes on both sides.

'Where're all the people, Baruch?' Yossel inquired as they passed a lonely mongrel raising its leg against a lamp-post.

'Eating their supper, or working still. But you should see it on a Sunday morning! And anyway, we're not really there yet.'

Moishe Lipkin had a perplexed look on his monkey face. 'Why're all the buildings painted black, Rabbi?'

'They weren't in Rostov,' young Lazar Lensky informed his middle-aged relative who had been born and bred there.

'Oy,' the rabbi sighed. 'The way a Jewish family gets split up nowadays, your children don't even remember me, Yossel. They're not painted black here, either, boys. They're coated with soot.'

'What's the soot from?' David wanted to know.

'Such inquiring minds these lads have! I hope they'll also apply them to studying the Talmud. The soot is from the smoke which belches from many chimneys. Everyone burns coal in their grate here and Manchester isn't short of factories. Cotton mills also they have in the area, they call it the cotton capital of England. You see that big lorry and the one behind it?'

A couple of vehicles were clattering past in the opposite direction, both piled so high with great lumps of cloth the drivers had to crack their whips to keep the straining horses on the move.

'That you'll get used to seeing. They're taking the cloth from the mills to the station goods yard.'

'You fancy working in a mill, Mr Sandberg?' Yossel asked Abraham.

Abraham looked startled by the question. 'How comes a cobbler to a loom?'

'My husband was the best cobbler in Dvinsk,' Sarah said proudly. 'If things had only been different, he'd have had his own shop.'

'Oy vay,' the rabbi groaned. 'If things had only been different! Everywhere I go they're singing that tune. As it happens there're no mills where our people live and work, but I promise you in every other street you'll find a garment factory.'

'We had boot factories in Dvinsk,' David told him. 'My Uncle Ephraim used to work in one, but they made him join the army and he hasn't come back yet.'

He never will, Abraham thought. And if the local police inspector hadn't spoken up for me because his wife said nobody could mend her fine slippers like I did, they'd have taken me also. What kind of world was it, when a woman's slippers could save a man from mutilation or death? It didn't require a war to cut down a Jewish lad who found himself in the Russian army. His Tsarist comrades saw to that.

Sarah moved closer to him, aware of what he was thinking. Whenever his brother's name was mentioned his handsome face tensed with pain. 'It was a long time ago,' she whispered comfortingly. David had never known his uncle, he only knew what he had been told.

'But nothing's changed, has it?'

'Something has, for sure!' Sarah chuckled with satisfaction.

20

'Fat Mrs Ivanovitch will have to find someone else to mend her slippers now.' She clutched Abraham's arm. 'What's that coming towards us?'

A very tall, narrow vehicle was rattling down the road.

'How is it moving, Abraham? I don't see any horses.'

'Only trains can move with nothing to pull them,' Shlolme Lipkin said confusedly.

Abraham eyed the passengers on the top deck, as the thing drew near. 'A train with two storeys? And no roof?'

Gittel held on to Moishe, in case he might try to leap over the side of the cart and board it when it clanked past. 'Nobody warned me to expect railway lines on the streets here!'

'Me neither,' Hannah Lensky wailed gathering all her children to her bosom.

'It can't be a train, there's no steam,' David said thoughtfully. He watched the vehicle recede into the mist. 'Whatever makes it go must come from that long thing sticking up on top. But what's it attached to?'

Everyone looked up and saw the wires overhead.

The rabbi was laughing so hard he dewed his beard with spittle. 'What greeners we are when we first get here from the old country!' he gurgled. 'In English they call that a tram, so you've learned your first English word. In Yiddish we don't have a word for it.'

'Tram!' all the children chorused delightedly.

'In the wire overhead, there's electricity, we don't have a word for that either.'

'Electricity,' the children repeated.

Their parents stared up at the wires nervously.

'They used to be drawn by horses and some still are,' Rabbi Lensky explained. 'But not the ones on Bury New Road, our district. So when you need a ride somewhere you'll take a tram.'

Sarah clutched Abraham's arm again. 'Never!'

The rabbi went on talking, but Sarah was no longer listening. She glanced at her sons who would soon be loose on this broad highway with its dangerous traffic, she couldn't go with them everywhere they went.

'Tram, Mamma!' Esther piped from her lap.

She smoothed her daughter's tangled hair, which flamed like

21

Abraham's and Sammy's, and smiled at how quickly she had picked up the English word. But Esther was quick for a child not yet three. It would be easy for the little ones to adapt themselves, they had nothing to compare things with, nothing to remember. Even the children of David's age would soon settle down into their new life. For their parents it was different. How would she ever get used to it here? Find her way about and do her marketing? Would the shopkeepers laugh at her because she couldn't speak their language? The ill-lit side streets seemed to be skulking in the shadows and had a mean, unfriendly look about them. Different from Dvinsk, with its cosy market place where she'd fed the pigeons in the days when there'd been bread to spare, before she'd grown up, and the river had looked fresh and clear as it flowed on its way to meet the Baltic, not like a mess of rancid soup fouling the air. Where she'd fallen in love with Abraham and borne her children and her parents lay buried beside her sister, who'd been prettier than her and so courageous. How had little Fredel, only fourteen, found the courage to walk into the Dvina, on and on until the current swept her away and covered her head? Their parents believed she had lost her mind, but Sarah didn't think so. All the young girls swore they'd drown themselves if they were ever violated by the soldiers who roamed the countryside. A good Jewish girl wouldn't want to live afterwards. Others had been ravaged, too, but Fredel was the only one who kept her word. Sarah looked at her daughter and shuddered. But Esther would grow to girlhood in a country where such things didn't happen, where the people weren't barbarians and nobody had the right to snuff out your life like a candle because you were a Jew.

'Stop daydreaming, Mother!' David gave her a prod. 'The rabbi wants to show us something.'

Sarah became aware that the cart had halted. She stopped fingering her brooch and listened to what Rabbi Lensky was saying. You couldn't bring back the dead and thinking about them didn't help you to go on living.

'You've been travelling so long, a minute or two more won't make any difference and this you have to see, it will make you feel at home.' The hanging lantern at the front of the cart cast its glow on the minister's face as he indicated a large, gracious building on their right, which seemed out of place in its humble surroundings. 'The Assize Courts, where all the worst criminals get tried,' he announced.

A tremor of indignation rippled through the vehicle and everyone looked at Yossel Lensky. The insult had come from his cousin.

Yossel found his tongue. 'We should feel at home there!'

Rabbi Lensky was enjoying himself. He had shown the building to new arrivals before and always played on them the trick which had been played on him the first time he saw it. 'Don't get excited, Yossel. You haven't yet seen who is up there on the top.'

'I don't care who is up there on the top. I demand an apology!'

'Have a look, all of you, just the same.'

The fine, Gothic structure was veiled in mist and the dusk had darkened into night, but a carved figure was just discernible perched on the apex of the gable which crowned the entrance.

'Who is it?' Yossel snapped, then the moon peeped from behind a cloud and lit the figure.

Everyone gasped.

'Moses in Manchester? How can it be?' Abraham rubbed his eyes and looked again.

'He's got the *Torah* in his hand, Father!' David exclaimed.

'What better than the Books of the Law could they have there?' Rabbi Lensky asked. 'When the Court begins a new session here, all the judges walk up the steps in a procession wearing their robes and wigs and trumpets are blown to herald them, but no judge is higher and wiser than the Almighty.'

'Will we be able to see the procession?' David asked eagerly.

'Never mind the procession, just keep your mind on the *Torah* and Moses.'

David glanced up the street beside the Court as they moved on. 'What's that big building at the back, Rabbi?' Something about its forbidding bulk made him shiver.

'You didn't see the bars on the windows? It's the county jail.'

'A nice cheerful place to have in your neighbourhood!' Shloime Lipkin quipped.

'Why do the Jews live near it?' David inquired.

'Oy, he's here with his questions again!' the minister said in mock exasperation. 'Well I'll tell you, little man. When I look at

Strangeways, the only reason I can think of why our people settled here is it isn't too far to walk from the station.' His beady eyes twinkled mischievously. 'Like most who are coming now, those who came first weren't escorted in a fine conveyance like this. Which my young congregant Menachem, who's driving us, borrowed from his boss, a greengrocer. And swept the rotting cabbage leaves out of, before he would allow me to get in. Those in whose footsteps you're following got off the train and *shlepped* on their two feet, with their bundles on their backs, and stopped when they got tired is my opinion.'

'You won't hear me and my wife grumbling, Rabbi,' Yankel Cohen said gruffly. 'Not after the place we lived in. You were either up to your ankles in mud, or choking with dust, according to the weather. Who knows from pavements even, in the *shtetlach* in the Pale? The wc excuse me for mentioning it, was a hole in the yard—"

'Ours had a screen round it,' Shloime interrupted. 'And for water we *shlepped* two miles.'

'Ours had a screen, also. You think we're not respectable?' Zelda Cohen joined in. 'And we too had to walk a long way to bring water.'

'How often did you clean your windows?' Gittel asked her with a smile.

'Never. And you?'

'The same.'

'How could anyone not clean their windows?' Sarah said in a shocked voice.

Gittel and Zelda shared a laugh, then Gittel replied for both of them. 'The houses didn't have any.'

'Except when a loose plank fell off the wall and then you had an open one,' Yankel grinned. 'So you see why we won't grumble.'

Rabbi Lensky had a special place in his heart for those of his brethren forced by imperial decree to live in the squalid, makeshift townlets within the Pale of Settlement, much of which was an arid wilderness along Russia's Western border. Five million Jews had been banished to the Pale, but God had begun to set them free and with His help more would follow. 'Who is entitled to grumble when the Almighty has granted them a new lease of life?' he said gently.

How lucky we were, living in a pleasant place like Dvinsk, Sarah reflected. There was always someone worse off than yourself. She felt for Abraham's hand in the darkness and entwined her fingers with his. 'Let's try to remember what the rabbi said, Abraham. He's right.'

'Some of the stores stay open late, to oblige people,' the rabbi said as they passed a couple which had their lights on. He peered through the windows inquisitively. 'Mr Halpern's not too busy tonight, people think twice before they spend money on a haircut.'

They could see the baldheaded barber sweeping the floor in the flickering gaslight. Next door, a greengrocer was weighing some carrots for a woman in a ragged shawl.

'Poor Mr Radinsky!' Rabbi Lensky chuckled. 'That's Mrs Kaplan he's serving.'

'Something's peculiar about her?' Gittel quizzed.

'If you get her for a neighbour you'll find out! Mr Radinsky's Menachem's boss, a man with a heart of gold. His wife's is made of iron.'

'I'm relieved the storekeepers're Jewish,' Sarah said.

'If they weren't you'd go without all the things you're used to. In England, the *goyim* don't know from blackbread and salt herring. Now quick! Show me the addresses, I've just given myself an appetite. First we'll take our young couple with the baby, it should be in bed already and its little mother also.'

Yankel cleared his throat awkwardly. 'It's like this, Rabbi—'

'All right, you needn't tell me,' the kindly man cut in. 'I see it on your face. Listen, it's nothing to be ashamed of, you're in good company, I too had no address to go to when I arrived. Tonight you'll stay at my house, it's not my house but where I live they're good-natured and it won't be the first time they've added water to the soup.'

Zelda was white with weariness. 'A thousand thanks, Rabbi.'

'Tomorrow we'll try to find somewhere,' Yankel promised.

'Tomorrow will take care of itself,' the minister replied with a pastoral smile. Because it invariably had to, it was an essential Jewish philosophy.

*

The Sandbergs stood outside their *landsleit's* house, their boxes and bundles cluttering the pavement, watching the cart trundle away.

'Knock on the door already!' Sarah said nervously to Abraham.

'I'm not sure which one it is.'

'I think Rabbi Lensky pointed to the one on the right,' David said helpfully. All the doors were in pairs.

'It's the one on the left,' Sarah said. 'The curtains're the ones Malka had in Dvinsk. They've still got the same hole in them.'

Abraham lifted the rusting knocker and gave the door a gentle tap. 'I wouldn't mention that to Malka, if I were you. I'd be careful what I mention.'

'We're not inside the house yet and he's already putting a muzzle on me.'

David was busy looking around. 'It's not very nice round here, is it?'

'He's the one you should put the muzzle on,' his mother told his father. She surveyed the short, narrow street. At one end was the main road, at the other a high, brick wall with broken glass on the top to keep out intruders. 'If the Lipkins' *landsleit* lived in this street, their Moishe would soon be cut to ribbons!'

Abraham stepped back and looked at the house, which was cramped in the middle of a grimy terrace of others just like it. 'You think maybe they're out? I don't see any lights.'

'The whole street can't be out at suppertime.' All the houses were in darkness. 'There must be two rooms and everyone uses the back one,' Sarah surmised. 'Give another little knock to the door.' She tried to control her nervousness but it showed in her voice. 'Though what we'll say when they open it . . . I feel like a beggar, standing here.'

'Beggars we're not, but choosers we can't be right now, either.' Abraham applied the knocker with a little more pressure. 'And even a *landsleit's* home isn't made of elastic,' he warned preparing Sarah and himself for the worst. 'You heard what Rabbi Lensky said about houseroom being hard to find, the Berkowitzes could be already full up.' He peered through the letterbox as if he expected to see a hundred newly-arrived immigrants crowded within.

Sarah pulled him away. 'A nice thing it'd be if Malka and

Chaim saw you spying on them! Knock again, louder. Remember how Chaim talks at the top of his voice? Maybe that's why they didn't hear.'

David reached up and pounded the knocker so hard the sound echoed down the street.

'Now they'll think we're trying to break the door down!'

'Calm yourself, Sarah.'

'How can I, when I don't know what kind of reception we'll get? And you know how I hate asking favours,' she whispered as the door opened.

Chaim's beefy face beamed like a welcoming lantern from the dim lobby, dispelling her doubts. 'Malka! Put down the soup ladle!' he bellowed excitedly. 'You won't believe who's here!' He clasped Abraham to his barrel-chest, half lifting him from the doorstep. 'So come inside, all of you! Why're you waiting there?'

Malka appeared in a doorway at the end of the lobby, clapped her hand to her cheek and shrieked. 'Ghosts from the past I'm seeing!' She rushed to greet Sarah whilst Chaim helped to bring in the Sandbergs' baggage. 'Worn out you look from the journey. You were seasick? Me, I was green before the boat moved. Give me your little one to hold while you take off your things. She wasn't born yet when we left Dvinsk! And your youngest boy was still in his cradle.' She snatched Esther from Sarah's arms. 'Come here to your auntie, darling.'

'Mamma!' the child screamed.

Malka stifled the cry with a flurry of kisses. 'Hang your shawl on the stair rail, Sarah. On top of my Cousin Chavah's. You remember Chavah and her husband Ezra? They're going to New York and who're they staying with till they'll get on a boat at Liverpool? Us, who else?'

Sarah exchanged a glance with Abraham. His warning that the Berkowitzes might have other guests had proved correct. She watched Chaim shove one of their boxes against the wall with his big foot, so nobody would trip over it in the narrow lobby, and hoped it was not the one containing her china.

'So let's feed these old friends, Malka, come on!' Chaim boomed. 'You've forgotten how hungry we were the night we arrived?'

'We were still hungry after we'd eaten,' Malka reminisced,

'Such a mean person that uncle of yours is.'

'But we only had ourselves to worry about then. Twin girls we've got now,' Chaim told the Sandbergs. 'Wait till you see them!' He led the way into the living room.

Malka watched Sammy limp ahead of her. 'He's had an accident, Sarah?'

Sarah's expression tightened. 'A permanent one.'

David clutched Sammy's hand and pulled him into the room so he would not hear them talking about him.

'Malka!' Chaim hollered. 'First the food, you'll gossip later.'

How can we accept their hospitality? Sarah thought as she followed Malka in. Chaim called us old friends, but we're only acquaintances, he just said it to stop us feeling embarrassed. The living room was also the kitchen and her pride dissipated in its steamy warmth. The meal had just been put on the table and the huge tureen of borsht, with thick slices of beetroot swimming in the pink liquid, seemed a vision of home. Tears stung her eyelids as she felt a strange emotion pulling her two ways. Russia was still home, but she never wanted to see it again. She looked at Abraham and saw that his eyes were wet, too.

For a moment there was silence in the little room, even the children's tongues were stilled by the charged atmosphere. Then Malka began briskly ladling the borsht into dishes, her blue-kerchiefed head bobbing up and down as she counted to see how many were required. 'An extra plateful for our *landsleit* we'll always manage to find.'

Chaim shooed four youngsters from the two chairs they were occupying, to make room for Sarah and Abraham at the table. 'We know how you feel, we've been through it ourselves,' he said spooning helpings of mashed potato into the bowls of soup which Malka put before them, his movements erratic as he strove to hide his emotion. 'So what can you do?' he added with a shrug.

'Eat already,' Malka instructed.

'How's by you, Chavah?' Sarah asked the pretty young woman seated opposite her. Like Malka, Chavah was fair and well-rounded. Sarah was always conscious of her own sallow plainness when in the company of women like these.

'How can a person be?' Chavah replied playing with the frayed cuff of her blouse. 'It wasn't enough we had to retch all the way to England in the herring boat.' She cast a resentful glance at her blue-jowled husband. 'Now in a banana boat, or whatever it will be, we have to go to where my Ezra thinks the streets are paved with gold.'

Sarah smiled her sympathy. From what she'd heard about England it would be good enough for her, gold-paved streets were not what she'd come for. Her sons had begun eating without saying the blessing which always preceded it and Abraham had not noticed the omission. 'The prayer, boys!' she scolded them. 'What will Mr Berkowitz think of you?'

David and Sammy put down their spoons guiltily and gabbled the words off.

Chaim sucked in a morsel of pink potato which had strayed to his moustache. 'To see a good hot meal again, it's affected their memories,' he chuckled tolerantly. 'And no more with the Mr Berkowitz, they can call me Uncle. So I wasn't their uncle in Dvinsk, it's different now.'

Sarah watched him tear some hunks of blackbread from the loaf at his elbow and toss a couple to David and Sammy. Bread had not been served that way in her home. Different it certainly was.

Esther, and Isiah the youngest of Chavah's three boys, were seated on their mothers' laps. The rest of the children had camped on the floor with their dishes of borsht and Malka had to step gingerly when she went between table and hearth to replenish the supply of food from the bubbling black cauldrons on the hob.

'You'll have a fall, be careful!' Chaim warned her as she almost stumbled over David's legs.

Malka laughed and mopped the beats of sweat from her face with a corner of her apron. 'A worse one I should never have!'

She was easy-going to a high degree, which Sarah did not fail to note as she observed the chaos around her. A matted hairbrush with a comb stabbed into it lay on the sideboard, next to a heap of socks and a basin of chicken fat. A saucepan and some shirts awaiting the smoothing iron kept them company and the iron was sitting on the mantelpiece with a couple of lemons, a string of amber beads and Chaim's Sabbath hat.

Despite her fatigue, Sarah itched to put the cluttered room to rights and remove the dust which was everywhere. But it was ungrateful to notice these things, she chided herself. A warm heart counted for more than a broom in the hand. Esther was lolling against her, too exhausted to eat, but the question of where the Sandbergs might sleep had not yet been raised. How unreal it all seemed, sitting around the table with people who had never crossed the threshold of her home in Dvinsk, or she theirs. In a house that bore no resemblance to any she had been in before. What strange situations being Jewish can get you into, she thought dryly. One day you were a little girl, skating on a frozen river in Russia, and the next you were in England, homeless, with your own little girl on your knee. Except that it wasn't quite like that, but thinking of it that way helped you to blot out all the terrible things that had happened in between. Esther was almost asleep. Why didn't Abraham ask if they could stay the night? She waited for him to do so, knowing that he would not. He always left things to her.

'Esther can't keep her eyes open,' she said to Malka not wantint to make a more direct approach.

'So you'll put her to bed,' Malka replied as if it was not a problem. 'She'll sleep with my girls, they've had company before.' She rose from the table and went to light the gas mantle in the lobby.

Sarah had to steel herself against the sudden change of temperature when she left the cosy kitchen and followed Malka upstairs. Her sleeve brushed against the shiny, brown wall and came away damp. She had thought the shine was lacquer, but now realised it was moisture seeping through from the brick. The feeling of unreality assailed her again. What was she doing here? Carrying Esther up this creaking staircase? Her house in Dvinsk had not had stairs and the wood stove which heated her living room had spread its warmth everywhere, finding its comforting way through the curtains which served as doors for the bedrooms. How like a dream this was. But wasn't coming to England a dream? A dream come true.

Malka led her into a tiny room and Esther was soon tucked up in the bed which filled it, her head at the foot to leave space for the Berkowitz children at the other end.

The treacherous gloss adorned the walls here, too, and Malka shrugged resignedly when she saw Sarah touch it. 'A palace it isn't,

Sarah. But your daughter could have worse places to sleep in.'

'Worse places she's already slept in, haven't we all?' Sarah said as they returned downstairs. The overcrowded quarters on the boat had reeked of vomit and urine and the train compartments on the journey from Russia to Germany had been little better. More than anything else, she longed to peel off the crumpled garments she had worn since leaving Dvinsk and scrub herself clean again.

'A hot bath will make you feel better,' Malka said reading her thoughts. 'You can bathe the children tomorrow, they don't feel the dirt like we do and it'd take all night to heat enough water for the whole family. For you and Abie, we'll boil some up now, by bedtime it'll be ready.' Everyone except Sarah called Abraham 'Abie'.

She opened the door of the parlour, which was unfurnished, and Sarah caught a glimpse of reddish lincrusta walls and muddy-looking tiles surrounding the hearth. Some bedding was spread out on the bare boards and a jumble of clothing lay in a heap beside a wicker skip.

'Here's where you and your family'll sleep after Chavah and Ezra have left,' Malka said in her matter-of-fact way. 'Tomorrow they're going.' She laughed good-naturedly, standing with her hands on her plump hips. 'Who knows, Sarah? Perhaps the day will come when nobody will need my parlour to sleep in any more, then I'll be able to put some furniture in it!'

When they went into the kitchen, the men were debating a passage from the Talmud.

'They're busy with their favourite pastime,' Chavah complained from a chair by the fire.

'Wasn't it the same at home?' Sarah smiled. The earnest group around the table was a familiar scene.

Ezra sat with his bony fingers clasped beneath his chin. 'Come then, said the fox,' he quoted thoughtfully, as if the words had a deeper significance than was immediately apparent. 'And live with me on dry land.'

Abraham stared into space as he considered the next line. 'But the fishes laughed.'

Chaim was contemplating the pin with which he had been picking his teeth. 'So why did the fishes laugh?'

31

'According to Rabbi Akiba—'

'I know, Ezra, what is according to Rabbi Akiba. But what is according to you and Abie?'

Malka cut the discussion short. 'Later they'll tell you. Right now, I need you to reach down the big boiling pot from the shelf and fill it with water.'

'Abraham will do it,' Sarah offered. 'Why should Chaim have to get our bath ready?'

'In my house the guests don't lift a finger.'

'I've had a holiday here,' Chavah laughed.

Sarah followed her hosts into the little scullery which adjoined the kitchen and tried not to notice the disorder. A bucket overflowing with garbage stood on the floor beside a cabbage and a can of milk; carrots, onions and bread lay side by side on the same shelf and the draining board was littered with unwashed cooking utensils. But the tap was an unexpected luxury, in Dvinsk there had just been a pump in the back yard.

Chaim shovelled a mound of potato peelings out of the sink and dumped them on the drainer. 'You've brought your *perineh* to England, Sarah?'

'Which Jewish wife would leave the main item in her dowry behind?' she smiled.

'So tonight you and Abie can roll yourselves inside it in the kitchen,' Chaim said as he filled an enormous soot-grimed vessel with water. His jowls shook with mirth. 'Beds we can't supply, but with all those goose feathers to pad your behinds, who needs one?'

'And the boys?' Sarah asked. The kitchen was so full of furniture, there would hardly be space for herself and Abraham to lie full length on the floor.

'Don't worry,' Malka said comfortably. 'The Moritzes next door have a son. David and Sammy can share his bed. Wouldn't we do the same for their *landsleit*?'

After her sons had been put to bed, Sarah followed Rachel Moritz downstairs, her legs aching with weariness. If only she could lie down and rest, but the bath water wouldn't be hot yet and even if it were, she and Abraham couldn't retire for the night until the Berkowitzes and their cousins had vacated the kitchen. Meanwhile, they must stay here and chat with the people who were accommodating David and Sammy, it was only polite to do so. She went with Rachel into the living room and found her husband perched awkwardly on the edge of a chair.

Sigmund Moritz was standing with his back to the fire, an amused look on his chubby face. He took off his pince nez and pointed them playfully at Abraham. 'Rabbi Akiba and the laughing fishes this gentleman's quizzing me about. Since my Bar Mitzvah I didn't give it a thought, I told him. And this evening my mind is occupied with Goethe.'

It was evident from the Sandbergs' expressions that they had no idea who, or what, Goethe was. Sigmund replaced his pince nez on his nose, picked up a book from the table and offered it to Abraham. 'You'll read him, I promise you'll never be the same again.'

'It's written in Yiddish?' Abraham asked and shrugged regretfully when Sigmund shook his head.

Such Philistines these people are, Sigmund thought contemptuously. A handful of intellectuals and a few brilliant writers didn't make up for the narrow ignorance of the mass of Russian and Polish Jewry. He opened the book, became immersed in it and forgot the Sandbergs were there.

Sarah could not recall ever experiencing such rudeness and would have left there and then, had her sons not been receiving the Moritzes' hospitality. She was aware of Abraham fidgeting with his moustache and knew he was hoping she would find an excuse to leave, but she avoided his eye and allowed her own to wander discreetly around the room.

Apart from the brass candlesticks used for the Sabbath lights, and the gleaming mortar and pestle with which apples and nuts were pounded for the Passover, not an ornament was in sight. Sarah had brought from Russia all the familiar objects she could cram into her bundles and boxes, unable to make herself abandon them; vases and trinkets; some wax fruit which had decorated her sideboard; a penstand and inkwell never used, but they were part of the bric-a-brac of her life. The Moritzes appeared to have

33

brought nothing but the barest essentials from their native Austria. And books. The walls were lined with shelves and shelves of them.

Rachel sat with her hands folded on her lap, perfectly relaxed, as if conversation with these strangers was not expected of her and Sarah thought her snobbish. She was wearing a black dress with a white lace stock and the way her creamy neck rose in a proud column above it enhanced this impression. Housewives in Dvinsk kept their good black dresses for special occasions and always wore an apron at home.

'You'd like something hot to drink, maybe?' Rachel inquired, but her voice lacked the persuasiveness with which a Russian woman would have asked.

Sarah rose to leave, she had stayed for the length of time politeness required. 'We're putting you to enough trouble, you don't have to give us drinks also,' she replied with a stiff smile.

'It's no trouble,' Rachel assured them.

Sigmund did not raise his head from the book when they left the room.

'You had to sit there so long?!' Abraham exploded whilst they waited for the Berkowitzes to let them in. 'A man like that I've never met.'

'If we'd left any sooner, our manners would be as bad as his,' Sarah retorted. 'What've they got to give themselves airs about? They're refugees, like us.'

It was their first encounter with Jews of a different culture from their own and what Sarah had judged snobbishness was a certain sophistication the Moritzes had acquired from living in Vienna, which she was not equipped to recognise. 'For my part you can keep the Viennese,' she muttered as Chaim opened the door.

'You should've told me they were leaving. I didn't wish them goodnight,' Sigmund was at that moment saying to his wife. 'What will they think of me?'

'If I'd told you, would you've been listening?' Rachel smiled. 'They'll think like everyone else, that you live in a world of your own. And since when do you care what the Russians think of you?' she added lightly though his intolerance sometimes upset her.

Sigmund snapped his book shut impatiently. 'Goethe they've

never heard of! Men with the brains to memorise the Talmud should extend themselves to other things also.'

The Moritzes had been in England for a year and it had not taken Sigmund long to become contemptuous of his Russian and Polish brethren. He had yet to learn the reason for their insularity, that the ghettos in which they had lived placed restrictions as insurmountable as barbed wire around the mind, as well as the body.

'That doesn't mean they're not nice people,' Rachel said quietly.

'Did I say it does?' Sigmund sat down in his wing chair and crossed his stumpy legs, as he always did when about to hold forth. 'Only two things we share with them, Rachel. Antisemitism and being Jewish. Would we have crossed each other's paths otherwise? Or had anything in common?' A heavy sigh escaped him. 'So now we have Strangeways in common. Life has set us down together side by side.' He opened his book again, but stared at the page without seeing it. 'Different we are, who could deny it? But it's right we should do what we can for each other. A Jew is a Jew.'

CHAPTER TWO

David awoke in the strange room and was momentarily afraid, then he saw Sammy's ginger head on the pillow beside him and the fear receded. He lay still, the *perineh* tucked high beneath his chin, his face exposed to the frigid air, breathing it in, tasting it. He was used to the cold, in Russia it had been much colder than this; crisp and clear, dry and biting. But the chill he felt now was different, moist and muggy, unclean. It was his first experience of a typical winter morning in Manchester, except that the rain had not yet begun to fall. He buried his face in the pillow to escape from it and from the general strangeness of which it was a part.

Last night, he had dreamed about Sammy and the Cossack again. It was three years since the dreadful thing had happened, but when he dreamed about it, it was as if it was happening all over again. Himself and his little brother sitting on the thick, green grass on the river bank throwing pebbles into the water. His own legs crossed, like Mr Seretsky, the tailor, when he sewed in his shop, and Sammy with one of his tucked under him and the other stretched out. They were a few yards back from the river because their mother had told them never to go there alone and when they went with her she always warned them to stay away from the edge. When the horses began to clip-clop past in front of them they had to stop tossing the pebbles and the one in his hand felt lovely and smooth when he stroked it. Even the flock of white birds overhead was there in the dream and the gleam of the horses' coats. And silver braid glinting in the sunlight as one of the tall, uniformed riders reached down and snatched Sammy's *yamulke* off his head and threw it into the river. Sammy's tears were real in the dream, too, plopping onto the pile of pebbles as they had that day; he'd known it was a sin for a Jewish boy not to have his head covered, though he was only two. Then the weeping changed to screams of pain as the Cossack turned back and rode the horse over his leg before he cantered away laughing.

The screams and the laughter were the most terrible part, and the guilty feeling because he'd taken Sammy to play by the Dvina, but his parents had said he mustn't blame himself, that Cossacks could be cruel to Jews anywhere. Later, his mother had warned him that Cossacks weren't the only ones, that Jewish children should be on their guard all the time, which she hadn't told him before because she didn't want to frighten him. He'd promised her he wouldn't feel guilty, but when he saw his little brother limping he still did.

He felt Sammy cuddle closer to him under the *perineh* like he used to at home. But now they had no home. He tried not to think about it. The boy whose bed they were sharing was lying on the other side of Sammy, reading a book, his spectacles perched halfway down his nose. Daylight had just begun filtering into the room and David was not surprised the boy needed spectacles; anyone would get eyestrain from reading in this light. He'd been sound asleep when they crawled in beside him last night, but finding them there this morning didn't seem to bother him. Unless his sight was so bad he hadn't noticed them yet?

'Good morning,' David ventured. You couldn't just lie in someone's bed and not say a word to them. Even if they hadn't said a word to you.

The boy gave him a vague smile, then continued reading.

Maybe I wouldn't be too friendly if I woke up and found two strange boys in my bed, David thought seeking an explanation for his indifference. Not if I didn't know they'd been driven from their own beds. 'It isn't our fault we have to be here,' he said with the words choking in his throat as memories welled over him. 'I bet you never had to hide in a barrel, like Sammy and me did.'

'I got my glasses knocked off, though.'

'When?'

'Before we left Vienna. That's why we left, my father thought it was time to.'

David digested this interesting information. Why had nobody told him that it wasn't only in Russia such things happened? Sammy woke up and gave him a good-morning kiss. 'I hope you don't mind us sleeping with you,' David said to the boy.

'The only thing I ever mind is being interrupted when I'm read-

37

ing. You'll find that out if you know me for long enough.'

'Well thanks anyway.'

'Why're you thanking him?' a cool little voice inquired. 'None of the other boys who've slept here did.'

David had wondered what was behind the curtains which divided the room in half. They had just been tweaked apart and he felt himself being appraised by a pair of pale-coloured eyes. The eyes were fringed by thick, black lashes which matched the tumbled locks framing the small white face.

'It's good manners to say thank you, Miriam,' a voice said primly from behind her.

'You and your good manners, Helga!' the little girl giggled. She leapt off the bed and stood shivering in her flannel nightdress for a moment, then drew the curtains back fully exposing her sister to David's view.

Helga was not as pretty as Miriam, but David liked her sweet smile. He judged her to be about his own age and thought she looked kind.

She thought him and Sammy somewhat scruffy-looking and hoped Carl wouldn't get nits from having them in his bed. 'Come back!' she chided as her little sister went to examine the guests at closer quarters.

'I'm only having a look at them.'

'Well you shouldn't, it's very rude.'

'I don't mind her looking at me,' Sammy laughed.

Miriam touched one of his springy curls. 'Your hair reminds me of the carrots my mamma makes the *tsimmes* with. Do you have *tsimmes* with your chicken on Friday nights, too?'

'Never mind!' David flashed. 'And your hair reminds me of dirty old coal!' Nobody was allowed to pass remarks about his brother, it was enough Sammy had to put up with being lame.

Miriam stared at him in bewilderment, then hurtled back to bed to be comforted by Helga.

To David's surprise, Sammy crawled over him and went to comfort her, too. 'You didn't mean it, did you, David?' He could not bear to see the little girl unhappy.

David could not bear it, either. 'No,' he muttered grudgingly.

'Then why did you say it?' Miriam gulped.

38

David remained silent, but later, when they were eating breakfast in the kitchen, he apologised for upsetting her.

'You've fallen out already?' Sigmund chuckled sipping his coffee. 'You've only just met!'

'It's all right, I've forgiven him,' Miriam said generously and gave David a hug to prove it.

Not yet six and look at her! Rachel thought as she poured hot chocolate for all the children. Such a madam that one's going to be.

David's face had flushed with embarrassment, the little girls he had known in Russia had not been so demonstrative. 'I thought your eyes were grey – but they're green—' he stammered watching them sparkle as she smiled.

'She's got cats' eyes like *Shmerel*, our puss,' Carl grinned and ducked when Miriam threw her buttered bagel at him.

'No she hasn't,' David retorted. They were the loveliest eyes he'd ever seen.

'Living with *landsleit* isn't easy,' Sarah sighed to Abraham at the end of the first week. 'Get a job already, then we won't be beholden anymore.'

'Nobody but you thinks of it like that.'

'Maybe they didn't have my upbringing,' she replied and the look on his face made her sorry she had said it.

Sarah's childhood was something they never talked about. Her family had once been comfortably off, by Russian-Jewish standards and her father had owned a sizeable piece of land until the oppressors seized it. Losing his property had not diminished his pride, nor did his new straitened circumstances prevent him from objecting to Sarah marrying a cobbler. Only after his younger daughter's tragic end, which broke his spirit as well as his heart, did he consent to the union. Abraham's expression told Sarah he was remembering this, too.

'In some ways you take after your father, the way you're so proud!' he exclaimed.

There were times when Sarah thought she did, but she would not admit it.

39

'And maybe you think I sit *shpeiling* with the cards all day, playing *pisha-paysha* like the old men in the marketplace at home, that I don't try. Get a job, she tells me!'

His last remark was addressed to the air. The Berkowitzes had gone to visit friends and Sarah and Abraham were minding the children, who had just been put to bed. Malka had been reluctant to allow Sarah to undress and wash her little girls, but had eventually been persuaded. One of Sarah's present troubles was that Malka never allowed her to do anything at all, but she could not make Abraham understand how uncomfortable this made her feel.

'Maybe we should go to New York, like Chavah and Ezra,' he said tentatively, absorbed in his own problems.

'Another seasick I can do without! And where is the boat money coming from?'

'So we're not going. But I heard it's bigger.'

'Bigger with people who can't find jobs.'

The rebuke in her voice brought a sharp retort from him. 'My feet are raw from the walking!'

'I'll make you a nice glass of tea.'

She rose to lift the kettle from the fire, brushing off the thick fur of soot which perpetually coated it, using the activity to calm herself. She was glad her boys were asleep in the parlour, where they could not see their father's despondent face.

'Tea she's making for my feet!' he joked half-heartedly. 'But cobblers nobody needs.'

Sarah infused the tea in a tall glass, set it in a silver holder which had been her father's and brought it to the table. Abraham avoided her eye, as if he had something to be ashamed of. She had seen fear in his eyes many times, but never this. She made herself shrug and smile carelessly. 'There's no law you have to be a cobbler.'

'Put in the lemon already!'

She slipped a thin sliver into the glass and watched him place a cube of sugar on his tongue, to sweeten the liquid before he swallowed it down.

'What else do I know?' he asked her.

'Listen to me, Abraham.'

'Don't I always?'

40

She stroked his hand. 'What did Chaim know when he came? A picture-framer he was in Dvinsk. Now he makes coats. What he can do, you can do. Already they have their own house. For two-and-six a week wouldn't we be able to rent one, too? So what is two-and-six and week and a few shillings for food, when you know how to get it? A man has to stretch himself, or where is he?'

'Living with *landsleit*.'

'Which he can't do forever. Malka's borsht is already getting thin from the extra water.'

'I tasted.'

'So I don't have to tell you. All right, you'll ask Chaim. In the place he works, or somewhere else, maybe they need someone like you.'

He sipped the tea thoughtfully and Sarah saw the light of hope enter his expression. Her own mind was busy with the details of how they would obtain furniture for their home when they acquired one. She had been one step ahead of him all their married life and sometimes wondered if he knew it.

'Caps and gloves they make round here, as well as garments. But getting a job's another matter,' Chaim replied when Abraham quizzed him.

'You got one didn't you?' Sarah put in.

'With his uncle,' Abraham reminded her.

Sarah was ironing the clothes she had washed that morning. In Dvinsk she had never had to iron in the evening, but her laundry had to take second place to Malka's by the fire and had not dried off until suppertime. 'I suppose that made things easy for you,' she said to Chaim.

Chaim grinned at Malka, who was mending her parlour curtains because Sarah had offered to do it for her. 'To get a job, yes. But in other ways? Don't ask!'

Malka put down her needle. 'It couldn't have been harder. Staying with us you have a room for your family to yourselves, don't you?'

'Listen, we're very grateful,' Sarah hastened to say.

'When we came five years ago, I was grateful to sleep on our

Uncle Mottel's kitchen floor with five other women lying alongside me. At night, Uncle had to put the table out in the back yard to make space for us. On his splintered wood floor. And my Chaim was grateful to share a room smaller than this with their also-grateful husbands.'

'Why d'you think Lakie and Bella weren't born until we'd been here nearly two years?' Chaim laughed. He leaned forward and pinched his wife's dimpled cheek. 'Until nine months before then, Malka and me never got to sleep together.'

Malka bent over her sewing again to hide her blushes. 'You didn't think it was so funny at the time!' She looked up and gave Sarah a poignant smile. 'I thought I'd never get the chance to have any more children. I used to help in the workshop with the button-holing, but it only kept my hands busy and all I could think of was how we'd lost our darling daughters in that epidemic. You remember, Sarah?'

'How could I forget? I nearly lost my David and I couldn't look you in the face when we met on the street afterwards, because I'd still got him and your little girls had died.'

'But God's good. He gave me two more, both together.'

'How could your own uncle treat you that way?' Abraham asked Chaim.

'When it comes to business, you'd be surprised what people can do. So he took advantage of me, if I'd worked for someone else they'd've done the same. At least he taught me the trade. When I'd learned it, he paid me a little better, my five room-mates also, and we could afford to rent our own homes.'

Malka giggled. 'The day after we moved out, I walked past Uncle Mottel's and saw him moving the next lot in.'

'He made a habit of it?' Sarah said incredulously.

'Made a habit of it is right!' Chaim told her. 'And plenty of others did, as well. It was how they kept their little pots of gold on the boil. Only an unskilled worker would let it be done to him. Once he became an expert machiner, or whatever, he was off to where he'd earn a bit more. I'm the only one of the six of us who shared that room who's still with my uncle, and I wouldn't be there, either, if he hadn't given me another raise and made me his righthand man."

'That a Jew could be like that with his own brethren is hard to believe,' Abraham said in a shocked voice.

'Oy, what babes in arms these Sandbergs are, Malka!' Chaim guffawed. 'They know from nothing. Believe me, Abie, it wasn't uncommon for a man who owned a little sweatshop to go to the railway station and offer room and board to immigrants getting off the trains, so the poor greeners would work for him for next to nothing. These days they can get their cheap labour without providing free bread and herring and a mattress thrown down in a stinking-dirty room. So many people're fleeing here from Russia just now, they're lining up to be underpaid. Did you think because we're all Jews there aren't some among us who'll grasp at the chance to exploit the rest? My Uncle Mottel goes to *shul* and says his prayers just like you and me, Abie, and maybe that means he's a good Jew, but it doesn't mean he's a good man.'

'My head's going round from all the terrible things he's telling me,' Abraham muttered to Sarah.

Sarah took the iron out of its tin casing and put it on the glowing embers to reheat. 'Chaim's talking about how things used to be.'

'You didn't hear the last bit?'

'I'm pretending I didn't and you'd better do the same,' she said with a firm smile. 'Because it doesn't matter how many people're lining up to find work, you've still got to get a job, haven't you?'

'I only told you for your own good, Abie, so you won't have to find everything out the hard way, like I did.' Chaim got up to fetch a pitcher of milk from the dresser and filled the cat's saucer. He watched the big, black creature leap from a stool by the fire and begin to lap thirstily. 'You know I'm getting quite fond of Nicholas, Malka. Even though we only got him to catch the mice.'

'Only my Chaim would name the cat after the Tsar!'

'What's wrong with calling one killer after another?' Chaim replied. 'It looked as if there'd been a massacre when I went in the scullery before you were up this morning.'

'Uggh!'

'It's the same every morning, he didn't get that name for nothing. Do you hear any scurrying about in the parlour when

you're lying there in the dark?' Chaim asked Sarah and Abraham.
'If so, we'll put Nicholas in with you for a night or two.'

'We don't hear a thing,' Sarah lied before her husband had
time to open his mouth. She was scared of mice, but the thought
of Nicholas' baleful stare riveting her from the end of the *perineh*
was too much for her.

'Tomorrow you'll leave with me when I go to work and I'll
show you where the factories are, Abie,' Chaim said. 'You can
rise at five, like I do, and watch me shovel up the corpses!' he
added rumbustiously.

Sarah thought most of Chaim's jests were in bad taste and this
one especially, but she was a guest in his house and forced herself
to laugh. Abraham did not even try to. She watched their host
give him an encouraging slap on the back which almost cata-
pulted him out of his chair.

'Tomorrow you'll start your rounds, all right, Abie? Listen,
you might get lucky.'

Sarah could not fall asleep that night and the scampering of
the mice seemed noisier than usual. She wanted a drink of water,
but was afraid of going into the scullery and finding the cat at its
nocturnal butchery. When she did doze off, she awoke with a
start, convinced there was a mouse inside the *perineh* with them,
but it was only Abraham's hand wandering on her thigh.

'Is it five o'clock yet? Or have I got time for another little nap?'
he mumbled against her cheek.

Sarah got up and put a match to the candle she kept on the
mantelpiece. They never used the gaslight because the Berkowitzes
were paying for it. She took Abraham's watch from his vest
pocket and held it near to the flame. 'It's a-quarter-to.' She
rubbed her arms and shivered. Getting out of bed in a freezing-
cold room she'd never get used to!

Abraham reached out and tugged at the hem of her nightdress.
She bent down to kiss him and laughed when he tried to pull her
down into his arms. 'I know what you haven't got time for!'

'You're sure?'

Sarah smiled and blew out the candle and he wasn't certain
whether she had done so because they never made love in the
light, even when their children weren't sharing their room, or was
taking off her nightdress to put on her clothes. He had never

44

seen her naked and did not expect to. Sometimes he wondered if
Chaim had ever seen Malka that way, but it wasn't the kind of
thing Jewish men talked about, not even when they'd had a few
drinks at a wedding. When Inspector Ivanovitch the policeman
had sat waiting for a rush job to be done on his wife's slippers one
day he'd talked about nothing else.

When Sarah relit the candle she was tucking her dark wool
blouse into her skirt.

Abraham admired her tiny waist for a moment and let his
eyes wander lustfully to her small breasts and the neat curve of
her hips which did not look as if she had borne three children. A
man was only human. 'So what can you do?' he sighed watching
her brush her hair to remove the night time tangles. 'I don't work
for Mr Chernik the cobbler anymore who didn't mind if I sometimes got to the shop late in the mornings. Did I ever tell you when
you stand in the candlelight your skin looks like silk and your
hair like satin?'

'Sure, but I don't mind hearing it again,' she laughed pinning
up her long tresses. 'Meanwhile you don't work for anyone anymore and you never will if you don't get up and start looking.'

'I've never been a lazy man, Sarah.'

'Don't I know it?'

'But it's like going out into a wilderness.'

Sarah kept her tone light. 'With all those two-storey trains and
the rest of the busy traffic?'

'I mean what I've go to do. Be something I'm not and first find
someone who'll give me the chance to be it.'

'You'll find the someone and you'll be what you have to be.
I know you. You'll do it.'

They heard Malka and Chaim clatter downstairs.

'Get up already!' Sarah glanced at her sleeping children and
removed Esther's thumb from her mouth, then she dropped
another kiss on Abraham's head. 'I'm going to the kitchen now.'

'But not to the scullery!' he joked as she was leaving the room.

'I wouldn't put a foot in there to wash my hands and face until
Chaim's been in with the shovel first!'

Abraham and Chaim left the house at 5.30. Nicholas was encouraged by Malka's foot to leave with them and went to join a
group of feline friends in the middle of the street. People in

Strangeways kept their cats in at night to serve their functional purpose and put them out during the day to get them from under their feet.

Some of Chaim's neighbours were also leaving for work. 'Good morning, Shmuel!' he called. 'How's by you today, Nocham? Your head cold's better, Mendy?'

'Tell me what's good about it.'

'How can a person be when they have to leave their warm bed and go out in weather like this?'

'My head cold is permanent in such a climate.'

Chaim watched them hurry away and laughed. 'Those three miseries say the same every morning, it never varies.'

Abraham glanced at the sullen sky and tucked his muffler into his coat to protect it from the drizzle. 'Neither has the weather since I've been here. A person can get fed up with it.'

'In Russia we got fed up with the snow, didn't we? Remember how we had to dig our way out of the house sometimes? It isn't that long since you were doing it. And when were we ever without chilblains? The reek of that stuff everyone put on them used to knock me over.'

'Nobody suffers from chilblains in England?'

'All right, so they do. But you can get a block of something nice and scented from the chemist, to rub on them.'

'Last night he tells me the brutal truth and this morning he's kidding to me!' Abraham snapped as they trudged along. 'What is it with you?'

'Listen, there's a time for the truth and another when people need cheering up, so this morning I'm cheering you up. Shoot me!'

When they reached the street corner, Bury New Road was seething with hurrying men in flat caps and long, floppy coats, darting between the trams and carts before disappearing into the side streets like ants on their way to the ant hill. Abraham had not ventured out this early before and the scene had a depressing greyness which chilled his heart. 'There must be a lot of factories, to make work for so many people,' he said to Chaim while they were crossing the road.

'Sure, but you'd be surprised how many workers will fit into one small room. You'll walk with me to Uncle Mottel's. We don't need any extra help right now, I wish we did, but there're plenty more places near there.'

'This is a factory?' Abraham said when Chaim halted outside a small, terraced house. 'It's got curtains at the windows, what kind of workplace is that?'

'The same as many others round here, also a home. My uncle and aunt live downstairs. Upstairs has got sewing machines. You want to see for yourself? Come, I'll show you, Uncle won't mind.'

Abraham followed Chaim into the dismal little place. They had to squeeze past some bales of dun-coloured fabric and almost tripped over a couple of underfed cats as they climbed the stairs.

'Uncle keeps two since the mice started nibbling the cloth,' Chaim explained.

He opened a door in the middle of the landing and Abraham caught his breath at the foetid atmosphere which came at him in a sickening wave. At first he thought the room was windowless. Harsh gaslight hollowed the workers' faces as they bent over sewing machines crammed into every inch of the limited space. The noise of the treadles was deafening and he was sure he could never learn to move his feet as fast as these people were doing.

Women were employed here, too, and a lad who could not have been more than twelve was crouched in a corner with a heap of coats beside him, sewing on buttons. The workers were talking to each other, shouting above the clatter and wiping beads of sweat off their brows with the backs of their hands without pausing in their work, as if it was a mechanical gesture and they were not aware they were doing it.

Chaim had taken off his coat and cap and was straightening his *yamulke* on his wiry dark hair. 'So what do you think of it, Abie?'

Abraham thought of the cobbler's shop in Dvinsk, where he had worked with just one other person beside a window overlooking the marketplace which had trees in it, leafy in summer, glittering with frost in winter. This room was not windowless he saw now, but the grime-blackened glass was like a shutter between the people who toiled here and the sky, denying the existence of any other world but this. He looked at Chaim and shrugged wordlessly.

'Listen, you'll get used to it, like I did. You should only be lucky enough to find a job.'

Uncle Mottel was standing at the cutting bench snipping away with his shears. Cutters had to be paid more than machiners, which was why he had never employed one. 'You've got time for social callers?' he rasped to his nephew without removing the cigar clamped between his yellow teeth. 'And also you're late. So who's your friend?'

'You don't remember Abie Sandberg from home, Uncle? Like I told you, he's staying with me.'

Uncle Mottel's codfish eyes surveyed Abraham. 'Now I remember him. It's ten years since I left the old country, but how many redhaired Jews do you meet? I wish you luck, Abie, but I'm not short of staff. Come back next week and who knows? You're a trained machiner?'

Abraham shook his head.

'In that case don't bother. You're going to stand there all day, Chaim? Plenty of people would like to be promoted to my right-hand man.'

'Go to it!' Chaim said encouragingly as Abraham opened the door to leave and clapped him on the back to help him on his way.

Abraham hurried down the narrow staircase and stumbled outside, gulping in air greedily. Even the smell of smoke and horse dung was a pleasure after Uncle Mottel's workroom. He eyed the other houses uncertainly. How was he to tell which of them were also factories? The only way was to knock and find out. He tried a house across the street.

A young woman in a rusty-looking black dress opened the door, dabbing at her swollen eyes. 'The funeral's not till this afternoon,' she sobbed. 'But you can come in if you like, all my brother's friends who aren't working are here already.'

Abraham was momentarily tongue-tied. What did you say when you'd intruded on someone's grief? 'You've lost your brother?' he stammered. 'I'm sorry to hear it?'

'You'd like me to lose him also? His friends are here to comfort him, but Job's comforters we can do without.'

He walked away with the sound of the slamming door echoing in his ears. It was not easy for him to knock on another one, but he made himself do so.

'I'll pay what I owe next week and if you don't like it you can take the china cabinet, or the sofa, or whatever it is you're too

48

mean to wait for the money for, back to the store!' an irate female voice told him through a crack in the door. 'Lousy debt-collectors!'

He ran down the street to escape from the voice.

'Where's the fire?' a familiar voice called to him. Shloime Lipkin was standing on the corner watching him run.

Abraham halted beside him and laughed. 'It's good to see you, Mr Lipkin.'

Shloime took off his wet cap, wrung it out and put it on again. 'Oy, if only some of the factories I've called at since I got here would say that! You found anyone who needs a cobbler yet?'

'Who needs a cobbler? Today I'm trying the garment places.'

'I've got competition! So we'll keep each other company, Mr Sandberg, we'll look together, why not?'

They plodded along the road and turned into another side street. Shloime made straight for a door which was ajar.

'How do we know it's a workplace? Walking in like this, without knocking, we could get hit on the head with a frying pan,' Abraham said as they entered. 'Two experiences I just had I wouldn't want to repeat.'

'When it's a factory as well, they always leave the door open,' Shloime informed him. 'To save the boss's wife from letting in callers all day.'

Some dejected-looking men were coming downstairs.

'Why're we bothering to go up, Mr Lipkin?' Abraham said scanning their faces. 'It's a waste of time.'

'Your friend's right,' one of the men said to Shoime. 'I'm an experienced machiner, I was a tailor's assistant in Kiev, but here nobody wants to know.' He rubbed his bloodshot eyes wearily. 'If I wasn't living with *landsleit* I'd go home and put my head under the covers, the way I feel, but you can't do that in someone else's house.' He thrust his hands into his coat pockets and rocked back and forth on his feet for a moment. 'So what can you do?' he sighed as he left.

'There's always the Benevolent Fund and the Board of Guardians,' another man called after him.

'What're they?' Shloime inquired.

'People who've been here long enough to save a bit give what they can spare to them, to help folk like us.'

'Charity?' Abraham said in a shocked voice.

'The rabbi at our *shul* told me about it. I didn't say I was going to ask them for anything, did I?' the man snapped. He took a soggy packet from his pocket and bit off some of the blackbread which was protruding from it, then walked away.

'So I'm wasting my time, but I promised Gittel I'd try,' Shloime shrugged.

'Didn't I promise my wife the same?' Abraham followed him upstairs.

They spent the rest of the morning trudging around Strangeways, trailing up rickety staircases and down them again after men in shirtsleeves, or bulky cardigans, who reminded Abraham of Uncle Mottel, had shaken their heads and turned their backs on them.

'Why don't we try a real factory?' he said to Shloime desperately.

'My *landsleit* Judah Mishnik said I shouldn't bother. They pay better, so they get the pick of the workers. We don't stand a chance.' Shloime led the way through yet another doorway. 'Here, they make waterproofs, I can tell by the stink. It makes me want to throw up.'

Abraham was trying not to breathe in. 'Me also.'

'It's the varnish they glue the hems down with,' Shloime told him when they reached the workroom. 'Judah's a *shmearer*, that's what they call those who do that job.'

Abraham got a glimpse of the *shmearers*' fingers swooping birdlike into cans of the malodorous substance, then flying lightning fast along the edges of garments amid the same clatter and confusion he had found everywhere.

'I wouldn't do that job for a fortune!' he declared when they were back on the street again.

'For that job they don't pay no fortune.'

'Whatever they pay I wouldn't do it.'

'Me, I'd do anything,' Shloime said flatly. 'Anything is better than nothing.'

By now, they were soaked to the skin and calling each other by their first names. They sheltered in the doorway of a baker's shop on the main road for a moment and stared in the window at the mouth-watering array.

'What d'you fancy, Abie? An onion bun, maybe? A hot poppy-seed roll, smothered in butter? Or just a nice piece of strudel?' Shloime drooled.

'Let's move away from here, Shloime. It's giving me an appetite. You're going home for a bite?'

'It's enough my *landsleit* have to feed me breakfast and supper.'

'I feel the same. Malka wanted to give me a sandwich to bring, but I said I don't get hungry.'

'That's what I told Becky Mishnik. A pair of liars we are,' Shloime said wryly. 'But a little break would do us good. Come, I'll take you where I always go at this time of day and we'll get a glass of tea there with the rest of the boys.'

CHAPTER THREE

'What're those lads doing?' Sammy asked his classmate Otto Rosenthal.

'What're the little glass balls they've got there?' Moishe Lipkin inquired.

They were in the playground at the Jews' School watching some boys who were crouched on the ground around an upturned cap.

'They're playing marbles,' Otto explained. 'That's what you call the glass balls when you go to buy them, but we call them allies. What you have to do is flirt them.' He flicked the tip of his grubby forefinger against his thumb. 'Like this, it makes them shoot away fast. You two don't know anything, do you?'

'I bet you didn't when you first came to England and it's only our first day at school,' Moishe said.

'I was born here,' Otto informed them. 'So was my big brother.'

'So why're you still speaking Yiddish?' Moishe demanded.

The chubby five-year-old gave them a withering look, 'You can't speak English yet, can you?'

'We know one word, don't we Sammy?' Moishe retorted.

'Tram!' they said loudly in unison.

'And my brother knows another word, the one that makes the trams go, he's remembered it,' Sammy boasted.

Moishe ran off to join some little boys who were kicking a ball and Otto chased after him.

David saw his brother standing alone watching the other children caper around and felt the same pang he always did at such times. 'Come over here, Sammy!' he shouted. He was leaning on a wall with some of the boys whose class he had joined that morning. One in particular, Saul Salaman, had been very friendly towards him.

'How would you like a sister to look after? That's worse than a brother!' Saul complained. A little dark-eyed dumpling in a dirty pinafore was tugging at his sleeve. 'Go away, will you?'

'I've got one, but she's not old enough for school yet,' David grinned.

'I've got two, haven't I?' Carl Moritz said without raising his eyes from the book he was reading.

'But they don't drive you mad like our Bessie does,' Saul declared.

'I don't let them.'

'Listen, brothers can drive you mad as well,' Leo Rosenthal put in as Otto came to show him a grazed knee.

David noticed Saul and Leo looking at how Sammy jogged from side to side as he walked towards them. Lazar Lensky, who was also in their class, did not stare because he had seen Sammy before, but everyone did the first time they saw him and David wished they wouldn't. 'How d'you like school, Sam?' he said ruffling his brother's hair affectionately.

'I'll be glad when it's home time.'

David laughed. 'Have you learned anything yet?'

'Why do I need to?'

'My father says he could teach me all I need to know,' Saul Salaman confided. 'He'd like me to help in his factory instead of coming to school.'

'But you're only eight!' David looked taken aback.

'He taught me to sew buttons on when I was six,' Saul yawned and David noticed he had dark circles under his eyes. 'I have to help him in the workroom every night.'

'Has your father got a job yet, David?' Lazar Lensky asked.

'No.'

'Nor has mine.' Lazar's moon face looked troubled. 'Him and my mother keep having rows about it.'

'My parents never have rows,' David replied as a teacher shook a big handbell to call them back to the classroom. Sammy glanced up at him, but he pretended not to notice. They had heard their mother and father whispering angrily to each other more than once recently, early in the morning when they thought David and Sammy were asleep.

The next day, David awoke and heard Sarah and Abraham quarrelling again.

'It's no use you telling me you can't find work,' his mother was hissing. Then she turned and saw David looking at her and went out of the room, hurriedly.

Abraham was draping his prayer shawl around his shoulders. 'What're you looking at, David? You've never seen me put on my *tallith* before?' he snapped. He adjusted his *yamulke* which was inclined to slip off because his hair was so thick and took the phylacteries which must be worn to say the weekday morning prayer out of a little draw-string bag.

David watched him flex his left arm and lay one of the small leather boxes on the upper muscle, opposite his heart like the Law instructed, then wind the long black strap attached to the box round and round, the required seven times, all the way down to his wrist.

'You've never seen me laying my *tephillin* either?' his father said tetchily.

'I like watching you do it.'

'All right, so watch,' Abraham sighed. 'I'm not angry with you, David,' he added though he ought not to be talking whilst preparing for the prayer. 'It's just the way I feel, why should I take it out of you?' He laid the second little box on the centre of his forehead and tightened its straps at the back of his head, to hold it in place. Finally, he wound the dangling end of the first strap around his fingers.

'When I was very little, I used to think you looked funny like that, Father,' David confessed.

'But a big boy knows it's a serious matter, that inside the boxes are holy texts. "And thou shalt bind them for a sign upon thine hand and they shall be for frontlets between thine eyes, as a sign that we are the sons of our Father in Heaven and members of the community of our great and holy people",' Abraham quoted gravely. 'We lay them opposite our brain and our heart so that our thoughts and desires will be subservient to God, David. After you are Bar Mitzvah, we'll do this together in the mornings.'

'Can you get *tephillin* in England? I haven't got mine yet, have I?' David said anxiously.

Abraham picked up his prayerbook and moved nearer the candle so he could read the print, though he knew the words by heart. 'Don't worry, wherever Jews are *tephillin* are made and everything else required for our devotions. In Russia, they think if they burn down the *shuls* with the scrolls inside them, they'll be able to wipe out our religion, but for every one they burn another will rise in its place.' He stared at the candle flame pensively for a moment, then bent over his prayerbook.

Something in his father's expression made David want to get up and hug him, but he controlled the impulse. 'I hope you find a job soon, Father,' he said quietly instead.

Sarah was watching Malka roll the dumplings for the chicken soup when Abraham arrived back one Friday afternoon.

'You're early today,' she said as he kissed her.

'The factories'll be closed in an hour for *Shabbos*,' he said listlessly. 'And in any case, none of them wants a machiner who's never used a machine. Haven't I proved it?'

Malka went on dropping the dumplings into a pot of boiling water. 'Make Abie a glass of tea, Sarah,' she instructed. 'I'd make it myself, but my hands're sticky from the *knedl* mixture.' Her pink cheeks creased into a smile. 'So you'll owe me another slice of lemon!'

The remark was meant to be a joke, Malka's shortcomings did not include meanness, but Abraham left the room without a word.

Malka shrugged. 'He's getting touchy.'

'Can you blame him?' Sarah followed on his heels and found him in the parlour, staring through the window.

It was not yet dusk, but the soft light which precedes it had muted the harsh brick of the houses opposite to a false mellow-ness and the streetlamp, to which the lamplighter had just applied his long pole, cast a friendly glow upon the pavement. Abraham watched a cat lope towards an open doorway and enter it. 'Even a cat has its own home,' he said bitterly.

Sarah went to stand beside him and linked her arm through his.

'Don't *shmooze* me,' he said in a gruff voice.

'Linking arms is *shmoozing*?' She reached up and stroked his fiery hair, standing on tiptoe because he was so much taller than her. 'Since when?'

'Since the day I first met you. When you sprained your ankle and asked me to walk you home.'

She laughed. They'd been skating on the frozen river the day they met, she with her sister and Abraham with a gang of lads. She had seen him before, through the cobbler's shop window, and wished she could get to know him, but her father always took the family's shoes to be mended. Once or twice she had caught sight of him in *shul*, too. The section where the women sat was screened off from the men's seats according to religious ritual, but during the part of the service when everyone stood his height had made him visible over the top of the screen. 'Without someone to lean on I couldn't walk,' she reminded him.

'Seven boys were skating there that day and she has to choose me to lean on!' He planted a kiss on the top of her head. 'She asks me to walk her home and now I'm living with *landsleit* in England.'

Sarah pulled away from him. Leaving Russia had been her decision, but what alternative had they had? Spending the rest of their lives like hunted animals? Never certain when they went to bed at night that they and their children would live to see the next morning? Life should be something better than existing from day to day, unable to plan for the future because you might not have one.

Abraham picked up his *tallith* and folded it. She watched him put it carefully into a blue velvet bag embroidered with the Star of David, to take it with him to *shul*. Their sons were already dressed in their Sabbath suits and soon he must change, too, and collect them from the Moritzes where they had taken to spending much of their time. After the men had gone to the synagogue, she and Malka would put on their best dresses and wait for them to return, as Jewish wives and mothers did everywhere on Friday evenings. These simple traditions were something solid to cling to and helped her keep her feet on the ground. Seeing her husband preparing for *Shabbos* helped her now. 'You'll talk to the men about a job, after the service tonight. Someone will advise you,' she said firmly. 'Chaim's a good person, but he doesn't know everything.'

David always looked forward to walking back from *shul* on Friday nights. His father would take him and Sammy by the hand

and talk to them earnestly about the sermon they'd heard, the way he debated the Talmud with his friends, which gave David a nice grown-up feeling. Other boys would be walking alongside their fathers, too, but Mr Berkowitz, who had no sons, always walked with Rabbi Lensky who had none either.

It was a night when only males were seen on the streets. A pleasant stillness hung in the air and candles flickered behind lace curtains, signalling a Sabbath greeting to those abroad in the dark. Sometimes, when you passed a house a savoury fragrance drifting from under the door made you think of the meal waiting for you and his father would quicken his footsteps and smile.

On this Friday night, he was grim-faced and silent.

'What is it, Father?' David asked, but received no reply.

Abraham was not himself during supper, either. David saw him toying listlessly with the food on his plate and noticed that his mother was watching, too, though she made no comment. His father's face had often worn a frown lately, especially when he arrived back in the evenings, only tonight it was not just his face which looked worried, but his whole body, as if he was hurting deep inside.

'Is Father ill?' he asked Sarah later, when she was tucking him up in the parlour.

'Such big eyes this child has! He sees everything! Your father's tired, David, that's all. He's worn out from looking for a job.'

'Why can't he find one?'

'Questions he asks, when he should be asleep! For people like us there aren't enough jobs to go round.'

David wanted to task her what she meant by 'people like us', but he knew she would not bother explaining because he was only a little boy. Perhaps Mr Moritz would tell him? Mr Moritz never minded explaining things.

Abraham was hunched by the stoked-up fire when Sarah returned from putting the boys to bed. Tomorrow, the *Shabbos-Goy* would call to pile on more coal; Jews were forbidden to do so themselves on the Sabbath and an elderly Gentile earned himself some coppers by knocking on doors in the ghetto and doing it for them. Cooking, too, was forbidden on the holy day, which necessitated meals being prepared in advance and left to simmer in the oven. Malka's *cholent* accounted for the appetising aroma of butter beans cooking in a rich, meaty sauce which filled the room and reminded Sarah of Friday nights in Dvinsk when she and Abraham had sat quietly together by their cosy wood stove.

The only privacy they had here was the time they lay cuddled in their *perineh* and even then they must talk in whispers so as not to waken the children. But tonight the Berkowitzes had retired early and they had the kitchen to themselves. A clock Malka had brought from Russia chimed the hour, puncturing the contemplative silence.

'You talked to the men in *shul* about a job?' Sarah asked.

Abraham's expression tightened. 'They advised me to be a *shmearer.*'

'Maybe it's a good idea, if they advised it.'

He looked at her for a moment, then bowed his head again, his hands clasped tightly on his lap as if he was trying to contain himself. A picture of the birdlike fingers swooping into the reeking varnish flashed before his eyes. Was this how he was doomed to spend his days? 'Once, I was a craftsman,' he said flatly.

'And once my father had money and my mother wore jewellery, but the Tsar thought they weren't entitled to these things and now they're both in their graves.' Sarah touched her brooch, which her parents had given to her when she was sixteen. In Dvinsk she had been afraid to wear it, in case it caught the eye of a roving *pogromschik.* 'What's the use of dwelling on the past?' she said simply. 'The future is what counts and how you'll feed and clothe your children now.'

'To dip my finger in varnish I left Russia!' Abraham exclaimed bitterly.

Sarah's eyes blazed and a surge of colour stained her high cheekbones. 'To live you left Russia!' she reminded him.

But looking for work as a *shmearer* proved futile, too.

'Why d'you think those know-alls advised you to be one?' Chaim, who had not advised it, scoffed one evening. 'Because it's easier to learn than machining. But every unskilled person who arrives gets the same advice. It's time for the brutal truth again and you might as well face up to it, the waterproof factories aren't just waiting for Abie Sandberg.'

Abraham got up from his chair and stalked out of the room.

Malka was quartering an apple to share between the four of them. She exchanged a glance with Chaim. 'Touchy he certainly is.'

'He's got feelings,' Sarah apologised.

'You think my Chaim hasn't?'

'It's all right, I understand,' Chaim shrugged, but he had a hurt look on his face.

They sat crunching the apple. Abraham did not return to the kitchen and his quarter remained on the table turning browner by the minute, a pointed reminder of his absence and, to Sarah, of how the Berkowitzes shared everything with them. They were kindness itself and sometimes she wished they were a little less so. Living in someone else's house wasn't easy and the feeling of indebtedness made it even harder. She wanted to go and comfort Abraham, but forced herself to sit and chat with their hosts until bedtime. When she retired, her husband was sound asleep.

'If you disappear like that again, they'll think you're ungrateful,' she warned him the next morning. 'You can't just walk out of the room like you can in your own house.'

'In my own house I wouldn't have to,' he replied. 'Chaim's a nice fellow, but in small doses.'

He should know how it is here for me all day, with Malka, she thought casting her mind back over the last four weeks.

After Chavah and Ezra left for Liverpool, she had set to with dusters and polishing wax taken from her own bundles, to clean the parlour.

'What're you doing?' Malka had laughed. 'It'll be the same again when your children have put their fingers on everything. A quick sweep with the broom is enough.'

But Sarah had cleaned the room thoroughly, then gone to the kitchen to assist with the daily chores.

'Put down the duster,' Malka had ordered. 'I told you I don't let my guests work.'

'It'll be a pleasure to help you. Look what you're doing for me.'

'That you'll please take for granted. And also, take the weight off your feet. If you won't sit down I'll have to get up from my chair and help you,' Malka gurgled in her happy-go-lucky fashion. 'And I don't feel like it. We'll have a nice gossip, you've only just got here. I'll clean and tidy tomorrow and you can watch me.'

It did not take Sarah long to realise that so far as cleaning was concerned, tomorrow rarely came in this house. Only once a week, before the Sabbath, did Malka make a desultory attempt to restore her home to order. But for Sarah, that was better than never and on the first Friday morning Malka found her about to scrub the scullery floor.

'A guest with a scrubbing brush in her hand? On her hands and knees?' She made Sarah rise and gave the floor a half-hearted tickle with a rag.

The same one used to wipe down the draining board where the vegetables were chopped for the stew, Sarah noted and tried not to remember this when she ate her meals. She could not help her nature, which was the very opposite of Malka's.

Her offers to assist with the cooking met with the same resistance.

'Let me at least bake you a sponge cake to have on *Shabbos* afternoon,' she pleaded. Saturday afternoons had been highlights of her childhood, with all the family gathering in her grandparents' home for cakes and tea. Never would times like those come again, she reflected with pain. But a person had to try. 'Give me the eggs and sugar, Malka.'

'In my home you'll eat my cakes. Take a rest! When you have your own household to look after, you'll wish you could have one,' Malka had told her.

That happy day could not come soon enough for Sarah, but meanwhile time hung heavily on her hands. Mr Moritz had taken David and Sammy to enrol at school and though she and Abraham had privately thought it too soon, they had felt unable to argue about educational matters with a man whose home was full of books. The boys' absence left her with only little Esther to care for, which was far from a full-time occupation.

'You're out of friends with me because I got a little huffy last night?' Abraham asked her.

She looked up and saw that he had dressed whilst she was standing daydreaming, feeling sorry for herself. 'That I'll never be,' she smiled shaking herself out of it. 'But maybe we should both remember what Rabbi Lensky said in the cart on our first night here, about not being entitled to grumble. We've let ourselves forget already, haven't we?'

After David and Sammy had gone to school she sat watching Esther play 'house' with the Berkowitz twins, determined not to allow the inactivity to depress her.

The scullery door was open and Malka was scraping vegetables at the sink, chattering away as usual, but Sarah could not concentrate on what she was saying. She could hear the tap dripping and the rasp of the paring knife as Malka moved it back and forth. The low ceiling seemed to be pressing down upon her and the stuffy little room, with its heavy furniture, closing her in. For a moment she panicked, she had never experienced such a feeling before. She fixed her gaze on a shiny, green chaise longue and tried to pull herself together.

This hideous piece had been purchased at the local secondhand shop, prior to the Sandbergs' arrival, and was destined for the parlour when they left. An emotion very like despair, but not quite, because hopelessness was not in her character, overwhelmed her. When, oh when, would that be? She became aware that Malka was standing beside her, wiping her hands on her apron.

'You've gone deaf all of a sudden, Sarah? I've been talking to you for five minutes! I'm out of onions just now would you believe?'

'So why don't I go to the store and get you some?' Sarah rose from her chair quickly, the chance to escape from the house for a while seemed heaven sent.

Malka hesitated, but Sarah had already fetched her shawl from the lobby and was slipping it around her shoulders. 'I've got to get used to marketing in England, you'd be doing me a favour,' she said persuasively.

'In that case.' Malka handed her a shopping basket. 'But you'll find it's no different from how you did in Russia.'

Maybe not, but other things aren't the same, Sarah thought as she walked slowly towards the main road. In Russia at this time in the morning everyone had their *perinehs* draped over the bedroom windowsills and it seemed strange to walk down a street and not see any. This had always been her first task after Abraham had gone to work, but Malka had said if she did it here, even when it wasn't raining, the feather filling would get so damp it would never dry again. Her house in Dvinsk hadn't been infested with mice, either, so she had to keep a cat like everyone here had to and it was funny to see so many cats roaming the streets.

Malka's neighbour Mrs Lemberg was cleaning her front door-step and looked up to smile at Sarah as she approached. 'So how're you settling in? Like the old country it isn't, eh?'

Sarah paused to speak to her. 'That's what I was thinking.'

'Listen, you'll still be thinking it when you've been here two years, like me! Did I ever think I'd miss Bialystok after what they did to us there? There's plenty I don't miss and that's what keeps me going.' Mrs Lemberg wiped her steaming hands on her faded black apron and rubbed her knobbly back. 'This donkey-stone they put on the steps here, oy vay, it breaks me in two rubbing it on!' She fished in her bucket of water for the yellow-brown slab and began applying it laboriously again. 'But in England you have to do like the English. Some people use the white, but you need to do it more often, it shows the dirt quicker.'

Sarah decided she would use the white when she got her own house. 'Why do they call it that?' she inquired.

'Who knows? Maybe because you get it from the rag-and-bone man who comes with a donkey and cart every week and gives it to you in exchange for whatever you want to get rid of.'

'Funny customs they have here!' Sarah laughed. Chatting with Mrs Lemberg had done her good.

On Bury New Road, she paused to look at the shops which were always closed and shuttered when she passed on her way to *shul* on Saturdays. It was the first time she had been out on a weekday, Malka always asked her to mind the children and slipped out to do the marketing quickly, as if it was a bother to her, but Sarah had always enjoyed that part of a housewife's duties. What could be more pleasurable than spending a little time selecting the food you gave your family to eat, making sure it was the best you could afford to buy?

She watched the butcher's treble-chinned wife plucking a fowl in a cloud of feathers, balancing it on her stained apron and talking to the customers whilst her husband, who resembled a side of beef himself, cut one into small joints. Some huge garlic sausages hanging up in the window made Sarah's mouth water. The aroma of fresh bread and cinnamon wafting through the open door of a bakery did, too, and she wished she could afford to buy one of the delicious-looking cheese cakes and take it back to Malka's for a treat after supper. England's going to my head, she smiled to herself. Wanting to buy cakes, when she'd always made her own!

There was only one greengrocery on the block, the one Rabbi Lensky had pointed out the night she arrived. It was also a fishmongery and Sarah had to push her way through the chattering woman who were clustered around a box of plaice near the door, flipping them from side to side to examine them.

'Without enough red spots on the black, they don't have the same flavour,' an angular lady wearing a man's flat cap advised the woman beside her.

'She thinks I was born yesterday!'

Sarah saw them move to a counter where the hake and haddock were displayed and begin digging their nails into the silvery fish to test its freshness. It's just like at home, she thought happily and went to where the fruit and vegetables were stacked, to press her thumb into the lemons, expertly, as she had at old Mr Katz's market stall in Dvinsk, even when she was not going to buy any. She watched a woman with wispy hair and a darned shawl brandish a bruised apple under the greengrocer's snub nose.

'This I'll take home, my husband will throw me out, like you should do with your fruit, you *ganef*!' the woman upbraided him.

'A thief Mrs Kaplan's calling me now,' the stocky little man said placidly. 'If I give it to you for half-price, will your husband still throw you out?'

'Enough already. I'll take it.'

'Your greengrocer in Russia gave you such good bargains?' Mr Radinsky inquired with a twinkle in his eye.

'Better than you gave your customers in Poland, believe me,' Mrs Kaplan retorted before she shuffled out of the shop.

Sarah had to smile as she sorted through the onions to find some nice big ones for Malka. How good it was, the way Yiddish spanned the gap between Jews of many different origins. And the way they did their marketing was universal! She took the onions to the counter where Mrs Radinsky sat purple-lipped beside a ledger, the glistening colour deepening with every lick she gave to her indelible pencil.

Nobody paid cash and Sarah considered having the purchase charged to herself, but feared she would be refused because she wasn't yet a householder. Malka had told her about some new arrivals who ran up bills with the local traders whilst living with *landsleit*, then disgraced their hosts by absconding to another town.

'Come again, we're always happy to see new faces,' Mr Radinsky said after he had weighed the onions and put them into her basket.

The warm words gave Sarah a pleasant feeling. One day she'd be a good customer here and pay her bills scrupulously. Meanwhile she must try to stem her impatience.

When she left the shop she met Rachel Moritz and was conscious of her shabby appearance beside the other woman's attire. 'That's a nice coat you've got on, Mrs Moritz,' she remarked as they walked home together. Her initial impression of Rachel was still with her and she could not think of anything else to say.

Rachel smoothed the soft brown pleats which flowed from her broad hips to her ankles. 'It shouldn't be?' she laughed. 'With a tailor for a husband?'

'Mr Moritz makes for ladies also?' Sarah said with surprise.

'Why not?'

'He measures them even?'

'What then?'

Sarah's expression was shocked. 'The bust and everything?'

Rachel pealed with laughter and Sarah had to laugh, too.

'If a woman let such a thing happen to her in Dvinsk, it wouldn't be a laughing matter!'

'Vienna is more broadminded.'

'It sounds it.'

They turned the corner from the main road and Rachel held on to her hat as a gust of wind came scurrying to meet them. Sarah gathered her shawl closer around her. She could see the blue chenille curtains at Malka's parlour window and wished she could delay her return to the house a little longer.

'How're you getting on there with my next-door-neighbours?'

Rachel asked. Always sensitive to the feelings of others, she was aware that Sarah's spirits had suddenly flagged.

'You lived with *landsleit* when you first came?' Sarah's tone implied more than she had intended.

Rachel shook her head. 'But I can imagine two women in one kitchen.'

Sarah found herself wanting to pour out all her frustrations, but managed to remain silent. It would seem like ingratitude to the Berkowitzes whom she could never repay for their generosity. 'I haven't had a cross word with Malka,' she said instead.

'That I can imagine also. You don't seem the type for cross words. Listen, I always drink a cup of coffee when I get home from the marketing. You'd like to join me? Since the night you brought your boys to sleep with Carl you haven't visited us. Here is an opportunity.'

Sarah drank only tea, but refrained from saying so. It was just one of the differences between Russians and Austrians she'd have to get used to if she was to have any Austrian friends. She was still far from sure she wanted any after that first encounter, but Rachel was certainly much nicer this time and the Moritz family was very kind to David and Sammy. 'A cup of coffee would be very nice,' she smiled.

As she sat sipping the bitter black liquid, which she meant to swallow down even if it choked her, the Moritzes' kitchen no longer seemed so austere. It was the same size as Malka's, but appeared more spacious. Rachel had not deemed it necessary to supplement the built-in dresser under the window with an addtional one, as Malka had; the dining set and Sigmund's wing chair were the only furniture in the room. There was no clock on the mantelpiece to point out the time and Sarah felt unusually relaxed.

'Well,' Rachel smiled. She was perfectly at ease, her elbow resting on the table, the leg o'mutton sleeve of her crisp white blouse ballooning out as she cupped her cheek in her hand.

She looks as if she never lifts a finger, Sarah could not help thinking. But her immaculate home said otherwise.

Rachel rose to bring something from the dresser, her movements quiet and unhurried. She's beautiful, Sarah thought. Why didn't I notice it before? It wasn't the kind of beauty a person would see immediately, ripe and blooming like Malka's, but the kind that grew on you. She was above average height for a woman and shapely without being heavy. Nondescript brown hair and a pale complexion did nothing to enhance her irregular features, but the eyes, dark and shining, illuminated her face. It's happiness that makes eyes shine that way, Sarah said to herself. But I'm happy with Abraham and mine're not like that. Happiness didn't always mean contentment, though.

Rachel returned to the table carrying a cake tin and sat down to open it, a smile hovering gently around her lips. Watching her, Sarah knew what it was that made her beautiful. Rachel Moritz was a contented woman.

'You must taste my Sachertorte,' she said taking some dark and sticky wedges from the tin and putting them on a plate.

Chocolate cake is chocolate cake, Sarah thought. Until she bit into it. The rich confection, tangy with an unexpected filling of apricot jam melted in her mouth, a culinary delight quite different from any she had experienced before. She wished Abraham could share it and felt a pang of guilt that she was enjoying herself whilst he was out looking for work.

'In Vienna we don't eat it in the morning. Usually with our afternoon coffee. You like it, Mrs Sandberg?'

'An ecstasy it is, Mrs Moritz. My name is Sarah.'

'And mine is Rachel.'

They smiled warmly at each other.

How could I have thought this woman stuck-up? Sarah thought. It'll teach me not to trust first impressions!

'With tea Sachetorte doesn't go so well,' Rachel told her.

'So here I'll drink coffee and you'll have tea with sponge cake, light as a feather, when you visit my house.'

The promise reminded her that she had no house and her expression clouded. Rachel noticed, but made no comment and they fell silent. The quiet room, the wintry sunlight burnishing a yellow tureen on the dresser to gold, the singing of the metal coffee pot on the hob, and Rachel's undemanding presence had a soothing effect upon Sarah. Troubles she had, but for a little while she had been able to forget them.

Rachel surveyed her over the rim of her cup and saw a tiny

66

woman, thin as a reed and yet with an undeniable strength about her. David, from whom the Moritzes had learned much about the Sandberg family, had said his mother was twenty-five, which was five years younger than herself, but Sarah looked older. Anxiety had etched premature lines on her broad forehead and a furrow had already begun to form above the bridge of her nose. The black hair, parted in the centre and dragged back severely into a bun at the nape of her neck, was winged with silver at the temples, giving her a striking appearance. Rachel had thought at first it was a *sheitel*, the wig which ultra-orthodox Jewesses wore after marriage, and wondered why she had chosen such an unusual one. Now, she saw it was her own hair. Rachel's mother had wanted her to wear a wig after her marriage to Sigmund, but she had refused and Sarah had evidently done the same, as others of their generation had.

Sarah sat quietly in her chair and her careworn appearance tugged at Rachel's heart strings. Thank God we left Vienna when we did, she thought. Carl's broken glasses and a brick tossed through Sigmund's workshop window were nothing compared with what the Sandbergs must have endured. There had not been pogroms in Austria and many people thought the current Jew-baiting would peter out. Sigmund had not disagreed, but one day it would erupt like a volcano, he had warned those who thought him foolish to flee. 'Why wait until your life depends on it?' he had asked them. As always with him, it was a considered decision and Rachel was now quite certain he had been right.

'Any coffee for me?' he said from the doorway. The parlour was his workroom, which was why the bookshelves were in the kitchen. 'How nice to see you,' he greeted Sarah and stood smiling at her, a thickset little man with pins jabbed hither and thither in his waistcoat, his tape measure festooned around his neck, the tools of his trade making him much less awe-inspiring than she had hitherto found him. 'Your sons we're already getting to know very well,' he chuckled. 'And let me tell you something. That David of yours has a head which will take him a long way. The questions he asks!'

'I hope he isn't being a bother to you,' Sarah apologised.

'There's nothing I enjoy more than a clever child.'

Sarah had always known David was clever, but in Russia it

had not been important. Jews who received an education in anything other than Hebrew were few and far between there and she had never met anyone who had. Sigmund's pronouncement opened up a new avenue of thought.

'He'll be something, take my word for it,' Sigmund declared sitting down to drink the coffee Rachel had poured for him.

'Maybe,' Sarah smiled. Then she pushed the idea away. For David to be something would cost money.

Sigmund took a book from a shelf he could reach without rising from the table, opened it at random and was immediately absorbed in it, but Sarah did not feel insulted.

'What can you do with him? He likes to read,' Rachel said. She sat watching him with the gentle smile about her lips again. She had taken no part in the conversation, almost as if her own presence ceased to matter the moment he entered the room, but her eyes had rarely left him. He seemed unaware of her, but Sarah felt he was not.

'What's the book he's reading this time?' Sarah asked her.

'Listen, with him it doesn't matter. Half of them he knows by heart anyway.'

In Vienna, Sigmund had used the workroom which had once been his father's. Here, his earnings were not sufficient for him to rent separate premises, but he had begun to like the improvised arrangements which allowed him to put down his needle and lose himself in his books whenever he had a moment to spare.

'Sometimes, I'm not sure if it's a tailor's shop we've got here, or a meeting place for professors, you should see what goes on with some of his customers,' Rachel chuckled to Sarah. Some of them were other Viennese of his ilk, armchair philosophers inclined to launch into intellectual discussions while he fitted their suits and working at home enabled him to dive into the kitchen and emerge with a volume which would prove his point and allow him to win the argument.

Sarah rose and picked up her shopping basket. 'Malka will think I've run away with the onions!' she laughed. 'Also I've stayed too long, taking up your time.'

'What's a bit of time between friends?' Rachel replied and Sigmund raised his head from the book to nod his agreement.

'A nice little woman, not a chatterbox,' he said after she had left. But Rachel had the feeling there was more to Sarah Sandberg than that.

CHAPTER FOUR

The *Chevrah Habimah* was one of the many small congregations which flourished in Strangeways and, like the *shuls* in the old *shtetlachs*, it was not just a building where prayers were said, but also a meeting place.

It was here that Shloime Lipkin had taken Abraham on the day they trekked round the factories together and since then he had often enjoyed a midday chat with Rabbi Lensky and others like himself who welcomed a brief respite from their search for work.

'The price of a glass of tea is a smile,' the little minister told newcomers to the circle. 'If you're going to be miserable, why bother to come in out of the rain?' Rabbi Lensky was a *Hassid*, one of the humanitarian sect who believe that sadness hinders devotion and that life is meant to be lived, rather than pondered upon. 'My personal bonus is you'll stay with your cheerful faces to say the afternoon prayer with me,' he always added.

Synagogue services required a minimum congregation of ten men and sometimes it was necessary to fetch some passers-by from the street to complete the number. However pressing a man's business might be, he would not refuse to make up a *minyan* for prayer. But these occasions were rare at the *Chevrah Habimah*, where the walls were more often than not lined with men leaning against them because all the chairs were occupied.

At midday, the rabbi served tea in the kitchen at the back of the dilapidated house. The front room was the *shul*. Upstairs was uninhabitable.

'Why don't you tell us how to keep cheerful, Rabbi?' Shloime said wryly one day. 'Without a penny in our pockets and sponging off *landsleit*.'

'When they throw you out you'll have something to cry about. A man can always find a reason to rejoice which tells him God hasn't deserted him.'

But sometimes you have to look hard to find it and you can't help feeling maybe He has, Abraham thought.

The minister refilled the kettle and put it on to boil again when Yankel Cohen came in with Yossel Lensky. 'No luck this morning, my friends?'

They warmed their hands by the fire and managed to grin as they shook their heads.

A lad with a craggy face and burning eyes, whom Abraham had not met before, took his glass to the sink to rinse it. They had to take turns to drink their tea because there were not enough glasses. 'If God hasn't deserted us, why can't we find work?' he asked bitterly.

Everyone fell silent. There was not one among them who had not asked himself that question.

Rabbi Lensky glanced compassionately at the weary-faced men for whom this brief interlude in God's house was the only comfort in their fruitless daily round. Some had taken off their coats and steam was rising from their coarse wool shirts as they crouched by the fire to dry off. 'God wants to be sure you'll value it when you get it, Simon,' he said to the lad with conviction. 'What other reason could there be for the merciful Lord to prolong such misery?'

'How could He possibly think we won't?' Shloime exclaimed.

Talking about God as if He were a flesh and blood person was not unusual among members of this congregation. Another *Hassidic* concept is that even the commonest man can find Him in his everyday life and many *Hassidim* told Him their problems as they would to a trusted friend.

'He's had plenty of experience with people who don't,' the rabbi replied slicing up another lemon for the next lot of tea. He picked up a whole one and looked at it. 'Not everyone is like Mr Radinsky the greengrocer who gives my young congregant Menachem a bagful of these to bring to me for these gatherings. Mr Radinsky isn't even a member of my *shul*, but he hasn't forgotten when he too tramped his feet off looking for work.'

'Are you saying God wants us to suffer so we'll appreciate His help when we get it?' Simon demanded.

'How long have you been in England, young man?'

71

'Six months.'

'And already you've forgotten what suffering is?'

Simon's face flushed with shame.

'Listen, it's easy to do, my boy. The present is always more important than the past. I also have my lapses of memory,' Rabbi Lensky confessed. 'Who doesn't?' He chuckled as he handed glasses of tea to the late arrivals. 'Shall I tell you why I called this *shul Habimah*?'

Abraham laughed. 'When we came here the first Friday night and I saw just the rows of chairs before the Ark, with no *bimah* for you to stand upon, I and my sons wondered.'

'That's the reason for the name, Abie.'

Abraham exchanged a puzzled glance with the other men. 'The *shul* is called after something it hasn't got?'

Everyone laughed.

Shloime raised his eyes to the cracked ceiling. 'You think He also sees the joke, Rabbi?'

'Why not? It isn't on Him, it's on me and it isn't really a joke, it's a reminder. In my little *shul* in Rostov, where my Cousin Yossel here was married to Hannah, a carpenter friend of mine built me a beautiful *bimah*. You remember, Yossel?'

'Three steps it had leading up to it, with a banister to hold onto and a railing all the way round, of polished wood,' Yossel recalled. 'I also remember how those barbarians chopped it to pieces.'

'And now I'm here, in a *shul* with no *bimah*,' the rabbi said quietly. 'But one day, with your help my friends, we'll move to a better building and there'll be a *bimah* in the centre for me to stand upon. Maybe it'll be the finest *shul* in Manchester, but I, its minister, will not get too big for my boots, I'll have the name, like a piece of thread tied around my finger, to remind me from whence I came.'

A few days later, Abraham found a job and began work immediately. Sarah was overjoyed when he arrived back in the evening and told her.

'Have we got any money left?' he asked her urgently.

She looked in her purse and found a shilling, the change after they had bought their railway tickets.

'Give it to me.'

'Our last shilling? What do you want it for?'

Abraham took the coin from her. 'To buy a little tea and sugar for Rabbi Lensky and I'm going to buy him some every week for the rest of my life.'

Sarah looked bewildered. Abraham had not told her about the rabbi's midday gatherings and she was not the only wife in Strangeways who believed her husband's day were unrelieved gloom. 'You're going to buy tea and sugar for Rabbi Lensky every week for the rest of your life? Why?'

She was no less bewildered by Abraham's reply.

'Because he's not short of lemons.'

David could not remember when his father had last looked so happy. 'Will we be able to have our own house now Father's working?' he asked with a note of longing in his voice he did not know was there.

Sarah brushed a stray lock from his forehead and thought, absently, that it was odd how his sidelocks curled but the rest of his hair was as straight as her own. 'We'll see,' she said softly, though in her imagination she was already hanging curtains at the windows of her new home.

'Your mother won't stay here a day longer than she has to, David, she's had enough of us!' Malka joked.

Sarah smiled and felt guilty because it was the truth, but Abraham's finding work lightened the atmosphere in the house and there was an air of festivity when they all sat down for supper, as if the frugal fare was a celebratory meal. Esther and Bella and Lakie were allowed to stay up late to eat with the others and Chaim was even more boisterous than usual.

'A toast to the new presser!' he bellowed raising his bowl of soup and quaffing some down.

'You'll burn your tongue!' Malka screeched.

'Then he won't be able to talk any more,' Abraham laughed.

'You look nice when you laugh, Mr Sandberg,' one of the little Berkowitz twins piped up.

'It's nice to have something to laugh about, Lakie.'

'I'm Bella.'

'So who could tell the difference?'

'Lakie's got a spot on her chin,' Sammy said eyeing the rosy face opposite him.

73

'Only when she's eating blackbread with caraway seed,' Malka chuckled.

'When I get my wages, you'll let Sarah buy a bone from the butcher Malka, to help the soup,' Abraham said tasting the thin liquid.

'Why not, now you're earning? Independent I am, but not that independent!'

'Shloime Lipkin's working now, also,' Abraham told Sarah. 'Yesterday his *landsleit* ran to fetch him when someone dropped dead at the *shmearing* bench where he works and Shloime ran back with him without even putting on his coat and got taken on in the man's place. I'm sorry for him.'

'It's the man who dropped dead you should be sorry for.'

Abraham put down his spoon contemplatively. 'When it comes to being a *shmearer* I'm not so sure. Pressing's not what I'm used to, but at least it's a pleasure to make a garment look neat and nice.'

Sarah eyed the heaped basket of laundry awaiting her attention. 'So I'll let you do the ironing in future,' she said slyly.

'That much of a pleasure it isn't!'

'Listen, a trade's a trade,' Chaim declared. 'And getting into one's the hardest part. Thank God Abie's managed to do it.'

Abraham steeled himself to receive the clap on the back he knew was coming.

'You're a fortunate fellow, Abie!' Chaim pronounced as he delivered it.

'I know.' But sometimes before your luck can be good, someone else's has to be bad, Abraham thought. Like with me and Shloime.

When they went to bed Sarah fell asleep immediately, as if her worries were over. Abraham lay tossing and turning. He had not wanted to upset her by telling her his job might only be temporary. Nor had he mentioned the circumstances which led to him getting it, which try as he would he could not put from his mind.

That morning, he had wandered up Southall Street, a byway he had so far avoided because it was beside the jail. Someone had told him that murderers were hung at Strangeways and once he had seen a man with a black leather valise heading in that direction and wondered if he was the executioner carrying his rope. Who wants to be reminded of that every morning on their way to work? A nice start to the day! he had said to himself. But there were factories nearby and this morning he had forced himself to go there.

One of them had seemed busier than the others. Some men were unloading lumps of cloth from a cart and carrying them inside and the rattle of many sewing machines was loud enough to be heard in the street. When he entered there was no smell of varnish, which meant it was not a waterproof factory. Maybe I'm not fated to be a *shmearer* he had thought hopefully.

The place was bigger than most of the others at which he had called. Please God, let them need me, he had prayed as he made for the stairs. Then a scene he could not help witnessing through the open doorway at the far end of the long lobby stopped him in his tracks.

A woman lay shivering on a sofa, though she was covered with many blankets. She looked extremely ill and a fat little girl stood beside her, holding her hand. A boy of about David's age was bathing her brow, soaking a rag in a bowl of water and wringing it out carefully before applying it.

'The noise of the machines is like an engine in my head,' the woman moaned. 'I never have a minute's peace from it.'

Gaslight from a wall bracket above their heads cast an opalescent haze onto the trio and Abraham had the feeling he was looking at a picture. It was one he would remember all his life.

The woman raised herself and peered in his direction. 'Always people in the house. Close the door, Bessie!' she shrieked feverishly and the little girl slammed it shut.

The clatter of the sewing machines grew louder as Abraham mounted the stairs. A hot mist greeted him when he reached the landing, and the acrid smell of singeing cloth, drifting from the pressing room. Above the noise, shouts of rage could be heard and a choice selection of Yiddish curses. Abraham's instinct was to retreat downstairs, but he stood rooted when a portly man confronted him.

'Just today she has to take bad!' the man ranted as if it was Abraham's fault. 'When the underpresser has gone somewhere else to work, for more money. The pox take him!' He glared at

Abraham from beneath hooded eyelids, the cigarette in his mouth dripping ash onto his well-stained waistcoat. 'I ask you what can you do with someone like that?'

Abraham spread his hands for want of an answer.

'So this morning I let a boy do the pressing. Holes he burns in the garments! You're maybe a presser, I should be so lucky?'

Abraham thought quickly, an unusual exercise for him, but urgency spurred him on. 'I can do better than a boy who burns holes in garments.' He was sure this was not a lie, though what it implied certainly was.

'So come inside!'

He found himself being steered through the clouds of steam into the pressing room and thus it was that he entered his life's work. Years of cobbling had made his fingers nimble and his hands deft. He had no difficulty in manipulating the heavy flat iron and soon became adept at exerting just the correct amount of pressure where it was required. The steamy atmosphere was not pleasant, but compared with the *shmearing* he had feared would be his lot, it was paradise.

'He's a treasure! A find!' the excitable man exulted examining his work. 'So *nu*! Press the next coat already, there's plenty more where that came from.' He stemmed his enthusiasm shrewdly. 'Who knows? Maybe I'll keep you on. Half-a-crown a week I'll pay you, piece work I'm not interested in here.'

How many hours a week's work comprised he forebore to mention, but Abraham learned from one of the machiners that it sometimes meant all the hours God sends.

'Here, you've got to take the rough with the smooth,' the machiner shrugged.

'Listen, plenty of people would be glad of the opportunity,' Abraham replied.

'That's why he gets away with it. But at least with Isaac Salaman you know you've got a steady job and you'll find out his bark is worse than his bite. Also, in the places where they pay piecework rates they take home more than we do when business is good, but when it's bad they get next to nothing and we still get the same as usual. When things're very bad the whole trade is laid off, but our jobs're waiting for us when business picks up.

With the pieceworkers it's different, the job they had before the lay-off could be given to someone else when it's over. My name's Issie, by the way. I just popped in here to tell you it's dinnertime.'

'I'm much obliged.'

Issie grinned at him from behind horn-rimmed spectacles and adjusted the *yamulke* on his prematurely bald head. 'With my hairstyle you need glue to keep this on? So welcome to the mad-house. Bring your food to eat it with us in the workroom if you like,' he said as he left.

Abraham continued pressing the garment on the ironing board and tried to ignore the hunger pangs in his stomach.

'A worker who works in the dinner break?' Salaman said from the doorway. 'Didn't I say he was a find? You don't feel like eating, Abie?'

'I didn't bring anything with me, Mr Salaman.'

'So today you'll share mine, or where will you get the strength from to press all the garments I'm going to bring in here this afternoon?'

Salaman hustled him into the workroom. Though he lived on the premises, he always ate with the workers at midday, to ensure the break did not last too long.

The workroom was as chaotic as all the others Abraham had seen, but larger than most of them and with more staff. The machiners were eating at their machines.

'Mind you don't drip anything onto that garment!' Salaman barked to a lad who was biting into a pickled cucumber. 'Brine stains as well as holes burned in the coats is all I need. This is Abie Sandberg, everybody, who's helping us out in the pressing room,' he announced turning on a smile.

Abraham's heart sank because it did not sound very perma-nent. He sat down with Salaman beside the cutting bench and accepted the bagel and cheese the employer offered him. Eli the cutter had gone to chat with Issie and Salaman gave Abraham his undivided attention.

'What would I've done if you hadn't turned up when you did?' he said in a voice which made Abraham feel like a delivering angel. 'You look like an understanding man, who else've I got to talk to? Everyone's wrapped up in themselves, they don't care what trouble I've got. My wife, she's full of imaginary ailments but never before did she stay away from the factory. If she keeps on doing it, where will I be? She's my head presser who I've always relied on, Abie.'

Abraham recalled the ghastly pallor of the woman he'd seen lying on the sofa downstairs, and her feverish shrieks. 'She's seen the doctor?' he asked.

Salaman smiled disparagingly. 'Every other week she sees the doctor, he never finds anything wrong with her.'

'All the same, maybe you should call him.'

'And make a fool of myself?' Salaman wolfed down the last of his food and rose from the stool which creaked under his weight. 'All right already!' he bellowed to his staff. 'Back to work!'

How can a man who's kind enough to share his dinner with me also be the sort who shouts at his workers like dogs? Abraham asked himself as he followed Salaman out of the workroom chewing a bit of bagel. The machiners were still chewing, too, but their feet had begun treadling before their boss made his exit.

In many respects, Salaman was a harsh employer, but he would listen sympathetically to a worker's domestic problems, his pasty face solemn, and had even been known to buy a bunch of grapes for somebody's dying mother. Sharing his meal with Abraham was one of these spasmodic generosities.

During the afternoon, when he was carrying a pile of garments into the pressing room, his little girl began screaming that her mother had fainted. He dropped the coats and rushed downstairs, but not without noticing the reproachful glance Abraham could not help giving him. This time his wife was really ill, but he had not believed her.

She was taken to the Jewish Hospital and Salaman accompanied her. He had not returned yet when the factory closed for the night and Abraham went home.

Supposing she dies? Abraham tortured himself as he lay awake thinking about it. I wouldn't want Mr Salaman's children to have no mother, just so I can have her job. 'Do me a favour, God,' he whispered to the ceiling before he fell asleep. 'And don't think I'm not grateful for the one you've already done me. Let Mrs Salaman get better and be her husband's head presser again. And if you could also arrange for me to be her assistant I'll be very obliged.'

When he went to work the next morning, Eli the cutter told him that Salaman was still at the hospital.

Abraham raised his eyes to the ceiling reproachfully. He did so frequently as three days passed by and his employer had not come back.

Eli, who had been with Salaman longer than anyone else, was doing his best to keep things going. 'There's something wrong with your neck, Abie?' he inquired on the fourth morning when he brought some garments and the news that the boss was still absent and Abraham raised his eyes to the ceiling again. 'A nervous twitch maybe?'

Abraham let the question pass and pressed a lapel so Eli would not see the guilt on his face. 'I keep hoping you'll bring good news.'

Eli dumped a pile of creased coats on the floor. 'The while I'm bringing you these, we don't want him to think we've taken advantage of his trouble, when he gets back.' He scratched his bulbous nose which looked like a large pink cherry on his long face. 'Mr Salaman's sister's taken the kids to her house. But an auntie isn't a mother,' he added ominously.

Abraham's gaze jerked upwards again.

'I'd get that seen to if I were you, it gives a person the creeps,' the cutter told him as he hurried from the room.

Salaman returned that afternoon and seemed unable to believe his factory had functioned without him. His wife was dead and he could not believe that, either. 'It's God's will,' he said heavily to his hushed employees.

Rabbi Blasberg from his *shul* was with him and nodded gravely. 'God's ways are mysterious. We mustn't question them.'

Mysterious is right, Abraham thought with mixed feelings. He would never question them again.

During the ritual week of mourning which followed his wife's funeral, Salaman sat on a low stool as custom demanded, receiving the condolences of his visitors, his son and daughter on either side of him. Little Bessie clung to his arm as if she would never release it, but Saul was seen to shrug off his father's hand when the grieving man placed it on his shoulder.

79

'So Saul doesn't want to be treated like a baby,' Sarah interpreted this when Abraham told her about it. But to Abraham, the boy's behaviour did not seem natural.

He visited Salaman every evening and joined in the prayers for Mrs Salaman's departed soul, which he felt was the least he could do under all the circumstances. His employer always clutched his hand, gratefully, before he left and looked at him with eyes that seemed to be trying to say something.

When Salaman returned to the factory, nothing was mentioned about Abraham's job being temporary and a few days later a youth was engaged to assist him. God and events had made him the head presser and his wage was raised to five shillings.

CHAPTER FIVE

Sarah began looking for a house, though Abraham had no immediate prospect of increasing his earnings. But once under their own roof, they would manage somehow. Years afterwards, she wondered how she had had the nerve and her grandchildren thought she had made the story up.

She decided on one with three bedrooms, which cost sixpence a week more than those with two. This would leave only two shillings with which to feed and clothe the family, but she was not daunted. She wanted a home in which her children could grow up. Eventually, little Esther would require her own room, it would not be seemly for her to share with her brothers. Meanwhile, the spare bedroom would be an investment. She would take a lodger, whose payment for bed and board would help out. By the time the room was needed for Esther, David would be earning and the lodger's contribution would not be missed. Her mind ticked away busily, planning for the future, which left her no time to brood about the present.

She found a house in Moreton Street. It would not become vacant until next month, but the Berkowitzes were now accepting payment for their hospitality and she felt better about receiving it. Malka's slothfulness ceased to depress her once she knew she would soon be leaving it, but the day she moved out was one of the happiest of her life.

'I can't bear you to go, it's been so lovely having you for company all day,' Malka said tearfully.

'They're only going a stone's throw from our street,' Chaim comforted her. 'We'll be able to run round and borrow things.'

'For you two we'd give our last,' Abraham said gruffly.

Sarah looked at the slapdash, noisy couple who were as different from herself and Abraham as oil from water and was ashamed of how she had sometimes felt about them. 'There's nothing we wouldn't do for you,' she told them sincerely.

'So let's get you moved into your house already!' Chaim bellowed to cover what was an emotional moment for all of them.

Removals usually took place on a Sunday, when friends and relatives were free to lend a hand, and the Sandbergs' was no exception. But first they had to buy some furniture and Chaim led the way to Bury New Road, trundling a big handcart he had borrowed from his uncle.

'Just look at all the people!' Sarah gasped when she saw the thronged pavements. Malka had allowed her to do the marketing most days since the time she bought the onions and she had also visited the Moritzes several times in the evenings, with Abraham, whose opinion of them had changed as hers had. But this was her first Sunday morning excursion and she could not believe her eyes. 'If a *goy* would get off the tram here, he'd think he was in a foreign country,' she laughed.

The air was throbbing with Yiddish voices raised in debate, or talking excitedly as people stood around in groups or milled around beside the shop windows. Housewives with scarves tied peasantwise around their heads nursed babies bedecked with red ribbons to keep the evil-eye away; elderly *Hassidim* conversed with friends whilst their pious wives, in ill-fitting *sheitels*, stood patiently by their sides; small boys in *yamulkes* chased each other in and out of Mr Radinsky's biting into cucumbers still dripping with brine from the greengrocer's barrel; marriages were being arranged, recipes and remedies exchanged, the Talmud earnestly and vocally delved into outside Mr Halpern's barber shop, and the garment trade heatedly discussed everywhere.

The Sandbergs and Berkowitzes pushed their way through to the secondhand shop where a motley collection of other people's discarded furniture spilled out onto the pavement. Tables and dressers. Bookcases and china cabinets. Sofas with the horsehair stuffing protruding, exchanged for something better by those who had gone up in the world and elaborate sideboards and gilt-framed mirrors, sold for a song by those whose luck was down. What a wealth of speculation it conjured up and sometimes an item envied in a neighbour's house would be there for the asking.

'There's Mrs Lemberg's fancy hearth rug!' Malka exclaimed espying one. 'I wonder how much he wants for it?'

'Don't bother to ask,' Chaim replied. Before he knew it a man could be steered into this Aladdin's cave by his acquisitive wife and find himself outside again, the owner of some monstrosity. Malka had acquired her green chaise longue that way, which Chaim had had no intention of buying. 'Once bitten!' he jested to Abraham though it was not a joke. Because no money changed hands, there was an air of fantasy about the transactions. Only when the dealer came knocking for his weekly payment did the purchaser come down to earth.

'So let's go inside,' Sarah said impatiently. 'With so many people in the shop, it could take all morning to get served.'

'Not the way you go shopping!' Abraham chuckled.

Sarah always knew exactly what she required and bought no more and no less. She could have furnished her whole house there and then, but she was not one to run up unnecessary debts and only the barest essentials were loaded onto the handcart. A deal table and some chairs for the kitchen; mattresses for the children which would lie on the floor until bedsteads could be afforded; a bed and a marble-topped washstand for the lodger they had not yet got, whose comfort was more important than the family's.

'What about a mattress for you and me?' Abraham asked her.

'We can roll ourselves in the *perineh* for a bit longer.'

'Oy vay!' he laughed ruefully. He knew it was useless to argue with her.

David would have liked a bookcase, but had not dared to ask for one. He knew what his mother would have said. 'Who has a bookcase when they haven't yet got a bed? Or any books to put in it?' He'd have a book soon though, he thought as he helped to push the cart to Moreton Street, as soon as he'd learned to read English without stumbling over the words. Mr Moritz had promised to give him one as a reward.

He wished his mother would ask him, sometimes, how he was getting on with his lessons at school, so he could tell her he was doing very well. Mrs Moritz always asked Carl. When Carl and his sisters got home from school, they had cake and lemonade and told their parents all about their day. Perhaps it'd be like that for him and Sammy now they were to have their own home. And he would have a bookcase, even if it wasn't a real one. An orange box would do and it could stand empty in the new room he was to share with his little brother, until he'd earned the prize Mr Moritz had promised him. His hopes and dreams went hand in hand with determination and a practical turn of mind, despite his tender years.

The Berkowitzes were invited to a wedding that afternoon and could not stay to help Sarah and Abraham settle in, but Sarah did not mind, she was pleased to have her new house to herself. Apart from the additional bedroom, it was much the same in size and layout as Malka's, but when everything was in place the kitchen echoed with emptiness by comparison.

'Here, I'll be able to put something down and find it again,' she said to Abraham.

'Here we can be ourselves,' he laughed.

Pleasure and satisfaction glowed in his eyes and their blueness sparkled as it had not done for a very long time. His hair was awry from the day's exertions and Sarah noticed that one of his sidelocks had grown longer than the other. I've hardly looked at him since we left Russia, she thought with a pang. What has life done to us? Looking at him now, she marvelled anew that he had wanted her. Weak he might be in some ways, but such a handsome man.

Abraham's delight in their new home was plain to see, but Sarah was secretly disappointed. The room looked cold and uninviting. The curtains she had brought from Russia had been hung at the windows, but the red chenille emphasised the bareness and she longed for her house in Dvinsk with its lived-in look, which years of family life had made that way. Would any house on this foreign soil ever feel like home to her? She sat down at the table and a tear coursed down her cheek, the first she had allowed to do so since her uprooting; even on the night they arrived in Malka's house, when homesickness suddenly overtook her, she had fought the tears back.

'Sorrel, the children are watching you,' Abraham said quietly.

He only called her by this pet name at intimate moments. But was this not one? When her heart was being wrung out of her? If they had been alone, he would have taken her in his arms and she knew he wanted to, but could not bring himself to do so whilst the children were there. He held her gaze for a moment, then inclined his head to where David, Sammy and Esther sat huddled together on the floor, their eyes riveted to her. They were feeling the strangeness too and part of it was seeing their mother weep.

She looked at them gravely, then a smile illuminated her face and she went to kneel beside them, gathering them into her arms. 'What a goose I am!' she laughed as Abraham put a match to the fire he had just laid in the grate and it began to blaze. Home is not bricks and mortar, she thought cuddling her children close. It's wherever a family is together.

After they had eaten the *kefulte* fish Rachel Moritz had sent round for their supper, and the children were tucked up in bed, Sarah unpacked the wicker box which held her treasures, she had not bothered to do so whilst staying with their *landsleit*. Nothing was chipped or broken, which seemed a good omen and when the ornaments were in place on the built-in dresser and the mantelpiece, the room had a different appearance and no longer seemed unfriendly and cold. Oval-framed portraits of her parents and Abraham's, reverently hung, looked down on them benignly from the dingy walls, as if wishing them luck in the years ahead. Sarah allowed herself to shed one more tear, remembering them, but vowed it would be the last. Their parents had been practical people, who would have told her not to waste her time crying for them.

She was drying her eyes when someone knocked on the front door. Abraham left her to recover her composure and went to open it. He was astonished to see Isaac Salaman standing on the doorstep.

'A nice surprise, eh, Abie?' Salaman said.

Abraham was not sure if he thought so or not as he invited him in.

Sarah had not met Salaman, but had heard about his unpredictable character and hoped he had not come to give her husband the sack. Who could know with a person like him? Abraham had said he was capable of anything. Any other boss would dispense with someone's services at the factory, but this one might not have the patience to wait until tomorrow. She felt sick with apprehension, building up the notion in her mind, waiting for Salaman to speak. She watched him appraise the room and was glad they had had time to give it the finishing touches.

'A nice place you've made of it, eh?' he said admiringly. Then his face puckered and he shrugged, spreading his hands.

He's stopped smiling because he knows what he's come to tell us means we won't be able to pay the rent, Sarah thought and was now convinced that her husband's dismissal was imminent. But Abraham knew his employer was thinking of his own lonely home now he was a widower.

Salaman's next remark confirmed this. 'Children aren't everything, he told them. 'And who would know this better than me?' He collected himself and beamed at them. 'So come with me, Abie. I've got a gift outside for you.'

A gift was the last thing they had expected and he chuckled at their surprised expressions. 'You thought I was a skinflint, maybe?'

Before they could deny this he waddled from the room, propelling Abraham with him. 'Come already! From this you'll get more pleasure than I'm getting.'

He had hired a horse and cart and brought them the double bed he no longer needed. Abraham had joked at the factory about not being able to afford one.

'So enjoy it is all I ask,' he said when they tried to thank him and departed as abruptly as he had arrived.

Sarah spent the rest of the evening polishing the tarnished brass bedstead until it shone like gold and when they retired for the night she stood in her nightdress admiring it. 'It's the most beautiful bed I ever saw,' she said softly.

'But beds are not for looking at,' Abraham smiled helping her into it.

He turned out the gaslight and got in beside her, stretching his long legs luxuriously.

Sarah snuggled close to him. 'Now we have everything,' she whispered as he took her in his arms.

The next morning, before the children were awake, they were drinking tea together at the kitchen table when Chaim walked in through the back door.

'Yesterday you said there's nothing you wouldn't do for us,' he reminded them without preamble. 'I didn't think I'd be asking you a favour so soon.'

'Whatever it is we'll do it,' Sarah assured him.

86

'We want you to take Nicholas,' Chaim requested.

Abraham looked at Sarah and saw her pale.

'I've brought him with me,' Chaim said opening his coat which he was holding around him. The cat was half-asleep against his chest. He lowered it gently onto Abraham's lap. 'It upsets me to part with him, but what else can we do?' He stroked his ferocious pet's silky coat regretfully. 'To take him with us to Leeds would be a cruelty, he'd be a stranger there and he might get runover trying to find his way back.'

Sarah put down her tea glass. 'What is Chaim talking about, Abraham?'

'How can he know when I haven't told him yet?' Chaim smiled. 'I didn't know myself until my rich Uncle Hershie, who's got a big trouser factory in Leeds, came banging on my door last night. He came to Manchester to the wedding we went to yesterday and fell out with Uncle Mottel for not putting him to sit beside the bride and groom when we had the meal. It was my Cousin Bluma, Uncle Mottel's daughter, who got married. My uncles're never going to speak to each other again after what they said to each other and to get his own back on his brother, Uncle Hershie decides to offer me a fat raise if I'll move to Leeds and be his righthand man instead of Uncle Mottel's. He knows how Uncle Mottel relies on me. We've been up all night, packing. In case I change my mind he wants us to move today.' Chaim blew his nose on a damp handkerchief. 'And I've caught a headcold on top of it!'

'You don't mind letting your Uncle Mottel down?' Abraham asked him.

Chaim grinned. 'After how he's treated me it's a pleasure.'

Sarah eyed Nicholas who was snoozing cosily.

'See how docile he is?' Abraham said to her encouragingly.

'When he's asleep!'

'Listen, I know how you feel about Nicholas, Sarah,' Chaim told her. 'But you'll get used to him, like Malka did. She even stroked him goodbye this morning and he didn't scratch her hand.'

'She was wearing gloves?'

'Cats like a little stroke now and then,' Abraham smiled.

'So I'll let you do it.'

'You'll take him?' Chaim smiled with relief. 'He knows you, so he won't run away and Malka and me will be happy he's got a good home. Also, you're getting the best mouser in Strangeways.'

'Don't remind me.' Sarah watched Chaim take a milk-crusted saucer from his pocket and sighed resignedly as he put it down beside the hearth. Nicholas was now in residence. She picked it up and took it into the scullery to scrub it before filling it. Even a cat would not be expected to drink from a dirty dish in her house.

'Such a big favour you're doing us, Sarah,' Chaim said gratefully.

Abraham watched her back away as the animal leapt off his lap and began lapping whilst she was putting down the saucer. 'Only for you and Malka would she do it,' he laughed.

'Listen, Abie,' Chaim said when Abraham saw him to the front door. 'Uncle Mottel's head presser Hymie is leaving next week, he hasn't told Uncle yet. You fancy the job?'

'It's nice of you to think of me, Chaim. But I'd rather stay where I am.'

'Uncle pays piece rates, you'd take home more money.'

'I don't want to leave Salaman's.'

Chaim eyed him incredulously. 'You're going to be a permanent fixture there? Where's your head? A presser can do all right for himself once he knows the ropes. With a bit more experience and a few contacts you'll be able to do like Hymie's got in mind, plenty of them do it. They set up a contract with a big factory for so many garments a week, then they get together a team of underpressers to do the work. The boss pays them and before they pay the others they take a nice cut for themselves. It's like having your own business without having any overheads, the work gets done in the factory. One of my neighbours has already paid off for all his furniture that way.'

'I'm very pleased for him, but me, I'm satisfied where I am. And do me a favour, Chaim, don't mention about this to Sarah when she calls round to see Malka before you leave.'

'Would I make trouble between a man and his wife? But why're you glued to Salaman's?'

Abraham shrugged and gave him no answer. Chaim would call him a fool if he explained how he felt and if Sarah knew she would think he was carrying gratitude too far, he would not be able to make her understand. The circumstances under which he had got his job and all the events of his first day there had forged an unspoken bond between himself and Salaman. He knew this was why his employer had given him the bed and the gift had secured his lifelong loyalty.

CHAPTER SIX

The Moritzes were part of a small circle of Viennese who met in each other's houses for coffee and conversation, as they had at home. It was not until Rachel befriended Sarah Sandberg that she became aware her other friends considered themselves superior to women like Sarah.

Why didn't I realise it before? she thought one Sunday when Paula Frankl was sitting in the kitchen with her, whilst Sigmund fitted her husband's new suit.

'You look like a peasant with that shawl round your shoulders,' Paula had just laughed disparagingly. 'But at least you don't walk out in the street in it, like they do.'

'Who do you mean by they?' Rachel asked though she knew.

'Jokes she's making!' Paula helped herself to a piece of Sachetorte from the dish on the table. 'How I wish I was back in Vienna.' Her expression grew nostalgic. 'The lilac will be in bloom just now, such a wonderful perfume filling the air.' She glanced through the window at the dingy brick wall which enclosed the back yard, then tilted the silver fob-watch pinned to her rust velvet jacket to see the time. 'Three o'clock on a Spring afternoon. The Kärntnerstrasse will be full of elegant people. Remember when we were girls, Rachel? How we used to stand on the corner beside the Palais Todesco and watch all the fine carriages go by? Once, we saw one of the Rothschilds drive past with his wife. How carefree she looked, I've never forgotten it.

'Nor have I. But she didn't live in Eisenstadt like we did, with a chain festooned across the street to separate us from the rest of the city.'

'Did you have to remind me?'

Rachel studied the other woman's pretty, petulant face and wondered, as she often had, why a gentle intellectual like Ludwig Frankl had married such a shallow creature. 'What's the use of only remembering the good things?' she shrugged. 'I too miss

Vienna. Who wouldn't? But folk like us, who weren't wealthy or important enough to be accepted in spite of being Jewish, weren't part of anything except the ghetto. So they did us a favour and allowed us to move freely outside it, to taste what Vienna is. Who wants their favours?'

'You didn't want to leave any more than I did. Why're you talking this way?'

Why am I? Rachel asked herself. Something was making her want to bring Paula down to earth, but she was also putting into words her own feelings. 'Because it's the truth,' she said quietly.

Paula played with her gloves edgily, crumpling them on her lap, then smoothing them out again. 'Sigmund's done a good job on you! When Ludwig said we were coming to England, I didn't speak to him for a week and I still think it was your husband who influenced him. Yetta Stein thinks he talked Max into it, as well.'

Max Stein was a mountain of a man, with an ego to match his size. 'Nobody could talk Max into anything,' Rachel smiled.

'And Ludwig?'

Rachel remained silent.

'My husband always gives in to me about everything, but I couldn't make him stay in Vienna.'

'Doesn't that prove how seriously he takes what's going on there? Sigmund worries about his brother who's still there, all the time.'

'My family're there, too. So they'll get their windows broken every now and then, it's not so terrible. They'll sweep up the bits of glass, go and have coffee and pastries in the Ringstrasse and forget all about it. Where can a person go here? In this miserable town? When we first came, we went for a walk in the centre one evening. Everything except the public houses were the drunks go was closed.'

'You haven't taken a tram in the other direction? To Heaton Park with miles of grass and the lovely flower gardens?'

'Sure. But where are the cafés and the smart people, and the feeling that's nowhere else but Vienna? Who wants to see nothing but flowers and grass? If my husband had used his brains to make money for himself instead of that store he was manager for, we wouldn't have had to leave, we'd've moved away from Eisenstadt and entertained the rich *goys* in our great big house.'

Rachel laughed. 'One like the Rothschilds live in?'

'You're making fun of me. I mean we could've been among those who're accepted by Viennese society.'

'Sigmund thinks the time will come when even they won't be.'

'Sigmund thinks!' Paula got up and paced the room. 'Such a pleasant apartment you had before and me also, even if we did live in the ghetto. What have we got now, because our husbands had a brainstorm and brought us to England, where they can't afford anything better than this? But at least I don't have to entertain visitors in the kitchen, like you do.'

'You object to being entertained in the kitchen?'

'Listen, I know the reason. It's not that I object.'

'Then what is it?'

'The way it doesn't seem to bother you. Your friends who knew you in Vienna find it sad.'

Rachel's soft lips tightened. 'I hope you enjoyed talking about me.'

'It upsets us to see how you've changed. You don't even mind mixing with people from dirty little *shtetlach* and it isn't doing you any good.'

'Was it their fault they had to live in them?' Rachel bristled. 'And if you mean the Sandbergs, they lived in a country townlet which was probably cleaner than Eisenstadt.'

'So they're not all alike,' Paula shrugged.

'All Viennese aren't alike, either,' Rachel told her. 'Some of us aren't snobs.'

Paula's gaze moved to the table. 'Once, you'd have put a lace doyley on that dish before you laid the cake on it. I still do. Is it snobbish not to lower your standards?'

Rachel thought of Sarah, who did not own any lace doyleys, but whose hospitality came from her heart with no notion of impressing anyone. 'You know I never realised until now how empty those standards are.'

Paula sighed and shook her head. 'So you've got a few funny ideas these days, but we still love you. Come to me for coffee tomorrow, some of the girls will be there.'

'I'm afraid I can't. Sarah Sandberg's coming here. Why don't you all come and join us? My coffee pot's big enough.'

It sounded like a challenge and Paula avoided her eye. 'I don't think so, thank you,' she said as her husband came into the room with Sigmund. 'So you'll come to me some other time.'

'I don't think so, thank you,' Rachel replied.

Ludwig Frankl's anxious grey eyes were fixed on his wife's frowning countenance. 'Something's wrong, Paula darling?'

'A little difference of opinion,' Paula said stiffly.

Rachel laughed. 'I'd call it a big one myself.' She turned to Ludwig. 'I didn't have time to ask how you are. You rushed straight into the workroom with my husband.'

'He was worried in case his suit wouldn't fit,' Sigmund joked to ease the strained atmosphere.

'The trousers were too tight round the waist at my last fitting,' Ludwig accused him. 'And this time they were too loose.'

'Am I to blame if you eat more *shnitzels* one week than you do another?'

'How can a person be, Rachel, with a tailor like him and a boss who won't let you read while you're working?' Ludwig smiled.

And a wife like Paula, Rachel added mentally.

'If he'd let you read while you work, you'd have no fingers left!' Paula snapped. Ludwig was employed at a glazier's in nearby Redbank, as quite a number of immigrants were.

'So you don't like me working there. I'm not full of joy about it myself, but what can I do?' he said placatingly.

'You should have asked yourself that before you left Vienna.'

When Sigmund returned from seeing the Frankls out, Rachel was staring through the window. 'Tell me something, Sigmund,' she said without turning. 'Do you still look down on the Poles and the Russians?'

'Where does looking down come into it? I think like Ludwig and Max, that it's a waste for them to be so narrow.'

'Is that why you take such an interest in David Sandberg?'

'If I don't, who will? All Abie cares about is feeding and clothing him and preparing him to be Bar Mitzvah. What else does the poor fellow know?'

'You don't think it's beneath us to have the Sandbergs for friends?'

'King Edward I'm not!' Sigmund chuckled. 'So that's what that foolish Paula's been saying to upset you. Come, Rachel, I'd rather talk to your lovely face than your stiff back.' He turned her around and settled her beside the table, then sat down in his wing chair.

'You're getting ready to give me a lecture?' she asked as he crossed his legs and took off his pince-nez thoughtfully. 'I'm not the one who needs it. I had a shock today and I haven't got over it yet. I used to think my friends from home mixed together to talk about old times, but it isn't just that.'

Sigmund smiled. 'I'm surprised it took you so long to find out. Their husbands I like, but those women have always been impossible.'

'But Paula is one on her own. Shall I tell you what I think about her?'

'If she wasn't Jewish she'd be anti-Semitic,' Sigmund said before she had time to.

'How did you know what I was going to say?'

CHAPTER SEVEN

David was late coming out of school and found Sammy, Miriam and Esther waiting for him as usual.

'I thought you'd gone without us,' Esther piped accusingly.

'I didn't.' Sammy's trust in his brother was absolute.

David wiped Esther's runny nose.

'I lost my hankie,' she snivelled.

'How could you, when Mother fixed it to your pinafore with a pin?' he asked exasperatedly.

The two little girls clutched his hands as they began the trudge home. To reach Strangeways from Derby Street, where the school was situated, they had to traverse a stretch of Waterloo Road and it was not uncommon to find Gentile children from adjoining Hightown waiting to jeer at them.

'Moishe Lipkin got spat at yesterday,' Sammy informed the others.

'Well David won't let us get spat at,' Miriam said confidently, skipping to keep up with his long-legged stride. 'Why were you late, David?'

'I'll tell you later.' He wanted to hug his wonderful news to himself for a little longer. 'You didn't have to wait for me, did you?'

Miriam looked hurt. 'But I always walk home with you. Just like Helga goes with Saul and Bessie Salaman.'

'Helga and Saul're sweethearts,' Esther giggled.

David knew they were. Saul was his best friend.

'I bet Bessie won't ever have a sweetheart, she's a dirty thing,' Miriam grimaced. 'She never wears a clean pinny and Helga said I might get nits because I sit next to her in school.'

'It's because she's got no mother,' Sammy said charitably.

'Saul hasn't, either, but he's nice and clean,' Miriam replied. 'Or Helga wouldn't love him.'

Esther was lagging behind, pulling at David's hand. 'Give me a piggy-back down the hill, David,' she whined as they turned into Waterloo Road. 'My toes are hurting.'

'It's because your shoes're too small,' he told her. He hoisted her onto his back and wished his parents could afford to buy her a bigger pair. 'What'd you two do if you didn't have me to look after you?' he asked taking Miriam's hand again.

'Don't be silly, David!' Miriam laughed. She could not imagine not having him there. Her brother could not be relied upon. Once, he had almost got her run over by a horse and cart because he was reading while they crossed the main road. She tightened her hold on David's hand.

The soft little fingers were warm and confiding and David felt ashamed of his joy about what his teacher had told him. It would mean deserting Miriam and Esther. And Sammy, whom the Gentile children ridiculed because of his jiggling walk. What would his mother say when she heard? His father's opinion did not seem important, it never had. He made up his mind to tell Mr Moritz before telling his parents. Somehow it seemed right he should be the first to know.

A February fog had descended during the afternoon and the acrid thickness was in the children's throats, making them cough. David had hated the fog, initially, but now it was just part of Manchester. He pulled his muffler around his mouth and told the others to do the same. This made talking impossible and allowed him to concentrate on his thoughts.

Tonight, if he wasn't too tired, he would light the stub of candle he kept hidden in the bedroom and read *Oliver Twist* again when everyone was asleep. He wasn't supposed to read in bed, but if his mother ever caught him doing it she wouldn't be able to accuse him of wasting gaslight, which cost money. *Oliver* was his favourite, because it was the first book he had ever owned, his reward from Mr Moritz when he'd learned to read. Mr Moritz was the only person he knew who spent money on books, and had given him three others, too, for birthday gifts. There was still plenty of room in his orange-box bookcase, but last month when it was his eleventh birthday, he'd worked out that if Mr Moritz kept on giving him one every year, by the time he was eighty he'd have seventy-three.

Sometimes he thought of the time Mr Moritz had met him and

Carl after school and taken them with him to the secondhand bookshop in Long Millgate. They'd gone by tram and it was the only time David had ever been on one, and also the only time he had ever been to town. Though it was within walking distance, his parents had forbidden him to go there in case he got lost. They had sat on the top deck and he'd watched the trolley-boy holding the long shaft in place and wished he could ride around town all day and see everything, the way the boy did. Mr Moritz had shown him a street called The Shambles, with very old buildings that had black and white gables, and a place called Poets Corner, which he'd thought was a lovely name, where one of the buildings had looked as if it was going to tip forward onto its bulging, black-beamed face. He'd seen a school called Chetham's Hospital, too, and Mr Moritz had said it wasn't because the pupils were sick. It had been near the Manchester Grammar School and they'd seen some big boys coming out of there with funny little round, peaked caps on their heads. David and Carl had said they wouldn't fancy wearing one and Mr Moritz had laughed and said they should only be so lucky.

But the best part of the outing had been going inside the bookshop, David thought as he plodded down Waterloo Road. It had been full of people standing about reading and some had left without buying any books, but the man behind the counter didn't seem to mind. David had thought what a friendly place it was, with its musty smell which wasn't unpleasant, but somehow exciting, and had enjoyed touching the worn leather bindings and wondering what the stories inside them were about. It had been before he'd learned to read properly and the next day he'd worked even harder than usual at his English lesson so he would be able to find out.

Now, it seemed a long time ago and he couldn't imagine not being able to read English. He wished his parents would go to nightschool, like Mr and Mrs Moritz did, so they'd be able to read and write, too. He sometimes thought they'd still be speaking nothing but Yiddish if they didn't have children who spoke English. At home, he and his brother and sister spoke a mixture of both with their parents, not like at the Moritzes', where only English was spoken at mealtimes so the parents could learn to speak it properly, like their children did.

'Thank goodness we're nearly home,' Sammy said through his muffler. 'My leg's starting to ache.'

David glanced compassionately at the thin little figure limping beside him. Sammy's leg must be hurting a lot, he rarely complained.

'And I want to get on with my carving, before bedtime,' Sammy added.

'Why don't you sit and read one of my books, for a change?'

'Reading's a waste of time.'

'You always say that, but you're wrong, Sammy.'

'Books take too long to finish.'

'So do the things you make, but you don't mind that, do you?' David could not understand why his brother had the patience to sit for hours carving things out of bits of wood with his penknife, but couldn't be bothered to use his brain.

'Those dolls you made for me and Esther're lovely, Sammy,' Miriam said. 'I like mine better than that big real one Bessie Salaman's father bought her.'

'I'll make you a big one when I've finished Mother's pin tray,' Sammy told her. 'If I can find a big bit of wood. Can I take my muffler off my mouth, David? It feels all wet.'

'All right. And I'll help you to find some more wood if you promise to try harder with your schoolwork,' David bargained. Three years of living in Strangeways had taught him you had to use your brains if you were ever going to get anywhere, but Sammy was like their father, who seemed satisfied to be spending his life pressing garments. What makes me think I'll get anywhere myself? he mused as they reached Bury New Road and walked towards the Moritzes' street. Then a tremor of excitement rippled through him. He was going to pass the scholarship exam, wasn't he? Go to high school. Boys who went there could become doctors and lawyers even if they were Jews. Hadn't his teacher said so, when he told him he was clever enough to sit the exam? It was that that had started him off thinking about being something better than Father was. Until this afternoon, he hadn't thought about it the way he was doing now.

Carl was also to write the examination and Sigmund promised to make school uniforms for both of them if they passed, which lessened David's apprehension about telling his mother. The expense of a regulation outfit had been worrying him, but now she would only have to pay for a badge to be sewn on his pocket and a cap like the Central High School boys wore.

Not for a moment did it enter David's head that he might fail the examination. He could already see himself striding to town in the mornings, with Carl beside him. He wished his best friend could go, too, but Saul Salaman wasn't the studious kind. So Saul'll end up owning his father's factory and be my father's boss, he smiled to himself. The smile was still on his face when he arrived home and walked into the kitchen with Sammy and Esther.

'You lost a farthing and found thruppence?' Sarah asked.

'Mother just said a whole sentence in English!' Sammy laughed.

'Well, David? Tell me why you look so happy, already.'

'Guess.'

'You didn't find thruppence, you found a pound note, we should only live to see one!'

'Better than that.' David told her his wonderful news.

'*Mazeltov!*' she congratulated him, then resumed stirring the borsht. 'So hurry up or you'll be late for *cheder*.'

David eyed her back resentfully. Carl's parents were letting him miss Hebrew class tonight, as if being one of those who were good enough to sit the high school exam was something to celebrate and he deserved a treat. He'd hoped his mother would tell him he needn't go because it was a special occasion, but it didn't seem to be one to her. His teacher had said it was an achievement, but she was behaving as if it was nothing. Most of the boys who took the exam had been born in England, Saul had, but he was bottom of the class. Why wasn't she proud of him, the way Mr Moritz was of Carl? Mr Moritz was proud of him, too, and he wasn't his son. He could feel his face growing hot with rage. If he'd found a pound note, or even thruppence, his mother would be dancing for joy!

Sammy and Esther had taken off their coats and were sitting at the table.

'Like a lemon he's standing there! You'd think he had all day,' Sarah exclaimed giving him a gentle shove.

He sat down with the others and she brought a loaf of black-bread to the table, cut a slice for each of them and spread it with chicken fat. They always had this to sustain them when they came home from school on winter afternoons and had their supper later, when their father returned from the factory.

David sat munching his sullenly, watching his mother fill Nicholas' saucer with milk, which she did at this time every afternoon so it would be waiting for the cat when it came home, the way she did everything that had to be done, no matter how tired she was. Living in their own house had not turned out the way he had hoped. His mother was always too busy to talk to her children about their school life. School was just somewhere they went in the mornings and returned from in the afternoons, what they did there didn't seem to interest her.

'Finish your bread and *shmaltz* already!' she said to him. 'The evening is short enough with all you still have to do.'

Usually, David did not mind his evening chores, but today he felt sick at the thought of them. He'd begun learning his Bar Mitzvah portion at *cheder*, Rabbi Lensky said it took a long time to become word perfect and his lesson now lasted longer than it used to. Afterwards, he'd just have time to come home and eat his supper, before he went to help Mr Radinsky clean up his shop. Other boys he knew had evening jobs, too, and some got paid in goods, instead of money, like he did. The fruit and vegetables he brought home were always a bit squashed or bruised, but they were fit to eat. Mr Radinsky wouldn't palm him off with anything that'd gone rotten, he was a fair man and had proved it when David went to cadge an orange-box from him. If it hadn't been for the orange box he wouldn't have got the job, Mr Radkinsky hadn't employed a boy before then, he'd managed with just himself and Menachem his assistant. Thinking about the night he'd got his orange-box bookcase gave David a nice, warm feeling and took his mind off how his mother had reacted to his news.

'When I want to give charity, I give it to the Benevolent Society,' Mr Radinsky had told him. 'So you'll do a little work for the box.'

He had put a broom into David's hands and asked him to sweep the floor. To get his box, David would have scrubbed the walls and ceiling.

'I like a boy who knows what he wants and even better one who doesn't mind working for it,' the greengrocer had approved

100

when David said what the box was for and had selected one which was not splintered for him. 'But a bookcase you can't eat. Tomorrow you'll come back and work for me again and I'll give you something for the *tsimmes*.'

The next evening, David cleaned the fish counter and left with his arms full of carrots and onions. His family had not gone short of fruit and vegetables since.

Sarah had shown more pleasure about this than she had about his scholarship entry and still smiled and patted his cheek when he handed her his edible earnings. Her priorities were the same as the greengrocer's, how could they not be? Day to day existence, with its material anxieties, obsessed all the immigrants, including the few who, like Sigmund Moritz, considered education equally important. They fed and clothed their children and if anyone had to go without it was themselves. Even those like Mr Radinsky and Isaac Salaman, who had established themselves and accumulated capital, did not feel secure. The feeling that what they had today would still be there tomorrow was one they would not acquire for a long time. David was aware that his parents had to struggle, but it was not until years later that he fully understood.

When he got back from *cheder* that night, his father shook his hand warmly and said how pleased he was about the scholarship. David had not expected his father's reaction to be any different from his mother's and wondered if there might be more to him than he had come to believe.

He was doing his homework at the table, after the rest of the family had gone to bed, when his mother returned to the kitchen.

'It's a pleasure to be without a lodger,' she said putting the kettle on to boil. Half-a-dozen had come and gone since they moved into the house. The last had left a few days ago and had not yet been replaced, or she would not have been walking around in her nightgown.

'Are you ill?' David asked her.

Sarah laughed. 'When am I ill?' She bent down and stroked Nicholas, who for some reason scratched everyone else but not her and she was no longer afraid of him.

Father can't be ill, or she wouldn't be laughing, David thought. So why had she come to boil the kettle at this time? The clock said half-past-ten.

'I'm just making you some tea,' she told him.

He looked at her uncertainly. He often did his homework late at night, but she'd never done this before.

'A boy who's studying for scholarships needs something to refresh him,' she said with a smile.

Everything was all right. His mother was proud of him after all.

'You've got ink on your face,' Sarah chuckled.

'What does it matter?' he said happily and went on writing his composition, choosing the words carefully because his teacher had said that was his only weak point.

Sarah got a glass from the dresser. 'Your pal Mr Moritz came to see us while you were out.'

'I sometimes think he's the best pal I'll ever have,' David said with feeling.

'Listen, we don't call him that for nothing, I think so also. He's going to make you an outfit, eh, David?'

'And the other things I'll need shouldn't cost too much.'

'Whatever they'll cost, you'll have. We'll buy.'

David recalled how his father had surprised him. Maybe he didn't know his mother as well as he thought he did, either.

'Before Esther's new boots we'll buy.'

'Miriam's got an old pair that'll fit her.'

'What the Moritzes are giving to you is enough!' Sarah said sharply. Her pride was as strong as ever. Providing the school outfit was Sigmund's way of helping David get ahead and not to be confused with handing down cast off clothing.

The kettle began to sing; kept on the hob all the time, it never took long to boil and tea could be made at a moment's notice. David watched her take a jar of blackcurrant jam from the cupboard and put a big spoonful into the glass, instead of lemon. So she's made him go to *cheder* as usual, but this was a special treat. He noticed she had let down her hair for the night and it looked like a silk cape, the way it hung over her shoulders, down to her waist. He knew it had not always been touched with silver at the front, but could not remember when the streaks had appeared.

'You look younger in your nightgown, Mother,' he said to her.

Sarah chuckled. 'In that case, it's a pity I can't wear it all the time!'

How lovely it was when she laughed and joked with him, David thought. If only she had no worries and then she'd be like this all the time. She looked smaller, as well as younger. He'd never realised how tiny his mother was. Perhaps it was because he had grown much taller? He was tall enough now to see his reflection in the mirror above the table, without standing up. It was the only one in the house and had been hung in the kitchen so everyone could use it. His mother was reflected in it, too, pouring tea into the glass at the hob. Why had he never noticed that he looked like her?

'When is the examination, David?' she asked.

'In two weeks' time.'

'So you'll pass it.' She brought the glass to the table. 'And be a high-school boy.' Such a thing to happen to a son of mine, she thought. Who would've believed it? She kissed his cheek and moved to the door. 'But don't get any big ideas,' she told him.

'Put the book down and come, Father!' Miriam said impatiently. They were going to Sarah's *Shabbos* tea party and she could not wait to get there. It was the only time she saw David, now he was at high school.

Carl, who saw him every day, could not understand why his sister got so excited about it, though everyone knew Miriam and David were sweethearts. She was still only ten and David twelve, but youthful alliances were not unusual in the ghetto. Children grew up side by side and married, as they had in the old country. Failing this, the matchmakers would lend a hand.

Sigmund closed his book and rose to put on his hat, chuckling at his little daughter who stood tapping her foot as she waited. How pretty she looked in the green velvet coat he had made for her. She'll be a real beauty one day, he thought. He shooed his family out of the house, as if he had been kept waiting by them, a habit to which they were all accustomed.

When they turned into Bury New Road it was thronged with people. On Saturdays, Strangeways changed character according to the weather. If the day was fine, the immigrants strolled decorously in their once-a-week finery, taking the air. On wet days it was like a dead city, nobody stirred from their homes except to go to synagogue or visit family. The Sabbath was strictly observed and stores remained shuttered from Friday evening until Sunday morning.

Most people had relatives living nearby, but the Sandbergs and Moritzes had nobody, which may have accounted for the closeness which had developed between them. The extended family was a long established Jewish way of life. Who needed friends if they had relations? Friends came and went, but family was a rock to lean on, always there. Other children had cousins and in lieu of these the Sandberg and Moritz youngsters had each other. It was the same with their parents, different in attitude and background though they were.

Since Rachel Moritz had sensed the Sandbergs' loneliness on their first Passover in England and invited them to share her table, the two families had come together on all festive occasions. Sabbath afternoons were always spent at Sarah's home and leavened the week's dull routine. Sarah and Rachel would chat together and Sigmund enjoyed talking with David and Carl. Helga played games with Sammy and Esther; she was now thirteen and liked to be in charge of younger children, who always adored her. Abraham would sit quietly, a contented smile on his face, happy that everyone was there.

All Miriam wanted to do was gaze at David. Handsome he isn't, she would think sometimes, watching him arguing the point with her father and brother, his Adam's apple wobbling in his skinny throat. He'd grown lanky as a string bean since he'd been at the new school and his nose looked beakier than ever. But he was David.

The tea party on this particular Sabbath went wrong from the very beginning. David was not there, which ruined it for Miriam. And as his absence was a source of distress to his parents, nobody enjoyed themselves. Even the sponge cakes were sad. Sarah had been making them the previous day when he had told her he could be out and the sorry repast on the table was the result.

'How can my hand be light to beat the mixture when my heart is heavy?' she sighed to Rachel pointing a quivering finger at the cakes. 'I'd have thrown them away, but who can waste eggs and sugar?'

The Moritzes had hardly stepped across the threshold when she began telling them.

'To who else but you would I pour out my heart? Like family you are.' She looked at Sigmund accusingly. 'And you are to blame for everything.'

'Tell us where David is already,' he replied. 'And for what am I to blame?'

'If you don't know, I'm not going to tell you.'

Rachel put a calming hand on Sarah's. 'Where is David? At least you can tell us that.'

'He has a *goy* for a friend now,' Sarah declared as if this explained everything.

Miriam knew this. Carl, too. The boy to whom Sarah had referred was in their class at school.

'Has David gone to Jim's birthday party?' Carl asked.

'And round the corner it isn't,' Sarah nodded grimly. 'A Jewish boy, who'll be Bar Mitzvah next year, buys himself a railway ticket and goes by train on *Shabbos*.'

Miriam saw her parents exchange a shocked glance, but all she herself felt was disappointment because David was not there.

'God will punish him,' Esther piped up. Then Sammy slapped her and she ran weeping to her mother.

Miriam burst into tears, too. She could not help it. David had let her down and now Sammy, who was always kind and smiling, had hit his sister and had an angry look on his face.

'So that's what he wanted the shilling for,' Carl muttered.

'He got the money for the railway ticket from you?' Sarah flashed.

'From where do you get money to lend?' Sigmund demanded.

Carl had been saving the penny-a-week allowed him when he started at high school. He now wished he had not lent some of it to David and sulked instead of replying.

Sarah got up to make the tea, but the water in the big urn kept on the hob throughout the Sabbath because putting the kettle onto the fire was forbidden, had gone off the boil and everyone got their mouths full of tea leaves. It was that kind of afternoon.

'So how come you think I am the criminal?' Sigmund asked Sarah when the Moritzes were leaving. Nothing she had said had explained the accusation and he could think of no possible reason for it.

Sarah did not reply.

When David returned home, his mother was the only one of the family still up, though it was not yet nine-o'clock. It had been that kind of evening for the Sandbergs, too.

'You had a nice time I hope not?' she said acidly.

David sat down by the hearth with a dreamy expression on his face.

'So what did you do there so many hours? Breaking the *Shabbos*!' Sarah had not meant to speak to him at all, but could not contain herself. 'Did your highty-tighty *goyim* friends give you a nice tea?'

'I had strawberries and cream,' he said rapturously.

'And bacon sandwiches?'

'Don't be daft, Mother.'

'Who is being daft? After you've taken one step, it's easy to take another.' She left the room without kissing him goodnight, a sign of her deepest disapproval, then popped her head around the door to deliver a parting shot. 'You want proof? Have a look in the mirror!'

For a moment David did not understand. Then he knew she was reminding him of how he had cut off his sidelocks before starting at high school. A new chapter had been opening for him and he did not intend to begin it with a handicap.

At the Jews' School all the boys from *Hassid* families wore them and many others did, too, but those like Carl, and Leo and Otto Rosenthal, who did not because their fathers never had, did not pass derisive remarks. Even boys whose families had joined the Reform Synagogue, which eschewed many of the old traditions, were not intolerant of the orthodox majority, but to Gentile lads the sidelocks were 'cissy' and David and Sammy had frequently had the offensive word hurled at them. They were called 'sheeny', too, as all the Jewish children were, but David had decided he did not have to look cissy as well. It would be hard enough in a Gentile school, without the sidelocks adding to it.

Despite this, the first day of term could not come quickly enough for him. He wanted to be something, though he did not yet know what, and going to high school would lead him to it. When the day arrived, he was full of trepidation. The life he had led so far made this inevitable. For the Gentile boys who enrolled on the same day, it was just another school. For boys like David it was another world. He was put into the same class as Carl, for which they were both thankful and the master allowed them to sit together. It might have been better if he had not. They felt like a small island in a foreign sea.

Carl did not look especially Jewish, but David was singled out immediately and examined with interest by the other boys, who had not met any Jews before. He did not learn this was the reason until he made friends with Jim Forrest, several weeks later. At the time, he thought it was anti-Semitism. But he had not previously encountered Gentiles who were not anti-Semitic and expected them all to be the same. When they had to call out their names for entry in the class register, Carl was similarly scrutinised, which confirmed David's impression.

'So?' his mother said eloquently when he returned that afternoon.

David managed to smile and did not answer.

Throughout the first week he had to steel himself each morning to face the day. Carl was less sensitive and was by now back in his customary trance. At the Saturday tea party it was taken for granted that both boys had settled down and David said nothing to indicate otherwise. Miriam was the only one to whom he told the truth. He wished he was back at Derby Street, he hated the new school.

'You don't have to stay there,' she said.

But David knew that he did. After a while, things improved. He and Carl became as familiar to the other boys as the classroom furniture and nobody treated them differently anymore. The work became all-absorbing and the gym a place they both loathed going to.

'You didn't pass the scholarship to jump over wooden horses,' Sarah said when David described the gymnastics to her.

He agreed, but had to endure it. Not only did he dislike the rigorous exercise, it seemed a waste of time when he could be cramming his head with knowledge.

Both David and Carl were recognised as brilliant from the beginning, but had they not been they could not have overcome the handicaps which were their heritage and won places at the school. Bar Mitzvah classes, sparetime jobs and material privation were part of this, but the ghetto had begun to breed scholars and the heights to which this would rise nobody yet dreamed.

The Jews' School was responsible for sewing the seeds. From a small establishment in Hanover Street in 1849 had sprung the flourishing educational institution now in Derby Street. By the middle of the twentieth century, men and women prominent in all walks of English life would be proud to say they were once pupils there.

Many boys took packed lunches to school and the food David

and Carl brought intrigued their classmates. The blackbread was not unlike wholemeal bread in appearance and passed without comment. But pickled cucumbers, eaten in the hand like chocolate bars? And chunks of smelly sausage and herring? One day, David brought two fried *kefulte* fish balls.

'Whatever are they?' Jim Forrest asked. He was a small, freckle-faced boy, destined to be a partner in his father's law practice. 'They look like Scotch eggs.'

'Perhaps they're Jewish eggs?' Hawkins, the class joker, quipped.

'Try one,' David offered.

Hawkins hesitated. 'I don't think so, thank you very much.'

'I will,' Jim said.

The others watched him bite into it.

'It's fish!' he announced.

David felt relieved it was recognisable.

'And absolutely scrumptious.' Jim gobbled it down.

'If they're that good, bring a few more next time, David,' Hawkins requested.

David wondered what his mother would say if he asked her to make a batch of fish balls for the Gentile boys and exchanged a grin with Carl. Jewish food had just been proved tasty and non-poisonous.

'You'd better have one of my sandwiches, as I've eaten half your lunch,' Jim said.

David could see something pink protruding from the bread. 'What's in them?' he asked warily. He had never seen ham, but had a feeling it might be.

Jim told him it was.

'I'm afraid I can't,' he said reluctantly. The pink meat looked savoury and succulent, but even if it had been beef he would have had to refuse. This kind of temptation had not come his way before, but he had not been out in the world before.

'Why not?' Jim wanted to know.

'It isn't kosher.'

'What does that mean?' Hawkins inquired.

David and Carl explained the Jewish dietary laws to the other boys and why they were required.

Moore, who was Catholic, took off his glasses and polished

them thoughtfully. 'It's a bit like not eating meat on a Friday.'

'Or giving something up for Lent,' Jim added, then had to tell the two Jewish boys what Lent was.

The next day, Jim brought David an apple in return for the fishball. 'Go on, eat it. It's kosher,' he grinned.

David got a warm feeling because Jim accepted what he was and respected it, and sat for a moment musing on the way knowledge helped people to understand each other.

'So bite into it already!' Jim said mimicking David's Jewish idiom jokingly. The way the Jewish boys spoke was a mixture of Lancashire accent and something peculiarly their own.

David did not mind Jim mimicking him, he knew it was not intended to be an insult. He munched the apple, which was sweet and unblemished, different from his earnings at Mr Radinsky's, he thought with a smile and told Jim about his evening job.

Jim looked astounded. 'When do you do your homework if you have to do that in the evenings?'

'Jewish evenings're longer than other people's,' David laughed. 'They have to be.' He explained about his Bar Mitzvah classes.

'Being Jewish isn't easy, is it?' Jim said thoughtfully.

David had never thought he would hear a Gentile say that. But Jim didn't know the half of it.

After this, the friendship ripened. Jim gradually learned of the Sandbergs' ordeal in Russia and began to look at the Jewish boys in school with new eyes. Although small for his age, he had a strong personality. Certain boys in the class had anti-Semitic tendencies bred in them by their parents and though not overtly so to David and Carl, revealed this in their absence.

'If you want to be a Jew-hater, don't be one in front of me,' Jim warned them and they watched what they said in his presence from then on. He thought of telling them what David had been through, but decided his Jewish friend would not wish this. And why should he have to be pitied, tolerated because he had suffered? He was no different from anyone else and should be accepted for what he was, in his own right.

Jim's mind was similar to David's, able to pick out the crux of a matter from the detail and act accordingly. When he spoke

110

of David at home, which he often did, his father said he would like to meet him; his law practice was expanding and David might be suitable material to be an articled clerk, as Jim would be after he had been to university.

Jim did not tell David about this immediately, but several times invited him home for Sunday lunch. 'I'll make sure we have fish,' he said reassuringly. 'My family won't mind doing without their roast beef and Yorkshire pud for once.'

But David always had to refuse. The whole of Sunday morning was spent at his Bar Mitzvah class. In the afternoon he worked at Mr Radinsky's and after that there was his homework, which could not be done on Friday night or Saturday because of the Sabbath. Even if none of these things had stood in his way, he could not afford the train fare. Jim lived in Cheshire, where many of the wealthy professional and business people of Manchester had their homes.

'Look, you've got to come to my birthday party, you're my best friend and it wouldn't be the same without you,' Jim declared when his birthday came around.

David had not realised the Gentile boy thought of him that way, or held him in such esteem, and was profoundly affected when he learned it. But they never saw each other outside school hours, how could Jim think of him thus? He reflected on his own friendship with Saul Salaman, which was on another level from his relationship with Jim. A purely Jewish level, born of their Jewish upbringing. Jim's life was not like his, it was all of a piece, school and home both part of an integrated whole. His own was split down the middle, the ghetto one half and his daily going forth to the world outside it the other. Would it always have to be like that? Until now, the ghetto had encompassed all of it and the problem had not arisen.

Jim's party was to be on a Saturday, which increased David's predicament. When he explained, his friend would not take this seriously, though he had always shown the greatest respect for David's religious observance.

'It's daft! How can you go through life never going anywhere by tram or train on a Saturday? It's the day when everything happens. Everyone has their parties then. And not riding on a

111

train isn't like not eating pork because pigs are mucky creatures, is it? That Jewish law makes sense, even though I eat pork myself.'

Eventually, David borrowed the fare from Carl and with his parents' wrath ringing in his ears slammed the door and went. Jim's reaction to the Sabbath travel ban had made it seem nonsensical to him, too.

Once on the train, his excitement mounted. The dingy buildings soon gave way to green fields and the snakelike glint of a river. Trees and bushes, creamy with a froth of blossom, flashed by and were instantly replaced by more, the leaves and petals of a richer hue. Hawthorn and laburnum, flowering cherry and copper beech, towering oaks and slender silver birch, a feast for the eye and balm to the soul of a boy whose horizon was the Strangeways ghetto. Then the houses began to loom up, solid and imposing. Not cramped together in humble little terraces, grimed by smoke and soot, with donkey-stoned doorsteps jutting into the street, but set in gardens; each one at least a mile from the other it seemed to David as he viewed them from afar through the window and wondered which of them was 'Forrest Dene'.

Jim was waiting for him on the station platform and looked different in his tweed jacket and flannels. David's instinct had told him not to wear his school blazer and he was glad he had obeyed it, though his outfit was not as smart as his friend's. He was still in knickerbockers, which were somewhat too small for him, but felt his Sabbath suit was presentable otherwise.

'It's not a bad little village,' Jim said as they strode down the High Street.

'Alderley Edge is famous, people come here for picnics, just to see it.'

'But you don't think of it like that when you live here,' Jim smiled.

Some of the shops reminded David of the ones he had seen in The Shambles, with black and white frontages, but these were freshly painted and everything about them smacked of quality. The pyramids of fruit in the greengrocery seemed to have been hand polished and the vegetables looked as if they had never seen soil. He couldn't imagine Mr Radinsky taking such care, or his customers having time to notice it if he did.

'My mum gets her dresses there,' Jim told him as they passed a window displaying a vase of roses and an elegant gown un-sullied by a price tag.

David thought that single garment would probably cost more than his mother had spent on clothes in her whole life.

Jim halted outside a confectioner's. 'Might as well start spend-ing my birthday money! I'll treat you to your favourite cake.'

'There's nothing here I recognise,' David laughed staring into the window.

Jim left him to admire the baker's art and went into the shop. 'Allow me to introduce you to a jam tart,' he said when he came out clutching a paper bag. 'Though I can't quite believe you've never met one!'

'How d'you do,' David grinned sinking his teeth into it.

They turned off the High Street and began to climb a steep incline.

'You'll see the Edge in a minute, we have to pass it,' Jim said carelessly.

How can he take living here for granted like he does? David wondered breathing in the fresh clean air as they walked past tall hedges, so thick and luxuriant they seemed like the outskirts of a wood. Behind them rose homes built of mellow brick and soft, grey stone, where boys like his friend lived with their families and every day was like this for them.

The view from the Edge took his breath away. To be able to step out of your house into this, instead of Moreton Street and Bury New Road. Meadows and copses, green and more green stretching below as far as the eye could see. Miles and miles of it, with the Derbyshire hills rising in the distance. How could anyone be so lucky, having this on their doorstep?

Jim dragged him away. 'Come on. My dad wants to meet you before the others arrive.'

David could not think why and his senses were so besotted with the beauty he had just beheld he did not bother to ask. Then they reached Jim's house and he stopped thinking, as the rest of the day assumed a dreamlike quality through which he moved in a trance, savouring the feel and smell and flavour of it, though his brain seemed to have stopped working and was recording nothing.

Years afterwards, when Forrest Dene was advertised for sale, in the *Guardian*, the day returned to his memory in detail, made poignant by the passage of time and he saw a gawky lad with too much brilliantine on his hair shaking hands stiffly with the smiling father, in a library which was a room in itself, not just shelves in a kitchen; the mother who smelled of lavender and was not careworn, but laughed a tinkling laugh as she served lemonade on a velvet lawn; the little sister playing with a puppy in a pool of sunlight, whilst a maid with a big bottom and a frilly cap and apron retied the ribbon in her hair. But all he could remember when he arrived home that evening was eating the strawberries and cream, which he had never tasted before. And he knew he wanted to live that way.

CHAPTER NINE

Sarah stood at the scullery sink, scrubbing the frayed collar of the lodger's shirt. Tonight she would have to tell Abraham, it could not be put off any longer. She tried to occupy her mind with other things, to set the new anxiety aside. Salaman was now paying Abraham fifteen shillings a week and thought it was a fortune. But older children ate larger portions than little ones and the Friday night chicken was no longer sufficient for Saturday also. Dinner on *Shabbos* these days was just *tsimmes* and gravy. Thank God for David's job with Radinsky. Next year he'd be earning money instead of the greengrocer's throwouts. But it was not yet next year. Why wouldn't Abraham leave Salaman and go where the pay was better? She knew he had had offers and turned them down.

She rinsed the shirt and sighed. Lodgers, What could you do with them? They expected to be waited on hand and foot for the little they paid you. She put the laundry into the zinc tub which the family took turns to bath in, once a week. Her lodgers she made go to the public baths, they could take it or leave it, though in other ways she tried to treat them like one of the family. Some she'd had in the past were pleasant fellows, but Manny Zelnik, her present one, was a churlish, middle-aged man and she wished she could afford to tell him to go. Soon, she'd have to, there wouldn't be space to accommodate him. After David's Bar Mitzvah he would be a man and Esther must be moved into a separate room.

What would David say when he learned his mother was pregnant? Boys of his age knew how babies were made. Would he be shocked to think of his parents that way? But first she must tell Abraham. When he knew there would be another mouth to feed, perhaps he would leave Salaman. The pregnancy was not welcome, but maybe it would do some good.

She was hanging the washing on a clothes horse in front of the fire when Sigmund walked in. In Strangeways, doors were left on the latch during the day and it was not unusual for someone to pop in for a neighbourly chat. But it was only women who did so.

'Something's wrong?' she greeted him. The last time he had paid her a morning visit it had concerned David and she felt apprehensive. What was going on with her high-school-boy son now? 'Tell me already!'

Sigmund shrugged, which meant there was something. Then he smiled, so maybe it wasn't anything bad?

'First I want to tell you David's Bar Mitzvah suit is ready for a fitting.'

'And second?'

He removed his pince-nez and studied them, then replaced them on his nose. 'He has it in his head to be a solicitor.'

Mr Forrest's offer to article him had been relayed to David after they met at the party. Jim had not wanted to build up his hopes until it was definite. As usual, David had consulted his mentor Sigmund.

'It's not such a terrible thing to be,' Sigmund chuckled when Sarah looked at him uncertainly.

Sarah sat down on the nearest chair, which fortunately was right behind her. Her legs felt weak and the room was spinning round. Don't get any big ideas, she'd said to him. And now this!

'He'll make plenty of money,' Sigmund informed her.

'And you have to be a millionaire before you can be one.' She picked up the poker and gave the fire an angry stir. 'Remember when he cut off his hair? So here is another result of it.'

Sigmund remained silent, but his eyes were twinkling roguishly.

'From one thing comes another,' Sarah said accusingly. 'Why d'you think I blamed you when he went on a train on *Shabbos*? Because it was you who came here to make peace between David and me after he cut the hair. If you hadn't talked me out of it, I'd have made him grow it again. He wants to look like all the other boys at the new school, you said. Don't make things harder for him, you said. And I let you persuade me you were right. Never before have I compromised on our religious teachings and the

116

first time I do, look what comes of it. I shouldn't have listened to you, the next thing he'll want to cut off his nose so he shouldn't look Jewish!'

'A nose he can't live without. And who says he doesn't want to look Jewish? So he wants to look English also, what's the harm? Here is not Russia or Austria. In this country a Jew can also be an Englishman. But this has nothing to do with him studying law.'

'Except that you encourage him to think everything he sets his heart on he can have.'

'If you don't want your son to be a solicitor, all right,' Sigmund shrugged.

Sarah took David's patched undervest from the clothes horse and turned it over to dry the other side. Sigmund must be *meshugah*, out of his mind encouraging the boy to aim so high. 'What has wanting to do with it?' she asked him bitterly. All the things she wanted for her family rose like a mirage before her eyes and drifted away. For the unborn child in her womb, who knew what the future might bring? But for David, now? Impossible.

After Sigmund had left, Sarah could not settle to her usual Monday routine and went to dust the parlour, though it did not need dusting. It was the best furnished parlour in the street and, not for the first time, she mused on how and why she had acquired it. Everything in it had come from Salaman. First, he had sent the sofa on which his wife had lain dying, though Sarah was not aware of this. The china cabinet and a pedestal with an aspidistra to stand upon it had followed, then he had brought the hearthrug and a small, octagonal table to stand in the middle of the room. Sarah had not wanted to accept any of them, but Abraham had insisted, and she had grown accustomed to having them.

For Abraham they were a constant reminder of his first day at the factory. Giving things away did not tally with his employer's penny-pinching nature and it was as if he had wanted to clear his home of everything that made him think of his dead wife. Abraham could not look at the sofa without seeing the picture which had engraved itself on his mind that morning and it deepened his compassion for Salaman, for whom the removal of these mementoes of his married life had done nothing to lessen his painful recollections.

It was in the parlour that Abraham learned Sarah was pregnant. The grumpy lodger had not yet returned from his day's stint *shmearing* waterproofs, but the children were in the kitchen and she beckoned her husband into the front room when he arrived home from work, unable to contain her secret a moment longer.

'Sit down, you look tired,' she said scanning his face.

Abraham could feel the chill of the room striking his lungs and began to cough, wondering in a distant part of his mind if the steam from the pressing irons had begun to affect his chest. They never used the parlour, why had she brought him in here? What was so wrong it couldn't be told in the children's presence, or wait until they had gone to bed? He remained standing, his back to the window. He could never bring himself to sit on the sofa because of its associations.

Sarah had lit the gas mantle and he was silhouetted against the darkness outside. His shoulders seemed more hunched than they used to be. Bending over his cobbler's bench had made its mark on his posture while he was still a youth, but wielding the heavy irons in the factory had added to this. Love for him welled over her, concern too. How hard he worked to provide for them. And now she must tell him his burden was to be increased. But was it not love which had brought this about? Hers for him and his for her? The knowledge strengthened her. It was the only solid, unchanging thing in their lives.

'There's going to be another Sandberg in the Spring,' she said simply.

Abraham's expression lit with relief. 'I thought it was bad news.'

'And who could blame you for thinking it isn't good news either?'

He was by her side in two strides, gathering her close. Then he held her away from him and smiled into her eyes. 'A child is a blessing, Sorrel. God is good to us.'

Salaman came into the pressing room and sat down on a stool. 'How goes it with you, Abie?' he asked morosely.

118

We're going to have another child, we don't have to struggle enough, Abraham wanted to say. His joy at the news had not blinded him to what it meant. And next week is David's Bar Mitzvah, he felt like telling Salaman. We'll have to provide cakes and wine for the whole congregation, or how will we hold up our heads? So it isn't a big congregation, even a small one is too large for our purse. He smiled and said nothing. By now he knew his employer came to him to pour out his own troubles, not to listen to his. And who else did the poor fellow have to talk to? His relatives had lost patience with him because he had not yet re-married and the loneliness was his own choice.

'The matchmakers have found me a widow. Like Venus de Milo she looks,' Salaman confided.

Abraham spat on his finger and dabbed the iron to test the heat. 'She can cook also?'

'Last night I had potato *latkes* at her house to melt in the mouth,' Salaman drooled ecstatically.

'I'm very pleased for you.'

'There's only one thing, Abie.'

Abraham knew what it was without being told.

'My Bessie, bless her, she doesn't like her.' Salaman sighed heavily and lit one of the cigarettes he chain-smoked to pacify himself.

Ladies of all shapes and sizes had been presented for his selection since the death of his wife. Several had taken his fancy, but none had taken Bessie's. Everyone but Salaman himself was aware that Bessie had no intention of having a stepmother. Her father introduced each new candidate to her with hope in his heart, but she found fault with all of them.

'If a man doesn't listen to his own flesh and blood, Abie, there'd only be trouble afterwards.' Salaman heaved himself off the stool and began pacing restlessly, weaving his way between the piles of unpressed garments which littered the floor, as if the movement might help him get whatever was ailing him out of his system.

'It's me my daughter's thinking of!' he declaimed halting by the ironing board, his fierce gaze challenging Abraham to deny this.

The underpresser had been sent on an errand, which always

119

meant Salaman wanted to talk to Abraham alone. After he had unburdened himself, he would waddle back to the workroom with his feelings temporarily relieved, but would return to repeat the process a few days later, when his inner turmoil was ready to erupt again.

Abraham would not have dreamed of denying his employer's interpretation of Bessie's motives, though he was sure it was incorrect. Salaman must be allowed to believe somebody loved him.

'Like her brother she isn't,' the unhappy man said sourly. 'I could get runover by a tram and Saul wouldn't care.' He blew his nose as emotion overcame him. 'Such a life I've got, Abie. So what can you do?'

Abraham thought there was plenty he could do about Bessie, who was now eleven and not a pleasant girl. Spoiled children were hard to find in Strangeways, but Bessie was a notable exception. He recalled how after her mother's death she had been petted by everybody, but had been quick to take advantage of the kindness showered upon her. Sympathy does not last forever and people came to realise she had been over-indulged all her life. How could a man as shrewd as Salaman be putty in her hands? Abraham had often asked himself when Bessie flounced into the factory as if she, not he, owned it and was rude to the workers. But Salaman would just pat her pudgy cheeks and beam with pride. And his meanness did not extend to her, there was nothing she could not have if she sat on his lap and asked for it, Abraham had seen her do this many times.

God help him when she grows up, he thought. As yet her wants were limited to having more of everything than her schoolmates had. The other little girls only had one Sabbath outfit and were glad to have that, but Bessie had two.

'You've seen my little princess in her new coat, Abie?' Salaman asked. 'She fancied one like Miriam Moritz's so I asked your friend the tailor to make it for her.'

Abraham started guiltily. It was as though Salaman had been reading his thoughts! 'Sigmund told me, he said it fitted her like a glove.'

'It shouldn't? With what I paid him for it?'

Abraham had not seen Bessie in the coat, but his children had told him she looked dreadful in it, because it was green, like Miriam's, and made her skin look the same colour. He tried to discourage them from disliking Bessie, but could well understand why they did. She never offered her sweets, though she was the only one who ever had money to buy any and he had once seen her wave a liquorice stick, tauntingly, under Esther's envious nose.

'Saul? He could stand on his head and I wouldn't have a new coat made for him,' Salaman suddenly flared. 'The old raincoat he has from the factory is more than he deserves, the way he treats me!' he added as he went back to the workroom.

But Abraham knew that Saul never asked his father for anything. He was the direct opposite of Bessie and would have given his last farthing to anyone in need. Eli the cutter had once told him Mrs Salaman had been like that and it had made trouble for her with her husband.

Saul had left school recently and was working in the factory, but spent his days watching the clock until he could go to see Helga. When his father returned from talking with Abraham, he treadled his sewing machine faster. Salaman had that effect on everyone.

'Remember, a boy who will one day own a business must be able to do every job properly himself,' Salaman said inspecting the garment in Saul's machine and frowning at a crooked seam. 'If I let you do the cutting, the garments would only be fit for humpbacks!' he exclaimed wrathfully.

Saul was to be taught every aspect of the trade, but his apathy was plain to see. If only he was like David Sandberg, Salaman thought as his son returned his gaze sullenly. A boy with a head on him. Ambitious. Who respects his father. The last thought was like gall in his throat. He was wealthier than anyone realised and it might seem strange that a man in his position should envy a presser earning a pittance. But Salaman did.

David rose on the morning of his Bar Mitzvah with all a young boy's excitement at the dawning of a great day. A January frost had powdered the rooftops and the pavements whilst he slept and he scraped the soles of his new shoes with Sammy's penknife so he would not slip whilst walking to *shul*, hoping God would forgive him for doing this on *Shabbos*.

His mother had laid out the blue serge suit and the pristine white shirt he was to wear with it in the parlour. He tiptoed downstairs and dressed there, in the biting cold, before anyone else was up.

The kitchen clock said 6.30 and the service would not begin until eight. How was he to pass the hour and a half which stretched between? He took down the mirror from the wall and balanced it against a chair, to admire his long trousers. Having his legs covered meant nobody would notice his knees knocking when he got up to read his portion of the *Torah*. Perhaps that was why boys had their first pair of long trousers for their Bar Mitzvah? Would the suit still fit him in five years' time, so he could wear it for university when he went there to study law? When Jim had first told him about his father's offer to article him, he couldn't believe his good fortune. Now, it was just the goal he must aim for. Sometimes, he daydreamed about sitting at a big desk opposite Jim, with legal documents spread all around them. But most of the time he kept his mind on his studies, which was the way to make the dream come true. He had to pass his matriculation exam, but did not doubt he would do so.

He was still gazing at his trousers in the mirror, deliberately thinking of everything but his Bar Mitzvah, when the rest of the family trooped in and roared with laughter. His mother served breakfast, then Mrs Moritz arrived to help her prepare the food for those who would come home with them after the service.

Cakes and wine for the congregation had been taken to the synagogue yesterday. Everything was under control, except David's nerves. His teeth began to chatter when they left the house and he said it was because he was cold, but nobody believed him.

Sitting on his hard, wooden chair, with his father and Sammy on one side of him and Sigmund on the other, he calmed down. The *shul* was full of men and being Bar Mitzvah had happened to all of them. He wished he could see his mother and Miriam, but they were hidden behind the brown-cloth screen. Isaac Salaman arrived with Saul and shook his hand solemnly. Then Rabbi Lensky took his place in the pulpit and he knew nothing could stop it from happening. Soon, Mr Rubens the beadle would beckon to him and he would have to stand up before the congregation.

When the moment came, he was not scared at all. His father was already standing beside the rabbi, waiting to receive him. The scrolls on which the *Torah* was inscribed had been taken from the holy Ark and their rich, velvet and gold covers removed. The one from which he was to read was open on the lectern, ready for him to begin.

At first, hearing his own voice chanting in the thick silence unnerved him, but he kept his eyes glued to the rabbi's silver pointer moving swiftly along the lines of Hebrew words and soon was conscious of nothing but being a Jewish boy on his Bar Mitzvah day, as the timelessness of the occasion washed over him.

His mother's face glowed with pride when she kissed him after the service. But first his hand was wrung by so many people it ached and the word *Mazeltov*! deafened his ears. The party at home was the happiest time he could remember. Except that Bessie Salaman was there and kept gazing at him like a sick cow, which embarrassed him.

Because it was *Shabbos*, the Berkowitzes had not been able to travel from Leeds, but had sent David a beautiful *tallith* bag. Isaac Salaman had given him a tie-pin and Mr Moritz's present was two books instead of the usual one, to mark the special occasion; *Treasure Island* and *Kidnapped*, which he couldn't wait to read. Most of the other guests had bought him prayer books, he had enough to fill a whole shelf of his orange-box bookcase. But the most significant gift was from his parents, a grown-up *tallith*, and a set of *tephillin* to lay upon his arm and his head every morning except the Sabbath and Holy Days for the rest of his life.

His mother had invited the three families who had travelled to England with them, which meant his friend Lazar Lensky was there as well as Saul. If only Jim could be here, too, he thought, but he had not dared suggest it to his parents. 'A *goy* in *shul*?' they would have said in shocked voices. And perhaps Jim wouldn't have been comfortable in a cramped little house, at a party where all the adults spoke a mixture of English and Yiddish. His Gentile friend's absence emphasised the difference between their two worlds, but he brushed his regret aside and enjoyed himself.

'So, David!' his mother said with satisfaction that night.

They were alone in the kitchen and she had just finished clearing up. It had taken her a long time, today they had used the parlour, too. The rest of the family were in bed, but David was too elated to feel tired.

'I don't have to worry about my Bar Mitzvah any more,' he laughed contentedly.

'Before it you don't have other worries,' she said stirring the dying coals into a last blaze. 'But now you're not a child any more.'

David knew the Bar Mitzvah ceremony traditionally admits a boy to manhood, but he did not feel any different from how he had felt before it and smiled at his mother's literal interpretation.

'How is the school work going?' she asked him.

'How's yours going?' he joked. 'I still can't believe you're going to night school, even though you are!'

'I know my ABC already,' she said proudly.

David grinned.

'But you didn't answer my question.'

He told her he was doing well. But she knew this, he always got good reports. Why was she asking?

'I wish it would be possible for you to stay there longer, David.'

He felt his stomach lurch. What did she mean?

'Next year you'll be fourteen. It's necessary for a boy of that age to be an earner, with people like us.'

People like us. The words reverberated in the room. His mother had spoken them once before, when they first came to England and he asked her why his father couldn't find work. Mr Moritz had said by the time David grew up he would have learned what she meant, that it was best to find out for himself. And now he understood. She meant people who weren't like the Forrests. Who had to try harder than others to achieve exactly the same thing and ought not to expect to achieve it. 'You want me to leave school,' he said flatly.

'It's not what I want, David, but the way it has to be.'

His mother looked pale and drawn and her knuckles gleamed white as she gripped the brass rail on the fireguard.

'Why?' he flung at her. 'So we're not wealthy, but I work, don't I? All the fruit and veg we have I bring home from Mr Radinsky's!'

124

'But this is not enough.'

'Enough for what?'

She gazed into the fire for a moment, then turned to look at him again. 'For a family where there's going to be another mouth to feed. I'm expecting a baby, David.'

He had not noticed her thickened waistline, but now he did. He brushed the shock aside. Sigmund Moritz had advised him to say nothing about Mr Forrest's offer for the present. But if he told her it might change her mind. It did not occur to him that she already knew.

'What's so special you want to be a solicitor?' she asked after she had listened to him enthuse about it.

'A professional man's somebody. You should see how the Forrests live, Mother, then you wouldn't have to ask. If I don't get a good education, I'll end up like Father.'

'Your father is a bad person to end up like?'

'It isn't the sort of person he is, it's what he's done with his life.'

'To bring up a boy to be Bar Mitzvah is nothing? Going without many a time, so he should have!'

'Achievement isn't just what you do for your family.'

'For your father and me nothing is more important.'

'Then why're you making me leave school?'

'I am not doing it. Life is doing it.'

The dream of himself and Jim together at the big desk crumbled to dust. He felt the hope ebb out of him and buried his face in his hands. When he looked up his mother was fingering her brooch and gazing at him pleadingly.

'So you'll be something else,' she told him.

'What for instance?' he asked dully.

'Who knows? You'll still have your brains even without an education. Maybe you'll be a businessman one day, like Salaman.'

David thought of how Salaman spent his days and felt suddenly sick.

'When the time comes for the new baby's education, if God gives me another son, perhaps the family will be able to afford it,' his mother said quietly. 'But for you such big ideas are too soon. Didn't I warn you, David.'

CHAPTER TEN

Nathan Edward Sandberg came into the world on 16 May 1910 and was welcomed joyously by every member of his family except one.

Because she had initially not wanted him, Sarah had been haunted during her pregnancy by fear that God would punish her by marring the child. When he was placed in her arms by the midwife and pronounced perfect, relief and gratitude mingled with the tenderness she instinctively felt for him. He was smaller than her other babies had been and strikingly beautiful. His features were regular like Abraham's, but his colouring was hers and even at birth he had a mane of silky black hair.

Her labour had been long and Abraham paced the house like a man demented, waiting for it to end. Sigmund, who kept him company, had not thought him capable of such powerful feeling. When he heard the child cry, he raced upstairs and burst into the room. At first, he only had eyes for Sarah, who lay back on the pillows exhausted.

'We've got an Englishman in the family now,' she whispered happily.

Abraham looked at his son and was moved to tears.

The children were spending the night at the Moritzes' and did not see their new brother until the next morning. Sammy and Esther stroked him gently and said how pretty he was. David barely glanced at him.

The baby arrived just ten days after the King's death and because he was the first English-born Sandberg was given Edward as one of his names, which accorded with the Jewish custom of calling children after the departed. Sarah's father had been called Nathan.

At his *Brith*, when Rabbi Silverstein the *mohel* came to perform the ritual circumcision, the house in Moreton Street was again the scene of a celebration, but this time it was David's baby brother who was the centre of attention.

The circumcision was to take place in the parlour, but first the baby must be dressed in his finery and Rachel, who was to be his godmother, helped Sarah put the finishing touches to it. They were in the kitchen with their daughters and some women neighbours.

'So give him to me already!' Rachel chuckled when the child was ready and Sarah still clutched him to her breast. 'The men are waiting to begin.'

Sigmund was godfather and nervous about the responsibility. He popped his head round the door. 'Come on already, Rachel!'

Rachel lifted the infant from Sarah's arms. 'Hold the pillow for me, someone. You've forgotten that's how I have to carry him in?'

Esther and Miriam and Bessie Salaman, whose father had brought her along, reached for the pillow together, but Helga took it and held it aloft for her mother to place the baby upon its snowy softness.

Rachel smoothed down her brown bombazine dress, everyone was in their best for the occasion, and carried the pillow, with its precious burden, to hand it over to Sigmund. She was glad that Isaac Salaman and not her husband had been given the honour of holding the baby's legs whilst he was circumcised, Sigmund had even less stomach than most men for such things.

'So tiny he is,' Sarah whispered as the darling of her heart was borne away to his ancient Hebrew fate. His robe and hat were those worn by David and Sammy at their *brith*, sewn by her mother who had held her hand both times until the ordeal was over.

Zelda Cohen, who had just moved into the house next-door-but-one, looked at her enviously. 'God should only give me a son. My Yankel would like another man in the family.' She emitted one of her nervy hee-haws and folded her arms on her pregnant stomach. So far, God had given her four more daughters to keep Naomi, born on the boat, company, but Yankel kept on trying.

'You think the baby's all right?' Sarah asked Rachel anxiously when she returned to her side.

Rachel took her hand, as her mother had done, and pressed it comfortingly. 'The first to have a *brith* he isn't, and he won't be the last either.'

Bessie began to giggle, but Miriam prodded her into silence. Only a stupid thing like Bessie Salaman would laugh when a little baby was having that dreadful thing done to him, Miriam thought contemptuously.

Everyone had fallen silent; waiting for the child's return was always a strain for the women, though they knew he was unlikely to feel the surgery because the *mohel* would dope him with kosher wine dropped onto his tongue from a bit of cotton which had been soaked in it.

'My dad says the baby sometimes gets *shikker*,' Bessie said giggling again. Drunken babies were the lighthearted side of every *brith*. Her eye roved to the cakes on the table. 'When can we have something to eat, Mrs Sandberg?'

Sarah was too preoccupied to reply.

Miriam did it for her. 'It's no wonder you're fat, Bessie. You can't have anything till the baby comes back, you greedy thing!'

Bessie made a dive for the dish of Sachetorte Rachel had brought as Sigmund entered with his godson.

'*Mazeltov!*' he beamed depositing Nathan in Sarah's arms. 'May you only have joy from him!'

Abraham and the *mohel* joined them with the rest of the men and the well-worn words were echoed over and over again. It was a weekday and friends like Moishe Lipkin and Yossel Lensky, whom Abraham would have liked to be there, were at work. But Rabbi Lensky had brought along some of his unemployed congregants to make up the necessary *minyan*. Now, they would drink wine with Abraham and join in the celebration of a new member of the Tribe of Israel, which was important enough for Salaman to have given his presser and himself an hour or two off.

'You want some wine, David?' Abraham smiled as he poured it into the collection of borrowed glasses.

David shook his head.

'So what can you do? My eldest son isn't a *shikkerer*!' Abraham laughed to the others.

Miriam watched David hovering restlessly in the scullery doorway and followed him out when he went to sit on the back doorstep. The day was fine and warm and they watched some sparrows hopping around in the sunshine. David did not turn to look at her when she squatted beside him. She'd hoped he might notice her pretty, new dress, but he seemed not even to hear the rustle of the taffeta when she spread her skirt around her knees.

How sad he looks, she thought and wished she could give him a hug to comfort him as she would've done when they were younger, but it wasn't seemly for a girl of eleven to hug a boy of thirteen. 'What's the matter, David?' she asked gravely. 'Since your Bar Mitzvah you're not the same.'

'Aren't I?'

'You're moody all the time and you don't tell me things like you used to.' The only one he seemed to want to talk to these days was her father, but she was careful not to say this in case David might fly into a rage, which he'd been doing for no reason at all lately. She moved closer to him to let him know she sympathised, though she had no idea what was wrong. Then Bessie came out of the house, pushing her fat legs between them to enter the yard, and David got up and went back inside.

Bessie stopped eating the piece of cake in her hand and watched him go.

Miriam went to stand beside her, but Bessie did not seem to notice she was there. She'd like David for her sweetheart! Miriam thought with shock. The way she's looking at him, though she knows very well he's mine.

They could see David through the kitchen window. His mother was holding out the baby for him to take, but he was shaking his head, refusing.

'He's frightened the baby'll pee on him,' Bessie said.

But there was something about the expression on David's face which made Miriam think there was more to it than that.

Sarah attributed David's indifference to his age. And boys did not usually fuss over infants. But she had seen him gazing at Nathan with a tightness around his lips. Was he jealous? She didn't neglect her other children, but the family's routine inevitably revolved around the baby. Sammy didn't seem to mind and Esther had learned to change his diapers and help bath him. David resented every inconvenience he caused.

That evening Nathan was fractious. David was sitting at the table trying to write an essay and threw down his pen when the wails grew louder.

'What can you expect after what he's had done to him?' Sarah said rocking the cradle.

'Take the brat out of here!' David snapped. 'I can't do my homework with him squawking his head off!'

'You're leaving school soon, what does it matter?' Sarah picked up the baby and kissed him. 'Such a sweet little dolly this is and his big brother behaves like he's a thorn in the side.'

Abraham got up from his chair and glared at her. 'Enough of that talk already!' he said with uncharacteristic force. He had seen the desolate look in David's eyes as he stared down at his books and now understood why.

PART TWO: REALITIES

CHAPTER ONE

David came out of the factory and slithered into the street. He could feel the slush seeping into his boots. His father and Sammy had left half-an-hour ago, but he had stayed behind as usual, sorting things out ready for tomorrow.

'David!'

He stopped and turned around.

Bessie had chased after him and stood in the lamplight wiping her hands on her apron, which was no cleaner than the one she had worn for school. 'Stay and have a bite with us.'

'No thanks.'

'We're having meatballs.'

For a moment he was tempted. Not many people had meat during the week, but the Salamans went short of nothing.

'They're your favourite,' Bessie said persuasively.

She knew this because she was always embarrassing him by bringing him tasty morsels to eat in the factory, it had become a joke among the workers.

David looked at his pocket watch, which had been his grandfather's. His mother had given it to him when he started work. 'I don't want to be late at Miriam's,' he said. He had promised to be there at eight-o'clock and it was now seven.

'Saul's going there, too. You can eat and go with him.'

'Bessie, I have to go home to wash and change first,' he said impatiently. Then her dejected expression touched him, though he had no time for her. 'Thanks, though,' he added with a smile and saw her face light up. Just because he'd said a kind word to her! He was conscious of her watching him as he continued down the street. She was still standing there when he looked over his shoulder, before turning into Bury New Road. Poor Bessie! Then the thought of all he had to do tomorrow crowded her out of his mind.

In the three years he had worked at the factory, he had become

Salaman's righthand man. This had not been a conscious decision on his employer's part; in his mind his son occupied that position. But Saul's apathy and David's natural ability had combined to produce the existing situation. Because David was Saul's friend and Abraham's boy, Salaman had offered to teach him the trade and had gradually come to depend on him.

The business had grown and was no longer just a matter of cash deals with whoever came in to buy a bundle of garments for resale. Retailers, both Jewish and Gentile, now sent in orders for goods to be delivered to their shops, which required organising. Records must be kept and transactions involved paperwork. Orders had to be honoured on time if they were to be repeated. David had instituted a system by which everything ran smoothly and efficiently, where previously Salaman had been out of his depth. It was not surprising that he relied upon David, though he was still only a lad of seventeen.

When David arrived home, his little brother was playing in the lobby with some small wooden figures Sammy had carved for him.

'How d'you like my soldiers, David?' he asked as David brushed past him. 'I'm getting ready for the war.'

David paused and looked down at him and the child's handsome face broke into a smile. David rarely had a minute to spare for him.

'Which war, Nat?' Nathan's name had been cut down while he was still in his cradle.

His smile faded as he saw David frown. 'You're not angry with me, are you?'

'No. But who told you there's going to be a war?'

'I heard Uncle Sigmund talking about it. What will the war do?'

'Never mind.'

Hearing Nathan mention it chilled David to the marrow. His little brother had a razor-sharp mind and ears that went with it. It was time he was at school, where he wouldn't hear adult gossip, but he was not yet old enough. Was it just gossip? The ominous clouds had been gathering in Europe for some time, but what had this to do with England? A small island on the other side of the Channel? David had not experienced a military war, but he had seen other examples of man's inhumanity to man and hoped never

133

to do so again. The family's ordeal in Russia had long since faded from his mind, but now it came flooding back, as if he was still a little boy hiding from the *pogromschiks* in a barrel. He saw Nathan staring up at him and shook the feeling off, then patted the child's head reassuringly,

'You've never done that before, David.'

'What?'

'Stroked my head.'

David smiled and went into the kitchen, where his mother had borsht and potatoes bubbling on the hob for him.

'So, David?'

She always greeted him that way, wanting to know about his day. As if any day was different from another, he thought wryly. The details sometimes varied, but the quality was always the same. 'Bessie asked me to stay for supper.'

Sarah said nothing, but thought a great deal. You could do worse, she wanted to say. Isaac Salaman's daughter, no less. But her son was in love with Miriam Moritz, the way she herself had given her heart to Abraham.

'Where's Father?' David asked as he ate his meal.

'Taking a rest. Where else?'

Abraham now had two underpressers, but still had to work too hard. Father's life's nothing but work and sleep, David reflected. Surely a man had a right to something more than just that? But his father had accepted his lot.

When he went upstairs to change, Sammy was in the bedroom, making something from a piece of wood as usual.

'What is it this time, Sam?' David grinned. He took off his shoes and socks to dry his damp feet and had to be careful where he walked, the floor was littered with chippings.

'A jewel box for Miriam.'

David laughed. 'She hasn't any jewels.'

'So she'll keep it until she has.'

One day I'll give them to her, David thought. And pay for Sammy to have special boots made, so he doesn't have to limp so badly. He couldn't imagine his brother ever earning sufficient to pay for them himself. Sammy's ineptitude at everything except wood-carving was well known, but David had managed to persuade Salaman to employ him. He could have coped with any of the tasks put before him, but, as always, would not apply himself to work he did not enjoy. He was now the odd-job lad, a position created by his presence, and just gave a hand where and when it was needed. Salaman'd fire him if he wasn't my brother, David said to himself as he put on his best suit. Why won't he buck his ideas up? It isn't as if he's a fool, what he lacks is backbone.

Sammy was sitting on the bed, painstakingly chipping away at the wood, wearing two old cardigans because there was no heat in the room.

'Why don't you do that downstairs? You'll freeze to death in here.'

'You know what Mother's like when I make a mess on the kitchen floor. Are you going somewhere nice to tonight?'

David avoided his eye. 'Dancing. I'd ask you to come with us, otherwise.'

'I wish every night was like this!' Miriam exclaimed rapturously as she fastened the bodice of her new dress.

'It wouldn't be a special occasion if we went too often,' Helga told her.

Rachel was seated by the window in their bedroom, enjoying their pleasurable anticipation as they dressed for the dance, and reflected as she often did on their contrasting natures. Miriam had inherited Sigmund's fiery impetuosity, but Helga was like herself, placid and practical.

'Let me do that for you,' she said when Miriam found she had missed the top button and had to undo the others and begin again. 'My fingers have more patience than yours,' she smiled as she completed the task in a trice. 'Come Helga, now I'll fix your sash. Very nice it looks, but I'll make it look even nicer.'

'Remember how Mother used to dress us up for *shul*, Miriam?' Helga reminisced. 'We always had bigger bows in our hair than the other little girls.'

'And being that kind of mother isn't something I can turn off like a tap now you're grown up.'

'So we've noticed,' Miriam laughed.

Rachel appraised her daughters proudly; the younger so tall

and shapely and with the bloom of womanhood about her, though she was not yet sixteen; the elder reaching only to her sister's shoulder, dainty as a china doll.

'How do we look?' Miriam asked her, pirouetting on the rug.

'*Wunderbar!*' she pronounced in the language of her youth, which such moments always evoked.

Helga had made the satin dance-frocks on Sigmund's sewing machine. Her own was lilac, Miriam's eau-de-nil and their full overskirts shimmered in the gaslight as they moved about the room.

'Like two jewels!' Rachel added extravagantly.

The girls laughed and hugged her until she pushed them away in order to catch her breath. 'Such an excitement! Your great-grandfather the rabbi would turn in his grave if he knew where you were going tonight.'

Helga sat down before the mirror and pinched her cheeks to colour them. 'You and Father don't mind, do you?'

'How can we mind? We're living in different times now. But some people will never accept it.'

Male and female dancing together was still frowned upon by the clergy and at weddings only the old Jewish folk dances were permitted. But it was 1914 and the immigrants' grown-up children had acquired a taste for the Veleta and the Lancers. Gliding on the polished floor at a local dance hall, amid the rustle of silk and taffeta and the heady mixture of scents was a blissful experience for the ghetto boys and girls. Between dances, they flocked to one end of the ballroom and the Gentiles to the other, as if by tacit consent, but when the stout lady at the piano began playing again and all took the floor together, the feeling of difference disappeared and everyone would smile and nod to each other as they danced by.

'Where did you and Father go when you were courting, Mother?' Miriam asked as he pulled on her long, white gloves.

'Often we would just take a stroll. Or sit in a café and drink hot chocolate when the snow was on the ground. Like Strangeways it wasn't.'

'I remember a very wide street, with lots of trees,' Helga said. 'Where you sometimes took us on Sunday afternoons in the summertime.'

'The Ringstrasse,' Rachel sighed. 'Your father's favourite street in all Vienna. Such a beautiful city! Everywhere a person looks is something worth looking at.'

The two girls exchanged a glance. There was a faraway look in their mother's eyes which they could not recall seeing before. She had been an only child and her parents were dead, but perhaps it was the place where she had been born and brought up which still held her fast?

Rachel emerged from her reverie briskly, she mustn't be like Paula Frankl who still hankered after what she had left behind. 'So in Strangeways nothing is beautiful, but there's no need for a Jew to be afraid,' she said to her daughters.

'There isn't in Vienna, either, now. Uncle Kurt says everything's fine every time he writes to us,' Helga reminded her.

'Your father thinks now is not forever and he always knows best,' Rachel declared as her husband appeared in the doorway, panting from climbing the stairs.

'You're talking about my brother? That *shlemiel* has his head in the sand!' Sigmund said. 'Come already, girls. Your young men are getting impatient. When I was courting your mother she never kept me waiting.'

'I'm looking forward to the day my son will start courting,' Rachel sighed as they went downstairs. 'Other young people go out sometimes and enjoy themselves, but where is he every night? Lying on his bed reading!'

Helga smiled at Saul, who was standing in the lobby with David waiting to help her on with her cloak. 'Carl hasn't met the right girl yet, Mother.'

'If we hadn't left Vienna, Helga and I wouldn't've met Saul and David, imagine that,' Miriam said looking at David as if she could not imagine it.

'Nicer boys you couldn't find,' Sigmund chuckled, then his voice grew grave. 'But I can think of more important reasons for leaving Vienna.' He took off his pince-nez and studied them reflectively. 'I hope I'm wrong, but one day, God forbid, you'll see.'

'You've been saying that for years, Father,' Miriam chided him. 'But things've got better, not worse. Why must you be such a gloom merchant?' At supper he and Carl had talked about the

137

war they thought was coming and spoiled everyone's appetites. She hurried David out of the house before her father had time to involve him in one of the lengthy discussions which sometimes made him forget she was there.

The slush underfoot had hardened to ice in the crisp, night air and the four young people had to tread carefully as they made their way to the main road.

Miriam slipped her hand into David's and looked up at the crescent moon which had silvered the humble rooftops. 'Even Strangeways is beautiful on an evening like this!' she exulted. 'When you're going somewhere special.'

The hood of her green velvet cloak had fallen back onto her shoulders and David caught his breath as he gazed at her perfect profile, smooth as marble in the moonlight, and the soft cloud of hair which she refused to pin-up, cascading around it. How lovely she was and soon he'd be holding her in his arms on the dance floor. Then he thought of Sammy, to whom such joy was denied and his smile of happiness tinged with guilt. If he hadn't taken him to play by the Dvina that day, how different his brother's life would have been.

'What's the matter?' Miriam asked softly when she saw his expression change.

'I was just thinking of our Sammy, sitting at home.'

'If you paid a bit more attention to Nat and a bit less to Sammy they'd both be better off.'

David stiffened. 'What do you mean?'

Didn't he realise how cold he was to his little brother? And the way he went on with Sammy! 'Sammy doesn't have to sit at home just because he's lame, does he?'

'I wouldn't've let him. But how can I bring him to a dance to perch on a chair watching everyone else waltz past him?'

'It's no different from seeing other people walk without a limp,' Miriam said bluntly. 'And Sammy doesn't need bringing, he can go anywhere he wants to by himself. You're stupid, David.'

David let go of her hand abruptly and the delicious excitement with which she had awakened that morning disappeared. 'Why did you have to spoil things?' she said resentfully.

They stopped walking and looked at each other across the barrier which had inexplicably risen between them.

Miriam could see Helga and Saul waiting for them on the corner. 'My sister's lucky having a boyfriend who never upsets her. I've been looking forward to to tonight for ages, to wearing my new dress and everything and now you've ruined it all!'

'Who has? What am I supposed to've done!'

'What does it matter? You've done it now, haven't you?' Miriam's eyes blazed like twin emeralds as her temper rose. 'And you're glaring at me as if it's my fault!'

'You're doing your share of the glaring, love! I had something important to finish off at the factory tonight, but I left it until tomorrow to take you dancing and this is what I get for it!'

'You and the factory!'

'And what's that supposed to mean?'

'The way you stay late every night. Anyone'd think your father owned it, not Saul's!'

'I happen to be the kind of person who takes his job seriously.' A bitter note entered David's voice. 'Even if it's a job I don't enjoy. It's the only way to get on.'

'That's all you think about! Getting on!' Miriam flashed. 'Well go and finish whatever you were doing, then. You don't have to take me to the dance, I'm going home!' She burst into angry tears and fled back along the street, her cloak billowing out behind her.

David stood reeling with bewilderment, as if he had received a short, sharp blow to the chin. He could not think of anything he had said or done to provoke such a furious onslaught.

Helga and Saul had retraced their footsteps. 'What did you do to upset her?' Helga asked reproachfully, halting beside him.

He laughed shakily. 'What makes you think it wasn't the opposite way round?'

They heard Miriam cry out as she slipped on the ice and lost her balance. 'Don't you come near me, David!' she sobbed as they hastened to her assistance.

David stopped in his tracks and watched Saul and Helga lift her to her feet and steer her along the treacherous pavement. Why was she treating him like a leper? Confusion churned within him again as he turned and walked away.

He spent a sleepless night thinking about it, but was no less confused the next morning.

'What was all that about?' Saul inquired in the workroom.

'You tell me! She just let fly at me out of nowhere.'

'Miriam's always been what they call temperamental, hasn't she?' Saul reminded him.

'Sure. But not with me.'

Saul shrugged. 'So for once you got a dose of what everyone else gets when she feels like giving it to them. She went straight to bed last night, without even explaining anything to her parents. I suppose they thought she'd come back because she fell on the ice.'

'And where did they think I was? In hospital with a broken leg?'

'You know the Moritzes. They don't ask questions.'

'With her for a daughter, it's as well they don't!' David flared.

Saul looked upset. 'It isn't off between you two, is it? Helga couldn't get a word out of her.'

'How do I know? When I've no idea what I've done.' David kept his voice steady, but the prospect his friend's question had conjured up made him tremble. The outburst had occurred when he'd been talking about Sammy. Was Miriam jealous of his concern for his brother? Fed up with the way he often brought him along and took it for granted she wouldn't mind?

'You're not feeling well?' Salaman asked when he saw him staring morosely into space.

'I'm fine,' David said tersely. What right had she to get him into this state! He tried to concentrate on the stock list he was compiling, but anxiety alternated with anger throughout the day. All he could think of was Miriam.

'I'd have it out with her if I were you,' Saul advised when he was putting on his coat to go home.

'Don't worry, I will!'

By the time he reached the Moritzes' house the anger had cooled and all that was left was the anxiety. He was glad it was Helga who opened the door. Miriam might not have let him in.

She was in the kitchen with her parents, who behaved no differently from usual. Except that Sigmund suddenly found he had something to do in his workroom. And Rachel asked Helga to go upstairs with her to look for something she had mislaid. The Moritzes were the essence of tact, not like Sarah Sandberg who would have wanted to know what was going on, David thought dryly.

Miriam continued to stare into the fire, which she had been doing since he entered the room.

'About last night,' he said in his direct way.

'Let's not talk about it,' she replied.

'Look at me, Miriam!'

She lifted her head but did not meet his eyes.

'I want to know why you suddenly lost your temper with me. It's got something to do with our Sammy, hasn't it? Only you always used to care about him the way I do. What's happened?'

'Nothing's happened!'

David could see a pulse throbbing in her neck as she strove to remain calm. 'But suddenly he gets on your nerves and you don't want him to go out with us anymore. Is that it?'

'I didn't say that, David.' You're the one who gets on my nerves, she wanted to tell him. Treating Sammy as if he's different from other people, just because he's lame.

David rose from his chair and went to stand beside her at the hearth. 'Get whatever it is off your chest and have done with it,' he said tensely.

The strong face she knew so well was contorted with emotion as his eyes searched hers questioningly. How dear he was to her. How much a part of her life. But one word too many and he might not be any more. Last night she'd spoken her mind impulsively and this frightening confrontation was the result. He wouldn't take kindly to being told what he couldn't see for himself. She had always sensed this and been careful not to risk it. Now she had proved it and must try to be even more careful in future.

He saw the secret thoughts flickering in her expression. 'Well?'

'I don't know what came over me.' She took his hand and held it against her cheek, staring into the fire again to avoid his gaze because she had lied to him. 'Let's pretend it didn't happen. I want us to be happy and never have another quarrel.'

Relief that he had not lost her surged over David. Everything's all right, he thought gratefully. There was a good deal he could not see for himself in those days.

CHAPTER TWO

'If I have to look at just one more khaki garment!' Abraham exclaimed as he tripped over a pile of them in the kitchen.

Sarah and Esther raised their eyes from their sewing, then their fingers flew fast again.

'We see enough of those buttons being sewn on in the factory,' David told them.

The war was only a few weeks old, but orders from the military had started pouring in months before it began. The workroom could not cope with them all and in company with other manufacturers Salaman was handing out sewing for the women and young girls to do at home. The extra earnings were a godsend to the immigrant families, but a sense of satisfaction was present, too. They were helping England to win the war.

'I bumped into Lazar Lensky and Berel Halpern today,' David said. 'They're home on leave.'

'Their poor mothers haven't had a night's sleep since they joined up.' Sarah began sewing on another button. 'Hannah Lensky looked dreadful when I met her in Radinsky's. I just hope the war'll be over before they start calling boys up, then you won't have to go, David.'

'A nice way for a Jewish person to talk! What would the *goyim* think if they heard you?' Abraham chided her.

'They feel the same, you think they're made of stone? Mr Pickles is dreading his grandson going, he said so last *Shabbos* when he came to stoke the fire.' Sarah looked at Abraham accusingly. 'You want your son to get killed, God forbid?'

Abraham looked at David and shuddered.

'Lazar and Berel were marching down Bury New Road as if they owned it,' David said. 'Showing off their uniforms.'

Sammy looked envious. 'So would I if I was a soldier.'

A lame leg has its compensations, Sarah thought. Sammy would never have to be one.

'I'd love to wear a uniform,' Nathan piped up.

'Me too,' Sammy sighed.

'Well I wouldn't!' David declared vehemently. 'Though it's on the cards I'll have to. Nat's only a kid, Sammy, but you're fourteen, you should have more sense. Remember the Cossacks?'

'Don't mention those barbarians!' Abraham said with another shudder.

'Why not, Father? We're talking about wearing uniform and killing's what it's all about.'

Nathan looked shocked. 'Will Lazar and Berel have to kill people?'

'If they're told to,' David replied grimly. 'They're in the Infantry and I could be put in it, too, because we came from Russia and the Russians are England's allies in the war. If Carl gets called up, he won't have to stick a bayonet in anyone, he'll get put in a Labour Battalion because he's from Austria so they won't let him carry a weapon.'

'Why should they treat him differently?' Abraham asked. 'His father is naturalised, like me.'

'I don't know why, but they do. Maybe they think if it came to it he'd help the Germans and Austrians.'

'He won't help anybody, because they won't make him a soldier, he's got bad eyes,' Sarah said practically as she fastened off a stitch.

'Would all a person's blood come spurting out if someone stuck a bayonet in them, David?' Nathan asked looking sick.

'What do you think?'

Abraham looked sick, too. 'A nice appetite my sons are giving me for supper! You've had time to cook something, Sarah?'

'Since when did my family not come first?' she retorted biting off the thread and putting down her needle. But the chance to boost their income could not be neglected, either.

Esther looked at her father reproachfully. 'You know Mother gets up an hour before the rest of us to prepare something for supper.'

'All right, so I shouldn't have said it! Let's eat already.'

Sarah went to the oven to take out the big stew which had simmered all day whilst she sewed. These days there was more meat in it, as there was in all the ghetto stewpots, but how hard everyone had to work for it. She was not surprised that her husband was irritable when he came home from the factory at night, he had only two extra pressers to help with his much-increased load.

Salaman had raised his employees' wages to encourage greater effort, a piece of astuteness which had not passed for generosity in their minds. The cash he must by now have in the bank was the subject of constant conjecture, but it was never discussed in the Sandbergs' home; Abraham would not allow it. He was the only one who did not begrudge Salaman his wealth. What else did the poor fellow have? Counting his blessings as the family ate their meal together in the cosy room, he was not envious. 'You're going back to the factory tonight, David?' he asked and sighed when David nodded. His son had a dynamo inside him which would not let him rest.

'If my boots are dry enough to put on!' David joked. He had taken them off when he came home and could see them steaming in the hearth. 'I could do with a new pair, Mother,' he said with his mouth full. 'We can afford to buy them, now.'

'And the money won't be there when we need it later,' Sarah replied.

David stopped chewing and look at her. Lately, he had worked such long hours he had not had time to think. It occurred to him now that despite their increased income, the family's standard of living had not changed. Other families had bought new clothes and some were refurbishing their homes. The Sandbergs still had only one mirror in the house. What was his mother saving so carefully for?

Sarah saw the unspoken question in his eyes. 'Nobody should know what we'll need money for better than you, David,' she said quietly.

Nathan was eating his meal, but listening to every word and sensitive to the atmosphere, which had suddenly grown tense. Sammy and Esther had put down their forks and were watching David.

Abraham gave his wife a warning glance, but she did not heed it.

'What happened to my eldest son won't happen to my youngest,' she declared with feeling. The thought of what David might

144

have been, had his education not been cut short, still taunted her.

'What happened to you, David?' Nathan asked apprehensively.

'Be quiet, Nat!' Sarah snapped.

'I'm your youngest son, I want to know what might happen to me.'

'To you we won't let it, don't worry.'

The child was not convinced and became hysterical, kicking and screaming. 'Tell me, David! I want to know!'

David's face had gone chalky white.

'Such a highly strung this little one is, bless him. A genius he'll be,' he heard his mother say as she went to comfort Nathan. But her voice sounded far away and a mist was floating before his eyes. He got up and left the room.

'Don't be upset, David!' Sammy called from the foot of the stairs, but he ignored him and flung himself on his bed, the resentment kindled in him four years ago, which he had tried to stamp out, flaring anew. His mother's words had brought everything back to him, the happiness of his Bar Mitzvah day and the way it had ended. He looked up and saw Nathan standing in the bedroom doorway.

'Mother says she'll keep your supper hot for you,' Nathan said in a subdued voice. He gazed at David appealingly, as if he was begging forgiveness for upsetting him.

David did not reply and the child went away, dejectedly.

His chance of becoming a solicitor had been lost due to Nat's birth and now his mother had revealed that most of what he earned at the factory was being hoarded for Nat's education. He lay back on the bed trying to make himself accept it. It went against the grain to let his mother do this to him, but what was the alternative? Leaving home? A split in the family? He would probably have to leave soon enough to join the army. Going for any other reason, apart from marriage, couldn't be contemplated.

He sat up and rubbed his unshod feet, which felt like blocks of ice. He could never be a solicitor now, no matter what. Why had it meant so much to him? Because there was a special status attached to it, as well as money. Money to buy his way out of the ghetto, to a life like the Forrests lived. His mind began racing, reasoning it all out. The status of a professional man he could never have, but money was within anyone's grasp if they had the brains to acquire it. The shrewdness and industry. The will to make what it could buy theirs. All these things he had and nobody could take them from them. Not even his mother, whom he loved in spite of everything. He would prove what was in him, to her and everyone else. When she cut the ground from under his feet she'd said life was doing it to him and this was true. It was wrong to blame her, she was just life's instrument. Wrong to blame Nat.

A kaleidoscope of scenes in which he had hurt or ignored his little brother shimmered into his mind and settled into shame. He had made the child suffer for something which was not his fault. The eroding resentment left him and something positive sprang into its place; he would make it up to Nat, help to give him his chance. Everything would be different from now on.

He did not return to the factory that evening, but undressed and got into bed and fell asleep immediately. Nobody detected the change in him the next day, it revealed itself gradually. His feelings about Nathan had softened, but his attitude to life had hardened irretrievably.

'Nobody's got a *succah* as nice as ours!' Nathan exclaimed excitedly to his mother.

'Except us,' his friend Lou contested. 'Nat and me've been round peeping in everyone's backyard, Mrs Sandberg.'

Sarah was in the kitchen, making her honey cakes for *Succoth*. It was the first Harvest festival of the war and ingredients were still obtainable in the shops. 'When I was a little girl in Russia, we had a garden and my father used to build a *succah* big enough for the family to live in, the whole seven days, like you're supposed to,' she told the two children.

'Will God forgive us for not living in ours?' Nathan asked her.

Sarah glanced through the window at the small lean-to David and Sammy had erected to commemmorate the departure from Egypt, as Jewish families did all over the world, every year. She smiled at Nathan. 'God doesn't expect the impossible.'

'The big one at *shul*, where we have a *nosh* after the service, is beautiful,' Lou declared.

'It should be! Your mother and me and the other ladies spent two evenings getting it ready.'

Sarah's next-door-neighbour, Mrs Plotkin, waddled into the yard and peered into the *succah*.

'You like it?' Sarah called through the window.

Mrs Plotkin came into the kitchen and eased her weight into a chair. 'Mine has red apples and also a bunch of grapes,' she replied.

'But no oranges,' Nathan said triumphantly.

'A competition it isn't.'

Sarah laughed. 'But who would know it? So how's by you, Mrs Plotkin?'

'I was waiting for you to ask. Oy, my back and also my bunions. I've been cooking all day and now I'm short of an egg for the chopped herring, but my feet won't carry me to the shop.'

She eased them out of her husband's carpet slippers to prove it and managed to contort herself into a position which allowed her to rub the grotesque protuberances twingeing beneath her wrinkled stockings. 'You've got an egg to spare?'

'Help yourself.'

'Before I go I'll take it. Last night I was up until two in the morning finishing my sewing for the factory, a little sit down won't do me any harm.' She eyed the dewdrop on the end of Lou's nose. 'Your mamma didn't teach you to use a handkerchief yet?'

Lou used his shirtsleeve instead.

'Very nice, I'm sure!'

'I haven't got no handkerchieves,' the skinny little boy told her.

'From your dadda's old shirts your mamma could make you some, like I did for my girls.'

'No she couldn't, my brothers're still wearing them.'

Mrs Plotkin shrugged. 'So there's no hope for you. A child that never blows its nose ends up with a lifetime's catarrh, isn't it so, Mrs Sandberg?'

Sarah added the flour to her cake mixture. 'In Manchester he'll end up with it anyway.'

'So how is your Tibby?' Mrs Plotkin inquired glancing at Nicholas' successor who was stretched out by the fire.

'She's expecting again,' Nathan replied.

'Mrs Plotkin knows she is.' Sarah looked at her neighbour reproachfully. 'Her Blackie's the father.'

'Can you prove it?' Mrs Plotkin retorted.

The two little boys looked puzzled. 'How can the kittens have a father when they're not born yet?' Nathan asked.

'Oy vay!' Mrs Plotkin averted her eyes from the cat. 'Never mind.'

'Our Tiger's expecting, too. I opened the cupboard where she always has them and watched them coming out, the last time,' Lou boasted.

Nathan grimaced. 'I wouldn't like to see them coming out. I wonder if it hurts?'

Mrs Plotkin had turned crimson and looked relieved when Sarah distracted Nathan's attention. 'Take the bowl out to the *succah* Nat, you and Lou can eat what's left on the sides,' she said finishing pouring her cake mixture into tins and handing him the basin.

'Listen, let them enjoy themselves while they can, we could all be finished off by a Zeppelin before next *Succoth*,' Mrs Plotkin said dolefully as the children went out to the yard.

'The while we're still here.' Mrs Plotkin was the neighbourhood pessimist, but Sarah never allowed her to get away with it. 'And we haven't seen any Zeppelins.' She put the cakes into the oven and began slicing apples for the strudel.

Mrs Plotkin cast a critical eye on the rich pastry Sarah had stretched into a large square in readiness for its filling. 'Mine I stretch even thinner. You're having company after *shul* tonight?' If company had not been expected, the pastry would have been half the size as she well knew.

'Our friends the Moritzes as usual and tomorrow we're going to them.'

'It must be terrible to have no family here,' Mrs Plotkin commiserated.

'To us they seem like family.'

'It isn't the same.'

'In some ways it's better. You can't choose your relations. How's that brother of yours you don't speak to?' Sarah asked with a dry smile.

'Don't even mention him to me! Your son's really going to marry Miriam Moritz?'

'They haven't been courting so long for nothing.'

Mrs Plotkin's expression grew gloomier than usual. 'You know I hate to say it, but in my opinion her and her sister don't look too healthy, with those white complexions. I'd be worried if my son was courting one of them.'

'You haven't got a son. And with consumption a person has rosy cheeks.'

'Did I mention consumption? My daughter Sivia has rosy cheeks.'

'And you'd like to make a match between her and David, Sarah thought as she filled the pastry with fruit and cinnamon.

'You think my Sivia has it?'

149

'Me, I don't think anything,' Sarah told her pointedly.

Mrs Plotkin snatched an egg from the basin on the dresser and stalked out.

Sarah folded the pastry and laid it on a baking tray, then went to the oven to peep at her honey cakes. 'What can you do, Tibby?' she smiled to the cat. 'It was the only way to shut her up.'

Tibby mewed a reply, as she always did when Sarah spoke to her. She was as gentle as Nicholas had been ferocious and purred when Sarah knelt down and stroked her bulging grey fur.

'I'm sorry we can't let you keep your kittens,' Sarah said to her. 'It isn't fair.' Having babies was a torture, but being parted from them afterwards must surely be a worse one.

Nathan brought the mixing bowl back, scraped clean, then went to sit on the *succah* floor with Lou again.

'If we did sleep in here, like they used to in Russia, we could count the stars at night,' he said gazing up at the roof which was made of loosely woven twigs.

'I wonder why you have to be able to see the sky through the *succah* roof, Nat,' Lou said thoughtfully.

'My father says it has to be like it was for the Children of Israel in the Wilderness.'

Lou looked at the fruit and flowers hanging in bunches and clusters above his head. 'Did they have apples and pears and oranges and chrysanthingemums in the Wilderness? My family never tell me anything.'

'Well mine don't often, they're always too busy.'

'Your David told you about the bayonets though, didn't he?' Lou said rolling onto his stomach and resting his chin in his hands.

'I wish he hadn't, it made me feel sick.'

'You even feel sick if you tread on a worm!' Lou scoffed.

'And you've got a rip in the seat of your pants,' Nathan retaliated inserting the tip of his boot in it.

'Now look what you've done!' Lou yelled yanking Nathan's ankle and making the rip bigger.

'You did it yourself.'

'And I'll get murdered, my mother's too busy doing piecework to mend things.'

'Mine does piecework, too, but she isn't.'

'Would she mind if we had an apple?'

'Take one each, boys!' Sarah called to them. She had come out to the yard to fetch a sheet which was drying on the clothes line and overheard their conversation. Talking about piecework at their age, but things like that wouldn't be part of Nat's life when he grew up if she could help it.

'We can't reach the apples down!' Nathan shouted to her.

'So I'll do it.' Sarah went into the *succah* and gave them each a golden russet.

'You wouldn't've been able to reach if it wasn't a very low roof,' Nathan teased her.

Sarah's children never let her forget how tiny she was and the height of her two elder sons made her wonder how she had produced them. How lovely it is in here, she thought glancing around. David had gone by train to Sale and returned with his arms full of greenery gathered in a country lane. But it was Sammy who had made the little lean-to look so beautiful, it had not looked like this when the children were all small and Abraham had decorated it.

Delicate fronds of fern and glossy laurel peeped from between the lattice of twigs overhead. Apples and oranges twinkled like coloured lights, each one affixed separately by Sammy's clever hands. Bronze and yellow chrysanthemum and crimson gladioli heads bloomed as if they grew out of the rough wooden walls.

'In Dvinsk, decorating the *succah* was no problem,' Sarah told the two boys. 'Nobody needed to take a train to find what they needed. We just cut off a branch from a big tree, leaves and everything, and it was a readymade roof. And all the little ones, like you, used to go with their parents on *Yom Kippur* night, when the *succah* has to be erected, to fetch a branch for their family. What a sight it was! First we'd go home and break the Fast, then everyone would be out in the street, the fathers pushing the children in a handcart to the river bank, where it was thick with trees. But the children had to walk back and help to push the cart because it was full.'

Nat and Lou were listening raptly as they munched their apples. Lou's grubby shirt was hanging out of his knickerbockers as usual. 'I like hearing stories about Russia,' he said wiping his fingers on it. 'It must've been very exciting to live there.'

'Such excitement we can do without.' In Strangeways there were no trees to make the *succah* roof from, but the last few years in Dvinsk the excursion she'd just described had not taken place. It wasn't safe for Jews to go out at night, Sarah recalled, or to put up a *succah* beside their house for fear of it being burned down. But even so, the Festivals brightened our lives, the way they do here, she reflected as she went to unpeg the sheet and blow the smuts off it. Maybe God wanted them to be observed not just to commemorate Jewish history, but to make us forget our everyday troubles now and then?

She returned to the kitchen just in time to rescue her cakes from the oven and was turning them out of the tins when a woman from across the street walked in. Did nobody else have anything to do today? 'Sit down, Mrs Kletz, I won't be a minute.' She put the strudel to bake and her cakes to cool. 'Your baking's all done?'

'I haven't even started it.' Mrs Kletz sat down on the chair Mrs Plotkin had just vacated and looked as though she was there to stay.

'You'd like some tea?'

'It's coming out of my ears, I've drunk glass after glass to settle my nerves, but it's done me no good.' Mrs Kletz choked back a sob and took a handkerchief from her apron pocket. 'It's my Manny, Mrs Sandberg. He's joined up.' She rolled the handkerchief into a ball with one hand, kneading it back and forth agitatedly on her lap. 'He told us just before he went to work this morning. A lovely present for *Succoth*!'

Sarah felt the goose pimples rise on her flesh. Though she spent her days sewing buttons on uniforms, the war seemed far away. Only at moments like this did the reality of it touch her. She watched her neighbour dab her eyes and straighten her bulky, brown *sheitel* which looked more like a matted fur hat than a head of hair.

'So what can you do? He's caught war-fever, like a lot of others. They think a Jew should fight for England after what England's done for us.' Mrs Kletz folded her chapped hands resignedly.

'Who could deny it? But also who wants their son to be a soldier? My life I'd give for England, but not my boy. Did I save him from the Tsar so he could be killed by the Kaiser?'

This is how it'll be for me, if David gets called up, Sarah thought with the chill still gripping her. Until now, she hadn't let herself contemplate it. Mrs Kletz was turning her wedding ring round and round on her finger. Usually, she looked neat and tidy, but today she hadn't even bothered to button the cuffs of her blouse, or put on the locket she always wore. Not all mothers were like herself and Mrs Kletz, taking a real pride in how they and their family looked. Mrs Benjamin from four doors away was the kind who wouldn't bother sewing up the holes in her Lou's clothing even when she wasn't busy and Hannah Lensky was another like her. But when it came to losing a son in the war, all mothers were the same, the thought of it shut everything else out of your mind. Please God, don't let there be conscription, she prayed silently. Let the war be over soon, it's bad for everyone. And for us especially. Haven't we been through enough?

'The Almighty will watch over your Manny,' she said quietly to Mrs Kletz, but she knew this was not a comfort to her and would not be one to herself if David had to be a soldier. Sometimes it was very hard to have faith in God, you couldn't help remembering those He had let die in the pogroms and asking yourself why He had.

In 1915 Sammy Sandberg and Mottie Benjamin took their little brothers to watch the 'Pals' Battalions of the Manchester Regiment march past the Town Hall. Lord Kitchener had come to Manchester to take the salute and stood like a ramrod in front of the huge recruiting posters, his medals glinting in the sunlight, surrounded by officers and civic dignitaries.

Albert Square was packed with citizens cheering their very own soldiers and the two little boys were seated astride their brothers' shoulders viewing the parade.

'Why aren't they wearing khaki?' Nathan inquired in a puzzled voice. 'Their uniforms look like the ones the tramdrivers wear.'

'That's what they are,' Sammy told him. 'They haven't got their proper ones yet, so the Corporation's lent them some.'

A beery-faced man next to them raised his shabby cap as the soldiers tramped past. 'Manchester's reet proud 'o thi, lads!' he roared. 'Good luck the Pals!'

'Why do they call them that, Mister?' Lou asked him.

The man laughed. 'Dust tha not know, son? Whir's tha bin? It's cause 'em amn't joint oop bi 'emsels like. Ter joint t'Pals tha 'as ter sagn on wi' thi frens.'

'You, me and Otto could all join the Pals together, only we're not old enough yet,' Mottie said to Sammy regretfully.

'We could sleep in tents in Heaton Park, like them,' Sammy added pretending he was not lame and barred from sleeping in military tents anywhere.

When Sammy and Nathan returned home, Zelda Cohen was there with her daughters.

'So how d'you like school, Natie?' she asked Nathan.

'Very much, thank you,' he replied politely wishing he could tell her not to call him that.

'Sit down and have some cake with us, Nat,' little Ruby Cohen invited him from the table.

'He doesn't need you to ask him, it's his house,' her eldest sister reminded her.

There were times when Nathan felt as if it wasn't. Lately, there always seemed to be ladies sitting in the kitchen with his mother, talking about the war. 'I'm not hungry, thanks,' he said to Ruby and went upstairs to escape from her. She sat across the aisle from him at school and smelt of camphor oil.

'Those two'll make a nice match when they grow up,' Zelda smiled to Sarah. She was pregnant again, ballooning vastly above as well as below her waistband, as she always did when in that condition, which was most of the time. She unfastened the top button of her skirt and sighed with relief. 'Who knows how long the war will last, eh, Mrs Sandberg? If my Naomi was a boy, she could even get called up.'

'The while nobody is getting called up,' Sarah said crisply because the subject upset her. 'And your Naomi is a girl like her seven sisters.'

Nathan wished he had stayed downstairs when he went into the bedroom he shared with his brothers. David was ticking

Sammy off about going to watch the parade and continued doing so as if Nathan was not there.

'What d'you think it was for, Sammy? To entertain people?' he said caustically. 'They're after more cannon fodder. It's all very well watching soldiers march past, but there's no glamour in the bleddy trenches!'

Nathan wondered what cannon fodder and glamour were, but was afraid to ask in case he got ticked off, too.

The day conscription was introduced, Abraham dropped into *shul* to see Rabbi Lensky.

The minister was huddled over a dying fire in the room in which he used to hold his midday gatherings. 'If you've come to ask me why the Almighty is letting this war continue, I don't know the answer, so don't ask me the question. I just told my Cousin Yossel the same.'

Abraham took the two small packets containing sugar and tea from his pocket and put them on the shelf beside the sink as he usually did.

'Listen, nobody's wet through and out of work anymore. I don't need them,' the rabbi protested.

Abraham smiled. 'But I need to give them to you.'

'Who am I to deprive a man of what he needs? You heard Yossel's son Lazar was wounded?'

Abraham nodded. 'And today I heard in the factory that Berel Halpern was killed in France.'

Rabbi Lensky paled, then he raised his eyes to the ceiling and shook his head slowly.

'You're reproaching Him?' Abraham asked.

'That's not for us to do. All I ask is He should help me to understand.' The rabbi stroked the silvery beard which made him look older than he was and gazed into the embers. 'Everything he does is part of a pattern, Abie, but we never see it at the time. When my poor first wife died, I thought why should he take a good woman like her? So now I'm married again and I have two daughters. Poor Reba gave me no children, but maybe God desired me to be a father, the pastoral duties of a rabbi demand the whole breadth of human experience. So that is what I've come to believe.'

'Wouldn't it have been simpler if He'd just let your first wife have children?'

'We can't concern ourselves with the things He doesn't do, Abie. It's enough to fathom out why He does the things He does.'

'You know the conclusion I've come to, Rabbi? And not without reason. It's better not to question Him at all.' Abraham looked at his watch. 'I'd better go, I want to be in time for prayers at the Halperns' tonight.' He stared into space for a moment, then collected himself. 'To say *Kaddish* for a son and not to know where his body is lying even – it doesn't bear thinking about.'

Rabbi Lensky clasped his knobbly hands on his lap and gazed into the fire again. 'We have to face up to it, Abie my friend. It won't be the last time such a *Kaddish* is said in Strangeways.'

'All my father bleddy cares about is raking it in, the war's done him a favour!' Saul ranted to David in the workroom early one morning.

David had just walked in and was shocked by the expression of hate on his friend's face. 'What's he done to bring this on?'

Saul was folding some khaki garments, slamming them onto a table as if to make them pay for the way he felt. 'My call-up papers came today. You'll soon be the only one left, David.'

'Don't worry, they're not likely to overlook me.'

'My old man's frightened if we don't get this big order off by tonight, the army'll stop dealing with him, so he won't give me half an hour off to go and tell Helga.'

'To hell with that, Saul! She won't've left for work yet, why don't you just go?'

Saul laughed abruptly and picked some bits of thread off his cardigan. 'It's a funny thing, David, but I've never been able to openly defy him. It sounds weak, doesn't it? But it's the way I am. The ructions it'd cause – well it never seems worth it.' He squared his thin shoulders and began folding again. 'But I'll tell you something. After the war I'm not coming back here to live with him. I'm going to ask Mr Moritz to let Helga marry me on my first leave.'

Sigmund gave Saul and Helga his blessing and a few weeks later, David, who was still a civilian, accompanied his friend on a wedding-eve night out. They went for a walk around Hightown, as a change from Strangeways, then sat drinking tea in a café where the only other customer was an old man who looked as if he had nowhere else to go.

The frizzy-haired waitress smoothed her soiled overall over her ample hips and came to give the oil-cloth-covered table a cursory wipe. 'On leave, luv?' she smiled to Saul.

'Embarkation leave, as it happens.'

'He's getting wed tomorrow,' David added with a grin.

'What's 'e doin' in 'ere then? Pub next door's t'place fer 'is last fling!'

'She's right, Saul,' David said as the girl took their empty cups away. 'So how about it?'

'Since when did Jewish lads go *shikkering*?'

'It's a special occasion, isn't it?'

'Pubs're all right when you've got no home to go to, like when you're a soldier in a strange town.'

'Shall we go back to your house then?'

'Not likely! We'll go to yours.'

It was after ten when they got to the Sandbergs' and everyone was in bed.

Saul watched David build up the fire and smiled wistfully. 'You don't know how lucky you are, David.'

'How d'you mean?'

'The sort of home you've got.'

David changed the subject. What was the use of harping on Saul's bad relationship with his father, which was what his remark had implied. 'Tell me what being a soldier's like, Saul.'

'You'll find out soon enough.'

'But I'd like to know how it feels.'

Saul watched the flames roaring up the chimney while he thought about it. 'As if you're marking time, more than anything else. I mean you're still the same, still yourself, aren't you, even though you're in uniform? Wanting the same things you've always wanted, only now you have to wait till the war's over.'

David looked at him uncertainly. 'But there must be more to it than that.'

'Not for me there isn't.'

'Don't you ever wonder what you're doing in the army?'

'I got called up, didn't I?'

'Exactly. Because someone assassinated an Archduke thousands of miles away, but what's that got to do with us? I can't fathom out what the war's for.'

'They say things'll be better for everyone afterwards.'

'But that's not why it started, is it?'

Saul picked up the poker and stirred the coals impatiently. 'What's the good of you and me breaking our heads about why it started? All I want is for it to end, so I can come home and be with Helga. That's when I'll start living. When I come back.'

David looked at his friend's yearning expression in the firelight and was touched by compassion for him. Saul's life had not been happy, who could blame him for longing for the time when it would be? But supposing that time never came? After his brief honeymoon he would be going overseas with his unit. 'Everything a person does is living, Saul,' he said impulsively. 'Even if they loathe every minute of it, it shouldn't be wasted.'

But Saul's mind was occupied with more immediate matters. 'Come round early tomorrow and keep me company,' he instructed. 'It's the best man's duty to protect the bridegroom on his wedding day. Especially from his father.'

David overslept the next morning and did not arrive at the Salamans' home until eleven o'clock. Bessie opened the door with a towel swathed around her head. Her pudgy face flushed with embarrassment when she saw David standing on the doorstep.

'I've just washed my hair,' she apologised. 'And I'm not dressed yet.'

David eyed the grubby wrapper she was wearing and tried not to show his distaste.

'It needs washing. I haven't had time, with all the excitement and everything.' She smoothed the wrinkled flannel, which had once been blue, but was now a yellowish grey, then folded her arms to hide the unfettered mounds of her bosom. 'Wait till you see what I'm wearing for the wedding, David!'

As if that could make up for how you look now, he thought. He had once called at the Moritzes' early in the morning, but Miriam and Helga had looked neat and fresh in their wrappers though they hadn't been expecting him. He was aware of raised voices echoing down the lobby, as he stepped inside and knew he was too late to perform the duty Saul had asked of him.

'Dad and Saul're at it again,' Bessie sighed shutting the door. 'It gets on my nerves!'

'So how d'you think it is for Saul?' David asked listening to Salaman's voice thundering through the thick wood of the kitchen door.

'Is it my fault if he can't get on with his own father? Saul behaves as if he hates Dad. Ever since my mother died.

This was not news to David and he had often wondered about the cause, which must be too painful to talk about or Saul would have told him.

'He thinks Dad killed her,' Bessie said casually as if this were not an extraordinary thing to say. 'Saul's never stopped blaming Dad for not fetching the doctor that day.'

The shouts from the kitchen grew louder.

'That's what I've had to live with since I was a little kid, David. You get used to it.' She went upstairs, clutching her makeshift turban which had loosened and slipped to one side.

David thought of what his friend had had to live with. A father he loathed, whom he held responsible for the death of the mother he had adored. 'Couldn't you have asked your father to leave Saul alone this morning?' he called angrily to Bessie. 'It isn't fair to upset him on his wedding day.'

'Why should Dad have to be upset? Or me? Nobody thinks about that, do they?' she retorted and flounced into her bedroom. A moment later she emerged again. 'I didn't mean to be rude to you, David,' she said contritely and returned to her room in another huff when he did not raise his head to look at her.

David hovered in the lobby, trying to find courage to walk into the kitchen. What a household, he thought. What with his father and his sister, Saul would be well out of it. He made his way along the dingy passage, wrinkling his nose at the mixed smell of new cloth and boiled cabbage which he did not have time to notice when he came here to work. When he reached the kitchen door he could not bring himself to knock and open it. The violence in his employer's voice rooted him to the spot.

'A son like you nobody should have!' Salaman was raging. 'I wouldn't wish you on my worst enemies!'

'And you've got plenty!' Saul shouted back.

'Who is the biggest one? You!'

David forced himself to turn the door knob and enter, but his presence went unnoticed. Salaman was standing in front of the fire with a whole smoked salmon clutched in his hand, gesticulating with it wildly, the veins on his forehead standing out as if they were about to burst. Saul had his back to the window and was wearing only an undervest with his khaki trousers. His pale

160

complexion looked tinged with green, as though he was gripped by a terrible nausea as he regarded his father.

'To bring his wife to live here after the war doesn't suit him!' Salaman bellowed to the air.

'That's right, it doesn't!'

'Why have a row about it now?' David interjected, but neither of them heard him.

'Who will you come to, to set up a home for you, Mr Clever?' Salaman rasped. 'You expect me to provide the money to keep you in comfort, when your work isn't worth an errand boy's wages!'

'I don't expect anything from you and I don't care what you bleddywell think of me, either!' Saul told him. 'Even today you couldn't let me alone, could you? You had to do something to spoil it for me! But you never have cared how you upset people. Just because you're rich, you think you can walk all over everyone. Well you're not doing it to me any more!'

Salaman began to tremble and the colour drained from his face so rapidly David thought he was going to faint. Then Saul became aware of David standing in the doorway and managed a sickly smile.

'Hadn't you better get dressed?' David said in the most matter-of-fact tone he could muster. 'We've got to be in *shul* at one o'clock.'

'Don't worry, I'll be there.' Saul pointed to the smoked salmon disgustedly. 'He wanted to take that bleddy thing to the wedding, David, to have at the reception. Can you imagine how insulted Mrs Moritz would be? Only the best for Isaac Salaman!'

Salaman looked down at the oily, pink fish in his hand and seemed surprised to see it there.

'No wonder my poor mother died young,' his son said with immense bitterness. 'But she's better off in her grave than married to him.'

Salaman lowered his bulk into a chair as though his legs would no longer support him.

'The grease from the salmon's dripping onto your trousers, Mr Salaman,' David said.

But his employer was not listening. He was gazing at Saul and now even his lips looked ashen. 'Honour thy father and thy mother, that thy days may be long upon the land which the Lord thy God giveth thee,' he quoted ominously.

David felt a chill of foreboding in the pit of his stomach and saw his friend blanch as his father pointed a quivering finger at him.

'A son who breaks the Fifth Commandment, what comes to him for doing so is on his own head.'

The synagogue bristled with excitement as befitted a wedding. David could see the flutter of handkerchiefs behind the grille where the women sat waiting to shed sentimental tears and was conscious of his stiff collar cutting into his neck.

Beside him, his father was fidgeting nervously with his moustache, which he had waxed for the occasion. A Jewish bride and groom must each be accompanied under the *chupah* by a married couple, usually their parents if both were alive. Salaman had asked the Sandbergs to deputise and would soon stand with them beneath the marriage canopy whilst they and the Moritzes handed sips of wine to Saul and Helga after the rabbi had blessed it.

Saul had gone with Sigmund to the room where Helga waited with her mother and Sarah and the bridesmaids. Before her father escorted her to the *chupah*, her bridegroom must gaze upon her face and afterwards lower her bridal veil himself, a custom dating from biblical times when Jacob was duped by Laban into marrying his elder daughter Leah, instead of the beautiful young Rachel whom he had been promised.

David could not wipe the scene he had witnessed that morning from his mind. The ludicrous sight of Salaman clutching the huge fish, and the chill evoked by his final words, were still with him. But Saul had been calm and smiling when they walked to *shul* together, as if no evil could touch him once he was married to Helga.

He returned down the aisle alone, the *tallith* which none but the bridegroom donned for a wedding draped incongruously around his uniformed shoulders. David saw him glance at his father, but Salaman appeared not to notice. Then the beadle ushered them to the *chupah* to await the arrival of the bride.

Not until his son performed the ancient rite of shattering a glass did Salaman show any emotion. As the sound of Saul's boot stamping purposefully upon the fragile goblet filled the hushed synagogue and the joyous shouts of *mazeltov*, which always followed, boomed from the congregation, the lonely widower was suddenly convulsed with sobs and had to be helped to a seat.

'Tears of happiness like that, I've never seen,' Rabbi Blasberg remarked whilst shaking hands with the Moritzes and the Sandbergs.

Only Abraham and David were aware that their employer was weeping sorrowfully, and for himself.

'Pull yourself together, it's a wedding not a funeral,' Saul said to his father and David was sure he had chosen the words deliberately.

Salaman blew his nose and kissed Helga. 'So how does it feel to be Isaac Salaman's daughter-in-law?' he inquired as if she had just become a member of the Royal Family.

'O Lord, who healest the broken-hearted and bindest up their wounds, grant Thy consolation unto the mourners,' Rabbi Blasberg intoned emotionally. Conducting mourning prayers for a lad you'd married to his childhood sweetheart only a few weeks ago was a painful duty and he could hardly bring himself to look at the bereaved bride.

Helga still had the War Office telegram clutched in her hand. It had arrived that morning when she was about to leave the house for work and her scream had chilled her parents' hearts. Afterwards, she had withdrawn into a pitiful silence whilst arrangements for the week of *Shivah* were made around her. Her husband's earthly remains would lie in a non-sectarian military cemetery near Ypres, beside those of the comrades with whom he had fallen on the battlefield, but Jewish prayers for his departed spirit must still be observed by his family.

Salaman, who had insisted on the marriage being solemnised in his *shul* instead of the small, Austrian congregation to which the Moritzes belonged, had surprised everyone by deferring to Helga's prior right as his son's widow and allowing the *Shivah* to be held in her parents' home.

The bleddy hypocrite! David thought savagely, watching him blubbering into his handkerchief as he recited the *Kaddish*, his sacred duty as Saul's sole male next-of-kin. How can he stand there mouthing the mourner's prayer, when he as good as put a death-curse on Saul?

The house was packed with friends and neighbours who had come to console the family. Visiting the bereaved was an honoured tradition, but the death of a soldier added an extra dimension to it. Most had someone of their own in the army and lived in fear that their turn to mourn might come next.

Sarah stood beside Paula Frankl, whose son Hugo had just gone overseas with a Labour Battalion.

'There's something wrong with your David that he hasn't been called up yet?' Paula mouthed from behind her chenille-dotted veil in a whisper which sounded more like a hiss.

Sarah adjusted the scarf with which she had covered her head to enter the house of mourning and avoided Paula's accusing eye. It's like when Malka Berkowitz lost her little ones in the epidemic and David got better, she thought. But her good fortune could not be expected to last. She pulled the scullery door open to let some cool air into the kitchen and saw Esther leaning against the sink with her friend Sophie Plotkin and some other young girls. They can't bear to be in the same room with Helga, she reflected with a pang; it's as if they don't want what's happened to her to touch them.

Salaman's voice, and the great sobs which were making it difficult for him to say the *Kaddish*, drifted through the open doorway to those who were crammed into Sigmund's workroom and the lobby. The sorrowing man dabbed at his swollen eyes with his wet handkerchief as the time came for every man present to join in the prayer and the house resounded with the ancient chorus.

Helga was seated beside Bessie, her black-kerchiefed head emphasising her pale composure. Miriam had told David her sister had not shed a tear, as though her feelings were too private to share with others. Her low stool was by the window, where she had stood with Saul to receive their wedding guests, radiating the happiness which had lent her beauty for so brief a spell. Even

Miriam, graceful as a long-stemmed rose in the bridesmaid's dress which had made Bessie's identical one look like a sack, had not outshone Helga that day, David recalled.

'I have such lovely memories,' she said to him quietly when he took her hand for a moment before he left. 'And I'm thankful for that.'

But David could not stop grieving for the waste of his friend's life and thought of the conversation they had had by the fireside after their bachelors' night out. Saul had existed in misery for most of his eighteen years and was cut down before he had begun living.

David's conscription papers arrived the following week, when Sarah was alone in the house with Nathan. She propped the envelope against the candlesticks on the mantelpiece and remembered how she had tried to comfort Mrs Kletz when her Manny joined up. But God had not watched over Manny, He had let him be shell-shocked and mutilated at a place called Paschendale and Mrs Kletz had said there were worse things than death after she visited him in a military hospital down south.

'You can cry if you like, I won't tell anyone,' Nathan said gravely. 'Lou said his mother did when their Issie got called up and now she cries all the time, in case the war's still on when Mottie's old enough to go.'

Sarah dragged her gaze away from the envelope and began clearing the breakfast table. 'I don't believe in crying before there's something to really cry about,' she replied and made up her mind as she said it that this was the only way to be. 'You'll be late for school, Nat. Hurry up!' Things must go on as usual until David came back.

But that evening she could not keep her eyes off him.

'You'll get used to me being away, like other people's mothers do,' he said as he combed his hair in front of the mirror. He turned around and smiled at her. 'I'm no different from anyone else, you know.'

Sarah reached up and touched his lean face. Good looking he wasn't, yet a person had to look twice at him. 'To me you are,' she said softly.

'Don't make such a fuss, Sarah!' Abraham muttered tetchily,

but she knew he was as choked with feeling as she was.

'I might be late back tonight, Miriam and I have a lot to talk about,' David told them as he left the house. But when he got to the Moritzes' it was Sigmund, as usual, to whom he addressed his thoughts.

'It doesn't seem real,' he mused to his old friend. 'That I have to be a soldier.' A vision of the brutal Cossacks who had filled his early years with terror rose before him and he shuddered. Now he was to be cast in the role of killer himself, as if wearing a uniform made it all right.

Sigmund raised his hands in a gesture which embraced the book-lined walls and a bowl of fruit on the table, the glowing fire and those he loved who were grouped around it. 'Here is what is real, David,' he said eloquently. 'The rest is a madness.'

David looked at his friend's widow, sitting beside her sister who would one day be his wife and knew that day might never come. He was no more immortal than Saul had been, but he would not waste the experience as Saul had done. He hated everything war stood for, but whatever faced him when he went overseas was, while he still breathed, living.

He was up to his waist in mud in a trench in Flanders, wondering if he would see the morning, when the meaning of Saul's words became clear to him. What he was fighting for was still a mystery; he obeyed orders blindly as the rest of the lads did, but what mattered to them all in the end was their own survival. The feeling of marking time which Saul had described suddenly engulfed him and he knew it was part of the hope which enabled a soldier to endure the madness until he could return to the reality he had left behind.

In November 1917 Nathan gave his mother and two of her neighbours a terrible shock. 'There's been a revolution,' he announced when he came home from school.

Sarah felt her legs turn to jelly and her mouth grow dry as she watched Zelda Cohen snatch her newest baby from the rug, hoist its one-year-old sister under her arm and flee home without a word.

'Mrs Cohen didn't finish her tea,' Nathan noticed as he helped himself to bread and jam.

Mrs Plotkin sat wringing her hands. 'Who thinks of tea at such a time? I suppose she's gone to clear out her closet to make room for her girls inside it, with so many it'll be a squeeze. Oy vay, how it takes me back!'

'For just Nat, I won't need to clear mine, I'll put him underneath the linens and throw a *perineh* over him,' Sarah planned feverishly.

Nathan stopped eating and looked upset. 'Why're you going to put me in the linen closet?'

'Because I don't have any pickle barrels big enough.'

Mrs Plotkin clasped him to her bosom and planted a protective kiss on his head. 'Here we didn't expect to need them.'

Nathan removed himself from her embrace and the sour odour which reminded him a bit of lamb chops wafting from her armpits. He eyed Sarah reproachfully. 'What've I done to deserve it?'

'Oy, from the mouths of babes and sucklings come questions only God can answer,' Mrs Plotkin declared before Sarah could reply. 'A child of seven shouldn't even have to know from revolutions.'

'Teacher told us and we all clapped and cheered.'

'You clapped and cheered when our people will be the scapegoats like always?'

'And with the war on, where is there to run to?' Sarah said desperately. 'Even the King will have no place to hide.'

'You mean the Tsar,' Nathan corrected her.

'The Tsar? What're you saying Nat?' Sarah clutched his hand.

'Teacher told us they've got rid of him forever and the Jews in Russia're going to be free from now on.'

Sarah did not know whether to laugh for joy or cry with relief. Then she and Mrs Plotkin did a little of both and she sent Nathan to tell Zelda the revolution was in Russia.

'Mrs Cohen kissed me!' he complained when he came back. 'Why is everyone so sloppy today? And she said to tell you it's a good job, because the pail she brought with her to England's getting too old to travel. What's all the fuss about? Where did you all think the revolution was?'

167

Sarah was ashamed to tell him. Later, she saw the humorous side of the incident and shared it with her family over supper.

Abraham was more taken aback than amused. 'Mrs Plotkin, she's a scaremonger. But you, Sarah? How could you think it was here? You've lived in England for twelve years and you still know nothing about the English?'

'Listen to the expert!' Esther teased him. 'How many English people do you know, Father?'

'Mr Pickles and the rag-and-bone man,' Sammy joined in.

'And me,' Nathan piped up.

'You're Jewish-English,' his mother informed him.

'What does that mean?'

'Well for one thing, you eat *kefulte* fish,' Esther joked watching him tuck into it.

'And for another,' Abraham declared, 'no matter how English you are you've got a Jewish heart.'

'Aren't Jewish hearts the same as Christian ones?' Nathan felt his chest.

'Sure. But they feel a little extra for our own people,' Sarah smiled giving him another fishball to take his mind off it.

Abraham got up and brought the kosher wine from the dresser. 'Get some glasses, Esther. We have to celebrate the news from Russia and we won't be the only ones rejoicing in Strangeways tonight!'

They drank to the downfall of their old enemy and a few sips of the sweet, potent liquid sent Nathan straight to sleep.

'It's always the little ones you think of at times like that,' Sarah whispered to Abraham whilst he was carrying Nathan upstairs.

'Times like what, Sorrel?' Abraham was pleasantly hazy himself.

'This afternoon, when Mrs Plotkin and Zelda and me were frightened we'd have to pack our bundles and run again. You asked me how I could believe it possible. I suppose because for most of my life it was possible and a feeling like that gets too deep inside you to really go away. You only think it has while nothing happens to bring it out.'

Abraham put Nathan gently onto his bed and lit the gas mantle. They stood gazing down at the child's peaceful face for a moment, then Sarah began to undress him.

'Thank God our Nat will never know that feeling,' she said fervently, 'For a whole ten minutes this afternoon I only thought of him, I stopped worrying about David.'

Abraham smiled and kissed her cheek. 'Even you, Sorrel, can only worry about your children one at a time!'

'What is it, David?' Miriam asked softly when he had been home from the army for a month and the depression with which he had returned still persisted.

It was Sunday afternoon and she had called at his house, because he had not come to hers with his parents as he had promised. She found him lying on the sofa in the parlour, with a rare fire burning in the grate.

'Maybe you'd feel better if you talked about it,' she told him, but he did not reply.

She knelt down beside him, spreading the skirt of her pleated dress in a fan around her. It was one David had not seen before and green, because he always said that was her colour, but he hadn't complimented her on it, or remarked how pretty her hair looked as he used to. Instead, there was this unfamiliar feeling between them, as if they were suddenly strangers. She'd felt it when she met him at the railway station after he was demobbed and it was still there.

'I saw Manny Kletz today,' he said staring into the fire. 'Since they transferred him to that place in Manchester, his mother's been taking him his meals, but she wasn't feeling well and Mr Kletz asked me to go today.'

'Why didn't he go himself?'

David smiled grimly, 'Maybe he can't bear to see Manny. And what they're bothering taking his food for beats me. As if it makes any difference whether he eats kosher or not! They probably think God punished him for eating *trafe* when he was in the army, that's how our parents' minds work. But poor Manny doesn't even know what he's eating, he just sits there with a glazed look in his eyes while the nurse shovels it in. The place gave me the creeps, Miriam. Half of them are neither dead nor alive and some of those who've still got their senses haven't got arms or legs,' David tried to control the tic in his eyelid. The last time he had felt it had been in the trenches when sometimes there had been a waiting silence and they'd known it couldn't last. Seeing Manny and the others had brought back the horror full force.

'The place is a great big house in a beautiful garden,' he told Miriam. 'It was lovely and warm inside and the lads were surrounded by fruit and flowers from well-wishers. A lot of good it'll do them! They're finished. It made me think of Saul, and Berel Halpern, and the lads in my unit who aren't here to tell the tale like I am, but they're better off than those poor devils.'

Miriam took his hand and stroked it comfortingly, but the contact brought them no closer.

'Nothing's any different because all those lads're gone, is it?' David mused bitterly. 'Things aren't that bad in the garment trade, but the day after I got back to Manchester I had to go to Ancoats to see someone for Salaman and there was a long queue of men outside the Labour Exchange waiting for the dole.'

'I missed you while you were away,' David,' Miriam said simply. 'And I know how you must feel. It'll take you a long time to get over the dreadful things you had to see, all that useless dying.'

David shivered and looked at her unseeingly for a moment. 'Dying's always useless, especially to the one who's dead. I'll never get over it.'

'People always think that, but they do. Helga has.' Helga had continued working in a glove factory, her life seemingly unchanged by the tragedy which had befallen her. 'Her father-in-law'd support her if she'd let him, but she doesn't want to be idle, like Bessie,' Miriam added.

David's expression tightened. 'It's a pity he wasn't kinder to his son, when he had one to be kind to, instead of trying to atone for his sins by giving money to Saul's widow.'

'I'm sorry I mentioned it if it makes you angry.'

'Everything about Salaman makes me angry.'

Miriam touched the lines on his forehead which had not been there when he went away. 'I don't want you to be angry and miserable, David. I want you the way you used to be.'

'Some of the other lads' girls married someone else while they were away. Are you sure you still want me at all?'

'Don't be silly, David,' she said the way she had when she was a little girl and he had asked a question needlessly.

He took her face in his hands and kissed her lips gently. She was his and always would be, their love for each other was the one thing he need never doubt. She wound her arms around his neck and the kiss became warm and urgent, blazing like the fire in the hearth until David broke away and sprang to his feet.

'Let's go out!' he said running his fingers through his hair, which still had a shorn, military look about it.

Miriam pointed to the white swirl outside the window. 'It's snowing!'

'Who cares?' David lifted her from the rug and whirled her around.

'Where shall we go to?' she laughed clinging to him. The old David was back with her, close and loving and sure of himself.

'We'll think of somewhere.'

Sammy popped his head out of the kitchen doorway while they were putting on their coats and mufflers. 'Where're you off to, David?'

'Come with us and you'll find out.'

'Can I come too?' Nathan called. 'I've finished all my sums.'

'So do the ones on the next page. Remember they're entering you for Manchester Grammar,' David called back.

'That isn't till next year!' Nathan grumbled.

'With the competition you'll be up against, you can't start preparing yourself a minute too soon.' David went into the kitchen to get his gloves which he had left on the dresser. He picked them up, then stood for a moment watching his little brother writing in an exercise book and saw himself as he had been before his golden future turned to dross. 'We're going for a train ride,' he told Miriam and Sammy impulsively as they left the house.

In later years, David thought of the trip they made that day as a pilgrimage and remembered his voice sounding reverent when he pointed out Forrest Dene to the others.

'Only one family lives in a house that size?' Sammy gasped.

They were standing on a wooded rise, ankle deep in snow, looking at the house in the distance which made it seem more imposing than it was. David had not wanted to venture nearer and take the chance of encountering Jim, who had gone out of his life and whom for some reason he did not want to see.

'I shouldn't like to have to keep it clean!' Miriam exclaimed.

'You won't have to, love,' David replied. 'When we live in Cheshire we'll have a maid.'

Miriam pealed with laughter.

'What's the joke?' David's expression had stiffened. 'You don't believe it'll happen, do you?'

He was implying that she did not believe in him, which made the question difficult to answer. 'How can it?' she shrugged.

'It will if David wants it to,' Sammy declared staunchly.

'You're crackers, Sammy and so is he!' Miriam flashed before she could stop herself. Sammy still looked up to David the way he had as a child. As for David! 'What does it matter where people live?' she said looking into his eyes. 'It's who you live with that counts.'

'That's only part of what counts,' he answered tersely. Where a person lives proves to the world what they are, he thought, but did not say so because he knew Miriam would not accept it. Her standards were different from his and her wants much simpler. All the Moritzes were the same, they set no store by material things.

Miriam could feel the chasm widening between them. It was as if their brief closeness in the parlour had never happened. 'My feet are freezing, let's go home,' she said in a depressed voice.

Sammy did what he could to lighten the atmosphere and on the train to Manchester made them laugh by pulling funny faces and recounting jokes he had heard in the factory. But the charm had gone out of the day and for Miriam and David it never came back.

Esther Sandberg did not make her presence felt in the family until she was seventeen. As the only girl, she had helped with the housework from the time she was old enough to wield a broom and had always been amenable, if not exactly docile. It came as a shock to Sarah when her daughter emerged as a purposeful young woman with a mind of her own.

'I've had enough of working in a factory,' Esther told her

parents one evening. 'I want to be a shop assistant, where there's a bit of life.'

'Like Miriam Moritz, selling millinery to stuck-up ladies all day and bringing home next to nothing at the end of the week,' Sarah said dismissively.

'But she works in Cheetham Hill, doesn't she? All I ever see is Strangeways!'

'All of a sudden it isn't good enough for you?'

'Well you couldn't call it paradise, could you, Mother? And I'm fed up with spending my days machining caps.'

'When you find a husband you won't have to,' Abraham said placatingly.

'Maybe I won't find one.'

'P-p-p!' Sarah spat three times, which Jewish folklore guaranteed would ward off catastrophe. Her daughter having no boyfriend sometimes gave her sleepless nights.

'Since your mother's getting older, she's starting to behave like the old grannies did in Russia,' Abraham chuckled to Esther.

Esther laughed, too, though she was secretly as anxious about her lack of a suitor as her mother was. The childhood attachments which led other girls to the marriage canopy had somehow eluded her. Until recently, her friend Sophie Plotkin had been in the same position, but she and her elder sister had just got engaged to the Rosenthal brothers. Sophie had spent the entire day talking about how much Otto loved her, whilst she and Esther treadled their machines side by side, and Esther felt more of an outsider than ever and was determined to venture into fresh fields.

No more was said that evening and Sarah thought it had just been idle talk. She did not know her daughter. By the end of the week Esther had found a job at a gown shop in town and was to start work there on Monday.

Sarah had a chat with David as she often did about family problems. 'Such a trouble your sister's turned out to be.'

'So let her try, Mother,' he advised remembering his own hopes which had come to nothing. 'I don't blame her for wanting a taste of something better.'

'She'll only earn buttons there. Can we afford it?'

'Nobody's earning that much anywhere these days. The war's over!' David reminded her bitterly.

174

'But even when things get better, what could she earn?'

'They pay commission in those gown shops, on top of the wages.'

Sarah had not known this. 'Hm,' she said thoughtfully. 'So maybe we'll see.'

Esther did not earn buttons, she proved to be an excellent saleswoman. Unlike the working class, for whom the end of the war meant a return to poverty, the smart women who patronised the gown shop still had money to spend and the sum Esther brought home at the end of the first week astounded the family. Sarah began to view her with respect, but this did not extend to her new appearance.

Esther's figure had not appeared overtly shapely in the garments she had worn previously, but the simple black dress her employer gave to her to wear for work hugged her waist so tightly that her bust seemed voluptuous above it and her hips curved fetchingly below. She was not a pretty girl, the combination of Abraham's red hair and Sarah's aquiline features was not a fortunate one, but she began to make the most of herself as the other salesgirls did, tinting her sallow compexion with peach-coloured powder and a touch of rouge, bought with the meagre pocket money her mother allowed her to keep from her wages.

'You look like a *shiksah*!' Sarah exclaimed in horror the first time she saw her daughter's transformed face. In her experience, only Gentile girls used cosmetics. 'Your father will throw you out of the house!'

But Abraham merely shrugged as he did about most things and Esther's brothers thought she looked attractive. Sarah gave up and hoped nobody outside the family would notice.

The new Esther was too striking not to be noticed. Even Carl Moritz, who would probably not have been aware that the Town Hall was no longer there had it been whisked away from Albert Square in the night, looked startled when they met at a tram stop. Carl worked in a bookshop near to Esther's place of employment and they had once travelled home together. On that occasion Carl had kept his eyes glued to his book as usual. This time he did not even open it.

'What're you staring at?' Esther asked him. 'Anyone'd think you'd never seen me before!'

175

'There's something different about you,' he muttered as they boarded the tram and found seats side by side.

Esther swivelled her body round on the polished bench and smiled at him. 'Is there?'

He swallowed hard and nodded.

She had not yet begun wearing make-up when Carl last saw her, or the tight belt she had added to her coat, but had no intention of telling him so. 'Perhaps it's just that you've never really looked at me before,' she said instead and a strange tingle warmed her as their eyes met. The jolting of the tram threw her against him and when he put his hand on her arm to steady her he kept it there, in a way which told her he was feeling the tingle, too.

'What are you doing tonight?' Carl asked when they alighted at their stop, keeping his voice as casual as he could.

'Nothing much. What're you doing?'

'The same.'

They laughed and strolled along the main road in the rain, which had just begun to fall. Esther put up her umbrella and Carl took it from her and linked her arm, so it would shelter him, too.

I'd never have done that with a girl I'd only just met, he thought. And yet, in some ways, it was as though he'd just met Esther. He'd sat beside her hundreds of time, sometimes sharing a chair because there was never enough seating when their two families got together, but the experience had never been thrilling before. He wondered if there was any precedent in the great works of literature for the way he felt; as if someone had put a spell on him. Love at first sight was a common romantic theme, but he could not recall reading about love at the umpteenth thousandth meeting.

'You and I've never done anything much in the evenings, have we?' Esther said.

The words had a cosy sound for both of them, as though they were two of a kind.

'So we'll start doing, if you'd like to.'

'Of course I'd like to.' She looked up at him with a smile which asked how he could have doubted it. He was only a few inches taller than her, but with a stocky manliness, much as his father had been in his youth, fair haired and fresh complexioned. Quite

176

good-looking in a way, she noted with surprise. 'Why didn't we think of it before, Carl?'

He gazed at her earnestly from behind his horn-rimmed spectacles. 'That's what I've been wondering, Esther.'

'You know I never knew you had blue eyes.'

'You think I knew yours were brown?'

'But we should've known. Seeing we grew up together. It's daft!'

'Well it certainly seems it now! What shall we do tonight, then?' Carl asked jauntily, leaping over a puddle and steering her round it.

What a lovely word 'we' is, Esther reflected. 'I wouldn't mind going dancing.' She had never been, the ghetto girls did not go unescorted. Nor did she possess a dance frock, but perhaps her brown taffeta would suffice, if she tied a scarf around her waist to give it a sash like some of the gowns had in the shop?

'I can't dance, Esther.'

'You'll soon learn.'

'And I'm afraid I can't afford it,' Carl apologised.

'Never mind, we'll find something else to do.' Esther's disappointment only lasted for a moment. Where they went wasn't important so long as they were together, she thought as Carl smiled into her eyes and the delightful tingle warmed her again.

When she arrived home, she did not set the supper table as she usually did, but went upstairs and lay on her bed, savouring the wonderful thing that had happened to her.

Her mother appeared in the doorway and eyed her anxiously. 'Something's wrong, God forbid?'

Esther leapt off the bed and kissed her. 'No, Mother! Just the opposite!' She had a boyfriend at last, though she had not expected the faceless sweetheart of her dreams to materialise, if he did at all, as Carl Moritz. 'I'm in love, isn't it marvellous?'

'Some no-good traveller you've met at the shop? He's probably married,' Sarah said apprehensively. That such a fate would befall her daughter now that she worked in town had become one of her secret fears. 'He's Jewish, I hope?' The city centre was full of Gentiles and this worried her, too.

Esther was standing dreamily by the window, watching the rain pour down.

'So who is he already?'

'Guess.'

'I haven't got time to play games, the soup will boil over.'

'Carl Moritz.'

'Jokes she's making now!'

'No I'm not, Mother.'

'It's réally Carl?' Sarah sat down on the bed with a look of profound astonishment on her face.

'I knew you'd be surprised.'

'Surprised? I need smelling salts! I've never had such a shock as you've just given me. Carl knows about this?

'Of course. He's in love with me, too,' Esther said confidently. 'It happened to us both at the same moment. On the tram coming home from work.'

'Tell me how, I'm trying to believe you.'

'You haven't got time, the soup'll boil over,' Esther teased.

'Right now the soup is not on my mind. How could such a thing be? With someone you've known all your life? While you're riding on a tram to Strangeways?'

'You fell in love with Father on a frozen river! The place has nothing to do with it.'

'I loved him before then. It was there I made him love me.' Sarah eyed her daughter sharply. 'You made up your mind to catch Carl?'

'Why would I wait until now if I was going to do that? He's the last boy I would've thought of trying to catch, that's what's so wonderful, Mother.'

'It is?' Sarah said doubtfully.

'The way it just happened, like it does in story books. What does it matter how, so long as it did?'

The rest of the family were as taken aback as Sarah, but recovered quickly and supper was eaten in a festive atmosphere.

'I can't get over Carl asking our Esther to go out with him,' David grinned. 'He's always been scared stiff of girls, even the ones he's fancied.'

'Who were they?' Esther asked jealously.

'Never you mind. But he was too shy to speak to them.'

'Well he couldn't be shy with me, could he? He already knew me.'

178

'And as long as you won't mind spending your honeymoon in a library you'll be all right!'

Nathan laughed. 'She might as well go and live in a library as marry Carl.'

Esther took her brothers' good natured teasing in good part. She half expected to see a thick volume tucked beneath Carl's arm when he called for her after supper, but reading had momentarily ceased to absorb him, she had superseded it. And the way he looked at her and she at him confirmed without a shadow of doubt the unlikely tale Sarah had heard from her daughter.

'So now I've seen it with my own eyes, but I still can't believe it,' she said to Abraham later. 'All these years they don't even notice each other and suddenly they're struck by lightning!'

'You wish they hadn't been?'

Sarah did not reply.

'Listen, you wanted your daughter to have a young man, so now she's got one. And Carl couldn't come from a better family. Be satisfied.'

The following afternoon, Sarah went to discuss the phenomenon with Rachel and found her huddled by the fire, though it was a warm day.

'You're not feeling well, Rachel?'

'A little off colour,' Rachel shrugged. 'But we've got better things to talk about! Who would have thought it, Sarah? A double wedding we're going to have maybe.'

The assumption that Esther and Carl would probably marry was not precipitate. Jewish boys and girls rarely went out together if their intentions were not serious. And David and Miriam's betrothal was taken for granted by both families.

'Who would have thought it is right!' Sarah echoed.

Rachel laughed softly. The gentle repose which had first drawn Sarah to her was still there and her appearance had hardly changed; the same mellow contentment emanated from her and her eyes were as youthful as they had always been. Only the dusting of silver on her hair registered the years.

'How long have we known each other?' Sarah asked sentimentally. Her mind had flown backwards, as minds are inclined to do at such moments; the beginning of her daughter's courtship marked a milestone in her life.

'A mathematician I'm not!' Rachel chuckled.

'To me it seems like always. But what is a bit of time between friends, you said to me the day you gave me the Sachertorte to taste.'

'And such a future we have to look forward to together. Two lots of grandchildren we'll share, God willing.'

Sigmund came in from his workroom beaming. 'What do you think about those two! Rachel thought her son was going to be a bachelor and the right girl was there under his nose, waiting. We couldn't wish for anything better, eh, Sarah?'

Sarah was not so sure and was ashamed of her conflicting feelings, which she hoped she had successfully hidden beneath her smile. With David and Miriam, he would be the bread-winner. She didn't want Esther to occupy that position if she married Carl, but felt it was highly likely. Carl was a nice boy, brainy also, but the wage he received at the bookshop was barely sufficient to support himself, let alone a wife and family. Money he would never have and, like the rest of the Moritzes, seemed not to care about. She'd lain awake worrying about it the whole of last night, but swallowed her misgivings and nodded, with the smile still on her face.

'On a warm day like this my wife fancies having a big fire in the grate!' Sigmund said scattering pins on the rug as he un-buttoned his waistcoat. 'What can you do with her?' He looked at Rachel. 'You took the medicine?'

'Sure I did. Such a fuss he's making!'

'I need you to darn my socks,' he chuckled.

'Helga's already darned them.'

Sarah surveyed her friend anxiously. 'You don't feel well enough to darn his socks?'

'Ill she isn't,' Sigmund declaimed.

'So why does she need medicine?'

Rachel held out her hands and could not keep them still.

'The medicine will cure it,' Sarah told her confidently. But she had not liked what she saw. Trembling hands were not a cold in the nose.

'Dr Smolensky's a clever boy,' Sigmund said, 'Everyone swears by him.'

'P-p-p! We should never need him.'

Sarah made some tea, for which the Moritzes had long ago acquired a taste, and said Rachel could come to her house and do the same for her when she felt off colour. But intuition told her the condition was more serious than it appeared.

On the way home, she wondered if Sigmund knew more than his cheerful manner indicated and hoped Dr Smolensky was as clever as he said. She'd heard there was a new young doctor at the local surgery, but hadn't known he was Jewish. Sigmund's voice had been full of respect when he mentioned him. And why not? The whole world respected a doctor.

When she entered her kitchen, Nathan was sitting at the table engrossed in one of David's books. She gazed at his intent little face, the dark eyes drinking in the words from the page, and made up her mind what he would be.

CHAPTER SIX

Salaman stood outside the workroom listening to his employees discuss the unofficial strike which had brought some of his competitors' factories to a standstill. Harry Rothberg, who owned a place across the street, had called to see him last night and warned him not to stand for any nonsense.

'Let the others bang their head on the wall! They'll learn their lesson when they don't get their job back afterwards,' Eli was declaiming.

'Why would we strike? We're not even members of the Union here,' Issie shouted above the noise of the machines.

Salaman made a timely entrance. 'Which Union?' he guffawed.

The workers were surprised to see him. Since Saul's death he had largely withdrawn from life himself and gave the appearance of being a broken man, cosseting himself in his kitchen where he sat by the fire in a splendid leather armchair with a blanket around his legs, poring over the Talmud whilst Bessie fed him cakes and toffees.

Everyone tittered politely because it was the boss who had made the jest, but it was not a laughing matter. Several different unions represented the trade, which meant there was no real muscle in any of them. But the main reason for continued exploitation was the trump card held by the employers; the majority of Jewish garment workers still thought they were lucky to be employed and feared they would lose their jobs if they joined a union.

Salaman settled himself on a stool beside the cutting bench and caressed the gold watch-chain adorning his paunch. 'Who needs to strike when they work for Isaac Salaman?' he asked unctuously.

David was standing behind him and cast a glance of loathing at his beefy back.

'They're striking because their wages have gone down to what they were before the war, like they have here, even though there's still a bit of a boom in the trade,' a squat young woman said bravely from behind her machine.

You tell him, Millie! David thought savagely. He had pleaded with Salaman himself on the workers' behalf, but to no avail.

'And when the bit of a boom is over, what will I pay you with, if I dole out all the extra cash now?' Salaman treated Millie to an oily smile. 'Didn't I pay you the week you had off to sit *Shivah* for your poor mother?'

'I'm very grateful,' she muttered.

'Listen, I'm a charitable man, a person only has one mother.' Salaman allowed his smile to embrace the entire workroom. 'Wouldn't I do the same for any of you?' He waited for the chorus of assent to die out. 'And when do I ever sack anyone? Believe me, if Millie doesn't catch a husband she's got a job here for life!'

David saw Millie blush to the roots of her sandy hair and finger the unsightly mole on the side of her nose. He controlled the urge to throttle his employer for capitalising on her plainness and escaped to the pressing room.

Salaman heaved himself off the stool. 'How many garments have we finished this morning, David?' he inquired following him.

Since David's return from the army, the management of the factory had slipped painlessly into his hands, for which he was receiving an extra ten shillings a week. But the promotion was not formally acknowledged by Salaman and occasionally the employer would lift himself from the trough of despondency into which he had sunk and charge upstairs to issue instructions to the workers. David had expected him to do this when he entered the workroom and was relieved he had not. Afterwards he would have had to countermand them because Salaman had lost touch with the business and this usually entailed arguing with Eli, who had learned his trade at Salaman's cutting bench and still considered him the one who gave the orders.

He began checking some garments which had just been pressed, ticking them off on a list and tried to ignore his employer's presence.

Salaman smiled at Abraham who was working industriously. 'Here they know which side their bread's buttered on, Abie,' he declared with satisfaction. He rubbed some grime off the window in order to see through it and gazed at the Rothberg factory which was presently idle. 'Isaac Salaman's workers know a good boss when they've got one!'

David kept his eyes glued to the paper in his hand, but his father knew he was finding it difficult to contain himself. 'One of these days Salaman'll get what he deserves,' he seethed when their employer had gone.

'He hasn't suffered enough already?' Abraham sighed as he manoeuvred his iron into the armhole of a coat. 'To lose a wife and an only son?' He coughed and spluttered as a cloud of steam enveloped him.

David could hear the phlegm rolling around on his father's chest and watched him spit into his handkerchief. 'How can you be sorry for someone who pays you a pittance for ruining your health in a poky little room like this? You can't even open the window, he's got it nailed down because he's frightened the place'll be burgled. Sometimes I don't understand you, Father!'

Abraham shrugged and picked up his iron again. But David was sickened by the avaricious man's exploitation of the human beings who spent their days in the atrocious conditions he imposed upon them. Some of Salaman's employees had been with him all their working lives and had witnessed the rise in his fortunes from a few sewing machines crammed into the front room to the hive of industry now occupying most of his large house. Yet despite the expenditure of their own sweat and toil to achieve this, and the meagre recompense meted out to them, a grudging sentimental attachment to the place was evident in their attitude. They thought of it as 'their' factory and continued to respect their unscrupulous employer, the way a dog ill-treated by its master is grateful to lie secure at his feet.

The afterwards envisaged by Eli, when Salaman's workers would still have jobs and the strikers would not, was short-lived. Raincoats were the staple product and the long, dry summer of 1919 struck a near lethal blow to the trade.

All but key workers were laid off and the Jewish relief organisations beseiged; it was not in the immigrants' nature to queue for the dole along with the Gentile unemployed, in times of severe deprivation they preferred to turn to their own for succour, rather than receive what they considered charity from the English government which had given them refuge.

The Sandbergs and Moritzes were among those who did not seek relief from any source, their pride would not have allowed it. Consequently, both families found it difficult to survive.

Sigmund had no clients, or hope of collecting outstanding debts from men who could not afford to feed their children. His own family were existing on potato soup, except for once a week when Yankel Cohen, who owed him for a suit, would turn up apologetically with a couple of eggs laid by the scrawny hen the Cohens kept in their back yard, and that evening the potatoes would be grated and mixed with eggs and flour to provide a meal of 'latkes'.

One morning, Rachel found Sigmund standing in the middle of the kitchen surveying his books, with an agonised look on his face.

'Oh no!' she cried as he marched resolutely to a shelf. 'I won't let you!'

But Sigmund reached down a volume despite her protests and opened the dresser drawer to find some paper in which to wrap it.

Rachel picked up the book. '*The King of Shnorrers*? How can you sell it when your father gave it to you?'

'My father would understand why I'm selling this book first.'

'I would like to understand also. Tell me.'

'You've forgotten Yiddish? You don't know any more that *shnorrer* means beggar?' He took the book from her and began to wrap it, lovingly. 'What Zangwill has written here is engraved upon my mind and my heart, I've read it so many times. So why do I need to see the words printed on the page? From books you can't make *kefulte* fish, my dear Rachel and they won't pay the rent when the man calls to collect it this afternoon. You'd prefer me to ask for a handout from the Benevolent Fund?'

Rachel paled and shook her head.

'When things get better we'll buy back the book. I'll take it to Carl's shop and maybe he'll manage not to sell it. And meanwhile I won't have to be a *shnorrer*.'

After Sigmund had gone to the bookshop, Rachel slid the other volumes along the shelf to fill the space *The King of Shnorrers* had occupied; she did not want him to be reminded of its absence. But as time went by and more spaces appeared on the shelves, she was unable to disguise them and could not bear to

185

see the distress in her husband's eyes whenever he entered the room.

The Sandbergs had nothing to sell except the furniture Salaman had given them and Abraham would not part with it.

'We'll manage,' he said to Sarah. 'We've had hard times before.'

'This hard never,' she replied putting bread and herring on the supper table. 'When did we not have even a quarter of chicken between us for *Shabbos*?' She sliced the bread, for which there was no butter. 'And why you won't part with a sofa you've never once sat upon I don't understand!'

'Shall I ask Mr Radinsky if I can work for him in the evenings like David used to?' Nathan suggested, but his mother did not reply. A sparetime job would be a means of escaping from the house, as well as a help to his family. 'Why won't you let me, Mother?'

'It was bad enough your brother had to do it.'

'Just keep your mind on your schoolwork Nat,' David said sharply. 'That's all we ask.'

'David's right,' Esther echoed.

'I don't get much chance not to, do I?' Nathan retorted with uncharacteristic petulance. His mother and David made sure of that. Sometimes he felt as if the whole family cared about nothing except him coming top of the class and passing the scholarship. Lou was to take the exams, too, but his family weren't at him all the time, they let him go out to play marbles in the street sometimes after school. You'd think it was a sin for me to spend a single minute thinking about anything but school! he thought resentfully. It's a good job I enjoy reading, but they'd make me read even if I didn't.

'Any more grumbles out of you, Nat and you'll hear from me about it,' David frowned as his little brother cast a sullen glance at him. 'You don't know how lucky you are.'

Sarah went into the scullery and returned with a piece of cheese, which she put on Nathan's plate.

'Why're you giving this to me, Mother? When nobody else is having any?'

'Mrs Moritz sent it for you. They sold some books again today.'

Nathan's face flushed. 'You said that last week when I was the only one who had a fishball for supper.'

'It's the truth,' Esther said. 'Carl told me.'

'But it makes me feel terrible! And I won't eat it unless everyone else has a bit, too.' Nathan divided the cheese into six pieces and felt as if he was carving up a treasured volume from his godfather's library. 'I might be the youngest, but I'm no different from anyone else in the family.'

'Of course you are,' Sammy smiled. 'You're the one who's going to be somebody.'

Nathan saw his mother glance at David, then Sammy looked uncomfortable, as if he had said something he ought not to have said, and a sudden silence descended. 'What's the matter?' he asked scanning the strained faces which had not looked that way a moment ago. 'What did Sammy mean?'

'We'll tell you one day,' his mother said as she dished up the frugal meal.

Nathan sat with the cubes of cheese cupped in his hand, looking from one face to another, but nobody met his gaze.

'So give everyone a bit of cheese if you're going to, Nat,' Abraham said restoring the atmosphere to normal.

'He'd take the food from the child's mouth!' Sarah exclaimed.

Abraham chewed the flavoursome morsel his son had just handed him. 'He isn't selfish and that I like to see. It's also important he should stay that way.'

Sarah sighed as she cut into her herring. Tonight she had fried them. Last night she'd served them soused. And the night before that they'd had borsht as watery as Malka Berkowitz's had sometimes been. Would the way her family was living now ever be any different? Sammy had been laid off from the factory and Abraham and David were bringing home only a nominal sum, paid to ensure their allegiance to Salaman until business revived. Esther's commission at the gown shop had recently dwindled to nothing; even the ladies who lived in fine houses and wore smart clothes had begun to feel the pinch.

She watched Nathan anxiously as he ate his herring, afraid he would become ill unless she could provide him with a more varied diet. The scholarship exam he was to take would set him on the path she had decided was to be his, but where would the money

187

come from to keep him there? The sixpences and shillings and half-crowns which must be hoarded week in, week out, as a squirrel accumulates its store of nuts for the time of need. She couldn't remember when she'd last been able to save a farthing and the lapse in building up her doctor-son's education fund was an added anxiety; she already visualised him with a stethoscope around his neck, a dark and handsome young man whose name everyone would mention with bated breath. But meanwhile, how to nourish him was the pressing problem.

Wispy-haired Mrs Kaplan provided the answer when Sarah met her on Bury New Road clutching a bloodstained parcel to her flaccid bosom.

'Someone's left you a fortune you're able to afford meat?' Sarah inquired.

'I've got a lodger now,' Mrs Kaplan informed her.

Sarah knew several women who had taken lodgers recently, men and boys who drifted from town to town in search of work. These transients always had benefit cash with which to pay the landlady and this enabled her to supplement her family larder. The Sandbergs no longer had room for a lodger, but nor did Mrs Kaplan.

'You've got six children at home. What've you done? Rolled him in a *perineh* in the back yard?'

Mrs Kaplan bristled, which she was always quick to do. She had on the same darned shawl she had worn years ago, when she bargained with Mr Radinsky over the bruised apple, and it looked as if it had not seen soap and water from that day to this. The neighbours thought her dirty, loud-mouthed and arrogant and Sarah agreed with them.

'If a person doesn't have room they can still find it!' she snapped. 'You've forgotten the old days, when everyone lived with *landsleit*, how people always found a way?'

Sarah eyed the blowzy woman thoughtfully and with new respect. She had never before encountered anyone who was more resourceful than herself.

A few days later, David arrived home from work and found a strange young man seated by the fire. Sarah had decided to present her family with a fait accompli.

'His name's Ben Klein,' she said with a smile. 'He's come here from Leeds to find work, so he'll live with us while he's looking.'

Ben gave David a lop-sided grin. His face was long and sallow, but his eyes were intelligent, with a humorous glint which warmed his somewhat saturnine countenance.

The Sandberg brothers liked him on sight. Had they not, they would have objected to having him share their bedroom. That night Nathan moved into the big bed with David and Sammy, vacating his own for the lodger.

Ben fitted into the family as if he had always been there. This was partly because he had no home of his own and found the Sandbergs' a comforting place to be. His parents had died in an influenza epidemic soon after he left school and he had been fending for himself ever since. He was David's age, but looked older. In repose, his face was the kind which had never looked young.

'I've lost count of how many houses I've lived in,' he said at supper. 'Leeds, Bradford, Newcastle, back to Leeds again when I was demobbed and now Manchester!' He was enjoying Sarah's potato *latkes*, having paid her a week's money in advance which allowed her buy some eggs. 'But food like this, Mrs Sandberg, I've never tasted.'

'With my mother flattery will get you nowhere,' Esther told him from across the table and he shot his crooked smile at her. When he smiles he's not so ugly, she thought with casual interest, though her mind was on Carl whom she was meeting after the meal. She returned Ben's smile.

Sarah noticed the exchange as she slipped another *latke* onto Ben's plate to welcome him at his first meal with them. But it did not assume significance in her mind until the following week, when Ben came home and said he had found a job.

'You waved a magic wand, maybe?' she exclaimed in astonishment. The rest of the family were amazed, too. There were no jobs to be had.

Ben stood warming his behind at the hearth, smiling to himself about how it had happened. He found it hard to believe, also. 'I was hanging around Flat Iron Market this morning,' he volunteered. 'Spying out the land.'

Abraham chuckled. 'You're thinking of buying it?'

'Well not tomorrow,' Ben countered with a laugh.

There was something about the way he said it which made David prickle with interest. Ben was like himself. Ambitious.

Sarah had recognised this, too. 'The day after, perhaps?' she asked smiling.

'A shop's what I'd really like, but I wouldn't mind a market stall to begin with,' Ben said confidently.

Esther brought him down to earth. 'Tell us about the job already.'

'Well I saw this old *Goy* puffing and panting, trying to unload some crates of pots and pans off his cart. So I started to help him. At first he wouldn't let me, he thought I'd want paying for it.'

'You wouldn't have?' Esther asked.

'Listen, money I need, but I'm not that kind of *shnorrer*!' Ben said hotly.

'I'm glad to hear it.'

'If a person does a deal with me, it's different.'

'I'm glad to hear that, too.'

'When I said I was just trying to help him, he let me do it,' Ben continued. 'Then he asked me to lay the stuff out on his stall. "You can't expect all that for nothing," I told him. "What makes you think I do?" he said. He told me to get on with it and watch the stall while he went, excuse me, to the lavatory. When he got back I'd served some customers. The prices were marked on the stock, so I knew what to charge. He sat and watched me serve a woman who only wanted a cup and saucer, but I sold her a plate that matched them. "You've got a real Jewish head on you," he said when I handed him the money. "You can't expect me to have a Christian one, can you?" I told him. Then he offered me the job.'

'*Mazeltov*!' Sarah chuckled. 'So let's have supper, there's another working man in the house to feed!'

When Esther returned from her outing with Carl that night, her mother was waiting up for her.

'You've been somewhere nice, Esther?'

'For a walk in Heaton Park. What else can we afford?'

'With Carl nothing and never,' Sarah said bluntly. 'What will he ever be, that sweetheart of yours? Bad times or good?' It hurt her to speak this way about the son of her closest friends, but she had to think of her own daughter and the truth was the truth.

'Maybe he'll be manager of the bookshop one day,' Esther said loyally, knowing this was unlikely.

'Like a horse would fly if God had given it wings.' Carl had been born without drive and Esther knew it as well as she did. Where was her sense?

'I love him, Mother.'

'And from love comes children. Who will support Mr Carl Moritz's children while his wife is pregnant with the next one and can't go out to work?'

'Stop it!' Esther cried.

'You're the one who should stop it. You must've been touched with lunacy that day on the tram to close your eyes to what you're heading for.'

Esther stared at her with hatred.

'So you hate me for telling you the truth,' Sarah shrugged. 'I still have to tell it to you, I'm your mother.'

'I couldn't live without him,' Esther said flatly.

Sarah laughed. 'You think there's only one man in the world for you? When another is right here in the house?'

Esther looked surprised.

'And a boy in a million Ben Klein is.' She paid him the highest of compliments. 'Another David.'

'Where've you got this daft idea from?' Esther asked derisively. 'We're always lashing out at each other. I don't think he even likes me.'

'No?' Sarah smiled. 'He had a little chat with me about you tonight.' She did not tell her daughter it had been at her instigation, so she could sound out his feelings.

'Hm,' Esther murmured. Then she told her mother to forget it and went upstairs to bed.

The following week, when Carl was stocktaking at the shop and Esther had nothing to do, Ben invited her to go dancing. Sarah did not so much as blink an eyelid when she heard her accept.

David's determination to raise himself from the ghetto had not faltered, but by 1922 he was no further forward and there was no sign of another boom which would make it possible for him to demand a worthwhile wage from Salaman in return for managing the factory.

Many of the workers were still laid off, or on short time, and he could not shake off the feeling of stagnation which had been with him since he returned from the army. The lines they had manufactured before the war were still being made in the same old way, shapeless gaberdines to be thrown on carelessly to keep out the rain.

But that's what they're for, he cogitated watching the blessed torrent which had just begun to pour from the skies. The sun had been shining when he came to work, as it had all day long for the past week, and the familiar anxiety about a dry season had pervaded the workroom. David had come downstairs to escape from it and was standing in the doorway, getting a breath of air during the brief morning tea break.

Bessie brushed past him carrying a shopping bag. 'My dad fancies cucumbers with sour cream for his dinner today. All week when it wasn't raining he didn't fancy it!' she grumbled tying a scarf over her head. 'I'll get drowned, going to the shop. I left my umbrella at my Auntie Rivka's.'

'Where's your raincoat?' David asked her. She was wearing a beautifully cut beige coat, which Sigmund Moritz had tailored to her ample proportions.

'I wouldn't be seen dead in one!' she snorted as she set off down the puddled street.

When David went back upstairs he did not eat the bagel he usually had in the break, but stood by the workroom window thinking of what Bessie had said. He'd heard Miriam disparage raincoats, too and had never seen her wear one. Most women would rather get wet than wear one and who could blame them? He eyed a bale of fawn gaberdine. It was not unlike covert cloth in appearance, of which Bessie's coat was made. David's mind began to buzz. The factory could not reproduce the fine lines of a Sigmund Moritz garment, but surely Eli could cut something similar?

'You're not eating today, David?' Millie said to him. 'You forgot to bring something? So share mine.'

He looked up and saw her offering him a blackbread wedge. 'I'm not hungry, thanks Millie,' he smiled and went to get a pencil and some paper, gripped by an unprecedented excitement. Half-an-hour later, he had completed the first of the many fashion sketches he was to make in his manufacturing career.

'You've become an artist?' Eli put on his glasses and studied the clumsy drawing which David showed him. 'So what is it? It looks like a lady with no legs or face.'

'It's a coat.'

'Very nice,' Eli lied and handed the sketch back to him.

'I want you to make a pattern for it.'

Eli snatched the sketch and looked at it more carefully. 'I should make a pattern for this?'

'Why not?'

The cutter rubbed his stubbled chin nervously. 'But what will Mr Salaman say?'

'Let me worry about that,' David smiled.

When the pattern was made, David changed one or two details and instructed Eli to get on with the next stage.

'I should cut it from cloth?' He was still worrying about Salaman's reaction to wasting time and paper on the pattern, if he found out.

'That's what you usually cut coats from, isn't it?'

Eli surveyed the pattern. 'But this is a real coat for a lady, David. Who makes real coats to wear in the rain?'

'We're going to,' David told him.

'Mr Salaman knows?'

'Are you going to cut it, or aren't you? If not, I'll do it myself.' There was no aspect of the trade David could not tackle and the staff knew it. Everyone had stopped working to watch the exchange.

Eli stopped rubbing his chin and picked up his shears; he was not going to be usurped at his own bench.

David had won his first real battle with a worker and his authority was never questioned again. Issie was asked to sew the garment and complied without hesitation.

David paced the workroom like a father awaiting the imminent birth of a child and at dinnertime could barely contain himself, waiting for Issie to stop eating and resume work. When the coat was finished he took it to Abraham to be pressed.

'He's been like a lunatic all day!' Eli exclaimed to Issie. 'And when the boss sees that sample, believe me I don't want to be there.'

'Make a good job of it, Father,' David said watching Abraham wield the iron.

'If you'd stop breathing down my neck it'd be easier!'

'It's a very special sample.'

'That I can see.'

'And what do you think of it?'

'It doesn't look like a raincoat.'

'It's not supposed to, that's the whole idea. All I have to do now is convince Salaman it'll sell.'

'I wish you luck, David.'

When David took the sample downstairs his employer barely glanced at it.

'Do what is best, David. It's all right, I trust you,' Salaman said with the flicker of a smile. None of his days were good, but this was an especially bad one, his dead wife's birthday. He could hear her voice reproaching him for not sending for the doctor. He pulled the blanket closer about his legs and resumed reading the Talmud.

Bessie showed more interest. 'Let me try it on,' she requested.

David's heart sank. Bessie was the only person who had more influence over Salaman than himself and he knew the sample would not fit her, which would certainly prejudice her against it. But he helped her to slip it on.

'You're catering for skinny-Lizzies like Miriam Moritz I see,' she said acidly, popping a button off in her vain attempt to fasten it. 'It reminds me of my covert coat.'

'It was seeing you in your covert coat that gave me the idea,'

David told her employing the truth to his advantage. 'So if we do well with them, it'll be because of you, Bessie.'

'Why shouldn't we do well with them?' she asked with a pleased smile.

David left the factory early and went to meet Miriam outside the millinery shop. The weather had brightened during the afternoon, but the sky was now overcast again and he saw her glance up at it as she pulled on her gloves.

She's thinking she ought to have brought her umbrella, he smiled to himself as he crossed the road to where she was standing. The sample was her size, perhaps Salaman would let him have it at cost price when the range was made and then he could give it to her. Skinny Lizzie indeed! His pulse raced as he watched her smoothing down her jacket and skirt, the way she always did, then settling the collar of her frilly blouse. He allowed his imagination to remove them and a vision of flimsy lingerie and silky-soft curves sent his temperature soaring. He should be ashamed of himself!

She had on a green and white hat, made from some bits and pieces her employer had given to her, but David was sure she looked more fetching in it than the smart Gentile ladies who patronised the Jewish milliner did in the expensive concoctions she made for them.

'Is something wrong, David?' Miriam asked. He had never come to meet her from work before.

'No, something's right, love!'

'That's a change,' she said with the bitter edge which had crept into her voice lately.

On the tram, David began immediately to tell her about the sample coat. Her lack of interest was like cold water dashed in his face.

'Nothing excites you, does it?' he said eyeing her impassive expression.

'Well not the kind of things that excite you.'

She was as beautiful as she had always been, but the glowing vitality he remembered was no longer there. When had it left her and why? She hadn't been the same since the day they went to Alderley Edge. But nor had he. And events since then hadn't helped.

'How's your mother?' he asked.

'I can't bear to talk about it.' The trembling hands had been a symptom of Parkinson's disease, for which even the brilliant Dr Smolensky had no remedy. 'Every time I look at her I wonder how God could let it happen.'

They sat in silence as the tram turned into Waterloo Road, where a new ghetto had mushroomed in Hightown.

'And she could've done without what your mother did to her!' Miriam flashed accusingly.

David did not reply and sat cracking his knuckles, a nervous habit he had recently acquired.

'I wish you'd stop doing that, it sets me on edge!' Miriam snapped.

'Perhaps it's because you're always on edge that I started doing it.'

'Who wouldn't be? With one thing and another.'

'Look, it's a year already since Esther jilted Carl. She's married to Ben now, so why don't you try to forget it?'

Miriam laughed abruptly. 'With our parents still not speaking to each other?'

'We agreed not to let that come between you and me, didn't we?'

'It's easier said than done, David.'

David took her hand, but there was no answering pressure and he let it slip back onto her lap. 'By the way, Esther's expecting,' he said conversationally. His sister was a forbidden subject, but how could things ever be right with him and Miriam while he had to watch his words?

'I don't want to know.'

'Why not?' he persisted. 'You'll be the baby's auntie one day.'
'Will I?'

David felt as if a lump of lead had suddenly been deposited in his stomach as he heard her express the doubt they had both begun to feel.

Miriam turned to look at him, her eyes sparkling with challenge. 'If you really want to marry me, what're you waiting for? Until you can afford to live in a house like Forrest Dene?' She laughed humourlessly. 'We'll both be old and grey by then!'

'Even if it takes that long, I'll do it!'

196

'Why is it so important to you?'

'You wouldn't understand if I tried to explain. You're just like your brother.'

'There's nothing wrong with my brother!'

'Esther'd still be working in the gownshop if she'd married him.'

'From what I hear, she's standing behind her husband's market stall and it isn't even his yet.'

'But it will be, when the owner retires and Ben pays him off. Just like I'll have my own factory sooner or later. Esther's helping Ben to build their future, not trying to keep him stuck in a rut, the way you're doing with me! When do you ever give me a word of encouragement? Why can't you?'

'Because money doesn't matter to me. All I want is you.'

'Grow up, Miriam!'

She turned away from him and he sat cracking his knuckles again. Why must she always depress him this way? He'd been over the moon when he went to meet her.

When they alighted from the tram, raindrops the size of pennies were spattering on the pavement and David took Miriam's hand and ran with her to shelter in Mr Halpern's shop doorway. 'If you had one of my smart new coats, you could wear it to work even on fine days and still be ready for a downpour, Miriam.'

'They're not your coats. They're Isaac Salaman's,' she reminded him flatly.

'Damn you!' David exploded.

Miriam's expression crumpled, then she turned and fled as she had when they were a boy and girl on their way to a dance. David stood for a moment remembering it and it seemed to him now that one way and another she had always eluded him; even when her physical presence had been there, the person she really was had never been his.

Mr Halpern stopped lathering a customer and opened the door to speak to him. 'You've had a tiff with Miriam? So you'll make it up, don't worry.'

David looked at him unseeingly.

'So run after her already. Like a dummy he's standing here!' The kindly little barber shoved him into the street.

Miriam had almost reached home when David caught up with

her. He grabbed her arm and turned her to face him. 'If you weren't always trying to belittle me, I wouldn't've lost my temper. But it's not as if this was the first time, is it?' He touched her bedraggled hair and the sodden hat sitting like a bruised water lily on the back of her head and an aching tenderness thickened his voice. 'I suppose you think I met you from work to tell you about the sample?'

'Didn't you?'

'I know you well enough not to waste my time leaping on trams just to tell you things like that. It was just that it made the future suddenly look brighter. And I thought we should fix our wedding date.'

She stared at him mutely.

'But I couldn't bear rows every day of my life and that's how it'd be if you kept on like you are doing, love. A man needs a wife who'll give him some support, not the opposite.'

Miriam knew he was waiting for her to tell him she would try to be what he wanted and the promise almost slipped off her tongue. But she could not pretend to be other than how she was. 'You'd better not risk it, then,' she heard herself say.

For a split-second David could not believe she had said it, then it was as if the entire gamut of human emotion ripped through him; sorrow and anguish, despair and despondency, injured pride and disappointment, regret for the wasted years and for what was now not to be, searing jealousy of the unknown man who would replace him in her life, and the terrible finality of loss all had their way with him, one after another; sardonic humour, too, the bitter irony of himself and Miriam ending their love affair drenched to the skin because she had taken him down a peg about a raincoat. Anger gripped him last as he stared into the cool, green eyes which seemed to be mocking him. The words were still echoing in his ears. 'You'd better not risk it, then.' She might just as well have told him to go to hell!

The reply Miriam knew was the only one he could give her shot from his lips like a bullet from a gun, straight into her heart. 'I'm not going to!'

She did not allow the tears stinging her eyelids to gush forth until he had turned and walked away from her.

Nathan was lying on the bed reading when David entered their bedroom.

'Are you all right, David?' he asked alarmed by the look on his brother's face.

'Sure.'

'No you're not. Something's happened, hasn't it?'

David sat down beside him. 'Oh yes.'

It had to be something disastrous from the sound of David's voice. 'Who did it to you?'

'When you get older, Nat, you'll find there're some things we do to ourselves.'

'Mother says everything's fated.'

'Well don't let her fool you, it's not.'

'Have you done something to yourself?'

'And I'll probably regret it.'

'So why did you do it?'

David shook his head wordlessly and lay back to bury his face in the pillow.

Nathan touched his shoulder timidly. 'Can't you undo it?'

David glanced up at his brother's handsome face. Nat had a sensitivity none of the other Sandbergs had, how would he stand up to the knocks life meted out? His vulnerability wouldn't be an asset. Now he's at Manchester Grammar there'll be no stopping him, but things'll have to look up if we're going to send him to university, David thought, then he laughed at himself. Instead of moping about Miriam, here I am thinking of family matters, he reflected dryly. But at least that's something positive. He got off the bed and combed his hair which was still damp from the rain.

'Can you?' Nathan asked watching him.

'Can I what?'

'Undo whatever you've done to yourself. I'd do it for you if I could.'

'Would you?' David smiled. How childish Nat still was, but he'd been more sheltered than the rest of them.

'I'd do anything for you, David.'

David laughed, but the expression of devotion had touched him. 'When there's something you can do I'll ask you, Nat. Now let's go down for supper, it's no use crying over spilt milk.'

Since David had come to terms with his lot, positive thought and action had become second nature to him and even if he did not resort to it immediately, sooner or later this painfully achieved philosophy came to his rescue and saved him from sinking into despair. There was no hiatus in his acceptance of the break with Miriam. Subconsciously he had been preparing himself for it. When he went into the kitchen he told the family his romance was over. He knew that hearing himself say it would help to finalise it in his mind.

Outwardly, the others were more affected than he was. Sarah's heart ached for him, but it was his own decision. This time she couldn't be blamed, the way the Moritzes had held her responsible when her daughter had jilted their son.

Esther was thinking of this, too. 'We had sweet and sour mackerel for supper the night I broke it off with Carl,' she said quietly.

'And if I'd known Sigmund Moritz was going to cut me dead in the street the next day, it would've stuck in my throat,' Sarah replied serving her a double helping of the succulent fish because she was eating for two. 'And when I went to the house to make the peace with him, what did I find? The back door is bolted which it's never been before and he doesn't hear me knocking at the front, or see me through the window though he's sitting there hand stitching a jacket!'

'What's the use of raking all that up again, Ma?' Ben said practically. 'It's over and done with.'

'Tell me how it's over and done with when Rachel and Sigmund haven't spoken to us ever since? You think it doesn't hurt your father-in-law and me, just because we don't talk about it?'

'So what can you do?' Abraham shrugged heavily.

'They're not out of friends with me and David and Sammy though, are they?' Nathan reminded his parents.

Sarah sighed. 'After what's happened with David and Miriam, I wouldn't bank on it.'

'Will it still be all right for me to go there and borrow Uncle Sigmund's books?'

'It'd be best if you didn't,' David said beginning his meal.

Sarah was still standing with the fish server in her hand, staring into space.

'Sit down and eat already!' Abraham said to her tetchily.

'I'm not hungry.' She glanced at his plate and saw he had hardly touched a morsel himself. Who could swallow food when they were choking with memories? The lengths to which Sigmund's hurt pride had carried things she wouldn't have believed possible; it wasn't in Rachel's nature to prolong the rift between their families, but she wasn't a woman to go against her husband. Not a day passed by when Sarah didn't think of her dear friend languishing in near-helplessness, and being unable to lend the comfort and support she would gladly have given was a constant sadness. Now, David had rubbed salt into the old wound by casting Miriam aside. She sighed and replenished Esther's plate, which was still half full.

'Do'you think I'm expecting twins, Mother?'

Sarah looked at her smiling daughter, whom she had saved from a life of discontentment at so great a cost and managed to chuckle. 'You've eaten an egg with a double yolk, Esther? P-p-p! Where would we put them?'

CHAPTER EIGHT

News travelled fast in Strangeways, there were so many meeting places. Work and *shul*, the grocers, the butcher's and the barber's, and every street corner. David and Miriam's broken romance was a nine-day wonder, but it did not take nine days for Bessie Salaman to make up her mind. She had stopped mooning over David openly a long time ago, adult propriety demanded it, but she had loved him as long as she could remember and still did.

Most people, including David himself, thought she had got over it and her father had never been aware of how she felt. Even in the days when she had tried to woo David with food and dogged his footsteps in the factory, Salaman had been too full of his own frustrations to notice his daughter's and was taken by surprise when she told him what he must do.

'Come downstairs, David. I want a word with you,' he said one morning.

Their employer's presence among them intrigued the workers, it had been some months since he last showed his face. He smiled at them benignly and this was rare, too.

David was no less puzzled than the rest of the staff as he followed him into the kitchen.

'Sit down my boy.' Salaman gestured to the leather wing chair which was reserved for his own exclusive use and David's perplexity increased. 'Help yourself to a cigar.'

'I don't smoke, Mr Salaman.'

'So you'll have one anyway.' He thrust a box of Havanas under David's nose, compelling him to take one and remained standing with his hooded eyes fixed upon him.

It's like being scrutinised by an eagle, David thought. There was something predatory in Salaman's expression.

'You've become like a son to me,' his employer sighed averting his gaze.

A moment of silence followed and David could feel Saul's presence in the room.

Salaman blew his nose and dabbed at a tear which had trickled down his podgy cheek. 'I don't have to tell you how I've suffered. But I still have my Bessie, bless her.'

'I'm sure she's a comfort to you,' David said stiffly, unable to summon up sympathy for the man he despised.

'Please God I'll also have a grandson some day,' he added with a watery smile.

David ran his finger along the inside of his collar, which felt as if it was glued by sweat to his neck. Salaman kept a fire blazing in the grate even in warm weather. How much longer must he sit here? He knew Abraham had always been the recipient of their boss's confidences. Was the honour now to be his, too? He hoped not.

'And the factory will be his,' Salaman continued. 'Me, I don't care anymore. But first he must have a father.' He lit his cigar, which he had not yet done, and puffed out an acrid cloud. 'You'll learn to enjoy cigar smoke, with what I'm going to offer you,' he promised when David coughed. 'So why're we beating about the bush?' He stationed himself in front of the fireplace, his demeanour suddenly brisk, and offered David a half share in his business.

David felt almost too weak to climb upstairs. His mind was in a daze. He would have gone directly to tell Abraham, the unlit cigar still in his hand, but the underpresser was there. It was not until he reached the workroom and saw the curious glances of the machiners that he came down to earth and realised that the offer included Bessie.

Bessie spent the day in town deciding what she would choose for her trousseau. Shorter skirts were now in fashion, but she had not yet worn one. The Spring clothes in the shop windows were a froth of delicate colours and fabrics, but were all in the new style and the way this would reveal her dumpy legs was worrying her.

She pushed the anxiety away. Some of the dresses had pointed hems falling gracefully in folds, like a handkerchief clutched by its middle. She would have one like that for her wedding gown. What she would do if David refused the offer she did not allow her mind to dwell upon. She had come to town to avoid being there when her father spoke to him. The next time she saw David the uncertainty would be over, everything would be settled.

A small child passing by with a lady smiled at her and it reminded her of how her own mother had taken her shopping on Bury New Road and people had remarked on the way little Bessie was always laughing. Until my mam got ill, she thought. And then she died. Since then, what had there been to laugh about? She recalled starting school just before her mother's death and nobody wanting to sit beside her because her pinafore was dirty. But who had there been to wash it for her? And after a while she'd found out how to get her own back on the other children and stopped caring. They'd been sick with envy when they saw all the things she had and remembering it still gave her a triumphant feeling. My dad would have given me the world to make up for having no mam, she reflected as a fur coat all by itself in a shop window caught her eye. He still would.

There were only two things which Salaman's money had not been able to buy for his daughter. One was a new face and figure. The other was David, who was now within her grasp.

Salaman's proposition was not a bombshell to anyone in the family except David, but nobody tried to influence him either way.

Sarah wanted to tell him what a wonderful thing it would be for his father and Sammy, having him for their boss, but kept her lips sealed and Sammy had to bite his tongue to stop himself from asking how David could consider marrying Bessie Salaman, when all he need do was make it up with Miriam and she would be his girl again.

Because he knew how much material success mattered to his son, Abraham wanted him to have the half share in the business, but the prospect of Bessie being his daughter-in-law filled him with dismay. Nathan, who even at the age of twelve was a romantic, thought only of Miriam's beauty and Bessie's ugliness. But

Esther, whose similar quandary was now happily resolved, felt like telling David to do the practical thing.

'Let him make his own mind up, like Esther did,' Ben said.

'Nobody's trying to do it for him,' Sarah pointed out, avoiding her daughter's eye.

Supper had been finished an hour ago, but the dishes were still on the table. The matter had been discussed from end to end, without David receiving the guidance he had hoped for from his family. Didn't his mother always know what was best? Tonight she appeared not to and nor did anyone else. He felt let down and jittery. 'I'm going for a walk,' he told them and slammed out of the house.

'Tell him not to do it, Mother!' Nathan implored the moment he had gone.

'He doesn't love her,' Sammy declaimed. For him that was all that mattered.

Love, Sarah reflected, doesn't always bring contentment, nor does it feed and clothe people. She glanced at Esther's placid expression which a year ago had been passionate with conviction that she couldn't live without Carl Moritz.

Esther read her mind. 'You were right, Mother.'

'What about?' Ben quizzed, but received no reply.

What's right for one is maybe not right for another, Abraham thought. 'You think David should say yes to Salaman, Sarah?'

'I think he should do what's best for him,' she answered ambiguously.

David found himself on Bury Old Road, without having consciously headed in that direction. How many times had he traversed this route with Miriam, making the long trek from Strangeways to Heaton Park? Memories of summer days they'd spent together in the green haven which was so different from their own environment rose to taunt him. Miriam a little girl in a frilly pinafore, sitting in the long grass making daisy chains. Miriam watching the graceful motion of the swans on the lake, wearing her first grown-up dress. Miriam breathless with delight, absorbing the perfumed beauty of the rose gardens the last time they visited the park. Was this what she'd meant when she said she was excited by different things from those which excited him? Daisy chains, swans and roses? Miriam. How he loved her. He reached the park gates, but could not enter, they were locked for the night. And he would never walk by the lake and through the rose gardens with her again.

On the way back, he succumbed to an impulse and went to look at the Moritzes' house. He stood in the night stillness, his heart heavy with longing, staring up at the window of the room Miriam shared with Helga. If she had appeared at the window he would have hammered the door down and asked her to marry him tomorrow. Salaman's offer had been temporarily erased from his mind.

When he reached home the dilemma returned in its entirety. It was not just a question of whether or not to seek a reconciliation with Miriam, but of what he would have to forego if he did not marry Bessie. He eyed his weary reflection in the kitchen mirror and laughed because it was still the only one the Sandbergs possessed.

Sarah came in from the scullery and surveyed him. 'Something's funny, David?' His expression belied the merriment she had just heard.

'I was thinking if I marry Bessie I'll be able to buy mirrors for every room in the house.'

He's been walking the streets for hours and it's still only an 'if', Sarah thought. But at least he was now considering it. She put the kettle on the fire, raking aside the cinders with which she had banked it up to keep the room cosy for David's return.

'Why aren't you in bed?' he asked her. It was after midnight.

At a time like this would his mother go to sleep and leave him alone with his worries? She gave him a reproachful glance and got out a cup and saucer for each of them, then went to fetch a jug of milk from the foodsafe with the wire mesh door which was kept in the cool scullery. Except after meat meals, when the dietary laws forbade milk, the Sandbergs now took their tea English style.

'Tell me what to do, Mother,' David pleaded.

'You want me to have that on my head, too?'

He knew she was thinking of the time she had told him he must leave school. 'That's water under the bridge now,' he said without bitterness.

'This will be also.'

'But while it's flowing it carries you with it and all you can do is sink or swim.'

'To sink isn't in your nature, David. Sammy, yes. Nat too, perhaps. Even your father, maybe. But you? Never!'

David smiled. 'You know us all inside out, don't you?'

'You I know best of all, because you're like me.'

It's true, David reflected. Whenever life knocked him down he always picked himself up again and went on battling, no matter how much it hurt. And his mother did the same. She wasn't the kind to sink, either. He went to sit at the table with her and stirred his tea, thoughtfully.

Sarah put a cube of sugar into her mouth, even English style tea she still drank the Russian way. 'We're the strong ones in the family, David,' she said when she had taken the first scalding sip. 'Did I make an agreement with your father he should leave everything on my shoulders? But that's the way it is. Wages he brings home, decisions he doesn't make.'

David knew she was not denigrating his father, but simply stating a fact.

'But to whom do I come when I have a difficulty? To David. The others also. What did you think would happen at supper tonight? That everyone would rush to advise you? Who would dare, when you are the big adviser in this family? Perhaps they'd like to, but nobody would have the courage.'

'Except you,' David said looking her in the eye.

'Courage I've got,' she replied holding his gaze. 'More since I know you don't hold the past against me.' She reached across the table and gripped his hand. 'For that I thank God, David. Everyone should have a son like you. A brother also.'

David averted his eyes from hers. He had not known his mother held him in such esteem and the revelation affected him deeply.

'So,' she said giving his fingers a final affectionate squeeze, then becoming her prosaic self again. 'Arranged marriages are no disgrace. Without them Strangeways would be half empty. I myself would not have been born. Your grandparents came from two different villages and only met three times before their wedding.'

David knew now what she wanted him to do. It was the sensible course of action as all his mother's advice was, but his gorge rose at the idea of it. This was 1922 in England, not fifty years ago in Russia. His mind wandered irrelevantly to Jim Forrest. Maybe Jim was married by now. To a lovely refined girl whom he had chosen himself, money wouldn't have entered into it. It wouldn't have to. He checked the flood of envy before it had time to overwhelm him. Money didn't have to enter into his own choice of a wife. It was up to him. Know thyself, a small inner voice said to him. Money was what he wanted – and the things it could buy. 'You think I should tell Salaman yes, don't you, Mother?' he said finally.

Sarah did not give him a direct answer. 'Life is full of sacrifices, David. So let them be for something.'

CHAPTER NINE

Throughout David's engagement to Bessie, Sammy kept a secret. He sometimes met Miriam and let her talk her heart out to him. The first time it had happened by chance. He had gone to Heaton Park one Sunday afternoon and found her sitting dejectedly on a bench opposite the lake.

'We're both lonely now, aren't we?' she said when he sat down beside her.

It was a cool October day, grey with the depression of approaching winter. In spring and summer the park was alive with people, but today no lovers lay entwined together on the grassy slopes, there were no children to shatter the silence with carefree shrieks, nor parents to chastise them. Miriam and Sammy had the lake view to themselves.

'You don't go out with David and her like you did with him and me, do you?' Miriam said flatly.

'I wouldn't want to.'

They exchanged a glance, allies against the interloper.

'So she's got him now, what can you do?' Sammy shrugged and suddenly Miriam was weeping on his shoulder. If the person who had hurt her had not been David, Sammy would have hated him.

'He didn't have to let her get him, did he?' Miriam said through her tears. Then disgust fired her expression. 'And everyone knows why he did.'

Sammy stroked her hair gently and she looked up at him, recollection softening her anger. 'You did this once before. When you arrived from Russia and slept in our room and David upset me.'

A picture of himself as a little boy climbing out of Carl's bed to comfort her flashed into Sammy's mind and was followed by other pictures of Miriam with a distressed look in her eyes, put there by David. But he'd seen David upset by things she'd said to him, too. Why did the two people he cared about most have to hurt each other? 'It was because you said my hair was like *tsimmes*,' he recalled with a wry smile.

'It still is.' David's misguided protectiveness of his brother had affected their three lives. But it wasn't the cause of the break between herself and him, she reflected bitterly as a sudden gust of wind brought the leaves flurrying from overhead. She turned up her coat collar, gazing disconsolately at the trees on the other side of the lake, which were fast disappearing into a shroud of mist.

Sammy wanted to take her hands and warm them in his own, but something stopped him. He tried to smile again, but his cheerful resilience had temporarily deserted him.

Miriam turned to look at him and saw the tiny lines etched beside his mouth, then her glance moved to his lame leg stretched before him like a dead thing and she wondered if it caused him pain. At the same time, she sensed that he was suffering on her account, that he had somehow been injured by what David had done to her. She knew he had noticed her looking at his leg and wanted to tell him she didn't pity him. 'You're worth ten of David!' she said impulsively.

Sammy looked astounded, then embarrassed. 'Don't talk daft, Miriam.'

'It's true,' she insisted. 'You wouldn't marry Bessie Salaman just because she's rich, would you?'

'I don't think being rich is all that important.'

'That's what I meant.'

Sammy thought of the time they'd gone to Cheshire and Miriam and David had quarrelled. It had been about this, though the word 'rich' hadn't been mentioned. He knew what David wanted and admired the ambition he didn't possess himself. 'Everyone's different,' he said in mitigation.

But Miriam had idolised David and he had fallen from the pedestal. 'When are you going to stop thinking he's right about everything? If he'd broken it off with me because he loved Bessie, or because he didn't love me anymore, I could forgive him. But it was because I can't stand his ideas, and Bessie's the way he's put them into practice.'

On the way home she confided that Dr Smolensky had invited her out. 'He comes from a wealthy family, so he can pick and choose who he marries,' she told Sammy. 'But I'd be the same as David if I encouraged him.' Her eyes flashed with scorn. 'Courting someone for mercenary reasons.'

Sammy wanted to defend his brother, but relief that the doctor was not going to replace David in Miriam's affections tied his tongue. He felt hot and feverish. What was the matter with him?

'Your face is flushed, Sammy. Don't you feel well?' Miriam eyed him anxiously as the tram rattled down Bury Old Road.

'I'm all right.' But his voice sounded strange and he knew he was not all right. He was in love with Miriam. It had not happened suddenly, as it had to Esther with Carl. He had loved her always, but not let himself know it, because she was David's. 'I'm fine,' he reiterated and smiled when he saw her scanning his face to make sure. Miriam cared about him, if not in the way he cared about her. And she was not his brother's girl anymore.

'I bet our Sammy's got a *shiksah* girlfriends, the way he does himself up when he goes out these days,' Esther teased him at supper one evening.

Everyone laughed except Sarah, who paled with alarm. One of her sons committing the unforgivable sin of God forbid marrying a Gentile?

'Esther's joking, Ma,' Ben assured her.

'A nice joke!'

David had laughed with the others, but was soon reimmersed in his own preoccupations. The liveliness which his dominant personality brought to the family mealtimes had not been in evidence since his break with Miriam and the gloom which had replaced it was deepening visibly as his wedding day drew near.

Sammy glanced at him. Was anything worth what David must be going through? Why didn't he call the wedding off? Miriam was never spoken of in David's presence, but they all knew he still loved her. How could Sammy tell the family he was seeing her himself? It would seem like disloyalty to his brother. After David's marriage it would be different, he'd be someone else's husband and the chapter with Miriam officially closed. Sammy knew it would not be closed in David's heart, but even he couldn't have the ha'penny and the bun and wouldn't expect to.

That night, when he came home after seeing Miriam, David was sitting at the table poring over some ledgers. He had grown thinner lately and his face looked cavernous in the gaslight.

'What are you doing to yourself?' Sammy exclaimed. 'Night after night you work at the factory and now you're bringing the accounts home to do as well!'

'I don't have time to do them during the day.'

'So let someone else do it.'

David smiled wearily. 'That's what Miriam would say.'

Sammy averted his gaze and stared into the fire.

'A person either wants to get ahead or they don't, Sammy. If they do, they have to make sacrifices.' David picked up his pen and began checking a row of figures.

'Why did you finish with her?' Sammy had not heard David's version of the reason for the break.

'It's none of your business, Sam!' David ground out and was shocked by the harshness of his voice, lashing at Sammy whom he wouldn't hurt for the world. But the question had touched a raw nerve.

'Tell me, David.'

There was an urgency in Sammy's voice which made David raise his eyes from the ledger and look at him. 'What's the matter with you? I broke it off because we're not right for each other. And it's no use you being upset about it. I couldn't make her happy, Sam.'

'I know you couldn't. But I wanted to hear you say it.'

Intuition flashed a message to David. 'You think you could, don't you?'

The truth now lay bare between them and Sammy's face shone with sincerity. 'If she'd let me,' he said simply.

This was the kind of love Miriam needed and longed for. David knew it. The kind he could not give to any woman. Sammy would worship at no other shrine than his marriage and Mammon would not sully his devotion.

'Would you mind, David? I mean she's got to marry somebody, hasn't she? And you know I'll look after her if she'll have me.

The humility in his brother's voice brought a lump to David's throat. Sammy was prepared to be second best, to marry the girl David had discarded and would be grateful for the crumbs. 'I'm not entitled to mind, am I?' he said gruffly.

It was David who told the rest of the family and he did so in a manner which made it clear that he approved.

'He hasn't got her yet, David,' Sarah said to him in private. 'And in some ways I'm hoping he doesn't.'

'You think it could cause trouble, don't you?'

'It couldn't?' Sarah asked eloquently. 'How will you like it to see her struggling on the wages Sammy brings home? He'll never be a good earner.'

'He works for me now,' David reminded her. There would be no struggling for Sammy and Miriam with David to watch over them; he had already decided that.

But it was not yet 'Sammy and Miriam'.

CHAPTER TEN

When David awoke on his wedding morning, which was also his twenty-sixth birthday, his first thought was that he would not be receiving a book from Sigmund Moritz. He leapt out of bed when Nathan came into the room carrying an oblong package.

'It was on the front doorstep, David. He must've got up very early to put it there before we were awake.'

There was no doubt in their minds about what the package was, or from whom.

'Open it, Nat.' David was too overcome with emotion to do so himself and could not speak when he saw the beautifully bound volume of Shakespeare's complete works. On the fly leaf, a simple message was inscribed in Sigmund's meticulous handwriting: 'Good luck, David, in all you set out to do.' His old friend bore him no malice.

'Can I come to your house and read it whenever I like?' Nathan asked excitedly. He rushed downstairs to tell the family about the latest addition to David's library.

David looked at the orange-box bookcase, now empty. He had packed his books with his clothes last night, ready to be taken to his new home. Bessie had asked him to move all his things before the wedding, but he had refused. The finality of it was something he wanted to put off, part of the inner rebellion he still felt. He glanced out of the window at the leaden skies. The weather matched his mood.

Sammy was sitting on the bed, silent with sympathy. The admission of his love for Miriam had not damaged the brothers' relationship, but had inexplicably drawn them closer. If David had suddenly taken it into his head to leave Bessie waiting at the synagogue and elope with Miriam, Sammy would have aided and abetted him, putting his own feelings aside, and David was aware of this.

When they went downstairs the atmosphere befitted a funeral rather than a wedding. David's attitude to his marriage, matter of fact at its best, peppered with moody outbursts at its worst, made lightheartedness impossible. His parents were subdued as they dunked their bagels into their tea and Nathan and Ben munched theirs mournfully. David was not allowed any food, orthodoxy decreed a Jewish bridegroom must fast prior to the ceremony. He sat watching the others eat, feeling like the sacrificial lamb.

'So what can you do?' Ben said expressively.

'If anyone else says that to me today, I'll throttle them!' David flared and got up to polish his new shoes, which did not need polishing.

'I'm sorry for Bessie if this is how you're going to be,' Esther said quietly. She was by the fire, nursing her baby. 'Such a clever uncle you've got, Harry,' she told the infant. 'So where's his sense? When a person makes up their mind to do something they should make the best of it.'

'Like you and me,' Ben said winking at her. 'No use crying over spilt milk!'

Nathan glanced at David, who had said that to him the day he finished with Miriam. But this did not concern Miriam, it concerned Bessie. 'This milk isn't spilt yet,' he reminded everyone.

'Hush, Nat!' his mother snapped. She was only too aware that the wedding had not yet taken place and would not breathe easily until it was over.

David stood with the polishing rag clutched in his hand. Esther's words had echoed his own philosophy, which he had temporarily allowed himself to forget. He wasn't the kind to change his mind once it was made up, nor would he vent his feelings on Bessie. Sooner or later the feelings would dissipate as everything did with time and meanwhile he would try to ignore them. There were plenty of other things to absorb him and reorganising the factory, now he was a partner, was number one.

He thought about this during the marriage ceremony and when he slipped the ring on Bessie's finger it seemed like sealing a business deal. But he would honour his side of the bargain.

'How d'you think I look, David?' Bessie asked anxiously in the taxi which took them from the photographer's to the reception. She was fussing with the orange blossom headdress which crowned her mousey hair and fortunately did not see David's expression as he surveyed her.

Her dress was of white crepe-de-chine, with the handkerchief skirt she had promised herself, but she had destroyed its simplicity by having the entire garment encrusted with silver bugle-beads which glittered and gleamed on her massive girth.

David patted her hand and smiled, words had failed him. But she interpreted this as admiration and was content.

The reception was at the Cheetham Assembly Rooms, which those who could afford it now hired for weddings and Bar Mitzvahs. A four-course meal was to be served by kosher caterers and Sarah thought she had come to the wrong place when she arrived and saw the size of the gathering.

'The whole world is here!' she exclaimed to Sammy and stood fingering her brooch with a bewildered expression on her face. In the synagogue she had been too pent up to notice anything, beset by a fear that David might suddenly turn and run. 'Where is your father? And Nat?' she asked Esther who had appeared at her side with baby Harry in her arms. 'In a crowd like this a person could get lost. Who knows if we'll ever find them again?'

Sammy went to look for a seat. His leg was aching and his spirits were low. He had been his brother's best man as he had promised to be a long time ago, but he had not known then that the ring he would hand to David beneath the marriage canopy would encircle Bessie Salaman's finger, or that he would one day want Miriam for himself. Today David had renounced her forever, but they still loved each other and he could not rejoice, even though there was now a chance he might make her his.

Sarah was hemmed in by guests. She could see Mrs Kletz's *sheitel*, and Mrs Plotkin was talking to Zelda Cohen and Gittel Lipkin a few yards away, but most of the other people were strangers to her. She found herself being suddenly embraced by a large lady in a pink satin frock.

'*Mazeltov* Sarah! In *shul* I couldn't get near you, so many people?'

'Who is it, Mother?' Esther whispered, but Sarah did not have time to reply, she had only just recognised the lady herself.

'You don't remember your Auntie Malka Berkowitz, darling,

who gave you a bed your first night in England?' She clapped her hand to her cheek as she had when the Sandbergs appeared on her doorstep and blew at the huge osprey which covered her head and was tickling her nose. 'Little Esther a mother already and such a lovely baby, bless him! It was only by the red hair that I knew her. How many years is it, Sarah? Don't tell me, I don't want to know! So you couldn't manage to come to my daughters' weddings, but we haven't fallen out with you about it, we've come to David's.'

'Without you and Chaim here it wouldn't have been the same,' Sarah replied politely. She was as overpowered by Malka's ripe beauty as she had been years ago. It was now over ripe, but still formidable to a stringy little woman garbed in modest grey taffeta and with a plain felt hat upon her silver hair. 'So how are Lakie and Bella?'

'I'm a grandmother twice over now, thank God,' Malka said with satisfaction whilst casting her eyes on the long tables, which were set with heavy silver and decorated with flowers. 'You've put us to sit at the top table, I'm sure?'

'Where else?' Sarah smiled. She had not forgotten her debt to the Berkowitzes.

Malka surveyed the opulent room, with its crystal chandeliers and rich velvet banquettes. 'Your David's done a good thing for himself, eh Sarah?'

'He couldn't have found a better wife,' Sarah answered hoping it would prove to be the truth.

'And all that money,' Malka gurgled as she pushed her way through the throng to congratulate the bride and groom.

This was the Berkowitzes' first visit to Manchester since their hasty move to Leeds, and Chaim, too, had gained weight.

'You're looking very prosperous,' Abraham said when they shook hands, observing the big cigar tucked in his *landsleit's* breast pocket.

'There's never an ill wind, Abie. You know that one?'

'From the Talmud it isn't.'

Chaim sighed. 'These days I don't have time for laughing fishes. All I have time for is arguing the toss with my staff.'

'You're not with your uncle the trousermaker anymore? You've got your own place?'

'I have and I haven't. Also, I'm with him but he isn't with me.'

'Riddles he's telling me!'

'My poor Uncle Hershie had a stroke, Abie. He's paralysed, the whole of one side, we shouldn't know of it. And he's only got daughters, two, like me. It runs in the family. And his sons-in-law?' Chaim had to mop the perspiration from his brow at the mere mention of them. 'One, he's only busy backing the gee-gees all the time. The other? Him I won't even talk about! My poor Auntie Lottie is worn out with the worry and with nursing Uncle night and day, so she has a chat with me. "Listen, take what you need for yourself and your family, Chaim," she says. "I trust you to run the business, only don't let it slip down the drain." Could I say no to her? I said yes. So now we've got a nice house in Chapeltown.' He patted the gleaming watch chain which he had not owned when he left Manchester. 'And one or two other little things also.'

'Who's that enormous man talking to your father?' Lou asked Nathan. 'I sat next to him in *shul* and he smells under the arms.'

'My family lived with him and his wife when they first came to England and I bet you won't believe this, Lou, they had to sleep on the parlour floor.'

'So did my parents, you *shmuck*! Nearly everyone had to when they first came.' Lou scratched his pimply nose thoughtfully. 'It wouldn't surprise me if half the lads in our Bar Mitzvah class were conceived on someone's parlour floor.'

The two boys were standing on the fringe of the gathering, resplendent in the Manchester Grammar School uniforms which singled them out as young geniuses in the eyes of the immigrant community. Nathan was glad he had been allowed to invite Lou, or he would have had nobody to talk to. They could see David having his hand wrung by guest after guest.

'I wouldn't go through it for a king's ransom,' Nathan declared.

'You mean for King Salaman's mines, don't you?' Lou quipped.

Nathan blushed. It had not occurred to him that anyone outside the family had realised why David was marrying Bessie.

Lou changed the subject, but it sounded to Nathan like a snide insult to Bessie. 'Your mother looks very nice.'

David had told Sarah that the black wool dress she wore on the Sabbath would not do and she had not argued with him, though she had worn it for Esther's wedding. Esther's blue crepe was new, too, but not as splendid as many of the guests' outfits.

'Mrs Shneider the dressmaker's been busy,' Esther said handing her baby to Ben and adjusting the flounce over her stomach. She was pregnant again.

'Sigmund Moritz also,' Abraham sighed. He had just escaped from Chaim and was eyeing the array of pinstripe suits. 'You can tell his cut a mile off.'

'Why're you bringing the Moritzes into it today?' Sarah averted her gaze from her husband's distressed countenance. The Moritzes were the last people she wished to be reminded of. 'So who are these fancy ladies and gentlemen?' she asked brushing her own distress aside. 'I hardly know a soul at my own son's wedding. Salaman must be *meshugah* to feed all these strangers!' She glanced at a group of men standing with drinks in their hands. 'Whisky he's giving away, too!'

'He wanted to give his daughter a good send-off,' Abraham placated her.

'I could think of better ways to spend so much money.'

'And David also,' he lied diplomatically, recalling how Salaman had ranted when complaining how much the lavish celebration David had demanded would cost.

'Most of the people you don't recognise are customers at the factory and their wives,' Ben told Sarah with a shrewd smile. 'David said he was going to invite them. He's got his head screwed on all right, believe me!'

'So why didn't you tell me before?'

'Could I get a word in?'

Sarah began to enjoy herself. Such a good business head David had, getting on the right side of people so they'd buy from him instead of his competitors. With personal relationships she knew he would never *shmooze* someone for what he could get out of them, her children hadn't been brought up that way. But to swell your livelihood it was another matter.

When they sat down for the meal, she smiled at the Gentile waitress who was standing behind her chair and almost tumbled off it when the girl addressed her as 'madam'.

'This I don't believe!' Chaim Berkowitz boomed from along the table. He was gazing down at the hors d'oeuvre which had just been put before him. 'Malka and me *shlep* all the way from Leeds to come to a wedding, and no smoked salmon!'

'Blame David,' Bessie called to him. 'It was him who decided what we were going to have.' Her father was seated beside her and was also looking at his plate. 'All of a sudden you don't like chopped liver with olives and tomato, Dad?'

Salaman picked up his fork and began eating. But he had seen David glance at him through narrowed eyes and knew, as David had intended he should, that the absence of the expensive delicacy meant his new son-in-law had not forgiven him for the way he had treated his dead son.

Between courses, Eli and Issie came to have a word with David and Abraham and displayed the new deference which David's alliance had acquired for the Sandbergs. The president of Salaman's *shul* came to shake Abraham's hand, too, though he had done so twice already, and offered to co-opt him to the committee if he would like to join their congregation, which boasted many wealthy manufacturers.

'I wouldn't leave the *Habimah* for a fortune,' Abraham told him. 'All my friends are there.'

'So maybe you'll be making new friends from now on, eh? Come, I'll introduce you to my wife. Mrs Sandberg, too. You haven't met her yet.'

'After the lemon tea I'll come,' Sarah smiled seeing the waitresses approaching with their loaded trays. But Abraham allowed himself to be led away, with a bemused look on his face.

Bessie had gone to fuss with her appearance before the speeches began, which gave Sarah a few moments of privacy with David.

'Money talks,' she whispered to him. The prestige aspect of her son's marriage was just seeping through to her.

'News you're telling me.' David cracked his knuckles and stared at the tablecloth.

Sarah scanned his impassive expression. 'Try to be happy, David,' she pleaded.

'Since when does it buy happiness?' he said with an abrupt laugh and went to join his wife, who had paused on her way back from the cloakroom to speak to a relative and was beckoning to him.

Sarah watched Bessie link her arm through David's and smile up at him. Marriage drew a man and a woman together, how could it not? Children came along and acted like cement. A family was happiness and David would have that. Without the poverty his parents had known, which love could not always withstand. She ate some grapes from the large basket of fruit adorning the top table and comforted herself with her own homespun wisdom.

There was nothing except his new status as a businessman to comfort David, but when Rabbi Lensky, who had been accorded the honour of toasting the bride and room, rose to make his address, he played his part and slipped his arm around Bessie's shoulders. It reminded him that tonight he would have to steel himself to do much more.

'What a lovely way to start a honeymoon,' Bessie grumbled while they waited for a tram to take them to the boarding house in Blackpool.

Rain was pounding down on them and they could see the huge breakers leaping wildly over the sea wall.

'The last time I saw waves like that was when we came from Russia,' David recalled. 'And I haven't set eyes on the sea since.'

Bessie had never seen the sea at all. 'I wish we'd got married in the summertime,' she shivered.

'What does it matter?' David replied and she smiled thinking he meant all that counted was them being together.

'Everyone says the air's like wine here,' she told him.

But David felt the need of something stronger to boost his morale. 'We should've brought a bottle of booze with us,' he joked half-heartedly.

Bessie looked alarmed. There was a heavy drinker in her family and she had seen David take a couple of whiskies at the wedding reception. 'I won't let you,' she warned him.

'Won't let me what?'

'Get like my Uncle Aaron.'

'What're you talking about, Bessie?' David could not remember which of her several uncles this was.

'A fine time my Auntie Rivka has with him!' she declared.

Bessie had the kind of mentality which turns molehills into mountains. She could also put together a chain of imaginary events and confound or bewilder whoever had unwittingly provided her with the first link, as she had just done with David. He felt tired and empty. Despite having fasted all morning, he had not eaten much at the wedding, but the emptiness was not just lack of food, it engulfed his whole being.

Bessie's umbrella turned inside out as the high wind lashed the rain against them. 'Do something, David!' she snapped struggling to set it right. The collar of her fur coat was clinging to her neck like a drowning cat. 'We should've got a taxi! Why didn't we? You're too mean with my money, that's why!'

Providing the answers to her own questions was another of her characteristics, David had learned during their brief courtship. It had not occurred to him to travel other than by public transport, taxis were not yet of his world. But he did not waste time explaining this. There was something more important he had to set straight with Bessie. 'You're forgetting something, aren't you?' he said tersely.

'What d'you mean?' she faltered.

He looked her squarely in the eye. 'A bargain is two sided isn't it? I've got a half share in your father's business, but in return for it you've got me.'

He left her to digest this while he went to fetch a taxi from outside the railway station. Ignoring a sensible suggestion, because of the manner in which she had made it, was no way to start his married life.

Mrs Litvak's boarding house was one of the small, kosher establishments patronised by Jews from the Northern industrial towns. Situated in a side street on the South Shore, the absence of a sea view was compensated by the homely ambience. During the high season, buckets and spades and perambulators made the long lobby a hazardous place to negotiate; children swarmed like sandflies all over the house and the bathroom was perpetually occupied, sometimes by a guest for whom no bed was available, who would be invited to sleep in the bath.

In winter, the house was virtually a honeymoon hotel. It was rare for anyone other than newly-weds to take a holiday then and the place assumed a different character. Breakfast was served later and the evening beverage earlier. The gaslight was turned discreetly low in the parlour, so that hand-holding and intimate glances might go unnoticed. Everyone's favourite dish was inquired about and served at least once.

This was Mrs Litvak's way of ensuring the young couples had a week to remember. She was a businesswoman to her fingertips and knew the honeymoon memory would draw them back year after year, with the children they would surely have; the eldest would probably be conceived in her house.

The dumpy little widow was also kind-hearted and romantic and wanted to give them what she and her husband had not had themselves. In summer this was not possible, but out of season she did so devotedly. Her pièce-de-résistance was a coal fire in every bedroom, a luxury her guests never had at home unless they were ill.

'It's so lovely here, David,' Bessie exulted warming herself by the blaze on their wedding night. She gazed around the little room rapturously, admiring the violet patterned wallpaper, which matched the design on the rug. Even the cows in the gilt-framed pastoral scene above the fireplace seemed to be smiling a welcome.

David felt better after consuming Mrs Litvak's ample fare. He had stayed chatting with the other couples in the parlour as long as he could, but apprehension fluttered within him now he and Bessie were alone together. He was trying not to look at the big bed, wondering how he would find the courage to undress and get into it.

'Why don't you get undressed in the bathroom?' Bessie suggested. She did not want him there when she took off her corset.

When he returned she had put on her nightgown and was lying waiting for him. 'Get in already!' she laughed. 'I'm not going to eat you!'

David smiled. 'It should've been me saying that to you, Bessie.' Somehow the situation seemed the wrong way round.

'I'm not afraid of you. I love you, David,' she said simply.

Green eyes, tantalising, drifted towards him from the past.

Bessie looked at the bright band of gold on her finger. 'And we're married now, aren't we?'

He blotted the green eyes out, the past was where they belonged, and got into bed with his wife.

His sexual experience was nil and neither love nor desire were present to show him the way, but Bessie was brimming over with both and let them guide her. This time, David did not pause to think the situation was the wrong way round. Instinct proved stronger than intellect and once initiated into the magic rites, his maleness asserted itself over the womanly flesh writhing beneath him. Her moan of anguish mingled with his cry of triumph as he penetrated her maidenhead and entered the secret place which marriage had made his own.

Not once that night did David think of Miriam. It was as though he had been shipwrecked on an island of untold delight. Bessie's great white breasts pillowing his head, her velvety thighs opening to receive him, the generous curve of her hips which had seemed ugly to him when clothed, possessed him utterly.

'Have I made you love me, David?' she whispered when they awoke the next morning.

'You've made me want you,' he said telling her the plain truth.

'That's the same thing, isn't it?' she said happily.

That love and desire were not necessarily twin emotions had come as a shock to David and he did not disillusion her. Thank God they weren't, he mused gratefully, and that Bessie was a passionate woman who had enabled him to learn this.

By the end of the honeymoon he had made another discovery. Sleeping together at night forged a daytime bond. He had expected their conversation to be dominated by matters concerning the business as it had been previously, but found himself discussing personal things with Bessie. Sometimes, when they braved the weather and sat huddled together in one of the little shelters on the promenade, he would tell her of his plans for the future.

'Our future,' she always said contentedly. She could still not believe she was David's wife, that the miracle which had changed her life had really happened.

'Wait till we live in a mansion in Cheshire. That'll show 'em,

Bessie!' he said exhilaratedly as they walked back to Mrs Litvak's for dinner on their last day.

She did not say, 'Show who?' or laugh at his big ideas as Miriam would have done, but smiled up at him. He could feel her pride in him and warmed to her because of it.

When they arrived home, he went directly to see his mother.

'So, David?' she said anxiously.

'Don't worry about me, Mother. I'm a married man now,' he replied and laughed when he saw her relieved expression. Had she feared the marriage hadn't been consummated?

The new sensuality released in him had acted like adrenalin on his system; he could feel the blood singing in his veins, telling him there was nothing he could not achieve.

On the way to the factory, which he intended to begin re-organising immediately, he reflected that what he had with Bessie was not happiness, but it was not misery, either.

CHAPTER ELEVEN

'You've made up your mind to be a Mrs Sandberg,' Rachel said
to Miriam one Sunday afternoon.

Miriam was putting on her new cloche hat in front of the hall-
stand mirror. She turned and saw her mother watching her
through the kitchen doorway.

Rachel's illness had progressed rapidly during the past couple
of years. At first the trembling had just made her increasingly
clumsy, unable to perform domestic tasks, and Helga had given
up her job to keep house. Now her legs were affected, too, and
Helga had become her nurse also. A sofa had been put in the
kitchen for her to rest upon and sometimes she slept there at
night if she could not find the strength to climb the stairs.

Miriam came into the room. 'What do you mean, Mother?'

Rachel laughed. Pain and disappointment had not diminished
her gentle humour, or her appreciation of God's gifts. She was
lying beside the window in a pool of May sunlight, letting it
warm her. 'What do I mean, she asks!'

Miriam avoided her eye. 'You're talking about Sammy, I
suppose.'

'Who else? Nathan is only just Bar Mitzvah!' She smiled at
her daughter compassionately, but delivered the cruel reminder
nevertheless. 'And David is married.'

Miriam sat down in her father's wing chair, gripping the arms
tightly. Why did she feel as if she was drowning? She hadn't let
herself think about it. Think about what? Any of it.

'You love Sammy?' her mother asked though she knew what
the answer would be.

Love anyone but David? 'No!'

'So it isn't fair then.'

She looked at her mother resentfully because she had made her
think about it.

'The poor boy loves you.'

'There's no need to pity him, Mother!' She could not bear to see people's expressions when Sammy walked past them dragging his leg, or had trouble boarding a tram. In that way she was like David, but David pitied Sammy himself and she did not.

'It's only because of you I call him a poor boy,' Rachel glanced wryly at her own weak limbs. 'I'm not so good at walking myself these days, but I don't think of myself as a poor woman.'

Miriam rushed impulsively to kneel beside her and took her hands, which had once dealt so deftly with the most intricate tasks and now lay limp and useless. 'You're the bravest person I know, Mother!'

'What has brave got to do with it? But I'd like to see a grand-child before I go, Miriam,' Rachel said with a poignant smile. 'Helga will never marry again, some women are like that, so long as they're needed it doesn't matter by whom and she's needed here. Your brother? He's married to his books!' She surveyed her beautiful daughter. 'So you didn't want Dr Smolensky and now he's engaged to Naomi Cohen. You didn't encourage him so it doesn't matter. With Sammy it's different.'

'Why?'

'You've been seeing him for months. And also he's a Sandberg. I wouldn't want you to do to him what David and Esther did to you and Carl, he doesn't deserve it.'

'You still grieve about it, don't you, Mother?'

'For Carl, no, it was just a flash in the pan for him, his love affair with Esther. If it had been more he wouldn't have recovered so quickly, all that was hurt was his pride.'

'What about Father's pride?'

Rachel sighed. 'That we won't talk about, but believe me he misses Sarah and Abraham as much as I do.'

'Even though he blames Mrs Sandberg for wanting her daughter to have a husband with prospects?'

'That isn't what he blames her for. We always knew what Sarah was like, the kind of things she hoped for for her children, how much money mattered to her, but it wasn't important to us.'

'Until it rebounded on our family?'

Rachel nodded. 'Me, I could forgive her, but you know how

stubborn your father is. A viper in our bosom he calls her. What happened with Carl and Esther was very hard for him to take.'

'And me and David?'

'Your father will always love David. But it doesn't have to be that way with you, Miriam. And marrying his brother won't help you to get over it.'

'He hasn't asked me to marry him, we're just friends, the way we've always been.'

'That isn't possible for a man and a woman and you're old enough to know it. If you're going to finish with Sammy, you should do it now before it's too late.'

Was she going to finish with him? The drowning feeling she experienced when she sat down in the chair had gone and with it the urge to hold on. A quiet lethargy had replaced it, as if she was floating with the tide.

'Before there's anything to finish,' Rachel persisted.

Her outings with Sammy were usually tramrides to the park, or chats in a café. When had she first noticed that he was careful not to touch her hand anymore, that a subtle change had entered their relationship? She liked being with him, nobody could be miserable with Sammy around. He never imposed his opinions on her, or said things to upset her as David had frequently done. With David it had been an equal blend of joy and sadness. Sammy made her neither happy nor unhappy, she was just content to have him there.

Rachel lay back against her pillows. The effort of saying what she had felt must be said had left her spent. She had waited for Sigmund to speak to Miriam, but for once he had failed to take the initiative in a family matter and she had not wanted to hurt his pride, which had been injured enough already, by telling him what to do.

Miriam was still kneeling beside her and looked as if all thought and emotion had suddenly been drained out of her. Rachel watched her rise and straighten her hat, then button her jacket, her movements mechanical. 'You never wear green anymore, Miriam,' she said and received a wan smile. Something was missing which had once been present in her daughter. Even without it, she was a girl any man would be proud to make his wife, but David had chosen Bessie Salaman. It depended upon what the man wanted. It would be best if Miriam didn't marry into the Sandberg family and be always under David's eye. 'Find someone else and let Sammy do the same, Miriam,' she pleaded.

The sluggish tide was still carrying Miriam along and Sammy was a harbour within easy reach. 'I don't think I want to,' she said wearily.

David experienced no pain when he sat in the synagogue listening to the rabbi intone the holy words which would make Sammy and Miriam man and wife. He loved them both and wished them well.

Bessie had been querulous with him from the moment she learned Miriam was to become one of the family, but her apprehension remained unspoken and he was pretending to be unaware of it. Six months of living with her had taught him that some imaginary problem or other would always be hovering on her horizon, inspired by the lack of confidence which had dogged her all her life.

At first he had tried to reason with her, but this had only made things worse. Her fears were at present exacerbated by pregnancy and she asked him repeatedly how he could bear to look at her, twice the size she was. To him her bulging stomach was beautiful, because of what it signified, but she refused to believe this.

Sammy had asked him to be best man and had seemed relieved when David said the honour should be given to a bachelor. Though the marriage had David's blessing, he had recoiled from participating in the ceremony, afraid that the armour he had built around his emotions might suddenly crack.

Moishe Lipkin, who had been away working in Liverpool since the war, had stepped into the breach. David had not seen him since he was a lad and during the wedding party was struck by his engaging personality. He was as lively as his childhood exploits had foretold, small and dapper with a ready smile and a way of listening to what people were saying with his head tilted slightly to one side, as if he was really interested in them.

'So how d'you like Liverpool?' David asked him.

'I'd rather be back in Manchester, but I've got a good job there, what can you do?'

It was a hot July day and the gathering had spilled over into the Moritzes' back yard, which Helga made pleasant with the nasturtiums and sweet scented stock she grew in tubs. David was leaning against the yard door, careful not to brush his new suit against the whitewashed wall. He would be glad when the party was over; the way his parents and the Moritzes were being frigidly polite to each other was unnerving, like a truce called for the day which everyone knew was not going to last a moment longer than necessary. The way his wife's eyes kept darting between himself and Miriam was a strain too.

Bessie was lolling on a chair beside Esther and David turned his back towards her and resumed his conversation with Moishe. 'D'you work in a factory?'

'No, a big store. The boss is a pal of mine's father. Someone I was with in the army, that's how I got the job.'

'Do you earn much commission?' David inquired.

Moishe grinned. 'More than anyone else who works there.'

David was not surprised to hear this. His surmisal that Moishe was the stuff salesmen were made of had been correct. 'Look, why don't you come and work for me?'

'I'm in the retail trade now and you haven't got a shop,' Moishe countered, but a flicker of interest crossed his expression.

'I could use a good salesman all the same.'

Moishe glanced at Sammy who was standing with his arm around Miriam, talking to the Lenskys. 'Sammy's your salesman, isn't he? You're not telling me business is good enough to have two right now?'

'He deals with customers who come to the factory,' David explained. He had elevated his brother to this position because he was unsuited to any of the more technical jobs as had been the case when he was a boy. But what it amounted to in reality was Sammy displaying the garments whilst David conducted the sales talk. 'I need a travelling salesman,' he told Moishe. 'How would you fancy it?'

'All over the country, you mean?'

'Wherever you can sell my coats. It's up to you.'

Moishe's eyes lit up, he enjoyed a challenge. Then he looked cagey. 'What will I earn?'

'That's up to you as well.'

'Plus expenses?'

'Sure, but I'll want them in black and white.'

'You think I'm a fiddler, David?' Moishe said indignantly.

David grinned. 'Why d'you think I'm expecting great things of you?'

Moishe was not sure whether to react to the insult or the compliment, but David had intended neither. His bluntness was something to which his employees had to accustom themselves. He always spoke the unembellished truth, letting them know where they stood with him.

'It takes *chutspah* to be a fiddler,' he added. 'And that's what ninety percent of selling people what they maybe don't want is.'

Moishe was well aware he possessed the special combination of cheek and nerve which no English word could quite describe and had to laugh.

'But people will want my garments, wait till you see what I'm turning out, and they'll get even better,' David assured him confidently. 'Listen, business has got to improve, how much worse can things get? And there're still folk around with enough money they don't have to go naked, especially in what they call the county towns. That's why I'm making smarter coats, for the ladies who can still afford them. So what do you say, Moishe? If you come in now, while the factory's still small, maybe your commission won't be so big, but you could end up sales manager of a large concern one of these days. The sky's the limit, believe me!'

The shrewd little man did believe him. David's purposeful gaze left no room for doubt. And a man who would marry Bessie Salaman to get where he wanted had to be admired as well as sympathised with. 'It's a deal, David,' he said decisively. 'I'll give my notice in at the shop tomorrow.'

Sarah banked up the kitchen fire with damp slack so she would not have to relight it in the morning and sighed as she turned out the gaslight. Weddings should bring pleasure to a family, she thought as she went upstairs to bed, but the day she'd just put behind her she wished she could forget. Two sons married in the same year and both of them to the wrong girl. No, Bessie was

231

right for David, even if he didn't know it yet. But Miriam would never be right for any of them. Why had Sammy brought her into the family? Now there were two Sandberg daughters-in-law who hated each other. And Sammy's marriage had done nothing to heal the breach between the Moritzes and herself and Abraham. She'd hoped that under the *chupah*, when their children were being united before God, the feeling of togetherness would embrace all of them, but Sigmund had kept his eyes averted and Rachel – poor Rachel! It had been a shock to see what the sickness had done to her, she'd sat limply in a bath chair and had only once looked in Sarah's direction. Even at home, when they had had to speak to each other briefly, their eyes had not met.

'You worry too much, Sarah!' Abraham grunted when she entered their bedroom without looking at him. He was always the one who had to suffer for her feelings!

'Who will worry if I don't?' she retorted.

'Perhaps it's you who sometimes makes the worries!' he snapped back. 'You want to live everyone's life for them.'

Sarah recoiled as if he had slapped her face. 'Is that what you think of me?'

'Maybe,' he muttered afraid he had said too much.

Sarah unpinned her brooch and laid it carefully in the little box Sammy had made for her, then she began to undress, her fingers fumbling with the fasteners on her frock, which was the one she had worn for David's wedding. 'You think a mother should stop caring about her children when they grow up?' she asked tremulously.

'Don't cry,' Abraham begged. 'All I need right now is for you to cry.'

'Since when am I a crier?' she said blinking back the tears.

He had not seen her weep for years. 'So when you do I know it's for something.'

'And shall I tell you what the something is? We'll have trouble in our own family now Miriam is Sammy's wife. As if we didn't have enough with how things are between us and her parents.'

'You're getting like Bessie Salaman.'

'Who is now Bessie Sandberg. And how am I getting like her? A plump lady I'll never be.'

'You haven't noticed how she lets her mind run away with her and makes a great big hoo-ha out of nothing? And once she's made it, it's there for everyone to see, when it wasn't there before. Why don't you take a leaf out of your old book, Sorrel?'

The intimate name softened her and she let him put his arm around her when she got into bed, which she had not intended to do. 'What old book is that?' But she knew.

'See all and say nothing, until there's really something to say it about.' He stroked her hair gently. 'Me, I do it all the time. And who did I learn it from? You.'

He turned out the light and they lay side by side in the warm darkness, beneath the *perineh* they had brought from Russia eighteen years ago.

'I'm forty-three already,' Sarah said softly. 'And you're forty-eight.'

'Whenever there's a Bar Mitzvah, or a wedding or a birth in the family she reminds me of how old I am!'

'That's when you notice that the years have passed by.' Sarah sighed thinking about it. 'Once you held me in your arms and loved me every night.'

'I love you still.'

'But like that not too often.'

'You're complaining?'

'I'm not complaining. Whatever's happened with you has happened with me also.'

Abraham chuckled. 'What's happened with both of us is middle age.' He stifled a yawn. 'And who can have the strength for everything?'

'Even those who have, their children would take it away from them!'

'Go to sleep, Sorrel. I've got a big day tomorrow. David's turning the factory upside down, he's making a new pressing room and he wants me to advise him.'

'Who else but you would he ask? An expert and also his father.' Sarah turned on her side and tried to settle, but she could not. 'So I'll see all and say nothing. What good is it when my daughter-in-law Bessie won't do the same? One day she'll make a hoo-ha and a half if I don't stop her.'

233

Oy vay, poor Bessie, Abraham thought before he fell asleep. He had not yet met the person who was a match for Sarah.

'You're paying your layabout brother good money so a certain person won't go short!' Bessie shrieked at David the moment he arrived home from work. She never referred to Miriam by name and since Moishe had joined the staff, doing what she felt should be Sammy's work, had begun referring to her often.

There was sufficient truth in the accusation to cause David to avert his eyes. But how could he let Sammy, with his lame leg, drag a case loaded with samples around the country? He did not say this to Bessie, or tell her what she already knew, that his brother was useless as a salesman, but kissed her cheek as if her outburst had not occurred.

'*Shmoozer*!' she flung at him as she waddled into the kitchen where the table was laid for supper. She lifted the pan of soup onto the fire to bring it to the boil. 'But you can't *shmooze* me!'

'Calm down, love. It's bad for the baby,' David said soothingly.

'Everything's bad for the baby, but nothing's bad for me!' she retorted.

David walked through to the scullery to wash his hands and stared at his strained reflection in the mirror above the sink. Bessie had thought him crazy when he had insisted on hanging a mirror in every room, but he had not tried to explain, knowing she wouldn't understand. She hadn't understood about the orange-box when he'd tried to tell her what it meant to him and had only agreed to have it in a corner of their bedroom when he'd said he wouldn't sleep there without it.

Their lovemaking had slackened off during her pregnancy and was now nonexistent because the baby was due soon. The cessation had not severed the bond between them entirely, their unborn child still held them together. But David was now aware of a lack in his marriage which he had not felt too painfully until there was nothing to compensate for it. Throbbing inside him was a part of his being he could not share with his wife, the emotional motivation which inspired his material ambition and made him determined to prove his worth despite the obstacles life had

234

set him. The orange-box was the only memento of the past he had allowed himself, an ever-present reminder of his humble beginnings. The mirrors proved he was on his way.

They weren't the only things that proved it, he thought as he combed his hair before the one above the scullery sink. The house he and Bessie had chosen for their home was pleasantly situated near the Bellott Street park, in Cheetham Hill. No factories darkened the skyline here. The park was minute, but its greenness heaven to behold and the terraced houses were set back from the street, each in its own patch of garden. Cheetham Hill was the new ghetto, but apart from its predominantly Jewish residents bore no resemblance to the grey vista of Strangeways. To David it was the first rung of the ladder he had set out to climb.

The house was airy and spacious, with ornately carved cornices in the high-ceilinged rooms, painted gilt by a previous tenant, and mahogany surrounds framing the fireplaces. Panes of stained glass adorned the front door and upstairs there was not only a bathroom, but a separate lavatory perched like a throne on a dais beneath the window.

Bessie had asked her father to live with them, but he would not move from the factory premises in case someone burgled them at night, for which David was immensely thankful.

'So what's your brother done to earn his wages today?' Bessie resumed her attack immediately David sat down for supper.

He wanted to yell at her, tell her to shut up, but mindful of her condition said nothing.

'Without your generosity they wouldn't be living round here!' she said sharply.

David and Bessie paid 12s 6d a week to rent their superior home, but Bessie did not begrudge it. Miriam and Sammy's rent was 7s 6d and their house accordingly less grand, but knowing they were able to live in Cheetham Hill incensed her. She set a bowl of soup in front of David angrily, spilling some on her snowy cloth. 'Now look what you've made me do! As if my back isn't aching enough from being pregnant, I'll have to stand at the sink tomorrow scrubbing the stain you've made me make!'

David picked up his napkin to mop the soup from the tablecloth, but she snatched it from his hand.

'He wants to ruin the napkin, too!'

He thought of his mother's homely kitchen, where they had all crowded around the small table, leaning their elbows on it while they chatted after the meal, which his wife would not allow him to do. In Moreton Street they hadn't had napkins, but who needed them? There'd been none at the Salaman's table, either, when he was courting Bessie. But marriage was her incentive to refine her lifestyle. She had become more fastidious about her appearance, which he welcomed, and always laid the table carefully with the good china they'd received as a wedding gift from her Auntie Rivka, a lady with the same delusions of grandeur Bessie was acquiring. You can't have it both ways, he told himself wryly. It went hand in hand with wanting a mansion in Cheshire.

Bessie had reset his cutlery at the other side of the table and was putting an upturned plate between the damp linen and the polished surface which nobody ever saw because she kept it covered with a red chenille square. She returned to her chair and sat down with a thump, glaring balefully at him. 'What's a certain person done to deserve a house round here? I'll tell you what. Married David Sandberg's crippled brother because she wasn't rich enough to get him!'

David got up and strode into the front parlour. One more word and he would be out of the house! Through the window he could see a boy and girl sitting on a bench in the park with their arms around each other, in the quiet dusk. Why had he listened to his head instead of to his heart? But Miriam had given him no peace, either. Her disapproval of everything he was had eaten into his pride like dripping water relentlessly pitting a pebble. He turned from the window and saw Bessie standing in the doorway, her eyes imploring forgiveness.

'I didn't mean it, David. I'll never say anything like that again.'

'You might as well say it, if you think it.' Her self-induced hysteria latched on to everything. She would never change.

'It's because I'm not pretty,' she told him piteously, 'I'm frightened you'll leave me.'

He looked at her squat figure, the hand wearing the wedding ring he had put there resting upon the mound of her stomach which held his child. 'I'll never leave you, Bessie.'

236

She flung herself upon him, covering his face with kisses and that night they slept in each other's arms and were closer in spirit than they had been for a long time.

Three weeks later their baby boy was born dead and Bessie was inconsolable. Her Auntie Rivka moved into the house to look after her and David was left in no doubt as to why Uncle Aaron had taken to the bottle.

'My poor dollink niece, she should only be well and have a hundred more children, blames the tragedy on aggravation,' she announced dramatically one evening, returning downstairs with the invalid's supper tray.

Uncle Aaron cast his bleary eye on the plate from which Bessie had consumed every morsel of a large portion of pot roast and potatoes. 'Aggravation should only give me such an appetite!'

'For a liquid diet, who needs an appetite?' Auntie Rivka removed a half-empty bottle of whisky from under his red-veined nose. 'God alone knows what a married woman has to put up with!' Her long-suffering gaze moved to David. 'So what's this aggravation my poor niece keeps talking about? Don't tell me! It's enough that she has it.'

She began serving a meal to David and her husband, her fat lips pursed censoriously, every bulge in her well-corseted body quivering with righteous indignation.

David wanted to remind her that he too had been bereft of a son. For nights he had been unable to sleep, haunted by remembrance of the little white face, its features perfect in death. He had not even been allowed the comfort of sharing his grief with Bessie. Auntie Rivka had banished him to the kitchen sofa and was sleeping with her niece. At other times, the domineering woman stationed herself like a sentry at the bedside, preventing David from being alone with his wife.

'A girl who's expecting can do without aggravation like that.' She eyed David accusingly as they began eating.

David put down his fork. 'Like what?'

A nice gratitude he gives me for taking care of his sick wife,' she told Uncle Aaron. 'Like what my poor niece didn't say,' she informed David and carried her plate of food upstairs to escape from the enemy camp.

'So what can you do?' Uncle Aaron sighed commiserating as much with himself as with David; he had accepted defeat a long time ago. He picked some meat from between his dentures, which he would not have dared do in his wife's presence, then went to the sideboard to fetch his bottled comfort. 'I'll pour you a *shnapps*, David. It'll help you to forget.'

David shook his head. It was Bessie who needed to forget. The unspecified aggravation was rooted in the past, as always. Miriam.

CHAPTER TWELVE

There was much to occupy David's mind in addition to his traumatic homelife. Industrial strife was affecting the garment trade no less than others and though Salaman's was still not a union shop, some of the newer employees thought it should be.

David was unaware of this until he found them conducting a heated discussion in the pressing room, during the morning tea break. Abraham was drinking his tea with Eli and the agitators had the room to themselves. They stopped talking when David entered.

'So what's going on in here you don't want me to know about?' he joked, but sensed that whatever was afoot might not be a joking matter.

The three youths exchanged a glance. Jake and Mendel were machiners. Maxie was one of the underpressers.

'We'll tell you when there's something to tell, Mr Sandberg,' Mendel said brusquely.

David was taken aback by his antagonistic expression. He knew Mendel had been to high school like himself, that his education had been cut short for the same economic reasons, but boys to whom this happened were not rarities in Strangeways. He glanced at the book Mendel had in his hand with the instinctive interest books always aroused in him. 'What's that you're reading?'

The lad handed it to him defiantly, as if the question was a challenge; it was a copy of Engels' *Condition of the Working Class in England*.

'I see,' David said pleasantly, handing it back. But he felt that some kind of gauntlet had been thrown down and that Mendel was waiting for him to pick it up.

Jake and Maxie had dropped their eyes, sheepishly, but Mendel met David's gaze steadily. Is he trying to get my back up? David thought. The lad's lips had a downward curl at the corners and he seemed to be eaten up by an inner fire. It was there in the aggressive thrust of his chin, the way his sharp nose looked pinched at the tip.

'I'd like to read that book sometime,' David told him.

'Be a good idea if you did, Mr Sandberg.'

David glanced at his watch to put an end to the conversation, which felt like a confrontation, and the youths left the room. Mendel's receding back was as defiant as his face had been.

It was the first time David had experienced tension when talking to his workers and a feeling of disquiet assailed him. It was soon replaced by anger that they had made him feel that way. There was no shortage of machiners and pressers looking for jobs and his first impulse was to dismiss the three of them. Then his innate sense of justice prevailed. What had they done to deserve dismissal? Make him think trouble was in the air, and prevention was easier than cure. He stood beside his father's ironing board thinking it over.

'You've found something wrong with my work?' Abraham asked when he returned and found him staring down at a half-pressed coat which was draped on the board.

David turned on him hotly. 'How could you be in here all day with Maxie and not know something's going on?'

'What's going on?' Abraham parried.

'You tell me! Nobody talks to me anymore it seems. I'm only the boss.'

Abraham lit the gas jets to heat his irons, avoiding David's eye. 'So some of them want to join the union, maybe,' he said casually.

'Why didn't you tell me before?'

'You haven't got enough on your plate right now? With Bessie and everything? I should worry you more?'

David stormed back to the office cubicle he had had erected in a corner of the workroom. Immediately after returning from his honeymoon, he had engaged a firm of builders to reconstruct the factory layout. Salaman now slept downstairs and the bedrooms he and Bessie had occupied were part of the extended workspace.

Neat rails of samples, which buyers could examine when they called, stood at one end of the room in the uncluttered area where the cutting bench was situated. The sewing machines had been rearranged symmetically in rows and David was able to supervise the machiners through a pane of glass in his office wall. It was not the factory he intended to have eventually, but a vast improvement on the chaos over which his father-in-law had reigned and would do to be going on with.

Abraham came to eat lunch with him in the office that day, though he usually ate with the lonely Salaman. He was apprehensive about the effect of the latest anxiety upon his son.

'Look at those troublemakers!' David pointed his pickled cucumber at the three youths who sat munching their food with their heads together, in a corner.

Abraham separated two slabs of blackbread to see what was inside them. 'Cream cheese again, your mother thinks it's good for me. Why do you call them troublemakers?' he said tentatively.

David's reply was caustic. 'What would you call them?'

Abraham thought carefully, no better equipped for mental concentration than he had ever been.

'Well?' David barked.

But his father was not to be hurried into saying what perhaps he did not really mean. 'Boys who are sticking up for their rights,' he pronounced.

David was outraged. 'Since when do they need to? With me for a boss?'

Abraham eyed him warily. 'You'll think I'm a communist if I say any more to you.' He ate some of his sandwich, with a faraway look on his face. 'Times are changing, David. There could be a Labour Government in England soon, like never happened before.'

David glared through the glass panel at Mendel and his two henchmen, which was how he had begun to think of them. 'Is that what's making them so cocky?'

'Listen, Ramsay MacDonald, he's a godsend to the workers. He could do great things for them.'

'If I didn't know you can't read English, I'd think you'd been borrowing Mendel's books, Father!'

Abraham chuckled. 'So I didn't go to night school like your mother. She can do the reading for both of us.'

David turned his back on the glass panel and ate some of his lunch, though he was not hungry.

His father studied him surreptitiously, noting the new shadows beneath his eyes and the deep groove above the bridge of his nose, put there by anxiety and tension. His resemblance to his mother was more striking then ever, she too had begun to look older than her years at David's age. It was what responsibility did to some people.

'Even when you were a lad you were a boss, David,' he said wryly. 'Coming in here straight from school and telling Salaman what to do!'

'He needed telling.'

'Such a *chutspah* you had! You never thought like a worker. Me, that's what I've been all my life. And before I found this job, I saw conditions elsewhere to make your hair stand on end. This place, even in the old days, was a Buckingham Palace compared to how some factories still are.'

'There aren't enough factory inspectors to cope with the job, Father.'

'With you they don't need any.'

David thought of all he had done to improve conditions for the staff; yet it seemed there were some who were not satisfied! In addition to the structural alterations, the whole place had been thoroughly cleaned and a new lavatory installed with a handbasin beside it. The whole hour for lunch was also one of his innovations. Contented workers meant better output, as he'd told Salaman when he protested about the capital outlay, but David had turned a deaf ear to his father-in-law's grumbles. He'd learnt from Bessie that her father was not just a tenant, but owned the house and also those on either side of it and the revelation had excited him. Sooner or later he would acquire the adjoining property and extend the factory further. After that would come a brand new building. His mind had galloped ahead, plotting and planning. What Abraham had just said made him think of it again. His father was right, he had always thought like a boss. From the day he entered the factory at the age of fourteen. Never like a worker.

He bit into the apple which Auntie Rivka said a healthy man must eat for his bowels every day. 'I look after my workers, don't I Father?'

'And the ones who've been here a long time and known you since you were a boy trust you, David. For the others it's different, they don't trust bosses. How do they know you won't change? Or maybe sell the factory some day? To someone not like yourself, who will exploit them like they saw happen to their fathers? Like is still happening, believe me. And for the coal miners, Maxie my underpresser says it's terrible.'

'To hell with what Maxie says!'

David had never sworn in Abraham's presence before and his father looked shocked.

'What've the coal miners got to do with machiners and pressers, Father?'

The question was beyond Abraham. He knew what he was trying to tell David, but was unable to express it. 'A worker is a worker,' he shrugged. It was the best he could do.

And a boss is a boss, David thought glancing at the clock to make sure the lunch break had not over run the allotted hour. There were still ten minutes left. 'All right, Father. So maybe they have to band together to get better conditions and wages sometimes,' he conceded.

Abraham looked relieved. It was what he had been trying to say.

'But not in my factory,' David added emphatically.

'Of course not in your factory,' his father echoed, hoping there would be no trouble with those who thought otherwise.

After Abraham had returned to the pressing room, David could not concentrate on the designs he was making for a new range. Moishe had interested buyers as far south as Cheltenham and this was keeping the factory going, boosting the flagging local trade. Though David was no artist, he had a keen eye for the subtle detail which lifted a garment from the run-of-the-mill and his rough sketches were usually easy for Eli to follow through. Today they were hopeless and he flung down his pencil in disgust.

He could see Mendel and Jake busy at their machines. Ought he to dismiss them, or not? Times were changing as his father had said and a Labour government would lend strength to the unions. If he sacked his three troublemakers it would not stop the snowball from rolling, others would come in their place.

What had he got against the unions? He agreed with what they were fighting for, but other manufacturers, with union shops, had told him what this meant in effect. Rules and regulations which had to be strictly observed. Everyone going on strike if just one worker had a grievance, because grievances were taken to the shop steward instead of directly to the boss. A union shop would mean the end of the family feeling which even in bad times had always been present in the Salaman workroom. And delegation of authority to hostile hands.

A few days later the matter came to a head. A representative of the Tailors and Garment Workers' Union, which had been formed in 1920 and was the strongest organisation the trade had ever had, called and asked permission to hold a meeting in the workroom. David saw Mendel's satisfied smile when the man entered the office and guessed it was his doing, but did not refuse the request.

'Don't worry, David. I'll tell you everything that goes on,' Abraham assured him.

'How can you attend it? You're the boss's father.'

His father looked as if he had been deprived of a privilege and David had to laugh. 'You joined the enemy when I married Bessie!'

'But we were both workers before then and easy for us it wasn't,' Abraham reminded him. 'Even though one of us thought like a boss.'

The meeting was held during the lunch hour and they went downstairs to eat with Salaman, whose sister Rivka sent food for him every day as Bessie had previously done. The overbearing woman was still in residence cosseting her niece, thought it was now three months since the dead child was born.

David sat listening to his father-in-law upbraid him for what was taking place upstairs, but could not make the effort to defend himself.

'Give the workers an inch and they want a mile!' Salaman told Abraham adapting the cliché to his own exaggerated requirements. 'Before my son-in-law showed them the way, what did they know from better conditions? Tea breaks? Higher wages and excuse me, new lavatories? Mr Ramsay MacDonald should God forbid be the next prime minister they'll soon take over the building!' He cast a baleful glance at David, as though the prospect of a Labour government had been brought about by him personally. 'What kind of lavatories, excuse me, do they have at home? And newspaper they, excuse me, wipe their behinds on, not like the luxury we give them here!' David's purchase of toilet rolls had been the final straw to him and he had still not reconciled himself to good money being flushed down the drain.

The tirade continued, but washed over David. His father's reminder that they had once been working class had lodged in his brain. He had never really thought about class as such before. Of how it set people on either side of a barrier. Made them enemies. Did he feel different from the people he employed? Most of whom he'd known for years and years. When he was a boy, there'd just been the Jews and the Gentiles, the former struggling to establish themselves in the latter's country. That had been the difference between himself and Jim Forrest. But suddenly there were two kinds of Jews and the realisation shocked him. Those who were not his kind would never need to arm themselves against him, but now he was able to understand why some of them thought they must and did not blame them. The unions were their insurance for the future, as the acquisition of wealth would be his.

'If they want a union shop they're entitled to it,' he said cutting into something Salaman was saying and watched him turn blue in the face.

For several days the workroom seethed with debate, but David shut his eyes and ears to it. He had come to terms with himself and the situation and would make the best of it as he had done with everything else.

It was Eli who brought him the workers' decision. He looked up from some statements he was preparing and saw the cutter standing in the office doorway with his thumbs tucked into the pockets of his shiny serge waistcoat.

'I've got good news for you, David,' he said without bothering to step inside. Wasting time and breath was not his nature and in his view plenty had been wasted upon all this. 'We're not going to be a union shop. Who needs trouble?'

He returned to his bench without further ado, but not before David had noted the gleam of triumph in his eyes. Eli was as pleased about the outcome as he was.

David had expected Mendel to be the spokesman; he would surely have been the shop steward had the vote gone the other way. Eli telling him informally warmed his heart and he realised how much the family feeling among them all meant to him, that he'd dreaded the inevitable loss of it more than anything else.

At the end of the week Mendel gave in his notice.

'I've got nothing against you, you're entitled to your opinions,' David told him. 'What've you got against me?'

The intense youth looked at him contemptuously, but did not reply. Later, Jake and Maxie left, too, and David learned that all three had got jobs in a big factory which was a union shop. He put them from his mind, but something told him it would not be the last he would hear of Mendel.

Sarah stepped off the tram on Waterloo Road and pulled her scarf closer around her neck, to protect it against the March wind. Coats and scarves were not as warm as the shawl she used to wear. She crossed the road carefully, looking to the left and the right. There were more motor cars about, nowadays, lorries, too, and Abraham was always telling her to mind the road.

She had never travelled on a tram unaccompanied before, but had enjoyed the feeling of independence, paying her own fare and chatting with the lady sitting beside her. The tram began its journey in town and had been full when it reached her stop, but a young Gentile had offered her his seat. In Russia he would have expected me to get up for him, she had reflected dryly, and a nice kick I'd have got to remind me. She rarely thought of those days anymore, but occasionally something would occur to prod her memory, making her want to laugh or cry.

She turned the corner into Bellott Street, admiring the tall, terraced houses, some with privet hedges springing from behind the low, brick wall. Until last year, there had been no reason for her to venture beyond the perimeters of Strangeways, but now two of her sons lived in this pleasant neighbourhood and she was proud that they did.

Her expression tightened as she rapped on David's front door, letting the brass knocker bang three times. Her hand came away dirty from the contact and she glanced down at the steps which had not been donkey-stoned for some time. When a woman lost pride in the outside appearance of her home, what was going on inside her heart?

Auntie Rivka opened the door and raised her eyebrows. 'Today you're visiting us, Mrs Sandberg? So when do you clean your *Shabbos* chicken and chop your fish?'

Sarah would have to stay up half the night to complete these tasks. No Jewish housewife ever had time for social calls on a

Thursday, but she had wanted to come when David was not at home and no other ladies would be there. She smiled without replying, noting Auntie Rivka's use of the word 'us', which confirmed her suspicion that Salaman's sister considered herself part of David's household.

Auntie Rivka led the way into the kitchen.

'How are you keeping, Mrs Finkel?' Sarah inquired politely, sitting down in David's wing chair to remind his aunt-in-law of her own position in the family.

'Only middling, Mrs Sandberg.' The heavy woman lowered herself with difficulty onto the sofa, pushing aside the blankets David used when he slept there at night. She sighed wearily. 'Such a load I've got on my shoulders! But what can you do? Can I walk out and leave my own brother's motherless child?'

'I heard your daughter moved to Liverpool last year. So how is she?'

'How can she be with a husband like that? Who takes her to live away from her mother?'

David had told Sarah that if he were Auntie Rivka's son-in-law Liverpool would not be far enough.

'And Bessie? She's no better?'

'She'll never be better. What can you do?'

Sarah picked up the shopping bag she had with her and went upstairs to see her daughter-in-law. Auntie Rivka was right behind her, wheezing as she climbed the stairs.

'The poor little dollink looks terrible,' Auntie Rivka said when they entered the bedroom.

Sarah thought Bessie looked healthier than they did, but was careful not to say so. Everybody should have such a nice long rest, petted and pampered! But something had to be wrong before they would want to. 'So, Bessie,' she said cheerfully.

'I'm not feeling too good today, Ma.' All Sarah's children-in-law called her Ma. Ben, the first, had set the pattern.

'Who can feel good when they never breathe the fresh air? There's such a nice breeze outside this afternoon, you should take a stroll with me across the road to the park.'

Auntie Rivka looked at Sarah as if she had taken leave of her senses. 'You want her to get pneumonia?'

'Before pneumonia she'd have to catch a cold, and wrapped up warm in the fur coat she bought for her trousseau, she wouldn't catch one.'

Bessie's aunt sat tight-lipped on the only chair in the room, her folded arms resting on the table of her bosom.

Sarah was still standing. 'An invalid she isn't,' she said pleasantly.

Bessie slid lower beneath the *perineh* and closed her eyes to prove she was.

'She had a stillborn child is all,' Sarah added in the same casual tone sitting down on the edge of the bed.

A tear rolled down Bessie's cheek, then a great sob engulfed her.

'To come here and mention it, Mrs Sandberg!' Auntie Rivka rose from her chair belligerently.

'I'm entitled to come to my son's house, Mrs Finkel. And it's time somebody mentioned it.'

'My poor little baby,' Bessie gulped.

Auntie Rivka was outraged. 'All this time I don't let my poor niece break her heart! What good will it do? I tell her. It won't bring back the child, better not to think about it. And now what does her mother-in-law do?'

Bessie looked at Sarah wanly. 'Auntie's right, Ma.'

'Your auntie is always right, dollink. If my own dollink daughter had only taken her mother's advice, she wouldn't be married to that dogsbody and living in another town with my three dollink grandchildren.'

'Your auntie is wrong, Bessie,' Sarah said after the lengthy interruption. 'What are tears for but to wash away sorrow? And how can a person forget, if first they don't let themselves remember? The way to forget sadness is to put joy in its place. You should have another child, Bessie.'

'With the aggravation her husband gives her, how can she?' Auntie Rivka took up her customary position by the bed with a protective hand on Bessie's shoulder, as she had on Sarah's last visit.

Sarah's eyes were like daggers. How dare this interloper insult her beloved son whom everyone respected? 'You mean with you sleeping beside her every night in his place how can she!'

...,' Bessie said pitifully. The confrontation taking place
... head was too much for her and she was frightened by its
...ensity. 'Maybe you should go home now, Ma, before it gets
dark.'

'A good idea,' Auntie Rivka rasped.

Sarah moved to the chair and settled herself comfortably.
'Nobody is waiting to hit me on the head and steal my purse. And
I'm not in a hurry.' She would not leave until Bessie was ready to
begin living again. She had made up her mind about this when
she decided to come and too much was at stake for the mission to
fail. Also, she knew the stillborn child alone was not responsible
for the disaster David's marriage had become after little more than
a year.

'How old are you now, Bessie?' she asked putting a thoughtful
expression on her face.

'You know how old I am, Ma.'

'I'm sitting here thinking is it possible my daughter-in-law
Bessie is still only twenty-three, when she looks ten years older
than my daughter-in-law Miriam already.'

Bessie got out of bed to study her face in the mirror as Sarah
had known she would.

'You should be lying down, dollink! Your poor legs are so
weak,' Auntie Rivka protested.

'Weak with not walking,' Sarah added.

But Bessie was not listening to them. She turned to Sarah
anxiously. 'I'm six months younger than Miriam, Ma.'

'And if you put on one of your smart frocks, which she can't
afford, and comb your hair the way you used to you'd maybe
look it.'

Bessie sat down on the bed, but she did not get back into it.
Sarah had stirred her fighting blood as she had cunningly intended.

'Does Miriam ever take Sammy's dinner to the factory, Ma?
Like I sometimes took David's?'

'How do I know?' Sarah shrugged stirring it more. But she did
not want to pursue this tactic until she had softened it with the
next one. She took a package from her shopping bag. 'Here,
Bessie. Something to *nosh*.'

Bessie opened it eagerly, sweetmeats were still her only comfort.

'Your sister-in-law sent it.'

She eyed the Sachertorte as if it might be laced with poison.

Miriam had brought the cake to the Sandbergs' when she and Sammy visited them the previous Saturday and Sarah had asked if she minded a slice being given to Bessie to cheer her up. Saying Miriam had sent it wasn't really a lie, she told herself.

'Tell her thank you,' Bessie said biting into it. Her sweet tooth had won.

'You'll tell her yourself next time you see her. They come to me every *Shabbos* for tea. And this week David'll come because it's my birthday.'

Bessie stopped eating and stiffened.

'If you feel well enough he'll bring you with him.'

'They'll carry her back on a stretcher if she walks from Cheetham Hill to Strangeways,' Auntie Rivka moaned.

'So I'll go by tram, God will forgive me for riding on *Shabbos* after all I've been through,' Bessie said. Only over her dead body would David be in Miriam's presence without her! And her aunt was getting on her nerves. 'Why don't you go downstairs and peel the potatoes for supper, Auntie? I'll set the table myself.'

'She orders me about like a servant!'

Sarah maintained a diplomatic silence, she knew when to hold her tongue.

'After all I've done for her!'

'I'm very grateful, Auntie, but I didn't ask you to do it,' Bessie reminded her, getting her best dress out of the wardrobe.

The misguided woman's expression crumpled into distress. Why did her good deeds always reap this kind of reward? But her pride had been hurt as well as her feelings and she regarded her niece coldly. 'You're better enough to go downstairs and set the table, you can peel the potatoes also, I've got a house of my own to look after. Your uncle will come for my things.'

She left the room without glancing at Sarah and a few minutes later they heard her slam the front door.

Bessie stood in her nightdress looking suddenly lost. Auntie Rivka was the rock she had leaned upon for months. 'Stay for supper, Ma,' she pleaded, afraid she would be unable to cope alone after doing nothing for so long.

Sarah felt sorry for her, but staying would not be in accordance with what she had come here to do. 'You can give David a boiled egg to eat tonight,' she said kindly. 'It'll be better than a banquet to him, believe me, as long as you're there at the table with him, well again.'

Before leaving, she went into the kitchen with Bessie and pointed to the blankets on the sofa. 'Those you can put away in the cupboard now. And take my advice, let them stay there.' She kissed her daughter-in-law's cheek. 'While a man sleeps in his wife's bed every night nothing can go wrong.'

The next day, David took his sandwiches to eat at his mother's house in the dinner break.

Sarah gave him a bowl of soup to go with them. 'So how come you've left the factory to look after itself?'

'I wanted to see you on your own.'

'Yes?'

'Yes! What did you say to Bessie?'

'Who me?'

David laughed. 'I got a *feinkochen* for supper last night, but who cares!'

'She took the trouble to beat up the egg and fry it in butter is a good sign. To boil is easier.'

David put down his soup spoon and studied her placid face. 'How did you get her to dress and go downstairs? And don't pretend it wasn't your doing. Auntie Rivka gave up.'

'Auntie Rivka!' Sarah exclaimed dismissively.

'And how did you get rid of her?'

'He wants to know all his mother's secrets,' she smiled.

'Bessie said you didn't tell her to go, she went because she wanted to.'

'It's true.'

That was all Sarah told him and he never found out exactly what had transpired that afternoon, or that she had plotted it carefully in advance, move by move. But David was too overjoyed that his life was back on an even keel to care how it had happened. Living with Bessie was still not happiness, but not having to live in isolation any more made him thankful for what he had.

PART THREE:
CONSEQUENCES

CHAPTER ONE

Sarah's formidable reputation was enhanced by the ejection of Auntie Rivka from David's life. When the family teased her about it she would laugh with them, but her private thoughts she kept to herself. Being a mother didn't get easier when your children left the nest, the way you'd imagined it would when they were still young. You no longer had to cook and clean for them, but their problems were still yours.

Sometimes she thought about this at her *Shabbos* tea parties, when she looked at Esther with two small boys tugging at her skirts and a baby girl on her lap. Miriam and Bessie were mothers now, too, and Sarah would listen to the three of them discussing their infants' teething troubles as if this was the biggest worry in the world and smile to herself because their real worries hadn't begun yet.

But if being a mother was sometimes painful, to be a grandma was ecstasy. 'So!' she said with satisfaction from behind her teapot one *Shabbos* afternoon. 'Just look at those beautiful babies!'

'1924 was a very good year for our family,' David laughed.

Sigmund's eyes twinkled behind his pince-nez. 'In more ways than one!' He eyed his chubby grandson whom Miriam was cuddling on her lap. 'Without our Martin would we all be here like this together again?'

'You had to come to your senses sometime.' Sarah could never resist telling him so.

'I never lost them!' he retorted as he always did. 'I only made it up with you for Martin's sake, so he wouldn't be saddled with grandparents not speaking to each other, like I told Abie when I spoke to him at the *Brith*.'

'Sure you did,' Abraham said comfortably, exchanging a smile with Sarah and Rachel. They knew Martin's birth last September had been a welcome excuse for Sigmund to end the rift without losing face, but nobody expected him to admit it.

Sarah sipped her tea contentedly and watched Bessie lift the edge of little Shirley's diaper to show Miriam a patch of rash on the child's bottom. Children drew people closer as nothing else could and her daughters-in-law were now able to be in each other's company without strain, each fitting into her own place in the family.

'Who's a little angel?' Bessie cooed planting a kiss on Shirley's ginger head, happier than she had ever been in her life. Being the mother of David's child made her marriage feel secure and she exchanged a parental glance with him as the object of their mutual adoration threw her teething ring on the floor.

David hastened to retrieve it and give it back to her, shaking the silver bell attached to it to amuse her. She dropped it and gurgled when he bent down and picked it up again, not yet six months old but already aware her father was her willing slave.

Esther's baby was lying on the rug playing with her fingers, a grave expression on her tiny face. She did not smile much and her dark eyes always looked thoughtful. Marianne had come into the world with the umbilical cord twisted around her neck and according to medical opinion ought not to have been alive. At first she was considered delicate, no amount of feeding succeeded in transforming her into a chubby child; then it had occurred to Esther that her daughter was a minute replica of Sarah, whose birdlike proportions had always belied her strength. The resemblance became more marked as time went by and now everyone noticed it.

Sammy sat gazing affectionately at his wife and son, but Miriam seemed unaware of it. Her baby was the centre of her world and nothing else mattered. The inner glow, missing for so long, had returned to illuminate her lovely face and blazed like a lantern whenever she looked at Martin. She stroked the soft brown fuzz on his head, exulting that she now had someone she loved whom nobody could take away from her.

'Let Shirley and Martin lie on the rug with Marianne and kick their legs, it's good for them,' Esther instructed her sisters-in-law to whom she was the voice of experience.

The two babies set up a howl immediately and Marianne joined in.

'Such fancy names these little ones have got, I can't get used to it,' Sarah told Rachel above the din. The children had Jewish names also, to be used on religious occasions, but were called by the English ones on their birth certificates. 'Their parents think they'll grow up to be film stars!'

'A Charlie Chaplin in the family'd suit Dad fine,' Ben laughed.

'So I like the pictures,' Abraham defended himself. 'Everyone needs to relax.'

'Such a relaxation I can do without!' Sarah snorted. She had been to the cinema once and pronounced it a waste of time. 'Who needs to pay money to be made to laugh and cry and get nervous palpitations from seeing nice young girls tied to railway tracks?' She watched Bessie and Miriam lift their babies from the rug and was not surprised when Marianne was left to continue howling. Esther was a strict mother.

'How can you let her?' David reproached his sister.

'When she finds out it gets her nowhere she won't do it. Why d'you think my Harry and Arnold're so well behaved?' She glanced approvingly at her two little sons. Three-year-old Harry was shaking a cocoa tin full of dried peas to amuse Arnold. The Kleins had no money to spare for toys, but Ben, who had not had any when he was a child, made sure they were not short of improvised ones. 'There! What did I tell you?' Esther added triumphantly to David when Marianne's screams petered out.

'I thought she'd never stop!' Nathan exclaimed. Being uncle to five was something to boast about at school, but at home on Saturdays he would gladly have disowned them. He was sitting by the window reading *The Iliad*. Carl sat beside him and was also reading. They occupied the same spot every Saturday and it had become known in the family as 'bookworm's corner'.

Sigmund never read when Martin was there, but sat feasting his eyes on him.

Sarah got up to offer a dish of strudel and paused for a moment surveying the human web which the years had woven around her. How clever Nature was, the way she arranged things; a headful of red hair here, a short nose there and a long one somewhere else, mixing and blending this way and that, making each new person in some way or other the continuance of their line. And how could it happen that her grandson Martin had

Rachel's face? That David's Shirley looked nothing like him or Bessie, but resembled Esther? Who had decreed that Marianne would be the image of herself? The wonder and mystery of it overwhelmed her.

'What's the matter, Mother?' David asked when he saw the expression on her face.

'I was just having a little think.'

'Hm,' he said ominously and everyone laughed. Sarah's 'little thinks' could have shattering consequences.

'So, Rachel,' she said to her friend hiding the sorrow which welled up when she looked at her. She began refilling the many teacups. 'We've got a nice big family now, eh?'

Rachel smiled contentedly. Her own family had only been extended by the addition of a son-in-law and one baby boy, but she thought of the Moritzes and Sandbergs as a single clan, as they all did. She was now unable to walk and had to be wheeled to the Saturday gatherings in her bath chair, but her spirit still burned bright. 'The Almighty is good, Sarah,' she declared. He had given her a grandchild who'd brought them all together again.

'Sure He is, Rachel. And you'll soon be better, out of that chair and dancing again,' Sigmund told her.

'Since when did I dance?'

'So you won't dance, you'll make the Sachertorte. Helga's isn't as good as yours.'

Helga smiled stiffly as she always did when her father spoke to her mother this way, and continued playing with Esther's boys. She loved children, but life had dictated she wouldn't have any of her own and sometimes she thought of the marriage offers she'd had during her years of widowhood. One had been from Moishe Lipkin, whom she liked, but she knew she could never leave her mother. The chances had come and gone, but while she was needed she had no regrets. She saw Miriam glance at her and knew it was because their father was still going on with his ridiculous talk.

'Remember how you used to walk faster than me, Rachel?' Sigmund was saying. 'You'll do so again, my dear.'

Why doesn't he stop it? Miriam thought desperately. Mother knows she'll never walk again, she's accepted it. Why can't he? How did Helga bear it? Seeing Mother slipping away and Father pretending she wasn't really ill, never being able to forget it for a minute because she lived with them.

It was not just in his wife's presence that Sigmund maintained the pretence. From the beginning he had refused to admit she was seriously ill, joking and laughing as he had when Rachel first showed Sarah her trembling hands.

He had not changed his habits, or paid her more attention, but still sat immersed in his books while she lay on her sofa, as if she was only inert because she felt tired and would soon get up to pour him a cup of coffee. It was as though believing it would make it real, that denying it meant it was not the case. How he had explained to himself his wife's absence from their marital bed nobody knew. Helga heard him walking the floor every night, but passed no comment.

The family found his behaviour unnerving and his daughters suffered because of it. Only Rachel understood. The one concession he had made was to move house, so she could see more of her grandchild, but Miriam suspected he had agreed because it was what he wanted himself.

They now lived opposite her and she took Martin to visit them every day. But sometimes Sigmund would take him out in the pram whilst she did her housework and Helga would have to go looking for him if a customer arrived for a fitting.

David had moved his parents from Strangeways shortly after his daughter's birth. It was inconceivable to him not to have them nearby. He had found them a spacious home on Heywood Street, which stretched between two points on Cheetham Hill Road, and Sarah was momentarily speechless when she saw the three-storey house with a much larger front garden than David's. It had one at the back, too.

'All this for your father and Nat and me? You could fit six families into it,' she had exaggerated.

'What about Esther and Ben and their kids?' David had taken it for granted that his sister would continue living with them.

'They want a place of their own and why not?'

'So your grandchildren'll come to stay the night and fill the rooms. And I'll pay the rent.'

'You think your father would allow you to?'

'It's you who gives the man his money when he calls. Father doesn't have to know.'

The new house had a large dining room and David had bought an enormous table to be used when all the family came together for the Passover *Seder* and other Festivals. His mother had told him to return it to the shop, she did not own a cloth big enough for it. He bought her an enormous tablecloth instead; he was not going up in the world without taking his family with him, though the climb was not proving easy.

Sarah's Sabbath tea parties were held in the front parlour and Salaman's sofa was much sat upon these days.

'So how's business, David?' Ben asked when the women had gone to the kitchen to wash the dishes.

'How can it be?' David replied cryptically.

'People have to replace their crockery when they break it, but even for me it could be better,' Ben complained. 'The folk who come to Flat Iron Market these days only come to look, they don't have a penny to spare in their pockets.'

'A lot that Ramsay Mac did to make things better!' Abraham snorted.

Sigmund smiled. 'You expected him to, Abie?'

The Labour Government had been and gone, Mr Baldwin was currently beset by troubles with the miners and the economic climate abysmal. David had never been more glad the factory was not a union shop. His employees were on short time, but the personal bond between him and them had helped soften the blow. Nobody had called him a bloated plutocrat whose greed had brought about their plight, as was happening in other factories. They knew that when times were good again for him, they would also be good for them.

'Rome wasn't built in a day,' Carl said lifting his head from the *Manchester Guardian* which he had been perusing. Abraham's remark and his father's reply had just filtered through to him. Politics interested him, but he viewed them dispassionately as he did life and seemed to have no desire for active participation in either. 'It'll take years for real Socialism to come to this country.'

David, who did not want it to, cut the discussion short by turning his attention to Nathan. 'How's school going, Nat?'

259

Nathan looked hesitant.

'Not getting bad marks are you?'

'Could we go into the dining room, David? I have to talk to you.'

Nathan could not recall when he had first known for certain he didn't want to be a doctor. The sight of blood, or being with someone who was ill, always distressed him. He couldn't look at Rachel without feeling guilty because he was healthy and she was going to die. And the thought of cutting up a human body in order to learn how it functioned sickened him.

This was how the deepening conviction that medicine was not for him had begun, but lately something positive had been added to it. Latin and Greek were his best subjects and the head of the school classics department had spoken of entering him for an Oxford Scholarship. Manchester Grammar sent boys to Oxford and Cambridge every year, but it had not occurred to Nathan that this was within his reach.

For a week he had existed in a euphoria, seeing himself capped and gowned cycling beneath the dreaming spires. He would devote his life to Homer and Plato instead of to the dreaded Hippocrates. But he had arisen this morning gripped by apprehension. Medicine was the goal the family had set for him and today there would be the *Shabbos* tea party. How was he going to tell David?

Somehow he found the courage to do so.

David stood by the window looking out into the back garden, then drew the curtains across with a swift, sharp movement though it was not yet dark. He had listened without interrupting, but the stiffness of his stance prepared Nathan for the worst. He had not been scared of David since he was a small child, but the fear returned now and the drawn curtains made him feel shut in.

'Are you out of your mind?' David thundered.

'Please don't shout at me.'

'I'll do more than shout if necessary, to bring you down to earth! Latin and Greek of all of a sudden!'

'That isn't true, I've always loved Latin and Greek.'

'Suddenly he doesn't want to be a doctor!'

'That isn't true either, I've never wanted to be one.'

'Well let me tell you something we both know is true, Nat.'

David's voice had sunk to a low pitch which was more alarming than his shouts. 'The family've scrimped and sacrificed. All of us. Mother. Father. Esther. Sammy. Not to mention me. So you can be Dr Sandberg.

Nathan averted his eyes. This was the part that made things so difficult.

'What have you to say about that?'

'I appreciate it. But wouldn't it have been better to wait and find out what I wanted to be?'

David took an apple from the bowl of wax fruit on the table and stared at it. 'The scrimping and saving to educate you began the day you were born, Nat. Mother decided your schooling wouldn't be cut short like mine was.'

A small bell rang in Nathan's mind.

'Her youngest son was going to college if it took every farthing we'd got and in those days we had buggerall. I can remember Sammy and me walking round in shoes that let water in during the war, when we were all earning good money.'

'Why didn't Father mend them? He was a cobbler in Russia, wasn't he?'

'Have you any idea of how hard he had to work? All he was fit for at the end of a day in the pressing room was to flop into bed, it used to break my heart seeing him like that. But even if he'd had the energy, Mother wouldn't have let him spend money on leather to mend them with. She hoarded every penny for you. Other people had new this, new that, but not the Sandbergs. Times aren't good right now, but there's still something going into the bank for you every week. I see to that. Esther and Sammy stopped giving when they got married, but that doesn't mean they haven't got a share in you.'

Nathan had paled as David loaded the weight of responsibility onto him and the bell in his mind was still ringing. 'What d'you mean by a share in me?'

'A doctor's a somebody and Mother wants a somebody in the family. The rest of us won't mind having one, either.

'It's bleddy disgusting!'

'You'd better watch what you're saying, our kid!'

'Snobbery, that's what it is!'

'Is that how you see it?'

'Yes! I do!'

David polished the wax apple on the sleeve of his jacket and replaced it in the bowl. 'Well you haven't roughed it like the rest of us, have you, Nat?'

Nathan sat down and put his head in his hands.

David wanted to tell him what it was like to scrub the scaley slime off Mr Radinsky's fish counter every night so your family wouldn't go short of fruit and vegetables; to say goodbye to school when you were fourteen and spend your days in a hell-hole like Salaman's used to be; to have your hopes and dreams trampled to dust and be left with nothing but ambition. 'The somebody in our family might have been me,' was all he said.

Something in his voice made Nathan raise his head and look at him, then the bell in his mind awakened a long forgotten child-hood memory. He was sitting at the kitchen table in Moreton Street, kicking and screaming because nobody would tell him what had happened to David which could also happen to himself. He had not found out what it was until years later, when he'd learned his big brother had had to leave high school to work in a factory.

'It might have been me, but it's going to be you,' David said flatly.

'I'm not going to be a doctor. I can't.'

David had bent his own life with the wind of circumstances when everything he yearned for lay in the opposite direction and the sacrifice was being flung in his face. He grabbed Nathan by the shoulders. 'There's no such word as can't! Look at me, I'm a living example of it!'

'Let go of me, David!'

David was trembling with emotion. He dropped his hands and Nathan slumped back into the chair. 'You'll damnwell be what the family wants you to be, you owe it to us after everything we've done for you,' he said curtly and strode to the door.

'I'm sorry,' Nathan whispered.

David turned to look at him, studying his forlorn countenance. He hadn't meant to let fly at him, but the boy had to get his feet on the ground or he'd end up an intellectual nothing like Carl Moritz and break his mother's heart.

Nathan tried to smile. 'I've let you down, haven't I?'

'No you haven't. And you're not going to. Tell your teacher Oxford'll have to manage without you, Manchester University'll do fine. And forget about Homer and Plato, they'll get you nowhere. Start swotting to get into medical school.'

The confrontation had brought David face to face with the past again and he was not himself for the rest of the day.

'Don't you love me any more?' Bessie asked him. He had hardly spoken to her during the walk home from his parents' house and was moody all evening. They had just come to bed and he was lying with his hands folded behind his head, gazing at the orange-box bookcase.

'Why do you think everything I do or say's got something to do with you, Bessie?' he said without looking at her.

'I'm your wife, aren't I?'

'But you're not my whole life.'

Bessie's mind leapt to Miriam and her new-found security slipped from under her. But David was not thinking of Miriam, he was remembering the far-off days before he had forcibly grown up, his daily escape from the ghetto to the world of school and books and his friendship with Jim Forrest.

'I'll kill her!' Bessie said feelingly.

He could not summon the energy to tell her she was on the wrong track. Women, he had learned, functioned only on one level and could not understand that men did not. He was still gazing at the orange-box.

'And I'll set fire to that thing!'

But you can't destroy the part of me you don't even know exists, he thought.

Shirley cried out in her cot beside the bed.

'You've made me wake her up!' Bessie rebuked him.

David laughed and touched his wife's plump cheek, affectionately. 'You'll never change, will you, love?' Her characteristic reaction had returned him to earth.

She got up and brought the baby into bed with them.

'But it doesn't matter. I'm used to you the way you are,' he told her. She was the mother of his child and he felt tenderness for her, the more so when her new confidence occasionally deserted her and made her seem ridiculous and vulnerable.

CHAPTER TWO

The section of North Manchester in which the family lived was a cultural and rustic fantasy. Ruskin, Wordsworth and Haydn lent their names to avenues of cramped terraced houses. Thirlmere and Crummuck Streets conjured up lakeland vistas the residents had never seen and humble thoroughfares where no trees grew had leafy namesakes ranging from Maple to Birch.

Miriam's home was back to back with Esther's, enabling them to pop in and out of each other's kitchens through the yard doors. At the rear of the houses was a cobblestone passage known as 'the entry'. Here, Mr Cohen the fishmonger and Tom the rag-and-bone man would come with their donkeys and carts, providing a door-to-door service. Jewish and Gentile children played whip and top side by side while their mothers gossiped together as if being of different religions was of no account and the new school on the main road was attended by both denominations.

The beginning of the Jews' integration into the general community was a natural consequence. Esther cautioned little Harry not to make a noise when he played in the entry on Sundays because it was the Christian *Shabbos* and the Gentile neighbours showed the same respect for Saturdays. It was no longer necessary to engage a *Shabbos goy* to stoke up the fires, people offered to do so as a gesture of goodwill.

The proximity of their homes engendered a closer relationship between the Kleins and the Sammy Sandbergs than might otherwise have been the case. Ben sometimes said Marianne had been born into the wrong branch of the family, she so obviously preferred Martin to her brothers.

As soon as she was old enough to crawl she began scuttling across the entry to visit him, or he would do the same to visit her. In the warm summer months, when back doors were left ajar, Miriam or Esther would suddenly find two babies on the kitchen rug when a moment ago there had only been one.

Miriam gradually came to rely upon her sensible sister-in-law and a warm friendship developed between them. Once, when Martin gagged whilst eating a chicken wing, she rushed with him in her arms to Esther. Her middle-aged next-door neighbour was leaning on the fireguard chatting to her when it happened and chased after her.

'Pull thiself tergether, Miriam! Bang 'im on t'back, luv, 'appen 'e'll cough it oop!'

'I'm no good in an emergency, Mrs Hardcastle,' Miriam said as she fled across the entry.

'Tha'll 'ave ter learn ter be!'

Esther calmly hooked her little finger in Martin's throat and dislodged the bit of gristle which had caught there. 'He's right as rain now, aren't you, pet?'

Mrs Hardcastle pushed her hairnet higher on her forehead and scratched the red groove the elastic had made. ' 'Is mam isn't!' She folded her scraggy arms across her floral-overalled chest and smiled at Miriam's tense expression.

'I can't help it,' Miriam apologised. 'Would you've kept your head and known what to do if it'd been one of your kids, Esther?'

'Well I wouldn't've sent for you! Look at you!'

'Like as not a nice cup o' tea'd set 'er reet, Esther,' their neighbour suggested.

'I was just going to make her one.' Esther wrinkled her nose. 'Something's burning somewhere.'

'Lawks! I left t'bubble'n squeak on t'stove when I popped inter Miriam's fer a minute!' Mrs Hardcastle dashed back across the entry.

'Mrs Hardcastle's minutes are like other people's half-hours,' Esther giggled. 'She once came in here when I was making *holeshkies*. "Wrapping minced beef up in cabbage leaves as though it were a parcel? I never heard the like of it, Esther luv," she said. "You have now," I told her, "just like I'd never heard of frying cabbage up with bacon and calling it bubble and squeak, till I came to live round here." "Well you'd never heard of bacon, had you?" she answered back! She's a good sort, Mrs Hardcastle.'

Miriam tried to smile as she sipped her tea.

'If you're going to fall to bits whenever some little thing happens to Martin, you'll end up a bag of nerves, love,' Esther

265

said to her kindly. 'You can't bring up kids without having a crisis every now and then.'

'He's the only one I've got and I'm not likely to have any more.' Miriam picked up her son and cuddled him, but he wriggled away to play with Marianne.

Esther looked shocked. 'Who says you're not?'

'Dr Smolensky sent me to a specialist because I took so long to get over Martin's birth. I was like a wet week for ages afterwards.'

'I remember.'

'You should, seeing it was you who ran my home as well as your own till I picked up.'

'I thought it was just because you'd had a very long labour.' Esther sounded upset. 'Why didn't you tell us, Miriam?' It was taken for granted that matters of health and welfare were the whole family's concern.

'I've kept meaning to. But with Mother getting worse all the time, I didn't want to upset everyone more.' Esther was studying her anxiously. 'He said I'm all right in every other way, so don't worry. But it was a miracle I conceived Martin.'

Esther looked at her nephew who might not have been born and knelt down to kiss his cheek. 'God's good, Miriam.'

Miriam smiled. 'You sound more like your mother every day! You won't tell Bessie about this, will you?' She averted her eyes when Esther glanced at her sharply. 'It's not because of David, in case you think it is. All that's over and done with, the way it is with you and Carl.'

'With me and Carl it was never like it was with you and David.'

'I'm happy with Sammy.'

'Why shouldn't you be? Our Sammy's a diamond.'

'You don't have to tell me that.' Nobody could have a better husband, even though they didn't love him, Miriam reflected warmly. 'But about the other, well I just don't want Bessie to know.'

Was it because Bessie was pregnant again? Esther wondered.

'I don't want her pitying me,' Miriam said quietly.

They'd always have it in for each other, deep down, that was it. 'I won't say a word,' Esther promised with a smile. So long as it stayed deep down nobody would get hurt.

Though David's home was barely five-minutes' walk away, Miriam and Esther rarely saw Bessie during the week. What she did with herself they never inquired, but Esther thought she just sat eating toffees and listening to the wireless. Nobody else in the family had one, but the others were not surprised that David and Bessie did. Though they were not really wealthy, they were considered the rich relations and the aura this carried with it set them apart. By the time they were toddlers Shirley's cousins had set her apart, too.

Esther and Miriam sometimes took their children to Bellott Street park in the afternoons, before collecting Harry from school and they would knock on Bessie's door. Miriam never wanted to, but Esther insisted they could not just walk by. Bessie always gave them tea and showed them new treasures she had acquired for her home.

'How can you afford to buy things, the way business is just now?' Esther inquired one day.

'My dad's got nobody to spend it on but me,' Bessie reminded her. 'He gives me a present every week, Shirley as well.' Shirley's teething ring with the silver bell attached to it had been a gift from Salaman, who made sure there was nothing his granddaughter lacked.

'Doesn't he ever give David a present?' The words slipped out before Miriam could stop them.

Bessie's eyes narrowed. 'Are you being sarcastic, Miriam?'

'Don't be daft, love. She's joking!' Esther said hastily and the awkward moment passed.

Shirley was playing on the rug with an assortment of dolls. Marianne, who only possessed the wooden one her Uncle Sammy had made for her, was trying to play with them, too.

'Mine! Mine!' Shirley screamed hitting her.

Marianne did not return the blow, but Martin did it for her.

'Say you're sorry to Cousin Shirley,' Miriam instructed him.

'No.'

'You must. It's naughty to hit someone.'

'Martin not sorry,' he informed her.

'He reminds me of your father,' Esther laughed.

He sometimes reminded Miriam of him, too, and she slapped his hand because she did not want him to grow up with Sigmund's stubbornness. His face puckered, but he did not cry.

'Auntie Miriam's naughty for hitting Martin,' Marianne said reproachfully and kissed him better.

'Trust our Marianne to turn your own words on you,' Esther said. Her tiny daughter's intelligence sometimes bothered her. 'They'll have to put her in the top class the day she starts school!'

Shirley continued playing with her dolls. Martin and Marianne sat quietly watching her. There was never a happy atmosphere when these three were together.

Bessie always entertained in the parlour. David had had a gasfire installed so it could be heated quickly in the winter, if anyone called unexpectedly. There was barely space to move between the many pieces of furniture and the rest of the family secretly called the room the Crystal Palace, because every inch of surface was bedecked with cut glass vases and bowls.

The moment the children entered the house they became noticeably subdued and Arnold would stay perched on the edge of a chair throughout the visit, swinging his legs nervously. When their aunt gave them cakes they watched her warily whilst they ate them, trying not to scatter crumbs on the carpet. Yet Bessie was never less than kind to them.

'There's something about David's house that gives me the willies!' Esther exclaimed after they had left.

'Bessie,' Miriam declared.

They laughed. Like the children, they were always relieved when the visit was over.

'Heaven help Shirley when she starts school,' Miriam said.

'What do you mean?'

Miriam's brow was puckered in thought. 'I don't really know, it's just a feeling. I don't get the willies there, Esther. I get stifled.'

'The window was open today.'

'I don't mean that kind of stifled. I mean it's like being in a sort of cocoon.'

Esther shrieked with mirth. 'Are you calling our sister-in-law a caterpillar, just because she looks like one at the moment? Don't be catty!'

'Well that's how she lives, doesn't she? All nicely padded with her expensive things, as if having them keeps her warm and safe.'

'She's got David to keep her warm and safe.'

'I told you that's over and done with!' Miriam flashed. 'Why do you keep giving me digs about it?'

'It was the last thing on my mind, Miriam. And I don't think I ever have done. Why should I?'

They walked along in silence for a moment, pushing their heavy prams. Esther had Arnold as well as Marianne in hers.

'I'm sorry, Esther, it's just that . . .' Miriam hesitated. 'Well in a way that's how David looks at life and it reminded me. We'd've been miserable as sin together, he was right to finish with me. Bessie's the right kind of wife for him, but I think it's sad.'

'What is?'

'The way neither of them can help being how they are.'

CHAPTER THREE

Bessie was the first of the family to have a housemaid. After the General Strike, young girls from the Yorkshire and Northumberland mining villages were sent into service by their poverty-stricken parents and many came to Manchester. They were paid five shillings a week and those who found jobs in Jewish homes lived *en famille*, often remaining to become pillars of the families with whom they had settled in their youth.

Lizzie Wilson was only fifteen when Bessie engaged her in 1927, but more capable than her employer. She quickly took Shirley and the new baby Ronald under her wing and accompanied them to the Sabbath gatherings, which set David's children apart still more.

Sarah let her wash the dishes and had no need to supervise her a second time; she followed Bessie's instructions scrupulously, as careful not to confuse the dish-rag and tea towel with those used for meat plates as if she had been Jewish herself. Everyone liked her and thought David and Bessie had found themselves a gem.

Only Miriam viewed it differently. To her, Lizzie was a status symbol. 'He's got the maid, even if he hasn't got the house in Cheshire yet,' she said to Sammy recalling how she had ridiculed David's aspirations.

'D'you wish you could have one?' Sammy asked casually, but his expression had clouded as it always did when she referred to the past.

Miriam's green eyes darkened to charcoal. Then they blazed. 'That'll be the day, when I pay someone to fetch and carry for me!' It was Thursday and she swept into the scullery to complete her pre-Sabbath chores.

Sammy's life with her was not undiluted joy, but he had not expected it to be and still considered himself fortunate to have married her. She had never really been his, even in their most intimate moments, and had seemed even less so since Martin was born.

Their son obsessed her and sometimes Sammy worried about the effect of this on the child when he grew older. But Martin was not really like an only child, he reassured himself. With his three cousins just across the entry there was a limit to how much Miriam was able to cosset him.

Miriam returned to the kitchen with a basin of carrots and sat at the table to talk to him whilst she scraped and sliced them, ready for tomorrow's *tsimmes*. 'I wish you didn't work for David,' she said feelingly.

Sammy looked taken aback. 'Don't be daft, love. He's my brother. And there's no other work I could do, is there?'

She watched him painstakingly carving a block of wood. He was making book ends for Nathan. 'Isn't there?'

He continued chipping away with the knife, without replying. The book ends were to be shaped like owls, a memento for Nathan of his schooldays which would soon be behind him; the school badge was an owl. The first one was finished and stood on the table, its perfectly wrought curves a delight to the eye.

'Who says there isn't?' Miriam persisted. She wiped her hands on her apron and ran her fingers gently over the wooden owl's rippled surface which looked like delicate brown feathers. 'What a mug you are, Sammy,' she said resuming scraping the carrots. Her husband was an artist and he didn't know it.

'I thought of being a cabinet maker once, Miriam.'

'When?'

'When I was a lad. I thought I'd do that when I left school.'

'Why didn't you, Sammy?'

'David said people who make furniture have to lug heavy blocks of wood around and what did I want to let myself in for that for?'

'It's a pity he didn't say what he really meant.' Miriam was tight-lipped. 'He does to everyone else, but he never has to you. It was because of your leg he didn't want you to do it.'

'I know, love.' Other people asked if his leg hurt, but David never mentioned it. Sometimes he thought it bothered David more than it did him.

'David likes to run people's lives for them,' Miriam said bitterly.

271

'What if he does? He helps them, doesn't he?'

'Does he?'

'David knows what's best for people.'

'You mean he thinks he does.'

'Look what he's doing for our Nat and he's been doing it for years. Nat never had to do a sparetime job like David did. Me neither.'

Miriam laughed harshly. 'Some doctor that kid's going to be! Your little brother was in here the other day when I pricked my finger on a needle and he nearly fainted. But he's going to study medicine because David says so!'

'So he won't be a surgeon.'

'You're telling me he won't!'

They fell silent and avoided looking at each other.

Was Miriam still in love with David? Sammy wondered. She had never talked about him openly before since their marriage, though she sometimes referred to the past in a general way.

'I know what you're wondering, but you're wrong. It's you I'm thinking of, Sammy,' she told him. 'And if you don't know that by now, I'm sorry for you.'

She had not said she loved him, but her words moved him nevertheless and he got up and went to kiss her cheek, then stood behind her chair with his hands on her shoulders. 'You mean the world to me, Miriam,' he said emotionally. 'But so does David and I've a lot to thank him for.' Not even she could turn him against the brother who'd protected him all his life. He knew she'd been trying to tell him it would have been better if David hadn't done so. But you couldn't turn back the clock. Things were the way they were and it was too late to think of how they might have been.

'I know he means well,' Miriam said. 'But sometimes it's the people who mean well who do the most damage.'

Sammy closed his mind to what she was implying. 'He's never done me any damage. Just the opposite. So I don't enjoy working at the factory, who can expect work to be pleasure?' He spent his days trying to do what was asked of him, aware of his own incompetence, waiting for the evening to come so he could go home. But a job was a job and Salaman would have sacked him the first week had it not been for David. He was damn lucky to have a job.

272

'Fool!' Miriam exclaimed.

He returned to his chair with the word stinging his ears.

She calmed down and watched him resume carving the owl. Their house was full of his work, lovingly executed. A stool and a horse on wheels for Martin. A fruit bowl with a bunch of grapes hewn in the centre, so perfect that she would not hide it by filling it with fruit. Candlesticks and a trinket set for their bedroom. The workbox on legs which was also a table, used every day. He had come a long way since he began making dolls out of firewood for herself and Esther.

'Such beautiful things you make, Sammy,' she said softly.

'But they don't pay the bills, do they, love? A job's how you earn your living, a hobby's just what you enjoy doing at home.'

Miriam sighed and began slicing the carrots.

Bessie had become a lady of leisure. Except for the cooking, she did nothing in the house. Lizzie Wilson raced through the chores with the energy which came naturally to her and the gratitude she felt showed in her work. David and Bessie had rescued her from the dire straits of Denaby Main and given her a good home. It did not enter her head that she was being exploited, but it sometimes entered David's.

'Have another fishball,' he would say to her at the supper table and Bessie would frown at him. She did not have his compassion for the underprivileged.

Acquiring a maid had enhanced Bessie's delusions of grandeur. She would have given Lizzie her meals in the scullery, but did not suggest it because she knew David would not allow it.

Shirley and Ronald loved Lizzie. She was tall and angular, but somehow exuded maternity from every pore and was fiercely partisan about 'her' children. Her plain, freckled face lit up when she looked at them and she was always telling Shirley how much prettier she was than her cousin Marianne. She knew how to crochet and made dresses of silk, trimmed with rabbit wool, for both little girls, but Shirley's were worked in a fancier design.

In the afternoons, Lizzie took the children to Heaton Park, or played with them in the house if it was raining and Bessie used her new freedom to improve her appearance. She had her hair bobbed and shopped in town for fashionable dresses, paying for them with the money her father gave to her.

She would pop into Fuller's for tea and encounter acquaintances who also had maids and plenty of leisure time. A new kind of life opened up for her and she learned from the women who lived it.

'Why don't we go to the State Café on Saturday night?' she asked David one evening. 'Like other people do.'

David looked up from the *Daily Dispatch*, which he had not yet had time to read and noticed that his wife had painted her fingernails red and was carefully made up. Her dress was the latest style. The short, pleated skirt revealed her thick calves and the new hairstyle didn't suit her large features, but nobody could say she didn't look fashionable and well turned out. When did the transformation take place? This was the first time he'd noticed it.

'What did you say?' he asked her, shocked by the knowledge that he could live in the same house, sleep in the same bed and be unaware that she had changed. It was not just her looks, but her whole demeanour, as though she was wearing a new personality as well as new clothes.

'I want to start enjoying myself, the way everyone else does,' she told him.

David laughed uneasily. He felt as if he was suddenly confronted by a stranger. 'Who's this everyone you keep talking about?'

She mentioned some of her recently acquired friends and how she spent her afternoons with them. She had not done so before in case he would disapprove of the children always being left with Lizzie, but knew she must tell him sometime if they were to become part of 'the crowd'. The other women saw each other in the evenings, too, gossiping in each other's houses whilst their husbands played cards together in another room, or going somewhere special in a group, dressed up to the nines.

'What's the good of me having my hair done and buying new frocks if nobody ever sees them?' she said petulantly.

'Since when was I nobody?'

'Don't be daft, David!' She put her arms around his neck and kissed his cheek.

Lizzie did not live *en famille* in the evenings, they sat in the parlour and left her to darn and iron in the kitchen, which Bessie had been advised to do by her new friends.

'But while we're sitting here by ourselves, other people are out having a nice time,' she informed him and flung herself onto the sofa, bored and restless.

'When I get home from work I'm too tired to go anywhere, love,' David replied. Letting her have a maid had been a mistake, she was getting big ideas. But a fine one he was to think that! His were bigger than hers.

'If we had a car you wouldn't have to walk anywhere, or go by tram,' she pointed out. 'All my friends' husbands've got cars, they've had them for ages.'

'How can they afford them, the way business is?'

'I don't know. But they manage it.'

The implied rebuke was too much for David and he lost his temper. 'I believe in making sure I can walk before I ride, Bessie! And it's not just cars I'm talking about!'

'But you can still pay wages to your good-for-nothing brother!' She did not know he also gave money to his mother every week. 'All the nice things I have get bought by my dad. What've I got out of being married to you?'

David felt sick. 'Aren't Shirley and Ronald anything?'

'I'm talking about things, not children!' She got up and put a jazz record on the gramophone.

David rose from his chair and knocked the needle sideways with his balled fist.

The violence of the movement frightened Bessie, but she stood her ground. 'If you won't buy us a car so we can start going out to enjoy ourselves, I'll ask my dad to.'

David's fury subsided into cold acceptance. 'Why not?' he said roughly. 'He bought me, so let him buy you the car, too.'

Bessie choked back a sob and rushed from the room. He heard her go upstairs into their bedroom, slamming the door so hard it reverberated through the house.

Lizzie came in from the kitchen and looked at him anxiously. 'Is summat t'matter, Mr Sandberg?'

David noticed her workworn hands, red raw from cleaning his home and washing his family's clothes, the way his wife's hands had sometimes looked before Lizzie came. But it was not possible to reach the heights to which he aspired without stepping on other people. Life was a ladder and those who got to the top could only do so by using the ones at the bottom. You had to be in one class or the other and he'd decided long ago where he belonged.

'Whatever is it? You look dreadful, Mr Sandberg.' Lizzie sounded terrified.

David managed to smile. 'Just a lovers' quarrel, Lizzie.'

She eyed him reproachfully. 'Don't tell me you'n t'missis 'as been 'avin' words? You should be like me'n count yer blessins every night. It'd do yer 'eart good. Don't let me ever 'ear you two at it rowin', or I'll be tellin' you 'ow lucky you both are!'

Lizzie marched back to the kitchen, leaving David close to tears.

'Why d'you give Lizzie work to do in the evenings?' he asked Bessie when he went upstairs to bed.

'She doesn't mind,' Bessie snapped.

That's the trouble, David thought. But when they start minding they get like Mendel. You couldn't have it both ways, as he'd told himself before.

'You're too soft with that girl!' Bessie said sharply. 'She must think you're crackers, the way you won't let her clean your shoes.'

This was David's way of expressing that he would not allow servility to sink below a certain level. But he was only expressing it to himself and he was not sure why. Perhaps because his own beginnings were similar to where Lizzie stood now, he mused, and part of him would always remain rooted where he began. His children would not have the same attitude. How could they when he was making sure they had no reason to?

'Are we going to the State on Saturday night, or not?' Bessie inquired in a surly voice. 'You have to book a table.'

'Whatever you want, love,' he said tonelessly. The socialising she desired was no different from having a maid, just one more facet of the pattern his ambition had set for them.

CHAPTER FOUR

The Sandbergs were not the only immigrant family who had struggled to educate a bright son and Nathan began his medical studies with his friend Lou Benjamin and several other Jewish students.

Lou now lived around the corner from Nathan and they went to enrol at Manchester University together, their necks swathed in the distinctive blue and gold scarves which proclaimed they were not just college boys, but future doctors. Lou, who was proud of this, flaunted his scarf like a flag and kept looking around on the tram to see if anyone had noticed it. Nathan sat gloomily beside him, full of trepidation which increased when they alighted on Oxford Road and made their way to the imposing seat of learning which would be their second home for the next six years.

'Pull yourself together, you *shmuck*!' Lou instructed. 'Look, the Infirmary's just down the road. All those beautiful nurses!' he added with an anticipatory smile.

'Think there'll be any Jewish ones?' Nathan asked trying to cheer himself up.

Lou winked. 'Listen, what the eye doesn't see.'

'Your mother should only hear you,' Nathan said as they passed beneath the archway into the university quadrangle and entered their student life.

The amount of personal equipment a medical student required had astounded David, but he had bought it for his brother nevertheless and gone with him to select it. He had also had a desk and a bookcase delivered to his parents' home for Nathan and had arranged for a gasfire to be installed in his bedroom to make the long hours of study ahead more comfortable.

Nathan knew he should feel grateful, but the only emotion aroused in him was shame because he did not. When all his new possessions were in place, everyone trooped upstairs from the Sabbath tea party to inspect the room, even Lizzie Wilson. The bookcase was already full of text books, but his personal reading matter, *The Iliad* and *The Odyssey*, Plato and Socrates, the poems of Catullus and other treasured volumes reposed on the desk between Sammy's twin owls.

David's instinct was to tell him to put them away, but something stopped him from doing so. Perhaps the books were to Nathan what the orange-box was to himself, a reminder of what was not to be, but some kind of comfort all the same.

Also on the desk was the costly miscroscope, the skull and the stethoscope, Sarah's pen and inkwell which she had brought from Russia and never used, a small leather attaché case from the Moritzes and two fountain pens, one from Esther and Ben, the other from Salaman. Everyone had given him something, but Nathan could still not feel anything but shame.

'It reminds me of our doctor's surgery!' Lizzie exclaimed when she saw the stethoscope.

'Well my brother-in-law's going to be a doctor,' Bessie informed her proudly and the maid looked awed.

Nathan's glory was already reflecting on the family, but only Miriam noticed the strained expression on his sensitive face.

Despite his misgivings he put his mind to his studies. A born scholar could not do otherwise and the academic work proved no problem. He did not allow himself to think about the practical aspect until the day they were due in the dissecting room for the first time.

'I can't do it,' he told Lou desperately.

'D'you think I'm looking forward to it? Nobody is.' Lou gestured towards some of their fellow students who were also in the café to which he had brought Nathan, hoping a cup of strong tea would calm him down. 'Look at that lot! Stuffing themselves with buns because they know they won't be able to face their dinner!'

'I couldn't even eat in advance, Lou. I didn't have breakfast. The mere thought of it knocks me over.'

'What's the difference between what we've got to do and being a butcher who sees carcases hanging up dripping blood all the time?' Lou asked trying logic where sympathy had failed.

'If you want me to be sick before we even start, you're going the right way about it,' Nathan groaned. 'And for your information, I can't even bear to see my mother drawing the *Shabbos* chicken.' He slammed his cup onto the saucer and strode out of the café.

Lou shrugged to a student who was sitting next to him. 'What can you do with him, Reuben?'

Reuben grinned and spread his hands. They walked back to college together and could see Nathan slouching along with his hands in his pockets ahead of them.

'Listen, not everyone can be like me with a strong stomach,' Reuben said.

Most of the students managed to put up a nonchalant front as they filed into the dissecting room. Nathan looked as if he was going to his doom.

'I've seen a dead body before, when my grandma died,' someone remarked casually.

'But I don't suppose she was naked and you didn't have to cut her up, did you?' Nathan reminded him.

The Professor of Anatomy was awaiting them with an expressionless face. He knew what to expect and was rarely surprised. The ones who appeared the most squeamish often coped better than those with confident smiles. But not always.

The sickly-sweet odour of formaldehyde, with which the cadavers were preserved, met Nathan's nostrils immediately he stepped through the doorway. He did not allow his gaze to fall upon the long tables, or what lay upon them.

Lou was gripping his elbow and brought him to a halt when they reached an end table around which several other pale-faced students were already grouped. 'This one's ours, Nat,' he whispered. The atmosphere was conducive to lowering one's voice. He dug Nathan in the ribs. 'It's a man.'

Why does death reduce a person to an 'it'? Nathan thought with one half of his mind. The other half was telling him to look at the body and remember it was now no more than that, the soul which had once animated it was present no more. He lowered his eyes and clung to the table. Then he retched.

'For God's sake!' Lou hissed. 'You haven't even got a knife in your hand yet!'

Nathan averted his eyes from the cadaver and tried to get a grip on himself.

'I wonder who he was?' Lou mused.

'I'm trying to forget he was ever anybody,' the lad next to him muttered.

Before commencing his introductory lecture the professor waited to see if anyone would actually faint. Fainting, if it did occur, did not generally do so until the students had each been allocated a section of the anatomy and made the first incision. But occasionally the odour affected them and he had noted some extremely grey faces this morning.

Nathan and the over-confident Reuben slumped to the floor simultaneously. Paul Latimer, the son of a leading surgeon, followed suit two minutes later.

Nathan found himself vomiting in a lavatory and could not recall how he had got there.

'Holy Mother of God,' he heard Paul moan from an adjoining cubicle.

'How could I be such a *shlemiel*?' Reuben exclaimed disgustedly from the one on the other side.

They all staggered out to the washbasins together to put their heads under the cold tap.

'I wasn't actually sick,' Reuben informed Nathan and Paul clinically. 'I just felt as if I was going to be.' He dried himself off and threw down the towel. 'But I'm going back in there if it kills me!'

'Good for you, Reuben,' Paul said as the tubby youth clamped his spectacles back onto his nose and charged out of the cloakroom. 'I intend to do the same. Coming Nat?'

Nathan was leaning limply against the wall, drying his hands and did not reply.

'You know what they say when you fall off a horse, Nat. Get back on and ride it again immediately, or maybe you never will.'

Paul had not been particularly friendly toward the Jewish students until now. Probably because he had been to a public school and the only Jew he had encountered was Shylock, they had surmised. There's nothing like vomiting side by side to bring people together, Nathan thought dryly. Even if one of them had never ridden a horse. He managed to smile, though he still felt queasy. 'I need some air, Paul. I'm going for a walk.'

Paul slapped him on the back encouragingly. 'Don't tell anyone else this, but what happened to us happened to my old man. He spent the rest of the morning sitting on a park bench, if it's any consolation to you.' His rugged features creased into a grin. 'It's a good thing he told me, or I don't think I could force myself to go back inside.'

Nathan got his coat and scarf and wandered along Oxford Road. If David had witnessed his debacle in the dissecting room, would he still say he must be a doctor? Was carving up a cadaver any more of an ordeal than the filthy sweatshop had been for his brother?

David had never mentioned the degrading conditions in which he had spent his youth, but Lou's father had also worked in a factory at that time and often recalled what it had been like. The boys today didn't know how lucky they were, he said repeatedly and Nathan's parents had said the same. Lucky by comparison with something worse, he thought mutinously as he trudged along the main road. His lot was never compared with something better.

A flicker of shame assailed him. His family had never known anything better, but were making sure he would. He glanced at his watch with the second hand, which David had bought for him because a doctor needed one to take the patient's pulse; it was too late to get back onto the horse this morning, the session would be almost over.

The watch had not been on the list of essential requirements, but David thought of everything. He was the kind of person who got things done while other people were still thinking about doing them. He had even rearranged Nathan's newly-equipped room the way he thought it ought to be, with the desk facing the wall, under the gaslight. Nathan had wanted it by the window, so he could look out on the back garden, but had not argued with him.

Why didn't people argue with David? Because he was unselfish and wanted the best for everyone in the family. But it was not just that. There was something indefinable about him which told you not to bother, you couldn't win. Nathan had only tried once and had not expected to win. It struck him now that none of them ever referred to his brother as 'our' David, the way they did when they mentioned each other. Nathan was 'our' Nat to the family, but David was just David whose name needed no qualifying.

A tram clanked by heading in the opposite direction and he wanted to leap aboard it, be carried homewards away from his problem. But when he got there he'd be faced with another; his mother would tell David, who would chastise him and send him back. He reached Whitworth Park and wandered inside to find a bench where he could rest and think. As Paul's father had done under the same circumstances, he thought wryly. Could he summon the willpower that eminent gentleman had found himself capable of? He sat down and tried to do so, but stress had wearied him and he fell asleep. When he opened his eyes he felt refreshed, but the problem was still with him.

'I was wondering when you were going to wake up,' a cheerful female voice said from the other end of the bench.

Nathan looked at his watch before he looked at her. He had slept for fifteen minutes. He turned to smile at the girl, whose expression was as perky as her voice. She was fair, with rosy cheeks. And not Jewish, a warning voice said inside his head. Why did he always think of people as Jews or Gentiles? Well how could he not when they did the same with him? She'd probably had him weighed up as a Jew-boy from Cheetham Hill even before he opened his eyes, his olive skin and black hair were enough to go on. But with girls there was an extra reason for the way he had reacted. Gentile girls were forbidden fruit and Jewish boys must never forget it.

'My name's Mary Dennis. What's yours?' she said with an engaging grin.

Nathan noticed that her mouth was too wide for the size of her face and her nose had a little bump near the bridge, but put together her features were pert and pleasing. 'Nathan Sandberg. And do you usually talk to strange men on park benches?' he quipped. Why had he said men? He still thought of himself as a boy, though he was now nineteen.

'I do when they're one of ours,' she laughed. 'I know you're a medic by your scarf. I'm a nurse at the Infirmary, so we've something in common, haven't we?'

Nathan slid along the bench to sit beside her. 'I wondered why you were wearing black stockings,' he said surveying her neat ankles.

'Well now you know! I've just come off duty and I'm having a breath of air.'

He saw the stiff white collar of her uniform peeping above her coat. His glance strayed to her small hands, which had a well-scrubbed look about them, then returned to her face. She did not smell of disinfectant, the way he had imagined a nurse would, instead the scent of lavender hung about her. 'How d'you like emptying bedpans?' he inquired.

She laughed again and Nathan sensed she was the kind of girl who enjoyed life.

'And sticking thermometers in people's mouths?' he added.

'Make up your mind which end you want to talk about!'

'Neither, actually.'

Mary studied him silently for a moment. 'What's up, Nathan?'

'Everyone calls me Nat,' he said without answering her question.

'I'd rather call you Nathan.'

The warning voice sounded in his head again. Why was he always hearing inner bells and voices? And feeling things? Like now, with this Gentile girl who was behaving as if they were friends, when they had just met. He either liked a person instinctively and they became important to him, or dismissed them immediately as not his kind. Occasionally his instinct proved wrong, as had happened with Paul Latimer of whom he'd seen a different side this morning. But it seldom proved wrong when he took to someone at once as he had to Mary. 'Call me anything,' he said stupidly, averting his gaze from her deep blue eyes.

'So long as I don't call you late for dinner!' she pealed giggling at her own joke, which he had heard before. 'Why've you got a face like a wet week?' she asked and giggled again when he looked affronted. 'I don't mean it that way, you're very good looking. But it's hard to see what you look like through the pall of gloom.'

He told her what had happened to him in the dissecting room.

'Is that all?' she grinned. 'Well don't let it worry you, I know some very good doctors who went to pieces the first time they came face to face with a cadaver.'

'I only know of one.'

'Wait till you're on the wards, you'll hear all sorts of stories about what happened to people when they were students.'

'If I ever get that far.'

'Now don't be daft, Nathan!' Mary's voice was soft-toned, but she could sound firm when necessary. 'How d'you think I was my first time in theatre? Out for the count with my pal lying beside me. But the next time we both stayed on our feet and after a while it didn't bother us. You get so you're standing outside it, if you know what I mean. Or how could anyone do the things doctors and nurses have to do? And someone has to, or sick folk'd just die for lack of treatment.' She smiled reminiscently. 'I'll never forget being sent to the lab for something when I was a probationer and seeing a pickled penis in a jar.'

She's as casual about it as if she was talking about a pickled cucumber, Nathan thought and was not sure which shocked him most, hearing her say that word or her callous attitude. 'A minute ago, I thought you were a compassionate person,' he said stiffly.

'Part of me is, but the rest's cool and objective,' she told him. 'And that's how you'll be sooner or later. The penis didn't belong to anyone any more, did it? And I had to smile seeing it floating about in the solution, even though I felt sick and sorry at the same time. I only mentioned it because that was the day I began laughing my squeamishness off and nothing's made me feel sick since.'

'It's strange hearing a word like that bandied about by a girl, all the same.'

'But you'll get used to it, Nathan, like you will to everything else. That's what I'm trying to tell you. Mark my word.'

'I'll let you know,' he said as if he took it for granted, as she seemed to, that they would meet again. He glanced at his watch and rose, conscious that he was reluctant to leave her. 'I must get a move on, Mary, or I'll miss a lecture.'

Mary rose, too. 'Come on then. I'll walk you to the door,' she grinned.

On *Yom Kippur* silence would lie thick as a blanket on Cheetham Hill. Only the rumble of the trams on the two main roads which flanked the district disturbed the solemn quietude.

The previous week, during *Rosh Hashanah*, a joyousness pervaded the air, friends and neighbours pausing in the streets to wish each other a happy New Year and chuckling tolerantly at small boys kneeling on the pavement to flip festive hazelnuts into their upturned caps, as they did with marbles on ordinary days. But the Day of Atonement was different. Even the children felt its awesome quality and walked to *shul* docile as lambs beside their parents, to make their peace with God.

The Sandbergs and Moritzes attended the new Central Synagogue which now graced the top end of Heywood Street, its presence there a testament not just to the Jews' desire to erect a house of worship worthy of their Maker, but also to how far they had advanced, both materially and as secure British citizens. It was not the first such testament and would not be the last, as freedom of religious expression and fading remembrance of past oppressions allowed the community to spread deeper into the city.

A thriving community of Sephardi Jews existed in South Manchester, but their Spanish and Portuguese culture was vastly different from the East European Judaism of their Ashkenazi brethren who had settled on the North side and the two lived separate lives.

On the North side, some of the original congregations still remained, rich reminders of the early immigrant days, and Abraham Sandberg preferred to worship at the *Chevrah Habimah*, where his boys had been Bar Mitzvah and his friend Rabbi Lensky was still the minister in a *shul* which had been rehoused, but did not yet have a *bimah*. He enjoyed the nostalgia evoked by the *Hassids*' old-style wool prayer shawls, edged with black and grey with use like his own, a world away from the sleek white-and-blue silk ones which Anglicised Jews had taken to wearing, his sons among them. The atmosphere was redolent of snuff and Russia; old bearded men, silk-hatted and swaying back and forth devoutly, incongruously shod in white canvas slippers as *Yom Kippur* piety demanded; remarks addressed in Yiddish when someone paused from prayer to speak to his neighbour. Sentiment mingled with gratitude in Abraham's heart as he gave thanks and atoned for his sins among them.

His children were humorously tolerant of his attachment to the traditions of his youth, which they themselves had gradually adapted to their *modus vivendi*. But his grandchildren were fascinated by the old ways and loved to go with him to the place where religion was so much more colourful and exciting.

On *Yom Kippur*, when there was never a seat to spare, they would cluster tensely around him, conscious of the invisible Almighty hovering above with a pen in His hand writing in the Book of Life whether or not they would live for another year, which the prayerbooks declared He decided on that day. But the Harvest and Tabernacles Festivals were their favourites and no-where were these more thrillingly observed than in 'Zaidie's' *shul*.

'Who's 'Zaidie'?' Marianne Klein's little schoolfriend asked when Marianne was telling her about it.

'Well you know how you have your Saturday on a Sunday, Marjorie?'

'It's you who has your Sunday on a Saturday.'

'Well anyway, we call our grandparents by a different name than what you do, like we do a lot of things different, it's because we're Jewish. So Zaidie's my granddad and my grandma's my Bobbie.'

Marjorie giggled. 'Don't Jews do funny things?'

'They do on *Simches Torah*!' Marian replied thinking of what went on at Zaidie's *shul* when Tabernacles time came around. Frock-coated old gentlemen paraded the aisles chanting joyfully as they held aloft the Scrolls and the symbolic fruits. All the children present received oranges, apples and sweets and were given wooden rattles with which to make as much noise as they liked. They could even play 'catchers' with the oranges if they wanted to and nobody told them to stop it.

Simches Torah was similarly celebrated elsewhere, but not with the same verve and abandonment. This included the ancients bending their creaking knees to dance a triumphant *Kazatsky* before the holy Ark and Abraham's heart would fill with regret because this generation of immigrants would soon be gone and with them the special something they had preserved from the old country. But at least his grandchildren would have it to remember all their lives.

In the Autumn of 1930, David sat in the Central Synagogue with his brothers and brother-in-law, allowing the timelessness of the Rosh Hashanah prayers to wash over him. Services always had this effect upon him, as though he was participating in something immense and mysterious. The first time he had felt this had been at his Bar Mitzvah.

He could see the women in the gallery above. The days when such distraction was prohibited by a screen were no more, though men and women still sat separately. His mother was the only woman in the family not wearing a new hat. Miriam had made her own and Esther's, but Bessie's had been concocted by an expensive milliner and had cost a guinea.

His mother sometimes said scathingly that the hats seemed more important than the prayers these days. She was dressed in black, as usual, and David noticed that the silver wings which sprang from her temples had spread so wide none of the dark sheen he remembered was visible beneath the shapeless felt hat on her head. But her hair had been predominantly grey for years. How old was she now? It took him a moment to work it out. Fifty! And he was thirty-three, with a few grey hairs of his own. Where had the years gone to?

Sarah was wondering the same thing as she looked down upon her three sons. The loftiness of the building, the sunlight spilling like molten gold through many windows, the monotonous murmur of male voices praying below and the subtle scent of cologne sweetening the warm air combined to lull her into a state of recollection. Twenty-five years had passed since she and Abraham stepped off the herring boat in Hull. They had six grandchildren to prove it! And an English-born son studying to be a doctor.

She gazed at the pale oval of Nathan's face. He was not reading from his prayerbook and chanting aloud with the others, but sat silently staring ahead. The way he had to study deep into the night sometimes worried her and she often heard him pacing his room as if a restlessness had beset him. But the privilege of being called Doctor had to be earned, was not something achieved without effort. Any more than being a businessman was, she reflected noticing David's frowning expression.

That her eldest son had business worries was no secret to his family. The finest raincoats in the world could not make a profit if nobody had the money to buy them and even the smart ladies in Cheltenham and Harrogate had to watch what they spent nowadays. Times were bad for everyone. When had they been good? Only once during all the years she'd been here. During the war. Did there have to be a war, men taking each other's lives, before ordinary people could have enough to eat?

Her own family didn't got short of food, but she knew there were those who did. Four years ago they had raised their voices and brought the whole country to a standstill, but it had done no good, nothing had changed. It was the same in other countries, too, she'd learned. Sometimes she read the *Daily Dispatch*, when David remembered to bring it for her and Nathan read the *Manchester Guardian* which Carl Moritz brought home for him from the bookshop each day.

Because Carl spoke German, his employers had sent him to see a publisher in Berlin recently and he had returned with disquieting news. People called Nazis were holding meetings dedicated to the glory of the Fatherland and it was said that their leader, a Mr Hitler, did not like Jews.

A cold terror had gripped her when Carl recounted this at a *Shabbos* gathering, but she'd comforted herself with the thought that Berlin was a long way from Manchester. When Carl had later mentioned an Englishman called Mosley who also disliked Jews, her fear became dread and seemed much nearer home. She had managed to put it from her mind, but today one thought had led to another and the feeling returned. She fixed her gaze on the Ark and pleaded silently with God not to let the evil happen again.

Walking home from *shul* in the September sunshine, past the convent which was its near neighbour and the redbrick English houses on either side of Heywood Street, her anxiety seemed

288

ridiculous. The pavements were thronged with Jews who had just poured forth from their temple and had no need to fear reprisals for being what they were.

Her neighbour Mrs Evans was sweeping the leaves out of her front porch when the family trooped up the garden path and wished them a happy New Year.

'They're nice *goyim*, the Evanses,' Abraham remarked at lunch. 'The way they respect our *Yom Tov*.'

'Don't we always wish them Merry Christmas?' Sarah replied.

'How could we not?' he teased her. 'When you stand by the parlour window watching for them to come out of the Welsh chapel across the road so you can open the door and say it?'

'What if I do? Mrs Watson opposite came specially yesterday to wish me all the best and I let her taste the chopping herring I was making. So she spat it out, what does it matter? She had a piece of strudel instead and asked me for the recipe. And she's going to show me how to make little cakes called scones for my grandchildren, like she does for hers.'

'We get those at home, Bobbie,' Marianne told her. 'Mrs Hardcastle taught Mam and Auntie Miriam how to make them.'

'You mix the flour with sour milk, Mother,' Esther said.

'It's a good way to use it up,' Miriam added.

'Sour milk I wouldn't give to my cat. I don't think I fancy those scones, but don't tell Mrs Watson. So you see, Abraham? If everyone was like me and my Christian neighbours and Esther and Miriam's also, the world would be a better place.'

'Is that what you're talking about?' Sigmund chuckled.

'I thought they were swopping recipes,' David said.

Abraham had also lost track of the conversation. 'What is she getting at me for? What have I done?'

'Never mind,' Sarah retorted. 'Just don't do it again. And who exactly is this Mr Mosley?' she inquired irrelevantly. Though her dread had receded, she resented the unknown figure who had caused it.

Her indignant expression made everyone laugh. 'A fine joke!' she told them hotly. 'He doesn't like Jews, so what's to laugh about?'

The family were seated around the big table in the dining room, the children together at the end nearest the door so they could run into the lobby and play between courses.

'What do you mean, who is he?' Sigmund said. 'He's a Blackshirt and they've already caused trouble.'

'Where?' Why had nobody told her about this?

'In the East End, Mother,' Nathan informed her. 'Can I have another *knedel* in my soup, please?'

'He talks about matzo balls and people who cause trouble for Jews in the same breath!' Sarah looked at Nathan rebukingly, then sent Lizzie to the kitchen to fetch some more *knedlach*. She had never heard of the East End. Was it possible Nathan had meant somewhere in Manchester. 'The east end of where?' she asked him.

'It's in London, Bobbie,' Harry Klein piped up before his uncle could reply. One of his schoolfriends had cousins who lived there and Harry had met them. 'Where they say Zaida and Buba instead of talking like we do.'

'Hm,' Sarah said thoughtfully.

Rachel was beside her in her bathchair and Helga was feeding her. She moved her limp hand with difficulty and touched Sarah's. Nobody noticed the gesture, but Sarah knew her friend understood how she felt. Why weren't the others taking her seriously? Enjoying their meal as if there were no such people as Mr Hitler and Mr Mosley!

'The Fascists aren't very strong in this country,' Nathan consoled her. As always, he was more sensitive to her feelings than the rest of the family and had now realised she was immensely disturbed.

'Yet,' Carl added consuming his third *knedl*. He saw Sarah looking at him and shrugged. 'If I don't eat my lunch, will it make any difference?'

Sarah knew it would not, but was preoccupied during the rest of the meal. She did not bother to inquire what Fascists were, or where they came into it. The word had an unpleasant sound and that was enough.

All the children except Marianne and Martin had gone to play in the lobby, but these two sat quietly together gazing big-eyed at Sarah.

'You don't want to go and play with your cousins?' Abraham asked them.

The sound of young feet racing up and down, and Shirley's shrill voice dictating to the others, pierced the silence which had fallen in the dining room.

Marianne and Martin shooked their heads. Something in the air held them fast, though they were not yet six years old or able to understand anything that had been said. The sensitivity of both had always been apparent. Marianne had a habit of flicking her fringe nervously away from her eyebrows and Martin's nails were bitten down to the quick. They were not just sensitive, but intense, in the way that kind of child can be, feeling things more deeply than others did, given to passionate outbursts for no apparent reason.

Esther's disciplining had made Marianne into a neat and tidy little girl, but had been unable to curb her turbulent nature and wild imagination. Only in looks and will power did she resemble her practical grandmother. Sometimes she invented stories which frightened Martin and her brothers, tales of horrors which had befallen children who existed only in her mind.

Martin composed little rhymes which rolled effortlessly off his tongue, but unlike Marianne's stories they were always about beautiful things happening to people he knew.

'If you didn't know them, you'd think butter wouldn't melt in their mouths,' David smiled breaking the silence. He found his niece and nephew quaint, as most of the family did. 'Sitting there like a little old man and woman!'

Ben laughed. 'Our Marianne was never like a baby.'

'They're going to be geniuses, the way they don't want to miss anything,' Sigmund declared.

'Nosy parkers, I'd call them,' Bessie put in. She did not like the way these two children were always stealing the limelight from her own. 'It isn't good for them, being in here with the grown ups when they've finished eating. I wouldn't let my kids have their own way.'

Esther and Miriam exchanged a glance. But you do about everything else, they were thinking.

Sarah had not said a word.

'What is it, Bobbie?' Marianne asked her. 'Who are you angry with?'

Her grandmother stopped crumbling the bit of bread on her

plate and looked into the inquiring dark eyes, so like her own. 'It's not so much with who as with what, Marianne,' she replied.

'Has something happened?' Martin said apprehensively. He wanted his world to be a pleasant place, where only good things happened. 'Something bad?'

'Of course it hasn't,' his mother reassured him. 'Tell him, Ma.'

'I can't tell my grandson a lie.'

'For God's sake, Mother!' David exclaimed. 'What's the matter with you?'

'That you need to ask is part of what's the matter with me.'

'Just because you've discovered there's such a thing as fascism is no reason to upset the kids.'

'The Fascists aren't outside the door,' Carl said with more flippancy than he felt.

Sigmund took off his pince-nez and studied them broodingly. 'You've made me go cold, Carl.'

Martin eyed his grandfather's grave face and burst into tears.

'All we need now is for Marianne to start!' Esther said exasperatedly.

Her daughter obliged with a convulsive sob, then everyone began talking excitably at the top of their voices.

'Only Jews could behave this way, getting hysterical!' Nathan shouted above the din thinking of his cool Gentile friends at college who had to be confronted by a cadaver before they showed their feelings.

Sarah put him in his place. 'And shall I tell you why, Nat? With Jews there's always something to feel hysterical about. Even when it isn't in front of our eyes it's still there. Waiting.'

Miriam and Esther removed their weeping children from the room and shut the door behind them.

'I thought it'd gone away forever, but I've been living in a fool's paradise all these years,' Sarah declared ruefully.

'So now you know better,' Sigmund, who had done no such thing, told her.

'And to know is to be prepared,' she answered. 'I lied to David and Sammy in Dvinsk, so they wouldn't worry or be afraid. The Cossacks won't hurt you, I said. If I'd told them the truth from the cradle they'd have kept out of the Cossacks' way and Sammy wouldn't be walking with a limp.'

'A nice *Rosh Hashanah* she's giving us here,' Abraham said gloomily.

'So what is *Rosh Hashanah*, Abraham? The beginning of a new year, when people take stock of what they have or have not. Let them also take stock of their lives.'

'A handful of Blackshirts in London's nothing to get worked up about, Ma,' Ben said placatingly. 'And I don't believe in frightening children.'

'I'll never lie to my grandchildren about what it means to be Jewish,' Sarah said firmly.

'They'll find out for themselves sooner or later, like we did,' Nathan told her.

'Anti-Semites're everywhere,' David endorsed. 'It's a fact of life.'

'Like those Blackshirts? That Mr Hitler?' Sarah said eloquently. 'So why didn't I know about them before?' She spat three times to keep the evildoers away. 'A snake doesn't lift its head to strike until it's ready, but the poison is still there.'

'Oy! Snakes she's giving us now after our meal!' Abraham sounded bemused. 'You think we could have some lemon tea, instead?'

But the discussion had gone too far to be cut short. 'And what do you think you can do about it, Mother?' David demanded.

Sigmund sighed. 'Soon there'll be nowhere for a Jew to run to.'

'Except Palestine,' Bessie said examining a chip in her nail varnish. 'But why is everyone talking about running, all of a sudden?'

'I am the only one talking about it,' Sigmund snapped. Bessie's exaggerations irritated him.

'And nobody's thinking about it. Here they don't need to,' David declaimed.

'But they don't have to be blind, either,' Sarah countered. 'Once it was the Tsar and now it's something else. Maybe in my time there'll never be a safe place to be Jewish in. In my grandchildren's time, who knows? Perhaps it will be better for them, But only if they always remember what they are and what could happen to them because of it, instead of waiting for someone to throw a stone through the window to remind them. So why're we still sitting here?' She rose from the table and smiled at Rachel.

293

'Come, I'll take you to the parlour, we'll drink our tea there.' She had said what she had to say and hoped it would have some effect.

'Ma's enough to put the fear of God into a person!' Bessie exclaimed after Sarah had wheeled Rachel from the room.

David patted his wife's hand reassuringly. But he felt uneasy.

CHAPTER SIX

'Mind over matter, that's all it takes,' Lou had counselled Nathan before the next session in the dissecting room. 'Forget you've got a stomach, use your bleddy brainbox!'

The second time proved less traumatic and before long Nathan found himself able to perform the gruesome tasks in a detached manner, as Mary had said he would. Determination not to let his family down helped him to follow Lou's advice and achieve this, but succeeding in Mary's eyes was an added incentive. From their first meeting her confidence in him had been absolute and helped to sustain him.

'Where were you yesterday?' she asked when she joined him on the bench in Whitworth Park where he had taken to eating his lunch on fine days. She had brought an apple to nibble during her break from duty and gave it a wipe with the corner of her cape.

'It was *Yom Kippur*.'

'What's that for heaven's sake?'

'The Day of Atonement, when Jews ask God to forgive the sins they've committed all year and fast for twenty-four hours.'

Mary bit into her apple. 'I don't think I could do it. I'd have to have something to drink, even if I didn't eat.'

'Not if you were Jewish you wouldn't, you'd be used to it. I've been fasting on *Yom Kippur* since I was thirteen. Before then you don't have to, though some kids do.' He grinned. 'I wasn't one of them.'

'You're not all that religious then?'

Nathan did not reply immediately; he was not sure if he was or not. Many of the rituals seemed absurd to him, yet he observed the basic ones. He could see Mary's blonde curls peeping from the front of her nurse's cap, her unmistakably Gentile profile despite the little bump at the bridge of her nose. One thing he wasn't observing was not just a ritual, but a sacred law. If he cared about his religion, why was he becoming increasingly involved with a Christian girl?

They had known each other for almost a year, meeting in the park when her schedule of duty and his lectures allowed it, or for tea in a local café if the weather was wet. They went to the pictures in the evenings sometimes and dancing more often. The first time he had held her in his arms at a dance, the contact with her sweet-scented softness had told him he was involved, though his brain had continued to deny it. Then he had kissed her goodnight and known for sure.

'You didn't answer my question,' Mary reminded him twining her fingers through his. 'Not that you need to, it isn't my business.'

If Nathan had been looking at her, he would have seen that her eyes were troubled, but he was too preoccupied. 'Of course I'm not religious, or I wouldn't be going out with you. Intermarriage is the number one sin for Jews.' He had said more than he intended. Why had he put it that way, when he didn't want her to take their affair, which was only one in the romantic sense, too seriously. Had he begun to take it seriously himself?

He recalled his mother warning the family after the *Rosh Hashanah* meal, telling them always to remember what they were, not to wait for someone to forcibly remind them. But being Jewish had built-in reminders. There were so many things which even a not overly religious Jew was aware he must never do and temptation would prod his conscience painfully.

If his mother knew about Mary she would say she'd rather see him dead than married to her. And if he did marry her, he would in effect be dead to his family. The week of mourning, exactly as after a bereavement, was observed by orthodox parents for a son or daughter who had committed the unforgivable sin and the sinner cast out of their lives forever. But he mustn't be like his sister-in-law Bessie and build up an imaginary situation like seeing the family seated on low stools mourning for him, which he'd just allowed himself to do.

'I was just explaining to you how Jews feel,' he said to Mary managing a smile.

She looked at him and for once was not smiling. 'I'm only interested in how you feel, Nathan.'

296

'Stop seeing her, Nat,' Lou advised as they rode home from college one evening. 'Be like me with half a dozen.'

'I'm not the half-a-dozen kind.'

'Nor would I be if they weren't *shiksahs*.'

'Don't use that word, I hate it!' Nathan barked.

'Only because you've fallen for one and that's why you've got to finish with her,' his friend said sagely. He glanced at Nathan's pensive expression and opened his *Gray's Anatomy* to read. There was no point in talking to a brick wall.

Was Lou right? Nathan mused. Was Mary the reason he'd begun to resent traditional Jewish attitudes toward Gentiles? A Gentile could be your friend, but he was different and you were aware he felt the same way about you. Never the twain shall meet no longer applied, but the fruits of conditioning remained and had begun to taste sour to him.

Once, *shiksah* had been a word he used himself, but now it grated on him as other such Yiddish words did. 'Why can't you just say Mr Watson across the road's a nice man, instead of a nice *goy*? What's the difference?' he had asked his father the other day and Abraham's reply came drifting back to him as the tram clanked along. 'The difference is their Messiah they've already had and ours we're still waiting for.'

Religion and nothing else was the cause of it, he thought bitterly. Without it people would just be people. If Moses hadn't been found in the bulrushes and Jesus born in the manger, Nathan Sandberg wouldn't be fraught with dilemma about a Christian girl called Mary.

He shared the conclusion with Lou when they alighted from the tram.

'And you'd've been born in Russia, your parents would've had no reason to come to England,' Lou pointed out logically. 'So you wouldn't't've had the dilemma anyway.'

When Nathan reached home, David's car was parked outside. He had not let his mind dwell on how his brother would react to the affair with Mary and always restricted his outings with her to the south side of town, to avoid any chance of discovery.

Sometimes Mary wanted them to go to the city centre, but nowadays David and Bessie had a social life which took them there and Nathan was not prepared to risk it. The clandestine nature of his relationship with a girl he was in no way ashamed of bothered him as much as her being Gentile. She was the kind of girl his mother would like, direct and cheerful, kind and intelligent. Deficient in only one way.

'What're you doing here at this time? he asked David. His mother was laying the table for supper.

'Mother wanted a chat with me.'

'What about?'

David lit a cigarette, a recently-acquired habit which had stopped him from cracking his knuckles, and avoided his eye.

'About you,' Sarah smiled. 'The big brains of the family!'

Nathan was always embarrassed when she talked this way, especially in David's presence. If his brother had had the opportunity he would probably have been the best solicitor in town.

'The *shatchan* has been asking about you, Nat,' his mother said lightly and laughed at his stunned reaction.

A matchmaker inquiring about him? As if he were a prize bull to be sold in the market place! 'You can tell him where to go!' he retorted hotly.

'It's a her.'

'And maybe she thinks she's still in Russia, but I've never even been there!'

Sarah continued laying the table, as though they were discussing some everyday matter. 'Marriage is the same everywhere.'

Nathan looked at David whose expression told him nothing. Was David going to support his mother? Try to make him do what everyone knew he had done himself? And what had he got for it? A load of business worries, a wife who bored him stiff, anyone could see it, and two spoiled kids.

'You haven't asked about the girl,' Sarah said.

'I don't want to know about her.' He sat down at the table and regarded his mother and brother coldly. 'If she'd agree to something like this, she couldn't be the right girl for me.' His dilemma about Mary crystallised into reckless decision to marry her, as he saw Sarah and David exchange a glance. They'd manoeuvred him into studying medicine, but they weren't going to deprive him of the girl he loved! Let them cast him out, it was just another of the archaic rituals born in the Wilderness which had no more place in modern society than the sin it was punishment for.

His mother took a photograph from the dresser and placed it on the table in front of him. 'So you don't want to know about her, but to see what she looks like is no harm.'

He glanced disinterestedly at the smooth, dark face. The eyes were almond-shaped and the lips delicate and smiling.

'She's better looking than Bessie!' David joked at his own expense.

Nathan jerked his gaze from the photograph. The girl was beautiful and probably had a figure to match her face, but she was not the girl he wanted.

'She lives in London,' Sarah said as if this made her an aristocrat. 'And money's no object. Her father owns property. The great-grandparents settled here in 1850. Such a refined family! Can you blame them for wanting a doctor for their daughter?'

A prize bull for a pedigree cow, Nathan thought with disgust.

'So what do you say, Nat?'

He glared at his mother as though he loathed her and wondered why he did not. 'No! With a Capital N!' he shouted and strode from the room.

After he had gone, Abraham came in from the scullery. He had been washing his hands there when Nathan arrived home and had decided to stay out of it. 'Listen, the boy's got feelings,' he shrugged. 'What can you do?'

'Wait and he'll get over them,' Sarah replied. 'He'll need a practice one day. They don't grow on trees and we're not a rich family like Dr Smolensky came from.' She set a platter of *kefulte* fish on the table and smiled at David. 'He'll see sense like his brother did.'

An arranged marriage for material reasons was a custom his parents took for granted, David reflected as he drove home. As he would have done if they'd never left Russia. He recalled how the idea of it had sickened him. How much more repulsive must it seem to Nat, even though he wasn't in love with someone else as David had been? The difference in their ages set his brother half a generation ahead of him and his boyhood had not been like David's own, steeped in the immigrants' early struggle to establish themselves in a new land. Nat was more English in attitude than the rest of the family, how could he not be when he'd never lived anywhere else? Despite his Jewish upbringing, the old ghetto traditions were bound to conflict with the English conditioning he'd absorbed.

If I hadn't married Bessie, I wouldn't be living here, I'd still be in Strangeways, he thought as he stopped the car outside his house. He wouldn't be the owner of a Morris Cowley saloon, either, he'd still be travelling by tram. How could he support Nat's refusal to consider the matchmaker's proposition, which he was tempted to do, when he'd married for money himself? And with the business barely holding its own, there was no prospect of David accruing the cash to set him up when he qualified. He made up his mind to remain neutral and leave things to his mother who had no doubt worked out how her doctor-son's practice would be bought the day she decided he was to be one.

When he opened the front door, Shirley and Ronald were playing in the lobby and rushed to greet him. By the time they grew up, arranged marriages would be unheard of, he reflected as he hugged them. Jews would become more Anglicised with each succeeding generation. Probably the beautiful London girl, who was third-generation English, had only agreed to be a party to one because Jewish doctors were still in short supply.

'You're late, David! And we're going out right after supper!' Bessie shrilled from the kitchen.

He went to kiss her cheek, with an arm around each of his children. Arranged or not, in the end marriage boiled down to family life and its strains and stresses. With a few patches of joy thrown in if you were lucky. 'Where're we going tonight, love?' He knew it was nowhere special or Bessie would have been wearing her smartest dress.

'To that meeting you want to go to,' she reminded him peevishly.

David ate a bit of bread and did not reply.

'And I still don't know why you want to bother with it,' Bessie grumbled handing plates of lentil soup to Lizzie to put on the table. But she intended to go with him, nevertheless. Socially she had maintained her policy of not letting him out of her sight.

'Remember what Mother said to us at *Rosh Hashanah*, Bessie? About there not being a safe place for Jews in her time? Well it got me thinking. I mean we've got a Jewish homeland now, haven't we? The Balfour Declaration gave us one in Palestine in 1917, but most of it isn't fit to live in and they can't make something of it without money. So I made up my mind to join a Zionist group and help to raise funds.'

'I think that's lovely of you, Daddy,' Shirley said.

David pinched her cheek and smiled. 'Every year at *Pesach* we say, "Next year in Jerusalem," don't we?' he replied quoting from the Passover meal tradition.

'But we don't really mean it,' Bessie put in.

'Zionists do and from now on so do I.'

Bessie put the soup ladle down and stared at him.

'I don't mean I'm catching the next boat, love! But I think there should be a Jewish homeland to be proud of for those who want to live there. Or need to live there,' he added significantly.

'You're getting as bad as Sigmund Moritz! And your mother with her Mr Hitler! I wish Carl'd never mentioned him to her, or any of that stuff about Blackshirts in England, either. Nothing terrible's going to happen to us here.'

'I don't think it is, either. But that's a bit of a selfish attitude, isn't it, love?'

Bessie glared at him.

'Sigmund's been expecting something to blow up on the continent ever since he left Vienna. I used to think he was an alarmist, but now I'm not so sure. This Hitler business could be the start of it and we can't just think of ourselves.'

'Your soup's getting cold,' his wife snapped.

'Let it. Why d'you think Shirley goes to *Habonim* on Sunday afternoons, Bessie?'

'To play with her friends, what else?'

'And dance the *horah*,' Shirley piped up.

'Like they do in Palestine,' David said. He glanced at the cardboard brick on the dresser which Shirley had made with the other children at the Zionist Youth Movement gathering and brought home as her personal symbol of what the Movement stood for. She had been very proud of it, though she was too young to understand what it meant. His wife didn't seem to understand its significance, either; to her the gatherings were just somewhere to send Shirley on Lizzie's afternoon off. 'When Shirley's grown up, she might want to go and work on a settlement in Palestine, like plenty of them're doing, it's the youngsters who're making it fit to live in. That's what Habonim's all about.'

'I never want to leave my mam'n dad,' his daughter informed him.

'And you're not going to,' Bessie assured her turning on David. 'Your mother started all this!'

'My mother's no fool, Bessie.'

'I should be so lucky!' Lou said when he learned about the beautiful rich girl matchmaker had found for his friend.

They were huddled over the gasfire in Lou's attic room, assigned to him because he was the youngest of the family and his two brothers were still unmarried and living at home.

'My brothers as well,' he added. 'Not that they're in the same bracket as you and me, Nat.'

'That's what makes it so bleddy disgusting!' Nathan exclaimed.

'You're always saying that about something or other.'

'It must be because there're so many things to say it about. Can you imagine a Christian family auctioning off their sons?'

Lou laughed. 'I wonder what my brothers'd bring? A machiner's worth more than a *shmearer*, so Mottie'd fetch the most!'

'That's what it boils down to, doesn't it?' Nathan got up and paced about angrily. 'I hate this whole damn Jewish preoccupation with status and money!'

Lou studied the threadbare design on the rug for a moment. 'If you stopped to think about it, Nat, you'd realise it's no different from the Christian one. It's just that Jews are that way openly. How much is this girl's family offering?'

'Well you certainly are!'

'I shouldn't be honest with my dearest friend? Hand her over to me if you don't want her.'

'You'd do it, wouldn't you?' Disgust was written on Nathan's face.

'How else am I going to get a surgery? You as well, you *shmuck*!' Lou popped a mint imperial into his mouth and crunched it noisily. 'If we both do it, we can go into partnership and I'll be able to keep your feet on the ground, like I've had to do ever since I've known you!'

Nathan strode moodily to the window and stared at the rooftops which looked as bleak in the moonlight as the future his friend had just described. He cared no more for medicine now than he had ever done. The thought of spending each day pursuing a career for which he had no heart, with only an anonymous girl he didn't love to come home to at the end of it made him shudder.

'Come back and sit near the gasfire if you're cold,' Lou said mistaking the shudder for a shiver.

Nathan smiled wryly. Lou was his best pal, but had never understood his deepest feelings, so different from his own.

'You've got a funny look on your face,' his friend told him. 'What're you thinking about?'

'Homer and Plato and Catullus. And what it'd be like to teach classics and be married to Mary.'

Lou brought him down to earth.

'If you weren't studying to be a doctor you'd never've bleddy met her. Listen, at least this London girl's good looking, she could've been cross-eyed and bandy.' He scratched his nose and winked. 'But you haven't seen her legs yet, have you?'

'You're talking as if it's a *fait accompli*!' Nathan flared.

'It would be if you hadn't met Mary. Your whole future's at stake and if it weren't for her you'd sell your pound of flesh for a bag of *shekels* and think no more about it,' Lou said bluntly.

'Thanks for the compliment,' Nathan retorted. 'And like hell I would!'

CHAPTER SEVEN

Marianne loved arriving home from school in the afternoons. When she and her brothers rushed in for their midday dinner, their home would seem a turmoil of incompleteness, the meal they were about to eat waiting on the table for them, tonight's supper halfway prepared, with its ingredients in a big dish on the scullery draining board, clothes laundered that morning strung around the hearth. But in the afternoons, all would be orderly and a sweet peace had miraculously descended upon the house.

Harry was now old enough to escort the younger children home and had learned to cross the main road with care. They would enter the kitchen and find their mother sitting by the window sewing, dressed in a dark skirt and a pale soft blouse, pastel-coloured with a frilly jabot falling from the vee-neckline. The boys liked their mother's pink and blue blouses best, but Marianne preferred the lemon one, especially on a sunny day when the light from the window deepened the shade to amber.

Friday was Marianne's favourite afternoon. Her mother would be darning or embroidering as usual, but the house had a special atmosphere. She could smell the *Shabbos tsimmes* simmering in the shiny, blackleaded oven and the candles would be already in the candlesticks, waiting to be lit when her father came home. Best of all, she liked to see the *lokshen* her mother had prepared for the chicken soup. A huge square of dough, rolled paper-thin and sliced into shoestring-width streamers, it would be lying upon a snowy teatowel on the kitchen table. No Jewish housewife in Cheetham Hill would have thought of buying a packet of vermicelli in those days.

One Friday, the children came home and found a strange man sitting in the kitchen. But he looked oddly familiar.

'Your Uncle Joe's come to visit us,' their mother said and Marianne thought she looked worried.

'All the way from London!' the man smiled.

'I can tell that by the way you speak' Harry told him.

He laughed and got up to kiss them. 'I haven't always lived there, but it must've been long enough to catch the twang! So these're our Ben's kids. I bet he's proud of them.'

Marianne did not usually like being kissed, but her new uncle reminded her of her father and she couldn't help liking him. 'Why've we never seen you before?' she asked gazing up at him.

'I didn't know Dad had a brother,' Harry said surveying him. He was a shrewd little boy, like Ben in both looks and character. 'I wonder why he didn't tell us?'

'It's a long story, kids,' Uncle Joe said.

'But there's no need to tell it to them, is there?' Esther put in hastily.

Marianne sensed a mystery and prickled with excitement. 'Why not?' she asked her mother, but the subject remained closed and she turned to her uncle. 'Why don't you live in Manchester like us?'

'Your uncle's a newspaper reporter and his office is in London,' Esther said before he could reply.

'What does a newspaper reporter do?' Arnold inquired tossing his shock of red hair away from his eyes. He was the quieter of the two boys, but would ask questions with a serious air and then consider the answers carefully.

'You've seen the daily papers, haven't you?' his uncle said.

The children nodded.

'With everything that happens everywhere written in them? Well how d'you think it gets there?'

'I suppose somebody has to find out what's happening,' Arnold said thoughtfully.

'And then write it down so it can be printed for people to read it,' Uncle Joe explained.

Marianne looked fascinated. 'Is that what you do?'

'And there's never a dull moment, believe me!'

'Hm,' Marianne said. 'I think I might do that when I grow up.'

'Girls have to get married and look after their children,' her mother laughed.

'Why do they?'

305

'Because they always have done,' Esther exclaimed impatiently.

'But I could do what Uncle Joe does before I get married, couldn't I?'

'Once our Marianne gets a bee in her bonnet there's no getting it out again,' Esther sighed to her brother-in-law.

'She's got a head on her all right!' Joe pulled Marianne onto his lap and smiled at her. 'I'll tell you what, chick. If you still want to follow in your uncle's footsteps when you're a big girl, you come and see me about it!'

'Go and change into your *Shabbos* dress, Marianne. And you two boys get ready as well. Your dad'll be home before you know it,' Esther said briskly. The last thing she wanted was for any of her children to emulate her brother-in-law and she was apprehensive about her husband's reaction to finding him ensconced in the bosom of their family when he walked in. Joe was Ben's only relative and had gone to London to seek work in his youth, as Ben had come to Manchester. Esther had never met him before and he seemed a nice enough man, but had committed the unforgiveable sin.

When the children had gone upstairs she felt uncomfortable with him, not just because of the circumstances which neither of them had mentioned, but because he was not like the men with whom she was used to mixing. His manner was smooth and self-confident and it made her feel a bit inferior, though she was sure he didn't intend to make her feel that way. It was difficult to believe he and Ben'd been brought up together. Perhaps living in London had made Joe different? Even his creased tweed jacket looked as if it was meant to be that way. 'Fancy you being a reporter,' she said searching for something to talk about. 'It takes Ben all his time to put a letter together!'

Joe laughed. 'He's like my father was. Father was the best tailor in Vienna, or so he used to tell us—'

'He couldn't have been. Our Sammy's father-in-law says he was,' Esther cut in with a smile. 'Ben once asked him if he'd ever met your dad, but he hadn't.'

'Vienna's a big place and there's more than one Jewish district. We lived in Leopoldstadt, if you can call it living.'

'You didn't have pogroms like us Russians.'

'But we were second-class citizens, even though not officially

306

and in some ways it's still the same. I went back to have a look at the ghettos when I was over there on a story.'

'You have an interesting life, don't you? Not like Ben.'

'He wouldn't enjoy what I do, he was always a home bird.'

'And he can't string two words together on paper, like I was saying.'

'That's what I meant about him being like Father. With a needle my father was a magician, but with a pen in his hand he flew into a panic! I suppose I take after our Zaidie who wrote Yiddish short stories.'

'Did he really?' Esther looked amazed.

'I bet Ben didn't bother telling you we've got artists among our ancestors, either,' Joe grinned. 'Two of our uncles painted religious pictures. They were quite well known.'

'Well I never!' Esther exclaimed. 'He certainly didn't tell me, the kids'll be tickled to hear it.'

'You know Ben, Esther. Things like that don't lie in his mind.'

'He's got other things on it,' Esther said loyally.

Joe leaned back in his chair and glanced around. A tear in the sofa had been carefully mended and the blackleaded grate shone as brightly as the brass candlesticks, which he recognised as his mother's. His sister-in-law was obviously a houseproud woman who did her best with the little she had, but there was barely enough space to swing the tabby lying on the faded hooked-rug and no amount of effort could disguise the room's shabbiness. He watched a big black beetle scuttle beneath the skirting board, but Esther didn't seem to notice it. There'd been a time when he wouldn't have done, either, when rooms much less salubrious than this had been all he'd known. Perhaps you had to move on before you became aware of quite what you'd left behind. His flat in West Kensington was just a modest one, but thinking of it now made him realise he'd moved on a very long way. 'With three kids, I'm sure Ben has plenty on his mind,' he said warmly to Esther.

Harry and Arnold were so intrigued by the unexpected arrival of a new uncle, they forgot their mother had not given them their afternoon tea. Marianne had noticed the oversight and the non-appearance of the scones and jam which always awaited them to stave off hunger until they had their proper tea, which on Friday nights they called supper, heightened the drama of the situation for her. Her father's expression when he arrived home and saw his brother did so still more.

Ben's swarthy complexion paled to parchment when he opened the kitchen door and his homecoming greeting to his family ended in mid-sentence.

'It isn't my ghost, it's really me,' Joe said with an apologetic smile. 'I had to come to Manchester on a story and it seemed like an opportunity to— well you know what I mean, Ben.' He moved forward and gripped Ben's hand between both his own.

Marianne could feel something rippling through the room, the kind of something that made her want to cry.

'So how've you been, Joe?' Ben asked gruffly, then he sat down and scanned his brother's face. Joe was the elder by two years and had been only twenty when they last saw each other. The time since their estrangement had aged him, his hair was thinning on top, the way their father's had and deep lines were etched beside his mouth. He looked more like forty-five than thirty-five.

'How've I been? Up and down like everyone else,' Joe smiled at the watching children and Ben became aware of them and pulled himself together.

'Why didn't you tell us about Uncle Joe,' Marianne asked Ben reproachfully.

'Don't keep asking questions!' Esther said to her sharply.

'Well you can't really blame the kid, can you?' Joe laughed. 'The way I popped up from nowhere!'

'You're here now,' Ben said in a resigned voice.

'And you'll stay for supper,' Esther invited.

'Look, I don't have to. I can eat at the hotel. The conference I'm covering doesn't end until noon tomorrow, so I'm in Manchester for the night.'

'You'll stay,' Ben told him brusquely, but the shortness was just a screen for his emotion. 'And there's no need for a hotel. Harry and Arnold can sleep with their cousin Martin, you'll have their bed.'

'We'll be late for *shul* if we don't hurry,' Harry reminded his father.

'Ben can't go to *shul* on Saturday, it's his main day at the market,' Esther explained to Joe. 'These days our living has to come first. But he always comes home early on Friday nights so he can go with the boys.'

'Tonight we'll give it a miss,' Ben decided to his sons' surprise. 'Because Uncle Joe's here.'

Harry looked upset. His Hebrew teacher always ticked off the boys who missed a service. 'Uncle Joe can come too.'

'Leave it at that, will you, Harry?' Ben avoided Joe's eye and looked at the clock on the mantelpiece. 'Time to light the candles, Esther.'

Marianne could feel the strange something rippling through the room again. Her uncle had sat silently staring at his fingernails while Dad talked to Harry. She watched his face as her mother said the *Shabbos* prayer over the candles and saw that he had tears in his eyes. Whatever the mystery was, it seemed to have something to do with *shul* and prayers.

Her father still wasn't looking at Uncle Joe and didn't glance at him whilst blessing the wine, either. After it was blessed, everyone had to take a sip from the glass and she noticed Dad's hand shaking as he passed it to his brother. Uncle Joe didn't take a big gulp like most grown-ups did, but barely touched the glass with his lips.

The feeling she experienced was tension, but she was too young to recognise it as such and stood behind her chair gripping the back of it tightly, wishing this part of *Shabbos* evening was over, though she usually enjoyed it. As the youngest present, she was the last to receive the wine and spilled some on her dress because her hand was shaking, too, but her mother did not rebuke her.

'So give my brother a nice big portion of chopped liver, love,' Ben instructed his wife when they sat down at the table and busied himself slicing the *chalah*. The golden-crusted bread, feather light and moist within, was shaped like a bulky plait. On Friday nights it stood on the table covered by a small, white cloth and custom demanded it be cut and handed out by the head of the family who first blessed it with a prayer, as he had the wine.

Joe received his slice of *chalah* and spread some of the savoury liver pâté on it, then his gaze moved to the candles.

'A fine night you chose to call on us, eh?' Ben said with his twisted smile and his voice had a tinge to it which Marianne could not recall having heard before.

'So what can you do?' Joe shrugged.

The brothers exchanged a long glance, then Ben averted his eyes. 'Try my wife's cooking already!'

'You can get chopped liver in the East End delicatessens.' Joe tasted Esther's. 'But believe me, it isn't the same.'

'A person makes their bed,' Ben said cryptically.

'I'm not complaining, Ben.'

'How many kids've you got?'

'One boy and he's the image of Father.'

Ben's eyes misted over. 'So what can you do?'

They used the old Jewish cliché over and over again during the meal, as if it conveyed all the things they were carefully not saying.

'And your wife?' Ben made himself ask. Years ago he'd wanted to strike this unknown sister-in-law dead for the way she had caused his brother to disgrace the family, defile their dead parents' memory. He never wanted to set eyes on her, but now Joe had taken the step towards reconciliation between them he was glad to see him and politeness called for the inquiry about his wife.

'Sally's fine.'

But the nephew was Ben's own flesh and blood. 'Your son had a *Brith*?'

Joe smiled. 'Which rabbi would circumcise him?'

'So he'll be a *goy* all his life.'

'Like his mother,' Joe replied.

'I'll dish the chicken and *tsimmes* up,' Esther said to distract them. The conversation was moving in a direction she did not like.

Marianne saw Harry and Arnold exchange a puzzled glance. She found what she had just heard hard to understand, too. Uncle Joe's wife and son were Christian. Only how could they be, when he was Jewish? Families had to be all the same. 'What's our new cousin's name, Uncle Joe?' she asked as she helped her mother to remove the empty soup plates.

'Christopher.'

Esther saw Ben blanch, but which Jew wouldn't be shocked to discover he had a nephew with the word Christ in his name?

'I'd like to meet him,' Marianne said.

'Maybe you will someday, chick.'

'Harry and me, too?' Arnold asked.

'We could come and stay with you in London, like my pal Asher Reubens does with his cousins,' Harry said excitedly. 'Then he won't be able to crow over everyone any more because he's the only one in the class who's seen Buckingham Palace. Can we, Dad?'

'We'll think about it,' Ben answered.

But the children knew the frown on his face meant no.

'Have you been to the cemetery lately?' he said to his brother. Their parents' grave in Leeds was the only reason they had retained contact. They contributed jointly to have it kept in good order and every year Joe sent his share of the expense to Ben.

'It's years since I was last up North,' Joe replied. 'But I'm going on Sunday.'

Ben played with some crumbs on the table, forming them into a neat square. A brother was a brother no matter what he had done. You could banish his presence, but not what he meant to you. They'd been suckled at the same breast, had wept together at their parents' funerals, two scrawny lads left with nobody but each other in the world. The *shiksah* wife he would never accept as a sister-in-law, but he could not exile his brother again. 'We'll go to the grave together,' he said touching Joe's hand.

The next afternoon, Joe went with Esther and the children to her mother's *Shabbos* tea party and Ben left his market stall in the care of his assistant in order to arrive at Sarah's earlier than he usually did.

It's like being pitched backwards in time, Joe thought nostalgically as he ate strudel and Sachertorte in the midst of the noisy throng. He had forgotten the special atmosphere, peculiarly Jewish, of such occasions. When he didn't have to work on a Sunday and he and Sally took Chris to her mother's for tea, how different it was from this! Sally's three sisters would be there with their husbands and kids, but there was never any noise. Everyone sat with plates of dainty egg and cress sandwiches balanced on their laps and afterwards they each received a slice of raspberry jam sponge. The conversation was bandied back and forth in polite middle-class voices and there were sometimes silences when you could hear the grandfather clock ticking in a corner of the room.

Did he miss this lusty ambience? There was no other way to describe it. It was not just the raised voices and the gesticulating, but an inimitable zest which the people exuded even when they paused for breath. How could he not have missed it, when he was one of them? But he hadn't let himself admit it until now. Judaism was more than a religion, it was a way of life in the fullest sense of the term and he'd never been more aware of it than he was in Sarah Sandberg's parlour that afternoon. It would take generations of everyone doing what he had done, to change it.

'Have some more strudel, Uncle Joe.' Marianne came to sit on the arm of his chair, bringing the dish.

'I prefer the Sachertorte, my mother used to make it.'

'There's a piece hiding under the strudel,' she whispered. 'Martin put it there for himself, but he won't mind you having it.'

Joe took the cake and smiled at her. He liked this little niece and felt she liked him. 'So when are you coming to London, chick?'

'When my mam and dad let me,' she said as if she had assessed the situation. 'If they don't, I'll come when I grow up. What's London like?'

Joe tried to tell her and her cousin Martin came to perch on the other arm of the chair, listening as avidly as Marianne.

'Heaven help you Joe, now those two've got you in their clutches!' Ben grinned.

'Give your uncle a bit of peace, Marianne!' Esther shooed the two children away, wishing the tea party was over. But Joe looked more at ease than she felt. She had called to see her mother while he was still at the trade union meeting he had been sent to report. She would not have brought the outcast to Sarah's family gathering without permission and when she received it had told her mother to warn everyone to be discreet. The only one who had not been warned was Nathan who had been at the library and had just arrived home. Esther watched Ben introduce him to Joe and hoped he would not say anything out of place.

She hoped in vain. 'You must be the skeleton in the Klein cupboard!' Nathan joked without pausing to think it might be the truth. 'I didn't know you existed.'

'It depends on how you look at things,' Joe replied wryly. 'Ask my brother to tell you about it sometime.'

Nathan did not need to, he was told by his mother when everyone had left. 'You mean he actually went ahead and did it, even though it meant cutting himself off?' He had never met anyone before who had found the courage to do so.

'And for what?' Sarah exclaimed.

Nathan went to the window and gazed at the houses across the street, so he would not have to look at her. His hasty resolve to marry Mary come what may, inspired by the matchmaker's proposition, had by now subsided into indecision again.

Sarah was cleaning the Sabbath candlesticks before replacing them on the mantelpiece. She scraped off some wax with her thumbnail. 'Now he has a wife who won't be able to sit *Shivah* for him when he dies and a son who won't know Hebrew to say the *Kaddish*. Only Ben, who he disgraced, can pray for him.

'Isn't being happy while he's alive more important?'

'Who could be happy with what he has on his conscience? Thank God his poor parents weren't alive to see it, it would have killed them," Sarah said irrationally. 'To be happy a person must first be at peace with the Almighty, or what should taste sweet will always taste bitter.'

Every word his mother said heightened Nathan's own dilemma. Oh Mary, he thought desperately. Why must it be this way? His medical studies were not yet halfway through and if he ended their relationship he would still have to see her, when he began working on the hospital wards. But he was not going to end it!

CHAPTER EIGHT

If the presence of the sinner at her tea party had not been so distracting, Sarah would have told Helga to take her mother back home and put her to bed. The sight of the frail figure drooping in the bath chair had made her want to cry out. She had not seen her friend for two days, but the deterioration in her condition during the short interval was marked.

Helga had not wanted to bring Rachel. Even the slight effort of being gently moved from the sofa into the chair had exhausted the sick woman and her hands had felt icy cold despite the warmth of the room. But Sigmund had insisted that his wife was fit to go out and Helga, who had never argued with her father, could not bring herself to do so now.

The next day, Sarah called at the Moritzes' house.

'You don't get enough of our company?' Sigmund chuckled when he opened the door. 'You saw us yesterday!'

Sarah often sat with her friend in the afternoons, but this was early morning and Sigmund knew the visit must have a special purpose. She had not entered through the back door and walked directly into the kitchen where Rachel lay, as she usually did. On Sunday mornings he was always busy in his workroom and it was there that he ushered her.

He had a gramophone by the window and worked with a record playing. Sarah shut the door and they stood silently for a moment, listening to the haunting strains of *Tales From The Vienna Woods*, then Sigmund looked at his watch elaborately.

'I'm expecting a customer for a try-on soon, Sarah.'

'You don't start with try-ons till ten-o'clock,' Sarah replied. 'Me you can't kid.' It was why she had come at nine. She moved a pile of canvas interlining from a stool and sat down. 'So, Sigmund.'

'You've come to say something, so say it,' he muttered resignedly.

Sarah picked up a piece of chalk from his bench and studied it. 'I've come to interfere, Sigmund. Like you once did with me, also early in the morning.'

Sigmund recalled the time he had called at her house in Moreton Street to tell her David wanted to be a solicitor. She had been putting her washing to dry, but had let him talk. 'It was a waste of time me interfering,' he said. 'And look what the boy has done with his life!'

Sarah averted her gaze. 'It wasn't my fault, you know that very well. And he could have a worse life than the one he's got.' She paused, then looked at him gravely. 'But what I've come to talk about is death.'

Sigmund put his hand on the back of a chair and managed to lower himself into it. The years of watching his wife suffer had taken their toll of him. His hair was now yellowish-white and dull, like the eyes behind the pince-nez, which had once sparkled. He knew why Sarah was here, but what she was going to confront him with he was not prepared to face. 'Who is dying?' he asked, avoiding her eye.

'We both know who is dying,' she said bluntly. The pain of saying it was excruciating, but it had to be said.

Sigmund's shoulders began to shake slowly, then faster as if what was causing them to do so was gradually increasing in momentum, but he did not shed any tears.

Sarah laid her hand gently on his and the tremors subsided. 'After she's gone we'll cry together. In between now and then you'll help her and I'll help you.'

'How can I help her when God doesn't want her to live?' The question sounded torn out of him.

'You can't argue with the Almighty. He's up there and we are down here, with her. You think Rachel doesn't know she's going to leave us soon? So she has to have the worry of how you're behaving, too! Perhaps she'd like to lie with her hand in yours sometimes, you could give her strength to go. Instead she has to pretend there's no reason to.'

Sigmund gazed at her dumbly, then got up to stare out of the window. The autumn sun cast its pale glow upon his stooped frame, but he felt no warmth. 'When she isn't here any more the sun will still be shining,' he whispered.

'Isn't it so for all of us?'

'But she's only fifty-five, she could have twenty more years.'

'You're arguing with God again. Listen, maybe what He takes in one way He gives back in another,' Sarah said quietly.

Sigmund turned to look at her.

'What is the length of a life compared with the quality?' she asked recalling the contented half-smile which had always made her friend seem beautiful. 'Our dear Rachel has been happier than most, believe me.'

'You think so?'

'I know so.'

'With a husband like me? Stubborn. Argumentative. His head in a book all the time.'

'Who can deny it? But a husband she loves all the same.'

A faraway expression entered Sigmund's eyes as he sat down on the chair again. 'It's October now and it was October when we met,' he said softly. 'She came with her father to my father's workshop in Eisenstadt and the sun was shining, just like today. "In such weather two young people should be out in the fresh air," my father said.' He sat listening to the music for a moment, as though the sound of the violins carried him back to Vienna. 'I put on my coat and we went together to the Ringstrasse to walk beneath the trees. She was sixteen and wearing a beige hat with a feather. Later we walked in St Stephen's Square to look at the latest fashions in the windows of Rothberger's store, but all I saw was Rachel standing beside me. Every evening we were together afterwards. Such a romantic my father was! He gave me money to take her to the Opera, Mahler was the director then. It was there I first held her hand. She had on a white silk dress, flowers in her hair. Oh how lovely she looked! It was an evening to remember.'

'Perhaps she'd like to remember it with you.'

'We've never been sentimental with each other.'

'Except in the beginning, when you held her hand at the Opera,' Sarah said gently. 'You had children together and came to a new country. With your daughters you stood side by side beneath the *Chupah* and now you have a grandchild. You've put the milestones of a lifetime behind you and it's time to be how you were in the beginning again.'

Sigmund knew she was telling him his life with Rachel had turned full circle. 'So what can you do?' he said heavily as acceptance mingled with the sudden emptiness within him.

'For you nothing.' Sarah rose from the stool to leave. 'This afternoon I'll bring Nat and he'll help Carl move Rachel to the bedroom.'

Knowing his wife would not return downstairs until she was in her coffin brought a cry of anguished protest from Sigmund.

Sarah ignored it. 'A woman is entitled to lie dying in her own bed, with her husband beside her to share the long nights,' she said firmly. 'The kitchen sofa is not the place.' She wanted to comfort him, but knew it was not within her power, that all she could do was be with him to help him endure what lay ahead.

The whole clan rallied around him as Rachel's life drew to a close and for the first time Miriam recognised her mother-in-law's dominating character as one which demanded respect.

Sarah returned that afternoon with Nathan as she had promised. Miriam came too and Rachel's transfer upstairs took place without fuss. Sarah had Sigmund's gramophone carried to the bedroom, so he and Rachel could listen to music together in the evenings and saw her friend place her hand in his when Carl put a record on to play.

During the day, Rachel was never left alone for a moment. The women took turns to sit with her and Martin and Marianne always visited her on their way home from school. Their mothers were initially reluctant to allow them to witness the approach of death, but Sarah spat three times and said it would not harm them. She did not believe in protecting children from the pain which living inevitably brought and thought they must experience the bitter along with the sweet, or why would the best loved of all Jewish lullabies, sung to them in the cradle, be a song about both almonds and raisins?

The matchmaker's offer remained in abeyance during the family crisis, but the photograph of the beautiful rich girl stayed propped up against a vase on the kitchen dresser and Nathan knew his mother would not allow him to forget.

Prior to this, being with Mary had brought him happiness and

317

he had hoped to postpone the day of reckoning until his studies were over. Now, the day loomed nearer and its imminence hovered like an ominous cloud over the time he spent with her. He knew he would have to make a decision soon.

One day he found himself alighting from the tram at a street which led through to Strangeways, instead of travelling all the way home. It was mid-afternoon, David would be at the factory and the impulse to talk to him was strong.

'What's wrong?' David said in alarm when Nathan entered the workroom.

Sammy stopped folding some coats and looked apprehensive too. Their brother had not been to the factory since he was a boy.

'I just wanted to see you, David.'

David was showing Eli some designs for a new line and the cutter put down the sheaf of drawings and smiled at Nathan. 'So how's the future doctor keeping?' he asked with respect. 'Your Nat's grown into a fine young man, eh David?'

The machiners had stopped work and were looking at Nathan with the same respect Eli had shown. Most of them had known him since his childhood and pride, too, was in the smiles they gave him.

'I remember when his mother used to bring him to Radinsky's wrapped in a shawl on a Sunday morning,' Issie reminisced. 'So who would've thought he could be looking down my throat some day?'

Nathan forced a grin as he followed David into the office. The aura his future profession carried with it never ceased to surprise and embarrass him.

'I didn't know you could draw,' he remarked noticing the sketches on the desk.

'I can't,' David shrugged. 'But they serve the purpose.' He smiled paternally. 'Shirley's the artist in our family. That kid's never without a pencil in her hand.'

Nathan was not very close to David's children, though he saw a good deal of Esther's and Sammy's. David let him know he was aware of this. 'You should come round on a Sunday sometime, Nat. You only see my kids on a *Shabbos* and in Mother's house on *Shabbos* kids aren't allowed to draw.' He laughed. 'In some ways she's still living in the dark ages!'

318

'I agree,' Nathan said quietly.

Something was wrong, David could feel it in his bones. 'So what brings you here? Got no work to do?'

Nathan saw the flicker of anxiety in his eyes. 'Don't worry, I haven't come to tell you I'm packing medicine in. Now I've got this far a doctor I'll be.' He paused and turned his back on the glass panel which made the office seem less private.

'So?' David said playing with his pencil.

Nathan thought he sounded just like their mother, but did not let this prevent him from continuing. 'Do I have to have my personal life mapped out for me as well?' He knew he was skating on thin ice and felt it cracking beneath him in the silence which followed.

David put the pencil down and lit a cigarette. 'Not if you don't want to, Nat. Me marrying Bessie was my own decision and who you marry's got to be yours. Mother didn't drag me screaming and protesting to *shul*, she just gave me her advice and then it was up to me.' He picked up an India-rubber and erased a thumbprint from the sketch he had been showing to Eli. 'If you can find another way of setting yourself up in practice, go ahead. But the way things are with the business I won't be able to help you.'

'I don't want you to help me. Why does everything always boil down to pounds, shillings and pence!'

'Would you be where you are without money?'

'I never wanted to be where I am, did I? And now I'm caught up in this bleddy vicious circle!'

'A lot of people'd be happy to be in your place.' David gestured through the glass at the machiners treadling monotonously. 'Instead of where they're sitting. That's what your family's saved you from and don't you ever forget it!' He softened his tone. 'Romantic notions are all very well, Nat, but nobody can have everything and you've got more than most. If you don't like the idea of an arranged marriage, and I don't blame you, see if you can find the right girl yourself. There's plenty of time before you qualify.'

'What if I've already found her?'

'Have you?'

'Maybe.'

David felt the colour draining from his face. This could only

319

mean one thing, or Nat would've brought the girl home. But he wouldn't make an issue of it, better to turn a blind eye and hope his brother's common sense and respect for the family would prevail. 'She's got to be right in every way,' was all he allowed himself to say and it was ambiguous enough to appear as a proviso about money.

'Right for me,' Nathan said and left abruptly, before David could reply.

After he had gone David could not work. Moishe Lipkin came in to collect some samples for a trip he was making to the Midlands and found him sitting pale and drawn at his desk, his ashtray overflowing.

'Has someone cancelled an order?' Moishe asked.

David shook his head and told him about the confrontation with Nathan. The little salesman had become his trusted friend.

'Listen, the lads today aren't like we were, with don't touch engraved on our brains,' Moishe commiserated. 'They don't think of God when they look at the sky, only how big the world is. They've come a long way from the old days in Strangeways. Would you or me've even looked at a *shiksah*? We'd've been frightened the Almighty would strike our eyes from our head!'

David thought of Joe Klein who had not been afraid to do more than look. But Joe and Ben had had no home life after their parents died, no family anchor, he comforted himself. From the age of sixteen Joe had been adrift in London.

'All right, so your Nat's looking, maybe he's also touching,' Moishe shrugged. 'A boy with his education wants to experiment. Don't worry, that's all it is.'

David lit another cigarette and tried to look cheerful. There was nothing he could do except hope that Moishe was right.

Rachel died a few days later, with the lilt of a Viennese waltz carrying her softly through to the other life and her husband and children beside her.

It was early in the morning and Sarah had shared the night vigil with the family, but left them alone in the room as the end drew near. Abraham and Sammy were with her in the kitchen when the others came downstairs and the emptiness Sigmund had felt in his heart when he finally accepted the inevitable echoed through the house.

'Fetch David,' Sarah instructed Sammy. 'Esther, too.' She put the kettle on to boil and busied herself getting teacups out of the cupboard. 'David will make the arrangements with the *shul*.' She took a loaf of bread from the enamel bin and began to slice it for breakfast. 'We must also think of the living,' she sighed. 'It will be a long day.'

The funeral was arranged for that afternoon, in accordance with the Jewish tradition of burying their dead immediately, and all the children were told to go to Bessie's house after school, where Lizzie would give them their meal. It was not customary for children to be present.

Nathan had left for the university when his father went home to tell him the news and at lunchtime David was sent to fetch him. He had never had cause to go there before and entered the quadrangle with mixed feelings.

The ambience of learning and carefree undergraduate life, which rarifies such establishments for those not privileged to attend them, was all about him and he stood for a moment gazing up at the archway through which he had once hoped to pass as a student.

Lads with scarves slung around their necks and books tucked beneath their arms were standing in groups talking together. They were all wearing blazers and he smiled wryly, remembering how he had wondered naively if his Bar Mitzvah suit would still fit him when the time came for him to start college. But for him the time had not come and the full realisation of what he had missed now struck him forcibly. The pleasure of sharpening his intellect against others just as sharp. The exchange of ideas and carefully acquired knowledge. The chance to extend his mind and personality, which bore no relation to becoming a solicitor and lining his pocket. All this had been snatched away from him, relegating him to the bread and butter echelon which was now his lot.

'What're you doing here?' Lou's surprised voice issued from across the quadrangle emphasising that this was not David's world.

'Looking for Nat,' he replied collecting himself as Lou ambled to his side with Reuben and a Gentile boy.

'Reuben you know. This is Paul Latimer, a friend of ours. Meet Nat's brother, Paul.'

David shook hands with the burly youth, who looked like a rugby player, but somehow reminded him of Jim Forrest. The same subtle quality emanated from him and David recalled wanting to acquire it when he had been at school with Jim. He had not known then that it was something a person had to be born with, the product of their breeding.

'Why're you looking for Nat?' Lou asked. 'Your father's not ill I hope?' Abraham's persistent cough was by now chronic bronchitis and everyone was accustomed to seeing him spitting into his handkerchief.

'It's Mrs Moritz,' David said and needed to say no more. 'So where is Nat?'

Lou and Reuben exchanged a surreptitous glance.

'He usually eats his sandwiches in Whitworth Park on fine days,' Paul told David.

'Oh I don't think he'll be there today,' Lou said hastily.

'Nor do I,' Reuben echoed, his reddish complexion suddenly more so.

'Perhaps you'd help me to look for him in the college, then?'

'He won't be there, Mr Sandberg,' Paul smiled, but stopped smiling when he felt Lou's foot on his toe.

'We'll find him for you, David, and tell him to go home right away,' Lou offered eagerly.

'Yes, leave it to us,' Reuben urged.

'Unless I take him in the car he won't get there in time. I'll chance him being in the park.'

Why had Lou and Reuben behaved so oddly? David pondered. As if they didn't want him to go to the park, though Paul had seemed certain Nat would be there. A sense of foreboding overtook him as he parked the car and entered the quiet enclosure. He had already surmised that Nathan's Gentile girlfriend was probably a nurse and the Royal Infirmary was not far away. He steeled himself for the encounter.

He cut across the grass to save time and heard Mary's laughter before he came upon them. The bench on which they were seated was shielded from his view by a clump of bushes and he did not see his brother until he stepped onto the path.

Mary's laughter petered out as she turned around to see what had arrested Nathan's attention. David had halted abruptly and seemed to be riveting Nathan with a frigid stare.

'Who is it?' she asked apprehensively. The expression on her lover's face was a mixture of rebellion and fear.

'My big brother,' Nathan said tersely. He got up and walked to where David stood. 'Why're you spying on me?'

'I came to tell you Rachel's dead. Unless you want to miss the funeral you'd better come with me.' David turned on his heel and strode off along the path, a picture of the girl's pretty, bewildered face floating before his eyes.

'I thought you were a united family,' Mary said in a strained voice when Nathan returned to her.

'That's the trouble!'

She played with a corner of her starched apron thoughtfully for a moment, then looked up at him. 'It's me, isn't it?'

Nathan averted his eyes.

'I'm the trouble.'

He picked up his attaché-case from the bench without looking at her. 'I've got to go, love. We'll talk tomorrow.'

Mary watched him run to join his brother as if he were being pulled by invisible strings back to the mysterious and powerful unit which dominated his life. The knowledge that this was so had dawned upon her gradually as her relationship with Nathan had deepened.

He could never see her on Saturday afternoons, or take her with him to the weekly gathering of the clan. Her Christianity prohibited it. Friday nights were struck out of the week, too. But she did not need these twice-weekly reminders of her enemy, as she had begun to think of it. Its power and presence hung like a protective pall around the man she loved, even when he held her in his arms.

How the power was wielded she could not fathom and doubted if anyone who was not Jewish ever could. Lately, she had felt Nathan fighting to free himself, but had said nothing to lend support. It had to be his decision, she did not want to be blamed if later he felt it had been the wrong one.

She got up and began walking slowly towards the park gate, numbed by intuition that Nathan would never be free, even if he alienated himself from the tribe and married her. The invisible strings would still exert their age-old pull on him. But she would give him all the love she had, to compensate.

David did not speak to Nathan when he got into the car. He was waiting for the apology he did not receive.

Both brothers stared tensely through the windscreen as though the other were not there, in a silence thick with animosity. Then David fumbled for the packet of Goldflake in his pocket, thrust a cigarette between his lips and lit it.

'A nice day to bury someone you love!' he said roughly as he started the engine. The sun was shining through the glass into his eyes. 'I can't believe Rachel's gone. It's like a light going out that's always been there.'

A sense of loss briefly replaced Nathan's anger, then he saw his brother's set expression and could not resist playing with fire. 'You almost had her for your mother-in-law, didn't you?'

David's hands tightened on the wheel. 'Almost is a very common word.'

He's telling me nothing's absolute until it's actually happened, Nathan thought. Warning me, but still skirting around the subject, even though he's seen me with Mary. 'Why don't you say what you really mean, David?'

'You might not forgive me if I do. In your present state.'

'I'm not going to finish with her.'

'Oh aren't you?' David was trying to control himself, but it was not easy. Was the young fool going to bring disgrace on himself and all of them, after what had been sacrificed to elevate him to a position of respect? 'What's she got that's different from the kind of girls you've been brought up with? Except that it's not kosher?'

'Stop the car!'

'What for?'

'I'd rather walk.'

'And miss the funeral of a woman who was like your second mother? You would, wouldn't you? Nothing matters to you right now except what you've got between your legs!' David put his foot down hard on the accelerator and the car shot forward suddenly as his temper rose. 'Believe me, it makes no difference where you put it! And you're hearing it from one who knows!'

His words shocked Nathan into silence. Crudeness was foreign to David's character. What had happened to make him reduce love between a man and a woman to nothing more than that?

'In a few years' time you'll be able to look at her and she'll be just another girl to you.'

'If what you're talking about was all I saw in her.'

'It wasn't all I saw in Miriam, either. But time's a great healer.'

'Don't give me platitudes!'

'That one's worthy of remembering. I've proved it. When I see Miriam now, she's someone I still care about, but not in the way I did. I'm married to Bessie and Miriam's just my sister-in-law, our Sammy's wife.'

'You couldn't have loved her the way I love Mary.'

'I loved her so much I'd have gone to the ends of the earth for her. But if I'd married her she'd have destroyed me. Just like in another way marrying this girl would destroy you.'

'I've made up my mind to.'

They had just turned from the main road into Heywood Street and David pulled up the car. 'You ungrateful little bastard! Just because you're the youngest you've had everything poured into

325

you, the blood, sweat and tears of the whole family. I won't let you do it!'

Nathan recoiled from his livid expression. When had he first begun to hate David? The sudden knowledge that he did was like a physical blow, knocking the strength from him. How could you hate the person who'd done everything for you? Even though you hadn't wanted some of the things he'd done. 'I'm not giving her up,' he heard himself say, but his voice sounded a long way off.

David looked at the fine-boned face and the new lines of pain beside the mouth which had a trace of weakness about it, and recalled the boy Nathan had been trying to comfort him after he ended his affair with Miriam. 'You once said you'd do anything for me, Nat. Here's your chance.'

'Not this. I can't.'

'Haven't I told you there's no such word as can't?' Fury and desperation caused the blood ro rush to David's head. Somehow he must stop Nat from committing the terrible sin he was contemplating. 'I had to swallow that pill because you were born!'

'What do you mean?'

'Why d'you think I had to leave school? It wasn't just poverty, they'd've kept me there somehow. But it was out of the question when Mother got pregnant with you. My earnings were needed to help to support the new baby. I'm still supporting him, aren't I? And the way to repay your debt to your family, Nat, is to bring them pleasure not heartache!'

He hated David because he gave with one hand and took back with the other, always demanded a price. 'I'll never forgive you for what you've done to me, David.'

'I thought that about you when you were a child.'

'A child isn't responsible for the effect it has on people's lives. A man is.'

'I hope you're responsible enough to do what you have to,' David said brusquely, starting the engine. 'Unless you want to put Mother where Rachel's going.'

The price of David's bounty was obligation. The everlasting family trap.

*

Marianne had guessed Bobbie Rachel was going to die last night. Martin was put to bed with her brothers and a scary feeling hung about the house after Auntie Miriam brought him and went away.

She had wished she needn't sleep in her little room alone, though usually she didn't mind. Being on your own let you think about things and most nights she lay making up stories until she fell asleep. But last night she'd thought about death and it reminded her of her friend Marjorie who had died a few weeks ago.

'I don't want to go to Auntie Bessie's for tea,' she said to Martin as they trudged along Bellott Street after school.

'They call it supper at Auntie Bessie's house.'

'So did we used to, but Mam says it's our tea now, like the Christian neighbours call it.'

'Auntie Bessie won't be there, will she?' Martin pointed out.

'I don't like her house, either.'

Lizzie was waiting for them on the doorstep. 'Trust you two ter lag be'ind t'others!' she chided them. 'They all came straight 'ome, like good bairns.'

'Could me and Marianne go to the park for a bit, Lizzie?' Martin asked her.

'I should think not! Playin' out'n mekkin' a show o' yerselves wi' a family burial goin' on!'

'We'll just sit down and talk,' Marianne promised.

'Please let us, Lizzie,' Martin pleaded.

The kind-hearted girl was touched by his expression and remembered that he was the one who had lost his grandmother, though all the other children had adopted her as theirs, too. 'All right,' she nodded. 'But don't go mekkin' a muck o' our Shirley's frock Marianne, mind!'

Marianne's navy-blue smocked dress was one of Shirley's cast-offs. She always protested to her mother about having to wear them, but Esther's pride was in accordance with her pocket and Marianne was told to think herself lucky she had a cousin several sizes bigger than her, who owned a different dress for every day of the week.

'I wear your Arnold's things, don't I?' Martin said to comfort her as she tramped by his side to the park.

'That's different,' she replied. She could not have explained why, but knew he understood.

327

There were many things Marianne could not explain, because they were just feelings which made her happy or sad. And sometimes they frightened her, like the time she had seen her father's shoes drying in the hearth, with gaping holes in them. She was too young to realise he could not afford to have them mended, but the sight of them somehow made her feel afraid.

She cared for her father differently from the way she loved her mother. Mam was the one who told them what to do and made sure they did it. She cooked lovely meals and saw that Marianne always looked nice, but never hugged her as she did the boys. Daddy didn't make a fuss of Harry and Arnold, but liked to kiss his little girl and once, when she had wakened in the night with toothache, crying because it hurt so badly, he had appeared magically in her room and rubbed her gum gently with his little finger until she fell asleep. They always had a special smile for each other and she felt upset when he came home very tired, looking as if he had a lot to worry about.

She had not mentioned the holes in his shoes, something had told her he would not want her to, but she still thought about them sometimes and a tenderness would well up inside her. Not until many years later would the incident fall into place in the full context of her childhood memories and cause her to weep.

'You're very quiet,' Martin said as they squatted on the grass beneath their favourite tree.

She had been thinking about the shoes again, but was unable to share the thought even with him. 'So're you,' she replied watching him select a blade of grass which looked juicy enough to chew. 'I wonder if there'll be blancmange for tea, like we have at Shirley's birthday parties.'

'Uggh!' he shuddered.

Shirley's parties were their yearly torture and not just because they loathed blancmange. Their cousin always ordered everyone around even more than usual and nobody could object as she was the birthday-girl. Some of the other guests were the children of Auntie Bessie's friends, who went to a private school and seemed to think it made them better than those who did not.

'I don't care what we have for tea,' Martin declared. 'I want to tell you about my dream.'

'When did you dream it?'

'Last night.'

'Why did you wait so long to tell it to me?'

Martin chewed the blade of grass thoughtfully. 'I've been thinking it over.'

Marianne smiled with anticipation. 'I hope it's as good as your last one.'

'It's better. You know how people go to Heaven when they die, Marianne?'

'Of course I do.' She looked up at the clouds. 'I expect Bobbie Rachel'll be there by now. I wonder if she's met Marjorie yet? I miss Marjorie, Martin. She was my very best friend, why did she have to get the diphtheria and die?'

'I don't know. I miss Billie Higgs and Johnny Watson.'

'Bobbie Sarah says they got it because Christians don't eat *tsimmes* and *kefulte* fish to make them strong.'

'But Andrew Lensky got it as well.'

'Perhaps he always left his on his plate.'

'Anyway, Marjorie's in the Christian Heaven, isn't she, Marianne? So Bobbie Rachel won't be able to see her. I dreamt about our Heaven, the one we'll go to when we die.'

'Hurry up and tell me what it was like!' She had not expected to find out until she went there.

'Very, very beautiful.'

Marianne felt comforted to hear this.

'The buildings were made of flowers, and music like Zaidie Sigmund plays on his gramophone was playing all the time.'

'Did you see God?'

'He had His back to me, but I knew it was Him because He was sitting on a big golden throne wearing a very long *tallith*. And listen to this, Marianne. All the angels were eating Sachertorte.'

'Perhaps the one who does the cooking made it because she knew Bobbie Rachel was coming today.' Marianne's eyes shone with excitement. The dream was as real to her as it was to him.

'If you had lovely dreams you'd want to fall asleep quickly, instead of lying making up horrid stories.' Martin dreamed often, but Marianne never did. 'Why don't you make up nice ones, instead?'

'Horrid ones are more exciting, I like to see everyone's face when I tell them,' she giggled.

'You shouldn't be laughing today,' he said solemnly.

'Why not? If Bobbie Rachel's gone to such a beautiful place? You ought to tell Zadie Sigmund about it, then he won't worry about her.'

'I'll tell him tonight, when we go to see him,' Martin promised as Harry came to fetch them for their meal.

Usually, Martin would not eat fish unless it had been filleted, but he ate the fried plaice which Lizzie gave them for their tea. Marianne thought it was because he was not worried about choking on a bone anymore, now he knew Heaven was such a nice place.

CHAPTER TEN

No flowers adorn the graves in an orthodox Jewish cemetery and the dead, whatever their station, are laid to rest in simple coffins of unpolished wood, vested with no more riches than those with which they came.

Rachel's son and the three Sandberg brothers who had loved her bore her to her resting place and lowered her into the earth.

The timelessness which David always experienced on religious occasions assailed him as he stood at the graveside between Sammy and Nathan. The grey, Mancunian sky above his head, the clay beneath his feet, the ancient Hebrew prayer the rabbi was intoning, would be unchanged by his brief span on earth. Only the earth's inhabitants changed, playing their infinitesimal parts in the scheme of things between the coming and the going.

Nathan stood with his head bowed and David could feel the emotion emanating from him. Was it affecting him, too? Causing him to see his love or duty conflict in its true perspective? Would he let duty win because that was how it had always been for Jews?

Sigmund leaned heavily upon Abraham, his face distorted by silent grief; he was not a man to weep in public. Carl, too, contained his sorrow within himself. Only the sobs of Isaac Salaman, who always wept at funerals, and the guttural voice of the rabbi punctured the solemn peace.

David became aware of Sammy putting a shovel into his hands. Jewish tradition is literally to bury their own dead, every man present taking his turn to pile soil into the grave, in the order of his kinship to the departed.

Sigmund had been unable to cast more than one shovelful and was led away by Abraham. In lieu of blood relatives, the Sandbergs were next in line to Carl and the brothers helped him complete the harrowing task when everyone else had left.

'We've been like one family, Abie,' Sigmund said feelingly to his friend as they stood together on a grassy incline watching their sons.

'Even the quarrels. So what can you do?'

'The caring makes up for it. Come, we'll say goodbye to her.'

The two ageing men walked slowly to the graveside.

David watched a bird soaring with timeless grace high above their heads as they made their final farewells.

Sarah had remained at the Moritzes' home with Miriam and Helga. Esther and Bessie were there, too, and several neighbours and friends who had come to comfort Rachel's daughters whilst they awaited the men's return. Custom forbade the presence of females at a burial and the interment of a Jewish woman was never witnessed by her own sex.

Every mirror in the house had been covered with a white cloth as tradition decreed. The four low stools for the mourners were placed in a row beneath the window and candles burned in the brass candlesticks Rachel had brought from Vienna in 1904. The *Yartzheit* light in its thick, glass tumbler, which was her ever-lasting memorial, flamed too as it would throughout the *Shivah* and every year another would be kindled on the anniversary of her death.

Sarah and Esther had prepared the ritual meal Sigmund and his children must eat on the men's return, though they would have no appetite. Hardboiled eggs which signified Life, salt herring symbolising tears and hard-crusted bagels, painful to swallow as the loss of a loved one, had been laid with primitive simplicity upon an upturned wooden box.

The black dresses Miriam and Helga wore had been jaggedly ripped at the neck with a knife by the rabbi, finalising their severance from the departed before she was carried from the house and Sigmund and Carl's waistcoats had received the same treatment. The days of sackcloth and ashes were long gone, but the spirit remained.

Rachel's old friends from Vienna, of whom she had seen little in recent years, were clustered around Helga.

'You don't know how much we loved your poor, dear mamma,' Paula Frankl sobbed behind the veiling of her smart hat.'

Helga remained silent, but thought a good deal. Like her mother, she had lost respect for them.

Miriam sat clutching Sarah's hand. 'You've been wonderful. Ma. I'll never forget it.'

Sarah brushed the dishevelled black locks from the lined forehead which used to be smooth as silk. She had never before felt tenderness for Miriam, but it warmed her now. Was a death required to enable people to bury the past also? The coolness between herself and the girl who had loved one of her sons and married another had been mutual, as if they had never trusted each other. She put her arms around her daughter-in-law and let the new feeling merge between them, asking herself no more questions, content that it was there.

After the evening prayers, when only the family remained, Lizzie brought the younger generation to pay their respects, and consolation entered the house with them. The six children filed past the low stools, uttering the traditional greeting, 'I wish you long life,' to each of the mourners in turn, as though the hands they were solemnly shaking belonged to strangers, not pillars of their own lives. Bessie's maid, by now well primed in Judaism, had instructed them in what they must do and followed behind them to do so herself.

Martin and Marianne stayed beside Sigmund, whom they sensed was the most in need of comfort.

'We'll always remember her, won't we Marianne?' Martin promised him.

'And we've got something lovely to tell you, Zaidie Sigmund,' Marianne said nudging her cousin.

Martin put his lips to his grandfather's ear and whispered the dream about Heaven to him, whilst Marianne looked on approvingly.

Sarah reflected on the closeness of these two grandchildren, the one resembling her dead friend, the other so like herself. Who needs a memorial light to be kindled for them once a year after they've gone? she thought feelingly. People lived on through those who sprang from their seed.

The children were quiet as mice and her youngest grandchild Ronald, who was the image of his Uncle Nat, came to nestle on her lap as the room grew still. Her fingers strayed to her brooch in the pensive silence and found a tiny dent in the delicate filigree which had worn thin with age. Tonight was Life's bitterness, but the sweetness would come again and then more sorrow, repeating the pattern relentlessly. Whatever the future held they would survive as they always had, strong, because they were together.

'What are you thinking about, Bobbie?' Marianne asked her softly.

How could she put it into words for this child who wanted to know everything? She glanced around at the faces she loved. A seed could take root anywhere, hadn't the Sandbergs and Moritzes proved it? And flourish anew, multiply itself, nurture its growth in alien soil yet still retain the God-given specialness which made it uniquely of one tree. 'The way it is with a Jewish family,' she replied.

GLOSSARY

Certain words and phrases have no precise English equivalent and the nearest possible definition is given. The original language is indicated by (*H*) Hebrew, (*R*) Russian, or (*Y*) Yiddish.

bagel (*Y*) Hard, ring-shaped bread-roll; adapted from the Russian 'bublitchki'.

Bar Mitzvah (*H*) Confirmation ceremony of a Jewish thirteen-year-old boy; also the term applied to the boy himself.

bershert (*Y*) Fated.

bimah (*H*) Platform in synagogue, from which prayers are led by ministers. Usually of imposing appearance and enclosed by a low railing, or panels of polished wood.

borsht (*R*) Beetroot soup.

Brith (*H*) Circumcision ceremony.

Bubbah/Bobbie (*Y*) Grandmother.

chalah (*H*) Traditional Jewish loaf.

chalutzim (*H*) Pioneers in the land of Israel.

Chanukah (*H*) Described variously as 'The Festival of Lights', 'The Feast of Dedication', and 'The Feast of the Maccabees'. Celebrated for eight days (in December). Instituted by Judas Maccabeus and the elders of Israel in 165 B.C. to commemorate the rout of the invader Antiochus Ephinanes, and the purification of the Temple sanctuary.

Chavurah (*H*) Group of young Zionists in the Habonim Movement.

chevrah (*H*) A small congregation.

cholent (*Y*) Butterbean stew.

chupah (*H*) Marriage canopy; a canopy supported by four poles, beneath which the marriage is solemnized, representing the home the couple will share.

chutspah (*H*) Cheek; audacity; brazen nerve.

droshky (*R*) Low, four-wheeled carriage.

feinkochen (*Y*) Omelet.

frum (*Y*) Religious.

ganef (*Y*) Thief.

gefilte fish (*Y*) Fishballs, fried or boiled.

goy(im) (*Y*) Gentile(s).

Habonim (*H*) (lit. The Builders) A Zionist Youth Movement.

Haggadah (*H*) The book containing the Passover Seder Service. (*see* Seder)

Hassid(im) (*H*) (lit. The Pious Ones) Mystic Jewish sect founded in the mid-eighteenth century by the Ukrainian Rabbi Israel Baal-Shem. Hassidim seek God in everyday life, believe sadness hinders devotion and cheerfulness aids prayer.

holeshkies (*Y*) Rolled cabbage leaves, stuffed with minced beef and cooked in a sweet-and-sour sauce.

Horah (*H*) Traditional Zionist song, and group dance performed in a circle.

Kaddish (*H*) The Mourner's Prayer, recited by immediate male relatives of the deceased.

kapora (*Y*) A folklore curse invoked by the superstitious to ward off evil.

kazatsky (*R*) A dance performed in a crouched position, stretching-out and bending first one leg and then the other.

Kiddush (*H*) The benediction recited over wine.

knedl (*Y*) Dumpling, usually accompanying chicken soup.

kosher (*H*) In accordance with the Jewish dietary laws.

kuchen (*Y*) Yeast cake.

landsleit (*Y*) Fellow-townsman.

latke (*Y*) Potato pancake.

liebchen (German) Darling.

lokshen (*Y*) Egg noodles.

Maoz Tsur (*H*) (lit. Rock of Ages) Chanukah hymn.

matzo(s) (*H*) Unleavened bread, eaten at Passover.

Mazeltov (*H*) Good luck; a congratulatory greeting.

megiyah (*H*) Conversion to the Jewish faith.

menorah (*H*) An eight-branched candelabrum used for the Chanukah Festival.

meshugah (*H*) Crazy.

mezuzah (*H*) Small, rectangular piece of parchment inscribed with the passages Deut. vi. 4–9 and xi. 13–21, written in twenty-two lines. The parchment is rolled and inserted in a wooden or metal case and nailed in a slanting position to the right-hand doorposts of orthodox Jewish homes (interior and exterior) as a talisman against evil.

minyan (*H*) Quorum of no less than ten males required to form a congregation for prayers.

mohel (*H*) The religious functionary who performs circumcisions according to Rabbinic rite and regulations.

nachas (*H*) Pleasure, pride and joy combined.

nosh (*Y*) Food; to enjoy food. Usually applies to sweetmeats and delicacies.

perineh (*Y*) Feather-filled duvet in a white cover.

Pesach (*H*) Passover. The Festival commemorating the Jews' liberation from their bondage in Egypt. Lasts seven days, during which only unleavened bread and specially prepared foods are eaten. (March/April)

pisha-paysha. A card game introduced by Jewish immigrants. Probably Russian.

pogromschik (*Y*) (derived from pogrom) One of the mob perpetrating a pogrom.

Rosh Hashanah (*H*) (lit. Head of the year) The Jewish New Year. (Autumn)

Seder (*H*) The religious service conducted around the dining table in Jewish homes, recounting the liberation from Egyptian bondage. Is celebrated amidst festivity on the first two nights of Passover. (Reform Jews observe only one night.)

Sefer Torah (*H*) (lit. Book of the Law) The Five Books of Moses, in which are written the Law.

Shabbos (Yiddish for the Hebrew word 'Shabbat') Sabbath.

Shalom Aleichem (*H*) Peace be unto you. A traditional Jewish greeting.

shatchan (*H*) Matchmaker.

sheitel (*Y*) Wig worn by ultra-orthodox Jewish married women.

shekel (*H*) Ancient Jewish silver coin. P'. colloq.: money, riches.

shikker (*Y*) Drunk.

shiksah (*H*) Non-Jewish female.

Shivah (*H*) The ritual Jewish mourning.

shlemiel (*Y*) Fool; inept person.

shlep (*Y*) Drag: make a tedious journey.

shluff (*Y*) Sleep; snooze.

shmaltz (*Y*) Chicken fat, usually refers to the rendered-down form.

shmearer (*Y*) One who spreads the varnish (glue) on seams and hems in a waterproof-garment factory.

shmerel (*Y*) Dolt; stupid person.

shmooze (*Y*) Cajole; flatter; sweet-talk.

shmuck (*Y*) Twirp.

shnitzel (German) Thin slice of veal, coated in breadcrumbs and fried.

shnorrer (*Y*) Beggar.

shpeil (*Y*) Play.

shtetlach (*Y*) Back-of-beyond townlets.

shtum (*Y*) Dumb; silent.

shul (*Y*) Synagogue.

simchah (*H*) Joyous occasion.

Simchas Torah (*H*) (lit. Rejoicing of the Law) The Festival celebrating the completion of the reading of the Law. (Autumn)

streimel (*Y*) Large, fur-trimmed hat.

Succah (*H*) A booth, usually in the yard or garden, in which Jews are required to dwell for seven days during the Tabernacles Festival. Only the ultra-orthodox still observe this law, but all synagogue congregations erect, and adorn with fruit and flowers, a large, communal 'Succah', in which to celebrate the Festival with sweetmeats and wine.

Succoth (*H*) The Festival of Tabernacles, commemorating the Jews' departure from Egypt when tents sheltered them in the Wilderness. (Autumn)

tallith (*H*) Prayer-shawl.

tefillin (*H*) Phylacteries worn by Jewish men for weekday morning-prayers.

Torah (*H*) Law; doctrine.

trafe (*H*) Non-kosher (*see* kosher).

tsimmes (*Y*) Carrot stew.

tsorus (*H*) Sorrow; heartache; troubles.

yamulke (Polish origin) Skull-cap.

Yidden (German origin) Jews.

Yom Kippur (*H*) Day of Atonement. The holiest day of the Jewish year. A solemn Fast Day.

Yom Tov (*H*) Festival.

Zaidie (**Zaida**) (*Y*) Grandfather.